D1329574

François Mai is an author, athlete, physician and musician. He was born and raised in South Africa of first-generation French ancestry and became a Canadian citizen in 1977. He earned his medical degree at the University of Cape Town, and completed psychiatric training in Great Britain and the United States.

Mai is author of a monograph entitled "Diagnosing Genius: The Life and Death of Beethoven."

He has been awarded a Fellowship of the Canadian Psychiatric Association and is a professional member of the Canadian Authors' Association. He lives in Ottawa.

Dedication

This book is dedicated to the original
Martin Mai
who inspired the story

François Mai

Father, Unknown

AUSTIN MACAULEY PUBLISHERS™
LONDON • CAMBRIDGE • NEW YORK • SHARJAH

A CIP catalogue record for this title is available from the British Library.

ISBN 9781786936080(Paperback)
ISBN 9781786936097(Hardback)
ISBN 9781786936103(Ebook)
www.austinmacauley.com

First Published (2017)
Austin Macauley Publishers Ltd.
25 Canada Square
Canary Wharf
London
E14 5LQ

Acknowledgements

I acknowledge the assistance of many individuals during the six years that this novel was in gestation.

To Richard Taylor and Bert Bailey, who helped spark this novel on its doubtful trajectory. Thanks also to Richard Aitken, Noel Burns, Cyril Dabydeen, Marybeth Drake, Sharyn Heagle, Anne Hennessey, Joce Kane-Berman, Yvon Lapierre, Vincent Mai, Stevie Mikayne, Liz Palmer, Joan Shorter, Marie Surridge and Sherrill Wark, who all read the manuscript at various stages of its uncountable drafts, and made many useful suggestions.

Special gratitude to Phil Jenkins, whose expert advice helped me navigate the shoals of writing fiction.

Finally, I am indebted to my wife Sarie. She read the manuscript and made countless suggestions about how to bring out the strengths, as well as the flaws and frailties of human nature. I could not have completed the book without her.

"Birth hath in itself the germ of death
But death hath in itself the germ of birth.
For there is nothing lives but something dies,
And there is nothing dies but something lives."

From "Ode to the Setting Sun"
by Francis Thompson

Contents

DISCLAIMER

The novel is based on events that took place in the towns of Vimy and Arras in the Department of Pas-de-Calais in France during the late eighteenth and early nineteenth centuries. Some of the characters are historical but the author has taken liberties with historical details and characters to ensure they fit the narrative.

DRAMATIS PERSONAE

X GABRIEL LACHÊNE: Peasant, widower and father of Marie-Anne, Darel and Alexis

X MARIE-ANNE: Youngest child of Gabriel and mother of Marcel

X MARCEL PIERRE (later changes name to MARCEL JUIN): Illegitimate son of MARIE-ANNE and PIERRE TREMBLAIS

DAREL AND ALEXIS LACHÊNE: First and second sons of Gabriel

HÉLÈNE: Nurse in Vimy

PHILIPPE, ROBERT, GRÉGOIRE and ALAIN: Citizens in Vimy

MONIQUE: Wife of Alexis

X PIERRE TREMBLAIS: Business man and ex-Army officer

CHANTAL: Wife of Pierre Tremblais

X FATHER ANDRÉ ST AMOUR: Parish priest at Vimy

HENRI LA FORTUNE: Owner and master of the Chateau and Estate in Vimy

MADELEINE LA FORTUNE: Wife of Henri

SIMONE, MIREILLE, HENRI-CHARLES AND LOUISE: Children of Henri and Madeleine la Fortune

LUC: Butler to M. and Mme. La Fortune

NICOLE: Tutor to the la Fortune children

X ADOLPHE GIROUETTE: Manager of la Fortune's estate. Later Police Chief at Arras

X CATHERINE LACHÊNE (TANTE CATHERINE): Sister of Gabriel and mother of Hubert

HUBERT LACHÊNE: Only son of Catherine and later husband of Marie-Anne

SIR WILFRED MONTAGUE: English businessman in London

STÉPHANE: Citizen in Arras, friend of Clementine

FR. CHARLES BARÉZ: Parish priest in Givenchy-en-Gohelle

ANTOINE DU MOULIN: Aristocrat in Arras

CHARLES AND PAULINE CAVIGNEAU: Friends of Catherine Lachêne and parents of Clementine

X CLEMENTINE: Oldest daughter of Charles and Pauline and wife of Marcel

X DEMY: Son of Charles and Pauline

FR. CLAUDE LADOUCEUR: Sulpician priest in Arras

FR. JEAN LEPIRE: Parish priest in Vimy

PIERRE PLOUFFE: Tobacconist in Arras

THÉRÈSE LAGRANGE: Citizen in Vimy

MAXIME and BRIGITTE BÉTHUNE: Residents of Arras

DR JEAN-PAUL POIRIER: Physician in Arras

DR VINCENT CADIEUX: Physician in Vimy

MAÎTRE AUGUSTIN GIBET: Notary in Arras

MICHEL LE GRAND: Representative of the Imperial Army

MADAME EULALIE TRICHEUR: Widow and resident of Vimy

CELESTE BOURDELLE: Citizen of Arras

LOUIS-MARCEL, JEAN-BAPTISTE, MARIE-ANNE, FRANÇOIS and CHARLOTTE: Children of Marcel and Clementine

X RAYMOND BATARSE: Ex-army officer who settles in Vimy

LAURE AND THOMAS COUPÉ: Citizens of Montréal

MAXIMILIEN ROBESPIERRE and JOSEPH LE BON: Revolutionaries

GABRIEL-JEAN BRASSIER} {Sulpician priests

JEAN-HENRI-AUGUSTE ROUX} in Montréal}

JOSEPH-GENEVIÉVE, COMPTE DE PUISAYE: French Aristocrat who migrates to York

X = Major Character

Prologue

Vimy 1837

The funeral took place on a wet and gloomy day in November. It was a dignified event befitting the passing of an illustrious member of the congregation. Father Claude Ladouceur celebrated a requiem mass, and the mournful melodies that echoed from the ancient walls of the church provoked sobbing from many of the bereaved who filled the church. The horse-drawn hearse hauled the coffin down the road to the cemetery, and the riders had difficulty controlling it on the muddy slopes. On the ridge of the escarpment above the town, a man on his way to the cathedral town of Arras, whose spires he could see in the distance, looked down, saw the now lost prosperity of the man in the hearse, and made the Sign of the Cross.

For some months Marcel Juin had complained of an irritating, hacking cough and shortness of breath. As the condition progressed he took to his bed and Clementine, his steadfast wife, called in Doctor Vincent Cadieux for advice. Cadieux was a fastidious man in his fifties, short in both stature and bedside manner, but familiar with recent advances in medical and surgical techniques. He proceeded to the sick room as fast as his short legs would take him and made the usual opening inquiries.

"I can stand the pain, Doctor, but my lungs feel like they're going to burst when I cannot get enough air," Marcel confided, the words coming, like his breath, in short bursts.

"You've a failing heart," said Cadieux after his examination. "This is causing fluid to back up in the lungs, legs and abdomen. I will give you an infusion of foxglove leaf to stimulate the kidneys and help get rid of excess fluid in the body. You will feel better also if you place extra pillows behind your back so that you sleep half sitting up."

These measures did indeed produce temporary relief but a week later, Marcel suffered a serious relapse and Dr Cadieux decided to use the drastic measure of 'cupping', a bleeding treatment. "This is going to be painful, Marcel," the doctor warned. He always thought it best to tell the patient what to expect. They screamed less that way.

"Go ahead, doctor. I'm used to pain," Marcel replied, with forced resignation. Cadieux clenched his knife in one hand and clamped down on Marcel's forearm with the other. Quickly he cut through the skin to expose and section the vein.

"O God, O God, help me. This is awful," moaned Marcel. The doctor ignored his complaint and placed a hollow cup over the skin and sucked large quantities of blood out of his system, while Marcel sweated profusely from the pain.

"That's good," said the doctor observing the sweating. "It means all poisons are being purged from your body."

Despite, or perhaps because of these heroic and well-meaning efforts, Marcel's condition continued to deteriorate. He remained conscious until near the end, and dealt with these painful treatments through prayer and stoic resignation, attributes he had learnt and employed early in life. Cadieux encouraged the generous use of cheap country wine to dull the worst of his symptoms. Ladouceur also visited to administer the Last Rites of the Church.

On the evening before his death, Clementine and the three surviving children - Louis-Marcel, the eldest, a farmer, François, a priest, and Charlotte, a budding pianist – sat around the death-bed. A fading wood fire heated the room and cast spooky shadows on the walls. The smell of sickness pervaded the room. Clementine clutched Marcel's moist hand and wept silently. "Is there anything we can do to make you more comfortable, Papa?" asked Louis-Marcel.

"I've had a rough but good life," he whispered, each word requiring its own breath. They craned their necks to hear him. He clutched his painful chest. "Ma mère - Marie-Anne - warned me it would not be easy. She was a simple country woman with a heart of gold, she knew what she wanted in life and none could sway her once she'd made up her mind. I'm a little like that too, I've been told," he added with a weak smile.

Clementine smiled in response. "I know mon chéri."

"The Revolution hurt me and many others. Things happened that cut deep into my soul. I tried to put them behind me but never did, completely. I tried to be a good father and protect you from the losses I had. You have to create your own lives and futures. You cannot build your happiness on the unhappiness of others. It will gnaw into you and make you miserable." He closed his eyes in pain and the children exchanged a familiar series of glances. They had heard this catechism of advice from their father before.

Marcel started coughing and clutched his chest again. Clementine winced in sympathy and helped him sit up to take a sip of water. He recovered his composure though was weaker still, then he continued, "To each of you, mes enfants, I give a small gift as a memento as they were passed to me from my mother and my father. Louis-Marcel, for you here is a neck band, François, this silver medal, and for you, sweet Charlotte, this ring. Take good care of your mother. Speak to Dr. Cadieux after I am gone and remember me to your children." With these final, drawn out words he fell asleep. He did not reawaken.

Father Ladouceur read the final obsequies as the pallbearers lowered the coffin and Clementine, as wife of the deceased, threw the first clods of earth into the pit. They sounded like a bass drum being struck. Gravediggers filled in the remainder as the mourners left the cemetery.

The day after he died, Marcel's two sons, Louis-Marcel and François, went to the Hôtel de Ville in Vimy to register his death. Marcel had spent all his sixty-one years in that small country town in the north of France. They met the mayor, Raymond Batarse, a gruff, corpulent man in his early sixties who ran the town with an iron fist. He and Marcel had disputed openly many times because of their differing political and religious leanings. Marcel had been a Catholic and a monarchist to the marrow, whereas the mayor was an atheist who strongly supported the revolutionaries and the Republic. Because of these conflicts, Batarse derived secret satisfaction from the fact that he had outlived Marcel, and from the knowledge that as mayor of the town, his function included recording details of Marcel's death for posterity.

He gave a broad, self-satisfied smile and chortled as he prepared the death-registration documents at his desk. "Give me the full name of the deceased," ordered the mayor jovially, jotting down Louis-Marcel's responses carefully and clearly in his elegant, cursive style. After writing each word in the Government-supplied logbook, he dipped the quill into the ink bottle near the edge of his desk, dried the ink with blotting paper to ensure no smudging, peeked through his pince-nez, and with deliberate intensity scratched out each word on the page under the heading of "DÉCÉS" (deceased) for that day.

"Marcel Juin," replied Louis-Marcel.

"Occupation?"

"Farmer."

"Date of birth?"

"June 6th 1776."

"Place of birth?"

"Vimy, in the province then known as Artois."

"Wife's name?"

"Clementine Cavigneau.

"Mother's name?"

"Marie-Anne Lachêne."

"Father's name?"

Louis Marcel hesitated before replying. "The name and identity of his father is not known. He knew n-n-n-nothing about his paternal roots." Louis-Marcel stammered with embarrassment as he uttered these words and looked down at the floor, while François beside him sat quietly, watching the mayor.

Batarse digested this information during an extended moment of shocked disbelief. His smile faded. Beads of sweat appeared on his brow. His shoulders slumped down as if a musket ball had struck him in the pit of his stomach.

After a prolonged silence, with trembling hands, he inked out the words "Father, Unknown."

PART ONE - 1759-1787

BIRTH, LIFE, DEATH

Chapter One

Here are extracts from the journal kept by Lieutenant Pierre Tremblais who served in La Nouvelle France for six years and witnessed the loss of the colony to the English. The journal was discovered amongst his papers following his death in 1794.

Québec, Thursday morning, September 13th, 1759

I am writing these brief notes before the battle begins. This morning, without warning, we woke up to find a large army of English soldiers lined up on the Plains of Abraham outside the Chateau. What an incredible sight! Where yesterday there was an open field, today there are hundreds of soldiers in formation, armed to the teeth and dressed in red like birds. How they climbed the heights of the precipice without alerting the sentries, I do not know. Montcalm is assembling his army to confront the invaders. He speaks strongly about throwing them back in the river but I'm not so sure. I shall be in the front line facing the redcoats. I have great respect for English fire power and resolve. I am not scared. I shall fight to the death. This is what I joined the army for.

Dear Maman and Papa; dear brother Nicolas: In case I do not survive I say goodbye. I have wonderful memories of our childhood on the vignoble; loved stomping the grapes with Nicolas using our feet and then sending the full-bodied wine to King Louis to drink! Playing pranks on the teachers at school; I remember locking Father Buisson up in the clothes' closet. It was hours before they heard his shouts and he nearly suffocated to death! They never discovered the culprit! Please say sorry to him. Special goodbye and thank you to Nana for looking after me so well and to Noirette, I still can feel his soft mane in my fingers and his special horse-smell! in my nose.

I love you all!

Québec, Saturday April 30th 1763

After six years in this blood-soaked beautiful place I am returning home to France, to my beloved family and village! I've had many wondrous experiences in this vast, lovely country, but also endured painful trials and tribulations. The immense spaces, endless trees and huge expanses of water make this land unique on earth. I love the beauty and the bareness. The sparse population and the adverse powers of nature compel the colonials to collaborate with each other in their work endeavours. I joined in and as a result made many fast friends whom I shall dearly miss when I depart.

However, we failed in our mission to protect New France from the English invasion. In September 1759, they took Québec following the Battle on the Plains of Abraham. A year later Montréal and the rest of New France fell to the English. The Conquest of Canada was signed and sealed at the Treaty of Paris early this year. The Treaty gave French army personnel the choice of remaining in Canada or returning to France. I chose to return. There is now no place for a French leader in the new Canada so next month, I cross the Atlantic in an English frigate. Yet I go back with mixed feelings, not knowing what awaits me in the land of my birth.

I come from a bourgeois family in the Loire valley that has spanned many generations. As a child, I was fascinated by history and especially French army history and I joined up at an early age. My favourite games were playing with toy soldiers. I would set up the soldiers, French on one side of the floor, English on the other, with rivers and cities between and around them, and replay the great battles of history. Hastings! Agincourt! Orleans! Calais! In my game the French always won even when they lost. Much blood soaked the family carpets!

My father, who had the same name as me, Pierre Tremblais, owned a successful vignoble. We produced elite wines that we've been selling to the Bourbons Royals for hundreds of years so as a child, I learnt all about wine-making. On occasion, my father would use my brother Nicolas and me to crush the grapes with our feet. We would first wash our feet (always!) and then climb into the huge vats filled with grapes. I loved the feeling of stomping on the soft grapes and then seeing the rising tide of grape juice as the solid berries became transformed into a pulpy, sticky fluid, this often accompanied by tickling on the soles of the feet from pips, skins and twigs. Our work would end with spasms of giggles. Nicolas and I got secret pleasure from thinking of King Louis sipping wine made from grapes squashed by our (sometimes) dirty feet!

I joined the army as soon as I turned seventeen and six months later, my father purchased a lieutenant rank for me. Very quickly they sent me across the Atlantic to take part in the defence of Québec. I was not sorry to come here. Action and adventure have always appealed to me.

The first two years in Québec were exciting. We spent hours training and target practicing. We built up the defences of the city and learned how to survive the rigours of winter. I took an active part in the lively social life of the colony and met many lovely young Canadian women with whom I had great relations. Unlike French women, Canadians are quiet and responsive and enjoy meeting the needs of French army officers. As a child I attended the local Jesuit school and my mother raised me with religious faith which I lost with the many temptations of army life in Québec.

I developed a great admiration for our leader, the Marquis de Montcalm. He appeared so wise and calm, just like his name. He had a huge fount of knowledge, not only about army tactics and procedures but about other topics as well. All in the colony knew about his difficult relationship with the Governor, the Marquis de Vaudreuil, who was also his superior. Vaudreuil knew nothing about the army yet interfered endlessly in decisions Montcalm had made about the defence of the city.

Things took an ominous turn in the spring of 1759 when a huge flotilla of English ships appeared on the river below Québec. For months they bombarded the city, ruining many beautiful old buildings and wrecking the surrounding countryside. We tried to set fire to their ships by releasing a flaming raft filled with explosives and letting it float downstream into the English fleet, but sailors placed grappling irons on the raft and hauled it away from the ships to safety. The attack was a failure.

In the Battle on the Plains, hundreds were killed on both sides and oceans of blood spilt that turned the field into a lake of fire. I managed to get Wolfe, the English general, in my sights, and gave him a fatal wound in his chest but it was too late. We'd already lost the battle. Later that day, the English entered what remained of the city. Montcalm also received a fatal wound in his stomach and died the following day. I spoke to him after the battle. He was moaning and in great pain. He took both my hands in his hands, looked me in the eye and told me to keep my courage after the defeat, return to France and live my life to the fullest. I will never forget his words. In his dying moments, he was still talking gently to me and giving advice to the totally confused Vaudreuil. His death devastated me. I loved him like a father and wept at his funeral. I too, got a bullet in my left arm that left a large bloody gash but continued fighting till the end. In the heat of battle one does not notice pain. To cap it all I lost my horse. They shot Magique in the leg and we had to destroy her. It was a fateful day.

I still do not know how we lost the battle. We had all the advantages: we knew the terrain and had a strongly defended Citadel sited on a high precipice. Our officers were well armed and trained though many in the militia were raw. We had powerful support from the population. If our sentries had alerted us to the fact that an army was climbing the heights during the night, the result would have been different. They must have been either asleep or were killed. Many months earlier Montcalm had ordered more cannon to be mounted on the ramparts, but Vaudreuil countermanded this order. Cannon fire would have decimated the English army. Wolfe had much luck in his victory but I lay most blame for the debacle at the door of Vaudreuil. I hope he will be charged and punished when we return to France. So be it. We lost. It was God's Will.

The winter of 1759-1760 was horrendous. In addition to our regular population of Canadians, Québec now had thousands of English army personnel to feed, clothe and keep warm. Much of the city had been reduced to rubble, many buildings burnt to a cinder. When walking in the streets, one had to step around mountains of masonry and broken timber. Les Anglais had destroyed the surrounding forests and farms so food and wood for fires had to be brought across the ice and snow from many leagues away. The Indians living in the countryside were allies of the French and harassed anyone who left the city to seek food or wood. A black market prospered so those with assets survived. Murray, the English Governor, introduced rationing and severe penalties for those caught pilfering supplies. Many received one thousand lashes and some were even publicly executed for theft. Canadians had to take an oath of loyalty to King George. Those who refused were forced at gunpoint to do so. Murray quickly realised he needed the support of the local population and the only way to secure their cooperation was through the Church, so he bribed Abbé Briand, the church leader, by offering freedom of worship and language.

Towards the end of winter, scurvy and other diseases became rampant. The Governor converted the Convent into a hospital and beds were filled to overflowing. The nuns, as always, were willing to help all who were sick including even soldiers from the English army. Meanwhile the cold and the ice bit into the bones of all. My best friend, an officer like me, died from scurvy. I survived only because I was taken into the home of a sympathetic old Québec family. They had stored both food and wood in their basement for just such an eventuality. Their supplies ran out and by winter's end we, too, had to catch, cook and consume rats. When faced with starvation and death, human nature takes desperate measures to survive.

We thought spring would bring relief but things got even worse after the ice broke up. General Lévis, who replaced Montcalm, had escaped to Montréal after the battle of the Plains the previous fall. A brave man, Lévis put together an army, sailed down the river and defeated Murray at the Battle of Ste. Foy outside Québec. However, he lacked resources to retake the city and the fate of the French was sealed when an English, not a French fleet, appeared from downstream.

For the next three years, I lived from hand to mouth. Les Anglais, under Amherst and Murray kept an iron grip on the city. They were resolved to prevent recapture by the French at all costs. I believe there was little danger of that. Because of defeats at sea when France tried to invade England during the Seven Years' War, the French navy had almost ceased to exist and there was no way a local commander could put an army together without access to military equipment. The population suffered greatly from disease and starvation and I shared their misery. During the summers, I helped with sowing and reaping in the fields. In the winter I dug down with the rest, trying to keep warm and fed. Before the battle, I had met a lovely young Canadienne called Marie-Anne whom I had hoped to take back to France with me and marry. She died from weakness and pneumonia last Christmas. It broke my heart.

If nothing else, the last six years has taught me the art of survival. One cannot fight the elements. I learnt how to lean to the wind so storms dented but did not destroy me. Escape and flight is sometimes better than strife and contention. I would likely have died or been killed if I had struggled and fought against the enemy and the weather.

I look forward to returning to France though hope to come back to Québec one day. My parents both died during my absence but Nicolas now runs the family vineyard and I shall see him and other relatives on my return. I have an intense interest in horses and in textiles and wish to move to the north of France, the centre of such industries, and purchase a business in one or other of these domains. I will live the life that Montcalm never did.

Chapter Two

Vimy, Summer 1775

Marie-Anne set the bucket down on the earthen floor of the rough sleeping quarters occupied by her two older brothers. Ahead of her was an afternoon of mopping up puddles that had deluged through the thatched roof that morning. Former pieces of the roof, moss and straw floated in small lakes, collecting in the valleys of the floor in all three rooms of the Lachêne home, valleys her brothers might have smoothed over for her. No chance of that.

The front of her hand-me-down long brown skirt quickly became sopping wet – yet again. Her pale yellow apron darkened as the muddy water seeped into it. The mopping motion loosened the pinching girdle she had worn since the onset of her womanhood and she could feel the sweat collecting under her bonnet. She rose from her knees and realised she needed to relieve herself. She crossed the sparsely finished main room, dried herself briefly before the woodstove, added a log, and stepped out over into the trees that marked the edge of the town where she jettisoned the night pot she carried. Anxious not to fill it again too quickly, she squatted on the ground to pee.

The Pox, a regular visitor to Vimy, had struck the previous year, and carried off her mother, Marguerite, and sweet youngest brother, Pierre. Wealth and position provided no immunity and even King Louis XV was swept away in its tide. Few families were spared the horrors of the epidemic that caused gross facial scarring and disfigurement to those who survived. Every day she counted her blessings that she had not got sick. As a young girl, she had worked as a milkmaid at the Chateau, and caught the cowpox, as had some of her friends. At the time she thought the cow pox dreadful but having caught it, it somehow seemed to protect her from the much worse pox later.

On her mother's death, to her disappointment, Marie-Anne had to stop her job as milkmaid. Instead she assumed the role of housekeeper to her father and two surviving brothers, Darel and Alexis, knowing they had few skills in this domain, and would not have practised them if they did. She had been assisting her Maman with such chores from the age of five, as her Maman had helped hers until marriage. It was the way of things.

The Lachêne family lived in a modest one-storey house amidst a cluster of trees on the northern outskirts of Vimy. In the front garden grew an ancient, gnarled oak tree as solid and old as the town itself.

Two narrow, hinge-less windows on either side of the front door allowed sunlight to peek through on cold winter mornings. The house contained three rooms — a large communal one in the front with a big black woodstove in the middle from which a chimney rose to the ceiling, and two small rooms at the rear that served as sleeping quarters. The main room contained little furniture; an elongated table flanked by wooden benches and rickety chairs without armrests occupied the centre. A smell of stale smoke and dampness spread through the house. Several times each day, Marie-Anne, as daughter and housekeeper, fetched large pails of water from the communal well at the end of the unpaved, dusty street.

At twenty years of age, she was the youngest of the original four children, and the only girl of Gabriel and Marguerite Lachêne. "Marie-Anne," her Maman often told her, smiling, "You are my youngest, my only girl and my special child." The dutiful daughter had an attractive, engaging face under her long dark hair, bright blue eyes, and the corners of her mouth curved upwards as if she had a perpetual smile.

She felt a great void in her life. The only woman in the house now, she missed the warmth and companionship of her mother. The epidemic had subsided gradually during the autumn and winter of 1774-1775 and the family adjusted slowly to the loss of Marguerite and Pierre. Gabriel Lachêne, Marie-Anne's father, found it especially difficult as he had become very dependent on Marguerite during their thirty-five years of married life. He felt as though an extra arm had been removed from him.

At sixty-one, Gabriel was the patriarch of the family, a role he had striven to perform fairly as he guided his loved ones through a hard life. Of medium height with a strong muscular build, his bushy, greying eyebrows overhung sharp eyes, and this, coupled with sun-tanned, wrinkled cheeks and roughened calloused hands, bespoke a life of hard labour. His expressive face and untidy beard made him look even older than his age.

After working in the fields from sunrise to sunset, Gabriel led the way into the home, the brothers Darel and Alexis falling into the kitchen and collapsing at the table. "Where's the gruel, then, Marie-Anne?" Darel demanded, shouting this out as if she were at the other end of a field. He spoke using the local patois, as did all members of the Lachêne family.

Gabriel frowned at his son. His mind was occupied with more important matters than filling his stomach, as Darel's should have been too. Like most of the local peasants, Gabriel had a share-cropping arrangement with

Monsieur la Fortune, the seigneur, lord of the chateau and lord of Gabriel's few arpents. The ancient arrangement required Gabriel to provide la Fortune with fully half of the annual sales of all produce of the land he worked. Nature had not been his partner this year, and coupled with the loss of his wife and son with the loss of four hands, he had fallen behind in his payments.

As they began eating Darel yelled again, "Marie-Anne, there is dirt in this gruel. It hurts my teeth. You're trying to slowly kill me, are you not?" His face became flushed and dilated veins visible in his neck.

"I am sorry Darel," she replied, looking down at the floor. "I dropped the bag of flour on my way back from the shop and it broke open. In order not to waste it, I gathered up the flour. I tried, but had trouble separating the flour from the grit."

Gabriel listened to the dispute between his son and daughter. And his mind rose from his apprehension to deal with it. "Darel, I too have got grit in my gruel. You will find if you just churn the gruel in your mouth using only your tongue, without chewing, you will not notice the dirt. Besides, it will not harm you. We take in dirt all day in the fields."

Darel mumbled to himself, pouted out his cheek and pushed the plate away, while the rest of the family churned away silently at the gruel.

As they completed the meal, they heard horse's hooves galloping up to the front door and all at the table froze, as if ordered to by an unheard voice. It was Marie-Anne who rose from her unfinished meal and opened the door to see a man on a sorrel stallion, cracking his whip loudly to ensure that all within were aware of his arrival. The family too left their bowls, Darel almost with relief, and lined up before the man who sheathed his whip. They all recognised Adolphe Girouette, the steward who managed the properties of la Fortune and collected the monies owed to the landowner. Girouette served the interests of la Fortune on the estate and in return received free food, fuel and housing. All four went out timidly to meet him.

A powerfully built man in his late twenties, Girouette had large misaligned features, short cropped hair, small penetrating eyes, a crooked nose and missing teeth, the result of a fracture in a bar-room brawl. Although he had never been in the army or faced a real enemy, he wore a military-type kepi with a sharp, pointed brim to give himself an air of authority. Without greeting Gabriel or dismounting, Girouette proclaimed, "You still owe me fifty livres from last season's crop. I expect you to pay the full amount by Saturday."

"I would have difficulty finding the money by then, Monsieur," replied Gabriel firmly but respectfully. "Please would you bear with me 'til the end of the month? By then the vegetables will be ripe, and can be marketed. The payment is assured. I expect you are aware of my misfortune this year and of others in the region. I offer this not as an excuse but as a reason."

It was as though Gabriel had not spoken. Girouette fingered his whip as if he intended to use it, smiled when the man beneath him stepped back, then said, "Unless the money is forthcoming by Saturday, I shall order the intendant to confiscate all your cursed belongings. Not that that will cover all that you owe." He smiled again, wheeled his horse, and rode off to the chateau, leaving a cloud of malodorous dust in his wake.

Gabriel shook his head and looked despondently at his children. "We know he means what he says. Remember what he did to Jean Petit and his family two weeks ago? Petit could not pay the share-cropping rent. Next morning Girouette and his gang from the chateau came and threw him, his wife and five children out on to the street. They had to leave town and now all live in the poorhouse in Arras. I have no wish to follow him."

The family went inside and resumed their meal. "We must find a solution," Gabriel said quietly, breaking the silence. "I do not like borrowing and owing money. We may have to do that, if there is no other way."

Marie-Anne waited for her brothers to speak, and when they did not, she said, taking her father's hand, "I could seek a position at the Chateau as a domestique or a bonne d'enfant. They often have visitors there and need extra help. I am sure of it." Despite his sometimes autocratic ways, Marie-Anne cared deeply for her father and hated seeing him humiliated. She also knew that despite his trustworthiness, he tended to yield when under pressure rather than fight back. She felt she could help him deal with this impasse.

The next day, after feeding the men, Marie-Anne went through the door with them, parted company at the edge of the fields and took the road to the Chateau, taking no notice of the darkening clouds to the west. Built during the Middle Ages the Chateau, as it was meant to, dominated the landscape, its turrets rivalling the spire of the church. She felt small standing beside its imposing door, but kept her spirits high. A servant kept her waiting a while, and then led her into a room the size of her home. On the far side sat Madame Madeleine la Fortune and Luc, the butler. Marie-Anne quickly took in and ignored her aloof, arrogant manner and her overuse of both rouge and perfume, while also noticing that Madame concealed her ample curves under elegant clothing.

Madame la Fortune looked at Marie-Anne from head to toe through her pince-nez. She pursed her lips and wrinkled her nose in disapproval of Marie-Anne's simple attire.

"What can you do?" Madame asked Marie-Anne, already shaking her head dubiously, as if Marie-Anne had already replied.

"Oh, I can do many things, Madame," she replied gaily. "I can cook and clean up; I can serve at table and love children. I don't mind working extra hours when needed."

Madame la Fortune glanced over at the butler, then said "Well, I do need a nanny. We had to let the last one go because she had a fight with Henri-Charles, my seven year-old son; she pinched him so hard that he cried."

"I know how to handle boys, Madame," Marie-Anne replied confidently. "I've two older brothers and one likes to have his own way but I know how to get around him without arguing."

Madame remained sceptical, but seemingly against her better judgement, after waving off a look of a sort from her butler, told Marie-Anne, "All right. I will take you on for a trial time of one month. You are to care for the four children, Mireille who is eleven, Simone, nine, Henri-Charles and Louise both aged three. You will work with Nicole who is governess to the children. She teaches them to read and write, and play music. I will also require you to help serving at table when we have guests.

"Oh, that is wonderful, Madame," replied Marie-Anne, smiling excitedly. "Can I start soon?"

"You can start tomorrow. I expect you to be here when the sun rises and if there are no guests, you may leave when it sets. Your pay will be five sous daily. Luc, take Marie-Anne and show her around the chateau. Please ensure that she meets Nicole and the children."

On her return home, Marie-Anne amused and entertained her father and brothers with a mocking version of the way that Madame la Fortune conducted the interview. She mimicked Madame's tone of voice, affected accent, gestures and haughty demeanour with witty accuracy. Even Darel, try as he might, could not help joining in the laughter.

Thus her employment at the Chateau began. Each day she got out of bed before dawn, walked the half-league to the chateau to serve the morning meal to the children, and helped give breakfast to visitors, who were frequent. Despite her early morning hunger, she enjoyed the walk through the misty, silent streets, listening to the murmurings of the flocks of sparrows hidden in the hedgerows, admiring the dew-covered plane tree leaves glistening in the dawn sunshine. She sang softly to herself the country folk songs she had learned as a child. Along the way, she would stop to pick wildflowers growing on the roadside to present to Madame la Fortune at the chateau.

At these times she reflected on the similar walks in the woods and countryside she had taken with her mother. Marie-Anne had come to love and respect nature. The recreational hunts for wild boar, deer and fox organised by la Fortune and his confreres distressed her greatly. As a troupe galloped noisily past their house, she uttered a silent prayer that the hunted animal would escape. She had a visceral hatred of hunting for another reason; it was an activity reserved for nobility and landowners alone. Although hunted animals destroyed crops, domestic animals and gardens of peasants, her father would have been severely punished if he'd killed them to protect his produce or feed his family. Despite the poverty of her family, she felt contented with her lot and knew what she expected of herself.

Marie-Anne's attractive features and engaging character caught the attention of young men in the town but none had gained her interest. A young man called Philippe tried to force himself on her the previous autumn. Late one afternoon the two were stacking hay in the barn and just as they were completing the task, he suddenly accosted her, "Marie-Anne: will you lie with me?"

"No, I will not," she responded immediately. Before she could provide any further explanation or resistance, he grabbed her wrists and arms and forced her to the floor, while dropping his breeches and exposing his genitals. She quickly realised she could not out-power him, so she screamed, clutched her arms in front of her and stiffened her body to withstand his attack as best she could. She saw his eyes, looking at her with an intense but vacant gaze. At that point she heard a horse neighing from outside the barn followed by a man's voice, calling, "Who is there? Who is shouting?"

"Sacré bleu," Philippe muttered angrily and he let go of Marie-Anne while quickly pulling up his breeches as the stranger entered the barn. She too got up, straightened and dusted down her clothing, and noticed the man's tall stature, penetrating eyes and elegant, equestrian clothing and boots.

"This man is forcing himself on me," she cried, pointing at Philippe.

Without a word, Philippe fled from the barn, followed by the stranger who, hindered by his heavy boots, quickly gave up the chase.

"You must watch your friends, young girl," he said on his return, shaking his head. "They sometimes do more damage than enemies."

"I thought I knew him and trusted him," she wailed. Then quickly collecting herself she added, "Thank you, kind sir. I shall be forever grateful." With an appreciative nod she hurried from the barn, clutching her shawl around her.

At the time of the assault, she had not experienced any pain but when she got home, she saw painful bruises and nail marks on her arms and wrists. She cleaned and dressed these as best she could then uttered a silent prayer of thanks for the timely arrival of the stranger. Marie-Anne told no one about this event, least of all her father. She also took care never to be alone with Philippe again.

She had been working at the Chateau for several weeks when Monsieur la Fortune ordered her to come to his room. In his mid-forties, of short stature, and overweight, he had a large nose, clean shaven face and thick jowls. He came from an aristocratic family that traced its ancestry to the Middle Ages. In a resolute, peremptory voice he said, "Marie-Anne, you are a very pretty girl and a good worker. But I have an offer for you, something that will help not only you but your family. There are some days when Madame la Fortune is away. If you are willing on those days to come and visit me in my room for an hour or so, I shall order Adolphe Girouette to forgive all amounts owed me by your father".

Marie-Anne half-closed her eyes, looked away and quickly made up her mind. "Monsieur" she replied, speaking quietly and firmly, still not looking in la Fortune's direction. "I like my work here, and I respect you and Madame. I am sure that if Madame happened to return early one day and found me here, I would be the one who would be asked to leave, not you. And you would then still expect my father to pay all the money he owed you. It is kind of you to consider my family, who would certainly be helped by the extra money. In addition, I've no wish to come with child, so must say no to your proposal."

"Think about it Marie-Anne" warned la Fortune with a threatening edge to his voice. "I may choose to force myself on you anyway, in which case you will lose both your virtue and your job."

With knees trembling she left the room. Once in the hall she leaned against the wall with eyes shut, wondering if she should have responded differently. It would be a big help for Papa to have no more worries about money. Then shaking her head and clenching her fists, she returned resolutely to the children's quarters knowing she'd made the right decision. She believed it unlikely that la Fortune would act on his threat.

One evening as Marie-Anne put the children to bed, nine-year-old Mireille suddenly let out a piercing scream and jumped out of her bed.

"Marie-Anne, come quick! There is something cold and wet in my bed!"

Marie-Anne rushed to her aid and when she pulled back the blankets, saw a squashed dead frog on the sheet.

"It's all right Mireille. It is dead and cannot harm you. Who could have done that?"

"It is Henri-Charles," she said through tears. "He's always up to mischief. Last week he put a beetle in my soup."

Marie-Anne went to Henri-Charles' room next door and found him looking at a picture book. He did not look up as she entered.

"Henri-Charles, did you place a frog in Mireille's bed?" she asked sternly.

He hesitated for a moment before replying. "No, I didn't. The frog climbed into her bed all by itself."

His eyes twinkled, and a smile played on his lips. Marie-Anne went up to his bed, took his hand in hers, sat on the bed next to him and said, "Henri-Charles, when I walked to work this morning, I saw a snake slithering in the grass. I remember precisely the bush where it disappeared. Tomorrow morning when I come to work I am going to find it, place it in a box, bring it to the chateau and leave it in your bed for you to find tomorrow night. Would you like me to do that?"

Henri-Charles shuddered. "Snakes are dangerous. They bite and kill."

"Yes, Henri-Charles, but they also scare people. Will you promise never to scare your sister like that again?"

"Yes I promise."

"And do you promise to apologise to her in the morning?"

"Yes, I will," he said meekly.

Marie-Anne squeezed his hand, kissed him on the forehead, said evening prayers with him and tucked him in for the night. She then returned to Mireille's room and discovered her still weeping and shaking. She found a small bag, and, using a large kitchen knife, while Mireille watched in disgust, she firmly scraped the frog's entrails off the sheet and placed the debris in the bag to discard. She then changed the sheets, consoled Mireille, helped her with prayers and tucked her in bed for the night.

Early next morning, Mireille accosted Nicole, "Specks, guess what Henri-Charles did to me last night. He put a dead frog in my bed and I squashed it with my feet as I got under the blanket!"

"What a horrible, naughty boy! I'll fetch him immediately and give him the strap!"

At that moment Marie-Anne entered and explained to Nicole the promise and apology that Henri-Charles had made the night before. She suggested Nicole ask Henri-Charles for an account of the story before punishing him, which Nicole did. She decided the beating was not required.

The children were cared for, taught and entertained during the day by Nicole, as governess, and Marie-Anne, as nanny. Each evening after the children had had their supper, but before the grownups had eaten, Nicole and Marie-Anne, with the four children in tow, trouped downstairs to the atrium where they meet with M. and Mme. la Fortune to discuss the day's activities.

Furnishings in the atrium were casual hence more suited to children than in the drawing room. Within ten minutes, both parents and children became visibly bored and irritable with each other so Nicole and Marie-Anne gathered them up and retraced their steps to the children's quarters, there to be bedded for the night.

During the autumn of 1775, the two older girls simultaneously developed a fever. They stayed in bed for a few days, had aches and pains, refused food then both broke out into a generalised itchy rash. When the physician from Arras examined the children, he immediately diagnosed measles.

"There is a serious epidemic," he told Monsieur and Madame la Fortune. "Many children are affected and some even die. Keep your girls warm and in bed. Give them plenty of fluids especially hot soup. This ointment will relieve the itch. Call me in a week if they're not better."

As Simone and Mireille recovered, the two younger children became ill. Little Louise especially became very sick with severe fever, vomiting and coughing up phlegm streaked with blood. The doctor diagnosed pneumonia and for treatment, applied leeches to suck out her blood, but she recovered.

Monsieur and Madame la Fortune barely changed their lifestyle during the weeks the children were ill. Once a day Madame, usually alone, would visit the children for a few minutes to enquire stiffly how they were doing.

Without being asked, Marie-Anne volunteered to stop returning home in the evenings, and slept every night on a blanket on the floor in Louise's room, getting up frequently to comfort any child who was restless, crying or could not sleep. She attended to their needs during the day and made sure they took their soup, their medicine and ointments.

Although not able to read, she regaled them with stories her mother had recounted when Marie-Anne was a child, embroidering them with entertaining details she created along the way, even acting out the roles of characters she portrayed. During their convalescence she taught them songs while Nicole accompanied them all on the piano.

The children grew very fond of Marie-Anne. Without her knowledge, Simone wrote a small song in her honour, the children secretly practised it together.

"Marie-Anne," Simone said with a demure smile. "We've a surprise for you. Sit down in this chair near the piano." While seated, with Nicole accompanying, the four children sang the following words, repeated twice and just a little off-key, to the tune of the nursery rhyme "Frère Jacques,"

Marie-Anne, Marie-Anne,

We thank you, we thank you,

Stay with us forever, stay with us forever,

We love you, we love you.

Marie-Anne wept with joy and gave them each a huge hug at its conclusion.

When they finally recovered from measles, Marie-Anne went to see Luc, the butler.

"Luc, I did much extra work while the children were ill. I slept here, got up at night when they called, and cared for them in many ways. Is it possible to increase my wage from five to six sous each day?"

"I shall talk with Madame but doubt it will be possible. Monsieur has many expenses and cannot afford such extras. He would go bankrupt if he gave everyone the increases they wanted. I shall speak with you tomorrow."

Marie-Anne heard nothing more from Luc. She suspected they decided if la Fortune rewarded her for her extra help, it would go to her head and lead to ever increasing demands. She consoled herself with the thought, "At least I know they love me."

In September 1775, Luc called Marie-Anne to his office, a small room off the kitchen. "We are expecting an important guest, a Monsieur Pierre Tremblais, who will be staying for three days and hunting with Monsieur la Fortune on his estate. Monsieur Tremblais fought as an officer in the French Army in Québec and heads a successful business in Arras. You are to work late on the next two nights to help serve at the dinner table. You are also to sweep and dust the dining and drawing rooms."

"Oui, Monsieur Luc," replied Marie-Anne. Her brow furrowed over with apprehension. "I have no difficulty working late but am not sure about serving high people at table. I shall do my best but please give me instruction on waitressing."

Pierre Tremblais arrived at the Chateau early in the afternoon and Luc met him at the door. "Come in, Monsieur Tremblais. Monsieur and Madame la Fortune are expecting you. Allow me to show you to the drawing room and I shall let them know you are here. In the meantime, I shall take your baggage to your rooms where you will find it later."

Pierre entered the drawing room just as Marie-Anne emerged from her cleaning duties. Their eyes caught with an immediate look of mutual recognition; she knew him as the stranger who had appeared at the barn the previous autumn and staved off the rape from Philippe. Pierre appeared to be in his mid-thirties and Marie-Anne observed his tall, handsome frame, well-trimmed sideburns and long, dark auburn-tinged hair, folded into a neat pony tail. He had brown, slightly protuberant and penetrating eyes, a large sharp nose with a small hook at the bridge and was dressed in tight brown breeches, white stockings and a beautiful silk cravat over his saffron-coloured shirt.

With a smile and a barely visible nod of the head, she curtsied respectfully before retiring to the kitchen area.

Pierre looked around the drawing room and saw its large size, location and contents. Situated on the south-west corner of the building it was furnished with beautiful period pieces from the reigns of Louis XIV and Louis XV. Several large Persian carpets covered the floor. In the centre of the room, an oak-lined fortepiano with the signature of Johann Stein of Augsburg, Germany, dominated the area. The room had a large grey-stone fireplace with a beautiful carved wooden mantelpiece. While observing these details, Monsieur and Madame la Fortune entered the room. Monsieur greeted Pierre Tremblais warmly and introduced his wife, "It is kind of you to accept the invitation to visit us, Monsieur Tremblais. We know of your illustrious career in the army and your business success in Arras; it is an honour to have you at our establishment. I have arranged our hunting trip for tomorrow, and am sure you will find it enjoyable. Luc will show you to your quarters, and on the way we would be grateful if you would sign our Visitor's Book. Tonight after dinner we will have a small concert at which my wife and two daughters will perform on the fortepiano. They are fine amateur pianists."

"It would be a pleasure, Monsieur. I am looking forward to the recital. I myself had some singing experience in the army and would be willing to participate if you are interested."

"That would be excellent Monsieur Tremblais."

That night as the company entered the dining room for dinner, Marie-Anne flushed when she caught sight of Pierre's well-dressed, debonair figure. She noticed him eyeing her as discreetly as she eyed him. During the meal, as she placed the main course plate in front of him, she knocked over his glass of wine. The beautiful crystal glass shattered and the rich 1765 Chateau Lafite turned the white, hand-woven silk table cloth a bloody red. Droplets splashed all over Pierre's tunic, culottes and stockings.

"You stupid girl! How can you be so careless?" yelled Monsieur la Fortune angrily. "That wine has been maturing in my cellar for ten years and you're wasting it! And look at the mess you've made!"

Marie-Anne rushed to the kitchen to fetch a broom and a damp cloth, followed closely by Pierre.

"Oh, my humblest apologies, Monsieur," she said trembling with embarrassment.

"It is nothing," he reassured her. "That wine was past its prime and should be thrown out anyway."

"I am so concerned. Monsieur will not think so. He and Madame are angry. They may let me go."

34

"I shall speak to them. Don't worry." And he brushed her cheek gently with the back of his hand. She flushed and felt wet in her palms and loins. After work that night she ran home, went straight to bed and slept fitfully.

The next morning, Madame la Fortune spoke to Marie-Anne severely. "You will be sent home for good if there is another incident of that magnitude and seriousness." Marie-Anne felt relief that she had not been told to leave. She suspected her work as a nanny had saved her position.

Simone demonstrated her expertise at the fortepiano that evening, playing a set of variations written by a nineteen-year-old Austrian composer called Wolfgang Amadeus Mozart, who was becoming famous throughout Europe at that time. Simone had visited Paris with her parents the previous summer and attended a concert given by the composer with his sister, Constanze. The family was dazzled by the performance and Simone attempted, with a little success, to emulate Constanze. After playing her piece, and with eyes aglow, she gave a vivid account of the Mozart recital. For his contribution, Pierre sang two songs: Monsieur de Turenne, a military song composed by Jean-Baptiste Lully, and another entitled "Marlborough s'en va-t-en guerre" that had recently been popularised by Queen Marie-Antoinette. He impressed the company with his firm and melodious baritone voice.

In one month's time, Pierre was scheduled to get married in a family arranged wedding in Arras. Despite his age, his meetings with Chantal, his fiancée, were carefully chaperoned to ensure no intimacy took place; this was not strictly speaking necessary because, in any event, Chantal made it clear to him that she intended to remain a virgin until their wedding. During his time in the army and occasionally thereafter, he had been with prostitutes, always taking care to avoid disease contamination. Unlike others of his class and generation, he drew a line against using servants for sexual outlet. Not sure why, he thought it more refined to avoid such complications and felt reluctant to face the realities of living in close proximity with a woman whom you paid to serve in your home, and with whom, you also made love. As a guest now in someone else's home, these impediments did not apply and in any event, he felt a high level of sexual frustration.

Marie-Anne knocked at the door that evening while Pierre moved about in his room, doing his toilette and preparing for dinner.

"Come in."

"I need to prepare the bed and the room for the night" said Marie-Anne, looking down at the floor.

"Certainly, go ahead Marie-Anne."

She folded back the counterpane and blankets, rumpled the pillows, picked up and folded the clothes he had dropped on the floor. Meanwhile,

Pierre watched her closely in the mirror. As she left the room, he took her hand and drew her firmly towards him in a warm embrace.

"I have been watching and admiring you, Marie-Anne, and see that you have a gentle, generous spirit. I see your engaging eyes and infectious smile. You have innocence in your soul that has touched me deeply." Pierre spoke quietly in a serious tone and looked into her eyes. His mind went back to the first Marie-Anne, the young Canadienne he had wooed in Québec and hoped to bring back to France to marry. It's strange. They even have the same expressive eyes.

"It is kind of you to say those words, Monsieur. I am but a poor peasant girl and have been confined to Vimy my whole life. I care for people, know how to look after them and love children. You are a successful man who has travelled the world. I love music and listened to your beautiful singing last night." Marie-Anne smiled demurely.

"I did what I had to do, what I was ordered to do." Pierre spoke with authority and conviction, gesturing with his arms to emphasise the point. "I also had times of desperate hardship when I felt cold and hungry. I've had opportunities and good fortune." Silent for a few moments he then added, "I love the way you smile and savour the merry twinkle in your eye! You seem always to be smiling."

"Monsieur, you are too kind." Marie-Anne looked away, embarrassed, though she sensed the truth of Pierre's words. She knew where the conversation was heading and tried to deflect its direction. "Despite hardships in my life I am content and do not seek adventures in distant lands." I respect and like this man, she thought. Even though he rescued me from Philippe, I must try to resist him. Yet I also have a strong desire to thank and please him.

"I understand Marie-Anne. I have lacked tenderness and love in my life and I felt from your manner and bearing that you possessed these qualities. I now do seek an adventure, but only in this land!" To emphasise the point he smiled and waved towards the bed.

Marie-Anne also smiled at his witty association and looked him straight in the eye. "You are not only successful but also smart and I like you for that!" Realising a little late that she now promoted the talk in a direction she had previously tried to avoid, she added, "I am young and still have much time for that sort of adventure." She looked down wondering if he could see that she didn't really mean what she had said.

Her resistance became a challenge to Pierre.

"Marie-Anne; I can see you are a gentle and unspoilt child. I care about you and would love to love you."

"Monsieur Pierre," she replied, after a brief pause, "I have much admiration for you but I am young and not ready yet to go with a man. I have made a promise to God and to myself to wait until I am married." She gently disengaged herself, avoided his eyes, and forced herself to turn and leave the room. Her heart beat uncontrollably.

During the hunt the following day, Monsieur la Fortune and Pierre Tremblais managed to kill a wild boar and Madame served it at dinner that night. Marie-Anne overheard la Fortune asking Pierre about his experiences in Québec.

"The battle on the Plains of Abraham was dreadful." He knew the company would seize a chance to hear a first-hand account of one of the epic battles of the century. As he spoke, he gestured expressively. "The English caught us by surprise ambush and we were ill-prepared. Our army fought with great courage but a bullet hit Montcalm in the stomach and he died the following day. We were demoralised. I was wounded in my left arm. Just look at the deformity I've developed in the palm of my left hand," He stretched out his left arm and hand to reveal the fingers curled over in the shape of a claw. Marie-Anne gasped silently in the background as she caught sight of Pierre's twisted hand.

"It started some years after the war and the wound," he continued, the group hung attentively on his every word. "Hundreds of soldiers on both sides were killed and wounded, and the soil soaked red as if cart loads of wine had been spilled. I managed to get the English General Wolfe in my sight and wounded him mortally but it was too late. We could do nothing. The English took the city. The fate of the French was sealed the following spring when the English fleet sailed up the river. . ."

"To me it is incredible that France sent no reinforcements," interrupted la Fortune, raising his arms and shoulders. "How could our Government have left its colony so poorly defended? They must have been thinking more about lining their own pockets than the welfare of the colony."

Pierre paused for a few moments before replying so that his words would have more effect. "It's a long story that started at least a century ago. England had sent nearly two million colonists to occupy their territory in North America whereas France had barely seventy thousand citizens in Québec, so we were totally outnumbered. Instead of persecuting and exiling the Huguenots, as we did, we should have sent them to New France where they would have built up the country and helped defend it when the crisis came. Finally, England's fleet controlled the seas, so we were unable to penetrate the naval blockade and send help to the colonists during the war."

"I am dismayed at the weakness and lack of preparation of our country," interjected la Fortune.

Pierre ignored the comment and continued, "After the battle, I remained in Québec for a further four years living the life of a pauper. I struggled to survive and often felt cold and hunger but Canadian friends and families helped me. The English ran the city by gaining the support of the Church and promising them freedom of religion. That of course was all the Church leaders were interested in. At the Treaty of Paris in 1763, France decided to keep the island of Guadeloupe rather than Québec. Canadians joked bitterly that France preferred sugar and black slaves to furs and white cousins. You can imagine how distressed the colons were at being abandoned in this way. The Treaty gave us eighteen months to decide whether to remain in Canada or return to France. I chose to return because a French leader had no role in an English colony. The English were being practical in allowing freedom of religion and the French language — they could never have governed the colony peacefully without making these concessions — but they are just marking time. It is a temporary expedient. It would have been very difficult to deport Les Canadiens as they did Les Acadiens ten years previously. There were too many of them and they were too entrenched in their land."

Pierre paused for a moment, looked at Monsieur and Madame la Fortune and then added in a lower voice for emphasis, "I have no love for the English or the way they have treated our people, yet I admire the manner in which they run their country."

"I agree the English are master opportunists and this has served them well in the development of their colonies." La Fortune struck the table for emphasis. "Do you think, Pierre, that the French language and culture in North America will be extinguished?"

"Times will be very tough for the colons. In my opinion the English will try to suppress both the religion and the language and they may succeed. I cannot say how it will end. However Les Canadiens will assert their culture as distinctively French and distinctively North American. Their religion will keep them together and united, and provide support and strength, acting like a bridge over the waters of these troubling times."

"Are you relieved to be back in France? Do you miss the Colony?"

"I do not miss the winter climate in Québec, though sleighing through snow-trails on a sunny day in the winter forests is an unforgettable experience. I loved the people and the life. Coming back to live in France has not been easy. The government made many promises about giving us land and money to set up businesses but in the end they gave us nothing. Of course the government is bankrupt from wars and corruption and they have no one to blame but themselves. Fortunately, I have managed to keep my army pension as a reservist and have met a woman with good family connections who is about to become my wife. I have set up a successful commerce in textiles."

Marie-Anne overheard Pierre's reference to his forthcoming marriage; her heart pounded and she felt a pang of jealousy.

"I must congratulate you, Monsieur Tremblais, both on your business accomplishments and on your upcoming marriage," la Fortune said with rare deference.

"It was nothing. I worked hard but also had good fortune. These two attributes often accompany and reinforce each other."

The company at the table sat spellbound at this tale of adventure and drama. Marie-Anne also overheard the narrative and the story of guts and daring enthralled her whilst she bustled busily over serving dishes, carrying loaded trays and replenishing glasses, but being supremely careful not to knock over or drop anything. Her experience of men had been limited to the narrow, demanding attitudes of her father and her brothers, the autocratic abuse from Adolphe Girouette and Monsieur la Fortune, and the sexual neediness of the country youths with whom she worked. Here was a man who had travelled, seen the world, and fought for his country, yet was also generous, supportive and forgiving. She also knew that he sensed, by the way their eyes meet periodically, that he was aware of the effect his words were having on her. She also noticed him peering down her dress at her breasts each time she leaned over his place setting.

The next morning she brought breakfast to Pierre's room and placed it on the table. She started to walk back towards the door when he took hold of her hand and placed it on his chest.

"Marie-Anne, my desire to love you has not changed and has grown even stronger. I loved you from the moment I met you in the barn six months ago. You are so beautiful! I love your sparkling young eyes and lips and your soft hands. I watched you serving dinner last evening. In my heart I felt as if I were talking to you alone, with no one else present in the room."

"I too had that impression, Monsieur. I listened to every word you uttered and felt you spoke only to me. I could not say anything, yet felt nervous and scared I would spill the wine again!"

"It is strange to think that it took a spilt glass of wine to bring us together. Did you spill it on purpose, Marie-Anne?" he added with a smile, knowing instinctively that this time she would not withstand his approach.

"Yes, I did. I needed an excuse to clean your tunic and cullotte," she teased back. "I have to make sure Madame la Fortune knows that I am always busy!"

Now she could not resist. All she could think about was her desire to possess Pierre, so different from other men who approached her. They thought of nothing but themselves; this man thought of nothing but her. His story at the dinner table the previous evening had touched her deeply, and she now had an intense desire to succumb to him. He drew her towards himself, enfolded her body in his arms, kissed her passionately, while she felt the bulge in his cullotte on her belly. She knew now what was coming, knew it was wrong and could have untold consequences, but felt quite unable to resist the exigent desire coming from the depths of her being. Her desire to remain a virgin until her marriage seemed to vanish.

The thought of pregnancy briefly crossed her mind. Her mother once told her that a woman would most likely fall pregnant if she made love around the time of her period. Her period occurred two weeks previously making a pregnancy unlikely. Anyway, I don't care if I come with child!

"Will you come and lie down with me, Marie-Anne?" he asked.

"Yes I will" she heard herself saying, as if the voice was coming from outside of her. Pierre Tremblais undressed her, caressed and kissed her; she noticed and was seized by the sweet smell of cigar smoke on his breath.

"Marie-Anne, I do not wish you to come with child. I shall withdraw before I complete the act and spill my seed."

Marie-Anne said nothing but nodded in understanding and agreement.

As he penetrated her she called out in discomfort but then relaxed with a profound sense of pleasure and satisfaction as he thrust gently and deeply into her. Pierre reached his climax too quickly and only then realised that in the intensity of the moment he had forgotten to withdraw. He said nothing and hoped it would work out well.

Marie-Anne then started weeping.

"Why do you cry, ma chère fillette?"

"I don't know. I care for you. I want you for me but know I am not going to see you again. You will go back home to your new wife and forget about me. Yet you have touched me like no other man has." Tears poured down her head to the pillow beneath.

"I too feel bad, Marie-Anne, that I have caused you to break your vow," Pierre said, pursing and biting his lip. "I thought too much of me and too little of you. We cannot undo what we have done."

"I will be well, Pierre" she replied. "I feel bad but am still not sorry I went with you. I've had other occasions to break my vow. If I'd said yes to them it would have been more hurtful than today. I'm glad I said yes to you. You did not force me. You were gentle and tender. Even if we never meet again, I'll always remember you. This is a special moment for me."

"This is a special occasion for me also, Marie-Anne," whispered Pierre. "You will always have a throne in the corner of my heart."

As she dressed, reality cleared the bliss she had experienced and she felt a complex surge of emotions; pain and guilt on the one hand, from breaking a vow to keep herself chaste for her future husband; joy and exhilaration, on the other, that she had experienced an unforgettable feeling with a man with whom she felt a special bond. She wondered if God was watching and criticising her and struggled to calm the emotional tempests embroiling her.

Eventually, Marie-Anne dried her tears; Pierre rolled over on to his side, and allowed her to get out of bed and dress. While watching her, Pierre unclipped a neckband attached to a silver religious medal that he wore, and removed a ring from his finger. He pressed them all into the palm of her hand.

"Keep these little gifts, Marie-Anne, to remember me."

"Thank you, Pierre. I will not — cannot — forget you."

She kissed him appreciatively on the forehead and left the room to return to her household chores. She pretended to the world that this was a day like any other, yet she had a feeling that people were looking at her and knew what she had done. When she arrived home that night she greeted no one and went straight to bed without supper.

With a feeling of tension-relief and satisfaction, accompanied by an ill-defined sense of foreboding, Pierre Tremblais left the Chateau that day and returned home to Arras.

Chapter Three

Christmas! A time for ceremony, singing and symbolism, time also for shivering, apprehension and resolutions.

Marie-Anne had continued her work at the Chateau throughout the autumn but Gabriél saw subtle changes. She had difficulty getting up some mornings and was late for work. On several occasions, Madame la Fortune chastised her but did not take more drastic action because her children had grown so fond of Marie-Anne. Many mornings she felt ill and even vomited at times.

"Marie-Anne, I've noticed you are not as cheery as usual. You look sick. What is the matter?" Gabriel asked her one morning.

"I am well Papa. It is nothing. It will pass," she replied.

"You must tell us what it is, my little one, because then we can help you," Gabriel smiled and pinched her cheek affectionately.

"I will be well Papa. Do not concern yourself" Marie-Anne looked away to make it clear she had nothing more to say. A puzzled Gabriel shook his head.

Next morning after she had vomited again he stated, this time more compellingly, "Marie-Anne, I want to take you to see Hélène. She is our town's expert in matters of health. I spoke to her at Mass this morning and she told me you look ill. I am sure she has a tonic or a remedy that will help you."

"No Papa. I shall be better tomorrow."

"If your mother were alive I know she would insist you see Hélène and you could not refuse. I wish that she were here. I no longer have the power to force you to do things even when I know it is good for you." He raised his arms in a gesture of helplessness.

Next Sunday Hélène took Gabriél aside and whispered, "My dear man; I believe your daughter is with child. Her face has changed and her stomach is swollen."

Gabriel shook his head vigorously. "That cannot be. Unless she is working she is at home all the time. She turns the young men of the town away when they approach her."

"I shall return home with you now. Let us talk with her together."

In the presence of her father, Hélène said, "Marie-Anne, both your father and I see you have not been well lately and I have noticed your belly is swelling. I believe you are with child."

Marie-Anne flushed, fell into a chair and with her hands covering her face, broke down in tears. Pent-up emotions from four months come flooding out. For several minutes she sobbed uncontrollably while Gabriel looked at Hélène helplessly.

"Why did you not tell us? How did it happen? I trusted you. You are bringing shame on our family! Who is the father?" sputtered Gabriel eventually, as her sobbing subsided. He sounded like several muskets firing off in rapid succession.

"I cannot tell you, Papa. Please do not ask."

Gabriel's voice rose angrily. "You have got to tell me. I want to murder that man."

"No, No." pleaded Marie-Anne tearfully. "It was all my doing. I could have said no and he would have respected me."

"Then you are a fool, my child, and deserve what's coming to you."

Marie-Anne started crying again and Gabriel looked at Hélène, his jaw and fists clenched, brow perspiring. Marie-Anne knew him as a phlegmatic man who pondered alternatives, then decided on a course of action. She heard him mutter under his breath, "If only Marguerite were alive to give me support and guidance!"

"Do you want us to take the baby away?" asked Hélène, quietly but firmly. "I know of a woman in Amiens who has expertise in that domain, but it is a dangerous procedure and some women are permanently maimed. As long as we do it quietly without involving Church authorities, there should be no serious consequences ...."

"Oh, no, no, no —. That's an awful thing to do to a child!" interrupted Marie-Anne, bursting into tears again.

By this time Gabriel had partially recovered his composure and said purposefully, "We can send you to the Convent for paupers in Arras, you can have the baby there and get someone in the city to adopt it. No one in Vimy will know".

"I would not do that," said Hélène, shaking her head. "Children born there often die. It is not a healthy place and they do not look after them well. Even the mothers sometimes get sick and die."

"No, Papa. I would like to stay home and have my baby here," Marie-Anne stated. She knew what she wanted and had no intention of letting her father make her decisions. "I would like Hélène to look after me."

"Do you realise the whole town will find out about you and you will never find a husband? This need not happen if you go to Arras, have the baby there and give it up for adoption."

"I know and accept that I am now a soiled woman and no man will want me, Papa. I will have the baby and I want to keep it. It is my child and my wish." Marie-Anne was not looking at her father or at Hélène but spoke firmly with her fists clenched.

"You have to tell us who the father is. He has obligations both to you and his child. I am your father and have a right to know."

Marie-Anne hesitated before replying. Her thoughts flashed back to that morning the previous September when Pierre held her in his arms, told her how beautiful she looked and invited her to lie with him. She recalled his words, "I shall withdraw and spill my seed so you don't come with child." He must have made a mistake or forgotten. How could she now betray him by naming him, incurring his wrath or even worse, his denial? She could never live with that. She preferred to cherish the memory of a unique experience that she could keep until the day of her death. Besides, to implicate him would also reflect on her own folly in assenting to his advances, when she knew he would have respected her refusal.

Oh Pierre, how I wish you could be here with me now!

She had no alternative but to accept responsibility, and deal with the situation as best she could. Eventually, after a prolonged silence she responded, her voice trembling with emotion. "I love and respect you, Papa. I appreciate your wise advice and all you do for me. But this is my secret and I am not going to tell anyone. Do you understand that, Hélène?"

Hélène hesitated a moment before replying. She placed her hand on Marie-Anne's shoulder while looking at Gabriel, and said, "I understand your decision and see you desire the baby firmly, Marie-Anne. You are not the first girl to whom this has happened and you will certainly not be the last. People in the town will gossip and whisper as they always do but in the end they will forget and get on with their lives. I am sure you will be happier if you keep the child, and the baby will be happier too staying with its own mother. I will look after you and I am sure everything will work out well."

"Oh, thank you, Hélène, thank you for your comforting words," Marie-Anne gave Hélène a hug.

"I do not believe everything will work out well, as you say, Hélène," groaned Gabriel, while shaking his head. "I see many things that can go wrong for both Marie-Anne and her child. I see that Marie-Anne's mind is set and she does not listen or does not want to hear what I am saying. I could never imagine this happening to our family. I will never live this down."

"I am sure, in time, you will understand," said Hélène. "God will help and support us all. You never know, eventually you may even come to love the child."

"That – will – be - difficult," he replied bitterly.

Next morning Gabriel went to the Chateau, met with Luc and told him that Marie-Anne had taken ill and would have to stop working. He gave no details.

Later, in the absence of Marie-Anne, Gabriel told his sons what had happened. Darel, the eldest, frowned. "Send her away, or throw her out", he urged. "I've got no time for women who abuse their privileges and then expect everyone to support them and solve the problems they have created for themselves." The right corner of his mouth twitched as it always did when he spoke strongly on an issue.

"I would like to send her to the convent in Arras but she refuses to go," Gabriel replied quietly. "I know she would be well cared for there and it would be easy to find a home for the baby in the city."

"If she does not go then I'm going to leave. I refuse to live in the same house as a woman who brings shame on our family."

His younger brother, Alexis, appeared more temperate in his opinions. Slighter in build than Darel, he could remain silent and withdrawn for long periods, sometimes even days on end.

"I love my sister and I think we must accept her," he declared eventually. "The same things happened to Madeleine down the street two years ago and look at her now. She has a beautiful baby girl that everyone loves. Besides, Marie-Anne takes good care of us. If we send her away would you do the cooking and the cleaning, and look after Papa and me, Darel?" He knew how Darel would respond to this question.

His brother fell silent.

"I agree with Alexis," said Gabriel, coming around to a more generous appraisal of the crisis. "Marie-Anne has been good to us. Hélène has promised that she will look after her and assist with the birth. I am angry she does not tell us who the father is, but what can we do? She seems to have respect for the man, whoever it is, so that is something. I hoped to arrange for her to marry Philippe, but I know that he will not want her now. No man will want her. Because she is a pretty young woman many are going to be jealous and angry at her."

"Philippe is not the right man for her," observed Alexis. "He seems a nice boy on the outside but he is mean and I've seen him hurt people. She is well out of his way."

"The next few months are going to be hard for us all," declared Gabriel, looking at both his sons for support. "I fear we are heading for some catastrophe. First we have the deaths of your mother and of Pierre, and now this. God seems to be turning away from us. I must talk with Father St. Amour. I am sure he has seen this before and will understand."

"Let us go and speak to him together, with Marie-Anne," said Alexis. "I am sure with his help and with prayer we can see this through."

The following day the family visited Father André St. Amour at the presbytery. A warm fire crackled in his sitting room as he welcomed them. St Amour was around forty years of age and had been a priest for perhaps fifteen years, most of them in Vimy. He had a full head of hair although streaks of grey were becoming visible about the temples. Of medium height, he had rounded symmetrical features, engaging eyes and a ready smile. He gestured with his arms, hands and fingers as he spoke to such an extent that his parishioners believed that a deaf person would understand his sermons just by watching his movements, without hearing the words. His knowledge of the finer points of canon law was tempered by years of practical parish experience. He also understood the fragility of human nature. He knew the family well and, to their relief, remained calm and supportive after hearing their story.

"I have seen this many times before," he assured them warmly. "It is a serious situation but there is much we can do to ease the problem. It helps that Marie-Anne wishes to stay in Vimy and keep the child, and I know that Hélène will be a good support. I suggest, Marie-Anne, that you stay home quietly during the day and ask your father or one of your brothers to take you out for short walks at night. I know there are those in our parish who will be shocked. They will also disapprove of me for seeming to condone immorality. Rest assured that I will deal with them. God knows that we often try our best and things still go wrong. You have to get up, and struggle on to the next stage of your life. Life is easy for no one, least of all in our community where there is so much poverty and injustice. God will help you if you ask, but you also have to do your share or nothing will change."

"I value your words of support, Father," said Gabriel, "but will you ask Marie-Anne to tell us who the father is. We have a right to this information and that man has a duty to us, to Marie-Anne, and above all to the child he has so recklessly fathered."

"You are right, Gabriel. But now is not the time to discuss this matter. I shall talk to Marie-Anne about it alone on another occasion. Marie-Anne, do you have anything else to say?"

46

"I know that I've brought sorrow and shame to my family, especially to my dear father for whom I have much respect." Marie-Anne addressed St. Amour and spoke softly but strongly. "I'm sorry for that. I usually think things out before I act. This time I let my passions take over. At the same time I am not sorry it happened. I love my baby now as part of me, and once born, whether a boy or girl, it will become someone special. I know it is hard for a woman to raise a child alone, and that most men will now not want me as a wife because of this. There is nothing I can do about it other than work hard for my father and my brothers and for my baby when it is born."

"You have spoken well, Marie-Anne," said St. Amour, smiling and punching the flat of his hand in the air. "Let's leave it at that for today." He got up and showed them to the door. Just before bidding them farewell he added, "Marie-Anne, we need to talk again. Come and see me tomorrow."

"Your father is quite right, Marie-Anne," St. Amour said when they met the next day. "It also could mean that you get help raising the child."

"That is not possible, mon Père. The man is not from these parts and I do not know now where he is." She had told a small lie. She knew, or strongly suspected, that Pierre Tremblais came from Arras, and therefore could be traced. "All I can tell you is that he is a man I loved, however briefly. I believe firmly that a child of his will be one that I can be proud of. That is why I wish to have and raise it. I shall work hard myself and will get help from my father and brothers. At least from one of my brothers," she added after reflection. St. Amour smiled and nodded knowingly.

"Have you considered that the child has a right to know who its father is?"

"I shall talk to my child about that when the time is right," she replied without hesitation.

"All right Marie-Anne. I will try to understand and will speak no more about it."

Marie-Anne felt much relief after St. Amour then heard her confession.

Although distressed about her condition, her father and brothers were not disappointed that Marie-Anne had to stop work. Their domestic skills were limited and they were dependent on her expertise in transforming the pasty, tasteless gruel that formed their basic diet into edible meals. The loss of her income also meant the family once again had to limit expenses to pay Adolphe Girouette when he next came by on his unsavoury visits. Winter brought more difficulties to the family; a combination of long, cold nights, boredom and diminished income had a depressing effect on them all.

In a small country town it does not take long for word to leak out about a scandal in any particular household. Every community has a handful of its members who thrive on spreading gossip and the juicier the better. As Marie-Anne walked towards her home one day she heard sniggering behind her. She turned and her face fell when she saw Philippe with a gang of three young men, all of whom she recognised.

"We heard you're in the family way," said one with a grin.

"That you have been very well served," added another.

"Bitten by a mosquito," scoffed the third.

Philippe placed his two hands in his crotch, thrust his pelvis in and out a few times, made a rounded gesture with his arms, and then, laughing, pointed to her belly.

The group giggled and jeered as they ran off.

Marie-Anne sobbed uncontrollably, her hands covering her face, as she hurried home. She went straight to her bedroom and buried herself under her blankets, hugging a soft toy doll she had cherished since childhood. It gave her more consolation than she would get from her father or brothers.

The next day, in Adolphe Girouette's absence due to illness, Monsieur la Fortune cantered up to the Lachêne home himself to collect cash owing from the share-cropper agreement. When the business dealings with Gabriel had been concluded he said, "I hear Marie-Anne is enceinte. What happened?"

"We do not know" he replied, his voice dropping. "She does not tell us."

La Fortune laughed aloud then said, barely able to control his mirth, "You cannot trust peasant girls these days or any women for that matter. They take liberties and then complain when they get into trouble. The only solution is to make them wear a waist-belt of the type they forced Anne of Austria, mother of King Louis XIV, to use. You would think that with such a belt they would be safe from seduction but even then you have to watch them. You have my sympathies, Lachêne. She is a stubborn young wench who thinks she knows everything. We have lots of louts in our town. One of them must have got hold of her."

He did not wait for a reply and, still laughing, galloped off to seek out the next share-cropper who owed him money.

For Marie-Anne the five remaining months of her pregnancy went by painfully slowly. She spent most days at home doing lace work, a skill her mother had taught her, but still got bored. She used this talent to bring much-needed cash into the household. After sundown one of her brothers or her father would take her for short walks. She attempted to conceal her swelling abdomen by wearing a baggy mantua but if they met someone on the street, she could tell what they were thinking by the curious way they eyed her. Because of the protective presence of Gabriel, Darel or Alexis, she had no further trouble from Philippe and his gang.

Hélène came to visit regularly. She brought infusions of tilleul, and feuilles d'oranger to give Marie-Anne strength and help her relax. But despite subtle hints and gentle persuasion, Marie-Anne gave Hélène no further information about the father of the baby.

Her spirits improved when spring and warmer weather arrived, but she felt frustrated that she could not go out to enjoy the aromas, flowers, fresh air, and blossoms. She felt better when she sensed the increasingly energetic activities of the infant inside her womb. This feeling of another life renewed her longings to see Pierre again, yet it also comforted her to know he had left part of himself inside her.

Gabriel stopped hectoring her and became increasingly supportive as the pregnancy progressed. Alexis also did everything to simplify her life, helping her prepare the gruel at meal times, washing dishes and pans, fetching water at the well and even taking out the piss-pots every morning. Darel said nothing but all could see and sense his sullen anger. He visited the tavern every evening to avoid domestic chores and often returned home late and drunk. He shirked every opportunity of taking Marie-Anne out for her evening strolls.

Marie-Anne had several episodes of false labour — recurring pains in her belly that subsided after a while — and went into serious labour when her waters broke early on the morning of June 6th, 1776. Alexis ran to fetch Hélène, and after her arrival the three men disappeared to the tavern for the rest of the day.

As the day progressed her labour contractions became progressively more frequent and intense. "Oh, Hélène, the pains are so bad," she wept. "I can bear it no longer!"

Hélène reassured her as best she could, but had no pills or potions to ease her distress. Marie-Anne got some relief from gripping the edge of the bed, clenching her teeth, and repeating endlessly, "O my God, O my God." The pains became more intense as the infant's head passed through the birth canal, and at this point she let loose piercing, uncontrolled screams. "Keep pushing hard, my dearest girl. It will soon be over!" Once the head emerged from the birth canal the baby's body quickly followed. "You have a baby boy!" exclaimed Hélène, as the child finally emerged and she inspected the small blue body. He drew in a few deep breaths then began crying lustily. Within moments, as if a magical chemical reaction had taken place, he became as pink as a rose.

"God be praised!" cried Marie-Anne as she cuddled and swayed the wrapped-up, crying child once he had been washed. For a brief moment she was oblivious to the myriad pains and sorrows she had experienced over the previous months and days.

"He is beautiful, is he not, Hélène?"

"He is the most beautiful baby I have ever seen, my darling Marie-Anne!" she replied as she embraced Marie-Anne on her bed.

Even Gabriel glowed with pride when he viewed and cradled his first grandson later that evening. He had forgotten how tiny were newborn babes, and shook his head with wonder as he gazed at the moving mite of flesh he held in his arms. He never referred to his wishes a few months earlier that Marie-Anne should be sent to a Convent in Arras and the baby be adopted once born. "Do you have a name for him?" he asked, finally. "Because of your situation you understand we cannot give him the Lachêne family name."

"I understand that, Papa. I would like to call him Marcel Pierre." replied Marie-Anne.

"I like the Pierre," Gabriel said enthusiastically. "He will remind us of our own Pierre who died two years ago."

Marie-Anne felt relief that her father did not press her for other reasons why she might like those names.

The baptism and registration were duly arranged at the Church that evening. Because she remained in bed recovering from childbirth, Marie-Anne could not attend, but she had no wish to risk that the child might die, as many newborn infants did, and its soul not be received into heaven because he had not been baptised. She received a copy of the birth notice which mentioned Alexis as godfather and Jeanne Belhumeur, a family friend, as godmother. The names of Gabriel as grandfather, Marguerite, grandmother (deceased) and Marie-Anne as mother were all mentioned. The father's name and identity were ignored.

The priest inscribed the child's name as "Marcel pierre"; he used lower case when writing the first letter of the family name to record for posterity that this child, born out of wedlock, was a bastard.

Marie-Anne quickly recovered from childbirth; she had to, to resume housekeeping for her father and brothers. But she noticed the home atmosphere and daily routine were transformed with the arrival of Marcel. The baby's plaintive cries disturbed sleep, expenses went up, and, most disconcertingly, the men sometimes had to prepare their own meals when she cared for or fed the baby. Despite these tribulations, both Gabriel and Alexis grew very fond of the child. They enjoyed listening to Marie-Anne sing Marcel to sleep with peaceful renditions of Frère Jacques, Au Clair de la Lune and other lullabies.

50

Darel, however, became increasingly sullen and withdrawn. The noise, baby smells and loss of space were the focus of his frustration and he spent more time drinking at the tavern, using money he extorted from his reluctant, hard-pressed father. Many days he woke up hungover and was unable to do his work in the fields. When drunk, he became belligerent and was involved in several street fights during one of which an assailant broke his nose. The months flew by. He did not respond to increasingly desperate entreaties from his father.

Late one night, he staggered through the front door, shouting loudly, slurring his speech, exhaling alcohol fumes, and rousing all from their slumbers, including young Marcel, just past his first birthday. He began wailing woefully for his mother.

"You're disturbing everyone, Darel. Can you not enter the house quietly when you return late," said Gabriel angrily, his nostrils flaring and arms gesticulating.

With flushed, contorted face, the corner of his mouth twitching and his fists clenched, Darel lurched threateningly towards Marcel. "Get rid of this shcreaming child," he spluttered. "He's wrecking our lives!"

Marie-Anne put up her hands protectively in horror while Gabriel and Alexis both rushed to restrain him. With difficulty they wrestled him down and pinned him to the floor.

"You will have to leave, Darel," said Gabriel, his voice still raised. "We cannot go on like this. You are upsetting the house."

"Get - rid – of – that - child!" He yelled again, the veins in his face and neck swollen with fury, his voice muffled by the floor and the weight of his father and brother. "He is disrupting the house. Everything went well until it arrived. You should have sent Marie-Anne off to the Convent when you found she was with child, and someone, anyone, could have adopted it. She should have stayed there to beg forgiveness for her immorality!" His voice grew hoarse.

This allegation struck Marie-Anne and she burst out, "Papa, Marcel and I can leave and find another home. I know I have done wrong and have no wish to vex you and the family. We shall leave tomorrow."

"Yes, you leave tomorrow," agreed Darel loudly from the floor, his voice still muffled by Gabriel and Alexis.

"Marie-Anne; you will do no such thing," Gabriel said firmly. "Tomorrow, when he's recovered his reason, I shall speak with Darel and exact a promise from him. If he did not scurry every night to the tavern we would not have this problem."

51

"Get off me. Go away. I can't breathe," said Darel as he vomited all over the floor, some of it landing on Alexis' coat and sleeve.

Gabriel and Alexis moved slightly to allow Darel breathing room but continued to sit on him until he fell into a drunken sleep. Marie-Anne threw a blanket over him and they left him on the floor for the night. She then cleaned up Alexis' coat and sleeve and wiped the mess off the floor.

With the exception of Marcel's periodic cries for food, a funereal silence fell on the house the following day. Gabriel and Alexis went out early, and Darel, once he recovered from his hangover, also disappeared without greeting Marie-Anne. She ruefully contemplated her options: stay and somehow survive this domestic turmoil, or leave, walk to Arras with Marcel in her arms, there locate a poorhouse and eke out an existence as a beggar and unwed mother. If she left she knew she risked abuse and exploitation, with enforced prostitution as a possible end result. With Marcel asleep and not requiring attention, she sat on a chair at the back door of the house, watching sheep grazing and bleating in the meadow. She felt the calming effect of the cool breeze blowing on her face and through her hair. What must it be like to think only of the present, and not be nervous about the future? I have less control over my life, and the life of my son than do those ewes and lambs. She shook her head in disgust.

That evening Gabriel took Darel aside and said tersely, "Darel, you might have harmed or killed Marcel last night if Alexis and I had not held you back."

"I do not remember what happened, other than I enjoyed myself at the tavern. I get very irritated with Marcel. He messes and cries a lot, but I do not wish to harm him."

"It is difficult for me also but we all have to accept the baby. If we each make small changes it'll have big results for all. If you are not able to stop drinking, you will have to leave and live elsewhere."

"I am sorry, I feel really bad about what happened Papa. Please let me stay. What can I do to make up?"

"You can say sorry to Marie-Anne and stop drinking."

"I promise to do that."

Both the threats and promises had been made many times before. Gabriel knew from past experience that a pledge from Darel to stop drinking had as much value as a handful of snow in winter, yet once again he accepted his son's assurances.

Alexis has been eyeing Monique at Mass every Sunday. Seventeen years of age, Monique had a thin frame and her face and hands were badly scarred

52

by small pox. But she also had twinkling eyes and an alluring smile that partially veiled her disfigurement. He glanced at her frequently and enjoyed her smiles and signals of recognition, which caused much distraction to neighbours at solemn moments of the Mass. The disturbed worshippers turned around and give them severe, disapproving, "keep quiet" glares. These had their intended effect for little more than a minute or two.

Thoughts about Monique monopolised Alexis' mind. He hid in the shadows near her house and when she emerged, he stalked her at a distance. He suspected she knew he followed her and pretended not to notice. But one warm and sunny Sunday, she led him to a remote clearing in a copse outside the town where they embraced each other tearfully. They were alone in the shadow of an oak tree with the wind quietly rustling its leaves.

"I've been longing to hold and hug you, Monique," Alexis whispered.

"I've yearned for you too, Alexis. I love your blue eyes, shy smile and big, strong muscles! But I'm not good enough for you. I feel bad about the scars on my face and cannot look in a mirror. I feel ugly and want to hide myself from the world, especially from boys. I try to cover my face with ointment and creams but they do not help much. I hate my appearance. I want to go into a convent, and even talked to Father St. Amour about becoming a nun. He thinks I am too young for such a decision."

"Monique, you have lovely long hair, bright eyes; your body is as slim and supple as a snowdrop. The scars are only on the surface; they do not trouble me so there is no need for them to trouble you.

"Besides," he added, "I have my own scar, though it is not so easily seen. I get discouraged. If I'm trying to accomplish something and there's a setback, I give up and lose hope in myself and my future. Two years ago, after a big fight with my brother, I even had an urge to end my life. I tied a rope around one of the beams in the barn, made a loop at the other end, placed it around my neck, and prepared to leap off the bale of hay. At the last minute I lost my nerve. I felt better after talking to Marie-Anne, my sister about it. As you know, she has had difficulties of her own. I wish I had her courage."

Monique hugged him more firmly when she heard his story. "Please don't ever think of doing that again. I need you too much. You are good for my soul, Alexis. But there are many who think differently about my scars, and I can see this by the way they gape at me. They discard me after looking without trying to find out what lies underneath. It makes me shy so I withdraw and avoid people."

"I understand, Monique. You are young, at an age when how you look is so important. I'm sure as you get older, you will come to accept your looks, especially once you get to use all your gifts."

"I love you, Alexis. You make me feel part of your spirit."

"I love you too, Monique."

They continued meeting secretly in the copse two or three times a week, exchanging confidences and small gifts, and kissing and hugging each other.

The strength of his feelings for Monique emboldened Alexis to approach Gabriel. "Papa, I've come to love Monique. Could you find out from her father if she would marry me?" His voice trembled as he spoke.

"I have seen the way you look at each other at Mass, Alexis; I do not think Monique is the right girl for you. She is still young and frivolous and has not recovered from her illness. Moreover, her father has not been well. Like Darel he drinks too much wine and I even heard it said that he has harmed his wife. I would suggest you think of Georgette, the daughter of Michel and Colette. She is older and more ready for marriage. I will talk to Michel and find out if they are interested."

"Papa, I am twenty-two years old, and am ready to settle down," he said raising his voice defensively. "I love Monique and have no feeling for Georgette. I have seen her in the company of Philippe and he has a reputation for using girls for his own ends. I want you to talk to Monique's father."

"I will think about it," replied Gabriel slowly and doubtfully, turning away to end the discussion.

In fact he thought no more about it. In his opinion it was the parent's duty and responsibility to find a suitable life-partner for his children, and in his own good time he would seek another eligible girl in the community. On such an important matter, he trusted his own judgement more than that of an inexperienced and emotional young man.

Alexis and Monique continued their clandestine meetings and their embraces became increasingly passionate. A few months later Monique found she was pregnant. She immediately informed her mother, Louise, who arranged a hasty meeting between herself and Roger, her husband, with Gabriel. Neither Monique nor Alexis were surprised or distressed about these developments, and even the three parents, once over the initial shock, accepted the situation. All could see they were committed and a quick wedding would legitimise the pregnancy. Discussions about the dowry were brief because neither family had any assets, or prospects of any. Of necessity, Gabriel was becoming accustomed to his children taking decisions about pregnancy into their own hands.

Roger and Gabriel agreed they would immediately notify Father St. Amour about the marriage proposal and traditional banns would be read out from the pulpit on the following three Sundays. If no impediments arose, the wedding would take place on the Monday following the third reading of the banns.

During this period, Monique and Alexis saw little of each other privately as their covert meetings were now no longer possible. However they did go and speak to St. Amour. He heard each of their confessions alone, and then met with them together.

"You do understand that the Church teaches that physical intimacy must be confined to couples who are married. This is because we try to follow Christ's example and this has been the Church's teaching from the beginning. Moreover, chastity is a virtue that encourages and promotes respect and honour between men and women who are not married."

"We know and understand that, Father," Alexis stressed, while shaking his head, "but we both have strong needs, we love each other, and we have a desire to express our love for each other. Even if we'd tried, we could not have stopped doing what we did. We knew that Monique might come with child. Before we became intimate, I asked Papa to ask Monique's father if we could get married. He said he would think about it but did nothing. This would not have happened if he'd said, yes, we could get married. We may have done wrong, but we are not sorry it happened the way it did."

"I love Alexis," added Monique, taking a deep breath, looking both Alexis and St. Amour in the eye. "He's helping me get over my disease that has been troubling me now for three years. I wanted to be his wife even before we became intimate."

"I understand and respect what you both have said," said St. Amour. "I see you have a genuine love for each other. From a human point of view, a state of honour and respect exists between you. It is good that you have made the decision now to get married in the Church. From an objective moral point of view, what you have done is sinful, but you are making amends. God is forgiving when confession is accompanied by an honest resolution to avoid sin in the future."

By the time of the wedding, all could see Monique's swollen belly. Only the two families were present at the Nuptial Mass to celebrate the occasion, and Father St. Amour made a brief but pointed homily.

"When writing about marriage St. Paul told us that love is patient and kind, that it is never jealous, boastful or conceited.

"I can tell you now that you will have difficult times, Monique and Alexis, because we all do. I can also tell you that the virtues of patience, love and charity will help you pull through those times, and this fact will help you grow in your natures and your love. Being a Christian means striving for the ideal of goodness. Most of us will not get there but you will be commended for trying.

"I look forward to welcoming a new member of our parish in a few months' time. You have my best wishes and hopes for a happy marriage. I shall remember you both in my prayers." He ended with a smile then embraced them both warmly.

Monique's parents still had four young children at home so after the wedding, the couple moved into the Lachêne house where there was more space. They used one of the two bedrooms; Marie-Anne and Marcel used the other, while Gabriel and Darel slept on separate blankets on the living room floor.

Tensions increased as the date for Monique's confinement drew near. It became clear that another crisis was brewing. Darel had resumed his drinking, and returned home late every night.

One evening Gabriel approached him before he went out and said, "Darel, I can see you are unhappy living here and this can only get worse once Monique has her baby. You have not kept your promise to stop drinking."

"You are always blaming me!" he burst out, his mouth twitching violently. "I do my best working every day in the fields, and give you some of the money I earn. Yet when things go wrong you blame me, as if I'm the cause of all the trouble in this house. Both Marie-Anne and Alexis have babies without being married yet you allow them to live here. And now you want me to leave, not them." Beads of sweat appeared on his brow and dilated veins were visible in his neck.

"Darel…... Darel…..." Gabriel implored, raising his arms in a desperate gesture.

Darel ignored him and quickly threw his few belongings into a bag. Gabriel, Marie-Anne, Monique and Alexis looked at each other helplessly as he stormed out the door. Gabriel saw that Monique was agitated and shaking.

"This reminds me of my father and mother when I was a child," she said, her voice trembling with fear, while clinging to Alexis. "Often it ended with Papa beating Maman, who then screamed with tears. Me and my brothers and sisters shook with fear then went to bed in our room and waited quietly until the storm passed. It was awful. What can we do? Darel may hurt someone or himself."

"Do not concern yourself, Monique," Marie-Anne replied, as if speaking to her naïve younger sister. "Darel can look after himself. He is the cause of much trouble in this house and it is best for us all that he lives somewhere else. By living alone he will learn how to take better care of himself. He might even find a woman who can either bear him or tame him. Then he can come back and stay with us."

Monique continued to pace restlessly. Her baby was due in two months but later that day her labour pains began and the waters broke. Alexis immediately fetched Hélène and next day Monique gave birth to a baby girl whom she called Marie-Louise after her mother.

"Look how tiny your baby is, Monique!" Hélène spoke, clasping her hands together with a sense of wonderment. "Although she now can move and cry her chances of living are poor. You'll have to keep her warm and feed her with your milk often and in small amounts."

"I have this small box we can use as a cradle," Marie-Anne's eyes sparkled with excitement. "We can use this lovely white shawl I crocheted and place the cradle near the warm stove in the living room. I will help you feed Marie-Louise. Together we will make her live!"

"That is good," Hélène replied. "I'll visit every day to help you until she is safe."

Until Marcel's first birthday Marie-Anne remained completely housebound, fearful of being taunted by the likes of Philippe and Adolphe Girouette. She almost convinced herself that the baby's small size and need for regular feeding made it impossible for her to go out... almost. It would have been a simple matter to tie him to her back using a shawl and he would have been rocked to sleep by her swaying body as she walked. She could have taken her stroll between his feeds. Despite St. Amour's well-intentioned assurance that he would deal with those in the town who deplored her pregnancy, she knew he could do little to protect her.

One lovely spring evening, an evening so gentle and fragrant she could not resist, she decided to brave the world and emerged alone with Marcel to enjoy the flowers and freshness of the air. She had barely reached the end of the street when she met Philippe with his equally callow friend Robert. It seemed to her that he had been lurking nearby for months, just waiting for the chance to bait her.

"A beautiful evening, Marie-Anne, an opportunity to put some colour in your pale cheeks," he said, grinning with thinly disguised scorn. "I see you have a beautiful baby boy. For long I've been wishing to congratulate you on his arrival, Marie-Anne," He smiled slyly, as a cat might as it toys with a mouse. "Who might the lucky father be? Surely a man with fine features, like his son. I should like to congratulate him too."

"Thank you, Philippe." She could hear the cowardly malice in his voice but decided to ignore it and respond seriously. "I'm glad you appreciate my little Marcel. He is a joy to our family. As to the father, that is a question between me and my Father in heaven, and no one else."

Her response silenced him for a moment, but he rallied. "We heard you," he paused, looking for the right word, "hired yourself out to staff and visitors at the Chateau when you worked there, to help your father pay accounts owed to M. la Fortune. I know you are an honourable girl," he added with a cynical smirk.

Now Marie-Anne lost her temper. Philippe was grossly insulting her and her family name. "That is not true, you wicked man," she shouted, and she felt Marcel startle at the heat in her voice. "When I worked at the Chateau I earned five sous, and five sous is what I gave my father." She took a step closer but did not lower her voice as she added, "You yourself tried to force yourself on me once and I resisted. I could never offer favours for money! And you, you! Dare to talk to me about my honour?"

"Now you're telling lies about me, Marie-Anne." Philippe also spoke loudly and brought his face close to Marie-Anne's, for emphasis. She saw his clenched teeth and protruding eyes, even smelt his smoky breath and sweat. "You – are – a - putain! If I hear any more of those stories about me around town I shall make sure you leave it for good... forever."

"You are right, Philippe," agreed Robert, nodding his head. He had been standing back from the exchange, silently enjoying it. "We'll march the slut out of town, with her shitty bastard," he said, jabbing a finger at Marcel.

Marie-Anne had made a valiant effort to defend herself and her reputation. She had been raised to believe that honesty would always prevail, and did not know how to respond to this double lie, that Philippe had not tried to rape her, and that she had prostituted herself to staff and visitors at the Chateau. His words were spoken vehemently, and the fact that Robert nearby echoed his voice with words, gestures and nods, gave them added credibility.

With a final, desperate, "You are wrong and you know it," she gathered up Marcel, who sensing his mother's distress, had begun to cry, and with tears on her own cheeks, returned home. There the ever present chores occupied her mind, and the wounding jeers of Philippe and Robert gradually receded

But Marie-Anne could not sleep that night. Although nearly two years had passed since her brief affair with Pierre, she realised she had not resolved within herself all the issues it raised. She had been to confession, made her acts of reconciliation, and no longer felt guilt. Yet her angry reaction to the false allegations from Philippe and Robert made her realise there were aspects of her situation she still had not dealt with. She decided to discuss them again with St. Amour.

The next afternoon, leaving Marcel in the care of Monique she went to the presbytery. On her way she encountered three women, all married and considered senior members of the parish. As they come towards her she saw them turning to each other, whispering and pointing at her, one whisper from the oldest of the three induced laughter in the other two. As they drew level she said, "Bonjour, Mademoiselle Putain. I hope you are done with your life of harlotry. If not, take that little bastard of yours with you and join your companions in Paris."

"Girls like you dirty our town," declared the one on her right, a straight-backed, thin-lipped woman. "We do all we can to keep the reputations of the women of Vimy clean, then you come along and throw mud in everyone's face."

"You bring shame not only on your family, but on us all. Tu es une sale garce," proclaimed the third, the smallest of the three, her voice not as sure as the others, her face reddening as she spoke.

Marie-Anne searched for a form of words, or an action, that would persuade them of her integrity and avoid antagonising them further.

"Mesdames, I made a mistake in a moment of passion," she said quietly, her lips tight with resolution. "I know other young girls have made similar mistakes. Perhaps you know of them even in our town and have advice for them as well. Because I conceived a child, my mistake is visible to all. I love my boy, will care for him with all my heart and raise him to fear God. I have no wish to make him suffer for my errors. This is my home, and his home, and here we stay."

"I don't care what you say, Mademoiselle Poule. You can make as many excuses as you like. You have sinned, you are a whore, and must certainly pay for it!"

Marie-Anne was done with these women, feasting on her perceived misfortune. Giving them each a look of pride, she carried on past and left them without responding, walking slowly with head and back hunched over, covering as much of herself as possible with her coat, as if trying to avoid recognition. She arrived at the presbytery gloomily, quickly found St. Amour, and recounted her experiences to him.

He placed his arm gently around her shoulder and said in an even voice, "You have to understand that people in the town experience one of two things about you; fear and envy. With the women it is mainly fear. They think that because you have allowed one man to seduce you outside marriage, you will allow others, including especially their own husbands. Their anger towards

59

you is directed to preventing this from happening. The women believe in their minds that by being vengeful, you will be less likely to seduce their men. With the young men it is more envy. They themselves would like to have been in the position of your seducer."

"But this happened two years ago," she replied tearfully. "Why would they still be fearful and envious after all this time?"

"There is something in human nature that makes people intolerant of those in their midst who are different, even though they present no threat or harm to others. The mere possibility of threat is enough to stir their fury."

"It is true that I have no desire to seduce their husbands so their fear is needless. There is little I can do about Philippe and Robert's envy. I have no desire to go with them. Even the idea makes me sick."

"Intolerance can be highly destructive." St. Amour spoke slowly in a serious tone. "The Wars of Religion in France during the 16th century provide an excellent example. They almost ruined our country. The wars ended because of the influence of Montaigne, the philosopher, and his friendship with Henry of Navarre, who later became King Henry the Fourth. Montaigne taught tolerance for those with different beliefs and, as a result, the king signed an edict, the Edict of Nantes in 1598 that brought peace to the country. It took many decades to realise that intolerance and fighting accomplished nothing.

"What is happening to you is similar, though on a different scale. It will take time, Marie-Anne and you will have to be patient. Eventually when women of the town realise you are not out to seduce their husbands, they will come to accept, perhaps even to respect you."

St. Amour's references to French history reminded Marie-Anne about the stories that Nicole regaled her with, when she worked as a nanny at the Chateau. "It is not easy for me," she replied eventually, her lips quivering with bitterness. "I no longer feel guilt for what I did. I loved and respected that man though I knew him but a short time. We were not married in a church but because of this love and respect, I believe in God's eyes we were married, so it makes me angry when people have so little sympathy, especially towards my little boy who has done nothing wrong. What you say helps me understand the townspeople but it makes me burn inside when I hear them attack Marcel."

During the prolonged silence that followed, Marie-Anne pondered the complexities of her situation. "There is another thing to consider, Marie-Anne," added St. Amour, finally. "People know nothing about your love and respect for your man-friend, and certainly would not agree that you were married to him. Even though you no longer have guilt about your affair and the baby, you may still have a sense of shame. Guilt is within you; shame is something you feel around people. It refers to your sense that people think less of you because of what happened, and it makes you want to avoid them. It is likely shame that has caused you to stay in your home for the past two years. It takes longer to overcome than guilt." He stopped to let Marie again absorb what he had said. Then he came to his point.

"I would like to propose a solution. It is hard to do, but the only way to overcome shame is to come out, face people and talk to them. They will in time come to see that you are one of them, you are like them, and they have nothing to fear by knowing you and coming close to you. By getting to know Marcel they will learn to love him, and they will then respect you, also."

"It's true," Marie-Anne said softly. She knew he was right, but felt too unsettled to expunge the final husks of her guilt. "I'm still ashamed but I cannot do what you ask at present. It is too embarrassing and hurtful to me, especially when I hear what they say about Marcel. Perhaps I shall be able to face them in a few months or a few years' time. But merci, Mon Père, you helped put my mind at rest."

"You have chosen a rough road to follow, Marie-Anne, but I am glad we had this talk. Pray hard and follow the Lord. You will rise above these tempests only by remembering the noble aims for which you are striving." He sat back for a moment, then rose and walked her to the door to say au revoir. He too appeared soothed by their conversation.

As she crossed the fields towards home, Marie-Anne spoke to herself about the proposed solution. She could not change the past, and did not want to. She could, perhaps, change the future, the future Marcel was heading into. But how could she do that?

Gabriel Lachêne cut and gathered cabbages from his garden on a threatening and overcast day in late autumn. The wind whistled through nearby trees and thrust dead and falling leaves along its path. Ominous clouds gathered pace from the west as Gabriel struggled to complete the task before the storm broke. He reached the end of the cabbage row when he heard horse's hooves galloping up the road, and saw that Adolphe Girouette had arrived on his monthly visit to collect the share-cropper rent.

"Monsieur Lachêne," he began. Gabriel knew that Girouette used the title "Monsieur" rather than "Gabriel" intentionally as a deceptive mark of respect, indicating a shock awaited him. Girouette's features were cold and expressionless. "Monsieur la Fortune has decided, as from today, to increase the amount required from his agreement with you to sixty percent of your monthly take. Therefore, I will expect an amount of twelve livres instead of ten as at present. I will be coming to collect the additional money tomorrow."

"As you know, Girouette, my income is less at this time of the year. Where do I get the funds to pay this amount? Both my son and daughter have young children and we have extra expenses. I cannot afford the increased rent."

"That is your bloody problem, Lachêne. Monsieur la Fortune also has additional expenses and has demanded the increase. It affects all share-croppers, not just you."

"I do not have the means to pay the extra amount," he replied, raising his voice unintentionally. "I have no source of income other than my work in the fields and my potagerie, neither of which is productive during the winter months. Monsieur la Fortune has more ability than I to both generate income and cut expenses. What is he doing in this domain?"

"I regard your questioning of Monsieur la Fortune's judgment and unasked for comments about the way he manages his Estate as impertinence of the first order, and will certainly pass this on to him. As a result he may increase your percentage even further."

Girouette dug his heels into the horse's flanks and disappeared down the road. He returned to the Chateau to report the result of his ride and met la Fortune in the yard near the barn. He raised his cap and bowed respectfully.

"Monsieur, mon patron. I had many complaints. Grimoux and Lasalle refused to pay so we will need to eject them from their homes. Lachêne questioned your judgment. He declared in an insolent manner that you should cut your expenses and leave the share-croppers alone. These lazy peasants spend their days slouching in their homes doing nothing. Then at night they carouse and lust with each other."

"And wonder why they're penniless," added la Fortune. "Perhaps they will come to their senses when they lose their homes. We struggle to support the king and his ministers while millions of peasants in the country sit back and do nothing."

"The king is our leader and he knows best what is good for us. We must follow wherever he takes us." Girouette smiled and slapped his fist on his hand for emphasis.

La Fortune shook his head. "The king vacillates and he will lose his authority if that continues. He pretends that he cares for the people but he looks after only himself. He has mastered the art of dissimulation. On the day he became king, he gave 200,000 livres to the poor but he did this only to ingratiate himself with them, not because of any sense of generosity. I do not trust him."

"You know him better than I do. I have no wish to serve a king who is self-indulgent. I have heard it said that he is not capable of satisfying his wife in bed, and then loads her with jewellery to make amends. That is why they have no children." Girouette laughed scornfully.

"He does that only to relieve his inadequacies." La Fortune also laughed as he contemplated the king's supposed impotence.

"Meanwhile we have to deal with our own situation. Do you wish me to throw Grimoux and Lasalle out of their homes? What must I tell Lachêne? He has that attractive young pussy with the bastard child."

"I heard about that. She's another peasant girl that couples with any goat that comes around. Yes, throw Grimoux and Lasalle out. And give Lachêne one day to change his mind, and if he does not, throw him out too."

"Yes, sir, right away, sir." He nodded his head vigorously, and then cantered off to immediately carry out the owner's orders.

Meanwhile Gabriel returned home slowly, his shoulders bowed. He hated the métayer system in which the share-cropper had no means to argue or appeal his case. He hated also the idea of borrowing money and having to pay interest to the lender. His approach had always been to live simply, husband his resources carefully and never get into debt. It seemed now he might have to break this resolution. It was an endless cycle with no escape hatch. He remembered that in a similar situation several years earlier, Marie-Anne had gone to work at the chateau. Although her earnings at the time were meagre, they were sufficient to make up the difference, and also buy goodwill. Was a similar solution available this time? Marie-Anne now had a child and less free time. He'd see what she thought.

At that point Girouette reappeared at the front door. Without dismounting he shouted, "Lachêne, I have spoken to Monsieur la Fortune. You have one day to pay the additional amount. I shall return at this hour tomorrow. If the cash is not here, you and your family will be ejected from this bloody house." He galloped off without waiting for a reply.

Gabriel went inside and described these developments to the family. "I do not know what else we can do," he ended, throwing his arms in the air. "Where will we live if we are thrown out of this house?"

"I could sell my lace work," said Marie-Anne, "I've learned new techniques using Venetian Gros Point design and am making a table cloth with a lovely floral pattern and matching serviettes. When complete it will provide a substantial sum, but that will not be tomorrow."

They looked at each other for a few moments in quiet desperation until Monique broke the silence. "I believe my mother can help us. Despite our troubles at home she is a strong woman. She told me that older women in

France can get credit more easily than men because money-lenders know they can depend on them to repay what is borrowed. She has had previous dealings with a Jewish money-lender in Arras and eventually repaid her debt, so will not have any problem borrowing money from him again. There will be extra charges, though he may be more reasonable this time, but she said you have to pay extra wherever you borrow money. It will enable us to last until Marie-Anne can sell her lace."

"That would be very helpful," sighed Gabriel with relief. "I do not like owing money to anyone, but we have little choice. Let us visit the money-lender with your mother tomorrow and we will repay him when Marie-Anne sells her lace, or at the latest next summer when my potagerie bears fruit. I only hope the additional charges will not be excessive."

Chapter Four

August 23rd, 1779

Impeccably dressed, yet sweating with impatience, Pierre Tremblais waited in the entrance hall of his home in Arras. To relieve his agitation he paced the floor, clenching then unclenching his fists as though deciding not to use them after all. Today was the king's birthday and he and Chantal, together with other regional notables, were invited to attend a gala reception given by the mayor to celebrate the royal fête. Chantal was always late for appointments and the bigger the occasion, the later she contrived to be.

Every detail of her dress and appearance, down to the smallest stitch and hair, had to be attended to and despite help from her lady's maid, this always took longer than expected. The lipstick, eye shadow, powder and perfume had to be applied exactly right. Even choosing the correct dress took several hours because each of three or four selected garments from her splendid wardrobe had to be tried on, sometimes twice, and inspected carefully in the expensive mirror that Pierre had imported for her, before she made a final decision.

"Hurry up, for pity's sake, ma crotte, we're late; the caléche and horses are waiting," yelled Pierre from downstairs.

"I'm coming, my darling. I'll just be one more minute," Chantal called back.

Pierre knew from experience that her one minute time estimates could be multiplied ten to fifteen times over. To calm his nerves, he entered the drawing room, grabbed Monsieur Voltaire's satirical novel, L'Ingenu, threw himself into his favourite love seat near the window, and immersed himself in the next chapter. It described the remarkable experiences of an artless Huron Indian from Canada who came to live in a sophisticated but hypocritical France. Meanwhile, he glanced anxiously at the mantel clock. Chantal had expensive tastes in furniture as well as clothing and equipped both their home and Pierre's office with ornate Louis XIV fixtures.

The Tremblais mansion rose three storeys above the wide tree-lined boulevard behind the west side of La Grande Place. The façade was suitably splendid with Doric columns on either side of an ornamental front door, and arched decorative frames on the windows at ground level. All the windows had stark green shutters. A large, well-maintained garden, surrounded by a solid stone wall higher by a head than their owner, occupied the rear of the house. In the garden's centre was a pond stocked with goldfish. The carefully cultivated pink and red rose beds, divided by an elegant system of symmetrically-designed pathways, were Pierre's pride and joy.

Chantal was the youngest of three daughters of Jean-Michel and Marie Sévigny. Jean-Michel had established the textile firm of Sévigny Frères, and developed it into one of the largest and most successful in the city. Distressed that he had no male heir to take over the firm, with only three daughters raised to act as sartorial ambassadors for the family business, Jean-Michel was delighted when he met and liked Pierre just as the latter was seeking an excuse to leave the army. Pierre paid a substantial dower to secure the hand of Chantal, and they had married in the autumn of 1775 and two children, Annette and Hughes, were born exactly twelve and twenty-four months later. Headship of the firm fell effortlessly into his lap when Jean-Michel died suddenly two years after the wedding. Pierre had natural business flair and the firm continued to prosper under his leadership. He was a rich man, with a grand home and influence. But as the marriage matured, he became increasingly dubious about benefits accruing from the other half of his agreement with Jean-Michel. Chantal showed little interest or responsiveness during physical intimacy; they performed the act as a reproductive chore, no more.

Fifteen minutes later Chantal very slowly descended the staircase. She wore an ankle-length mauve satin polonaise dress with low neckline and a wide waist, a crocheted white shawl with an authentic pearl necklace. She had done up her hair in a poof style to better emulate Queen Marie-Antoinette. Her maid followed her down the stairs and lifted the dress to ensure that her mistress did not trip on it during the descent. The rustle of her dress and the chatter of Chantal and her maid distracted Pierre from his reading. He sniffed her alluring cologne with pleasure.

"You look stunning, Ma Cherie," he said, almost forgetting the recent ruing of his marriage. "I can see you have not been wasting your time whilst I've been waiting. Let us go. The horses have taken my mood and are restless."

The carriage bearing Chantal and Pierre passed through La Grande Place and into La Petite Place, which though the smaller of the two town squares took several minutes to cross, passing the beautiful arches and baroque-style town houses, and arrived at the Hôtel-de-Ville at the far end of the square as several other latecomers also came to a halt beneath the belfry. They were escorted to the steps by their chauffeurs, whereupon serving maids ushered them to their seats. A string trio performed on a low dais at the far end of the hall and Pierre recognised the music of François Couperin, possibly the Grand Trio Sonata, Le Parnasse, but the clatter of plates and utensils, and hubbub of conversation rendered it barely audible. I wish they would play music only when people were quiet; how is it possible to enjoy lovely melodies when there is such a racket? He shook his head sadly, but said nothing. This was not a crowd who had come to have their musical tastes enriched.

Pierre and Chantal stood for a moment and surveyed the crowd, as a connoisseur might have surveyed the works of art in a salon. Among the familiar faces he spied Monsieur la Fortune, his wife standing beside him, performing the same surveillance. With Chantal in tow he passed through the forest of shoulders and arrived before la Fortune, the music quieter here. "Bon soir, Henri. Bon soir, Madame la Fortune, a pleasure to see you again. I have not forgotten the delightful hunting expedition we had on my brief visit, what, three, four years ago? Since then I have had the great good fortune to enter into marriage. Allow me to introduce you to my wife, Chantal."

As he turned to her, his arm extended, Pierre saw Chantal cast a swift, critical eye over Madame la Fortune's dress and appearance. He knew immediately that later that evening, perhaps even in the calèche, Chantal would, a triumphant smile on her face, say to him, "Pierre, did you notice Madame la Fortune's haughty demeanour and put-on accent? Her dress fits her too tightly making mountains where before there were only hills. The excess rouge is a red herring, perhaps to distract attention from her clothing. But I am grateful to her. She makes the rest of us look even better."

But even as his wife was looking outward at her sartorial rival, Pierre was looking inward, recalling his most cherished memory, the all-too-brief fling with Marie-Anne. I would love to know what became of her, yet I dare not ask Henri. He will be suspicious if I even show I noticed her. He allowed himself to drift into an erotic reverie.

Chantal saw the glazed, distant look in his eyes and punched him playfully in the ribs. "Pierre, wake up! We're at a gala, not a bathhouse!"

"Uh… Uh…. Yes of course, ma Crotte. I'm right here," he lied.

The two couples sat opposite each other for the meal, Pierre put aside his reveries and got into animated conversation with Henri about politics and horses. Periodically, if Pierre strained his ear, he could hear faint tones of the struggling musical trio in the distance. Meanwhile Chantal and Madeleine discussed the relative merits of Lille versus Arras lace and whether or not Queen Marie-Antoinette had the capability of producing a son and heir for the King. A few months earlier, the queen had finally given birth to a daughter after more than six years of marriage; at least that proved, or, Madame la Fortune thought it proved, in her humble opinion, that the king was likely not impotent, as had been alleged. She gave a knowing, ambiguous wink as she made this comment.

Between courses speeches were made by the mayor and others extolling the virtues of King Louis and of the royal family, each speechmaker jousting with the others with their eloquence and praise, and all wishing him a long reign. One by one they congratulated him on the birth of a daughter and hoped a son and heir would soon follow. At the end of the meal, a large group of musicians, including drums and brass, replaced the trio and, much more audibly, they accompanied the assembly for social dancing.

Late in the evening, as the exhausted dancers began to quit the dance floor, la Fortune approached Pierre with a business proposal. Both had to shout to be heard above the din of the music, singing and conversation that echoed through the hall, so they moved to a quiet alcove near the far end, with a bust of the king overlooking their conversation. Henri la Fortune straightened himself up to his full height so that his eyes were at a level with Tremblais' shoulder, and said, "I have been thinking of converting a portion of my estate into a larger stable and paddocks for breeding horses. My present stable, as you know, is more for domestic use only. With the limitless need of horses for armies and transport, it can only be a commercial success. I have no doubt of this. Would you, Pierre, be interested in collaborating with me in this venture? Harnessed together I believe we would make a fine team" La Fortune smiled with satisfaction at his own witty concluding turn of phrase.

Pierre held la Fortune's gaze for a moment, and then told him, "It's a proposal worthy of thought, Henri. As it happens, I've had considerable experience working with horses during my years in the army. We relied on them in Québec, in Nouvelle France, while the colony was ours, and it was an extraordinary experience to go sleigh-riding with them on bright sunny days in the winter snows." For a moment Pierre could feel the bite of the wind off the river on his cheeks. "But, alas, I am now confined to the city and, other than the mares I possess for personal use, I do not have the liberty to indulge in owning greater numbers. Your proposal interests me, to be sure, but I have to consider also my own affairs." He became more serious as he began to discuss money. "I took over the ownership and direction of Sévigny Frères after Jean-Michel died two years ago, and the position is a demanding one. It requires travel to such as Amiens, Paris of course, and even to London, during the rare times we are not at war with the English. However, if you wish to proceed I could be willing to collaborate financially, and with your assurance, obtain a return when the farm becomes profitable." Although

Pierre feigned interest in the project, and feigned it well, in fact he distrusted la Fortune's motives. He sensed la Fortune intended to use his contribution to promote his own plans for the estate, and at a later date would drop Pierre as a partner. Such was the way of business.

"Ah, that is good. And wise," replied la Fortune with a satisfied smile. "I believe we will not take more than a year or two to make a good profit. If you allow me some haste, I will communicate with my notary and draw up an agreement proposal. The extra income will enable me to purchase additional land and displace some peasants who have been threatening to encroach on my estate on its north side. 'Never Trust a Peasant' is my motto."

"I am not sure I agree with you," countered Tremblais firmly. "Many peasants are poor and struggle to feed their families. They till the soil for long days with little return, sometimes not enough to feed themselves. The country could not function without them. You could not function without them."

La Fortune's face was set in a grimace now, replacing the smile he had employed while making his equine proposal. "I have no wish to dispute with you on this matter, Tremblais. I have yet to see a peasant work hard in the fields, and their pay is more than sufficient for their simple needs."

"I agree there is no purpose in furthering this dispute and it does not pertain to our discussion. Let us leave it at this. Let me see the agreement proposal, and then I'll make my decision within the week," Pierre said calmly. La Fortune's mouth remained closed and he bowed low, as though showing Pierre the quality of the top of his wig, then turned and decanted into the crowd.

On reflection Pierre, who remained in the corner awhile, in no hurry to rejoin Chantal who was in a circle of expert gossipers, realised the digression about encroaching peasants did pertain, badly, to their more general discussion, and confirmed his earlier suspicions about la Fortune's motives. He all but made up his mind then to turn the man down, and then thought it wiser to delay a decision on such an important matter. He knew himself to be impulsive in love, but he was not so in matters financial. As Pierre was leaving at the end of the evening's festivities, his tired wife on his arm, many of the men, and some of the women, had to be supported by their butlers and maids as they staggered back to their carriages.

At the dinner table the following night, after the servants had cleared away the bones of the venison that Henri la Fortune had sent them as a gift, Pierre went over la Fortune's proposal with Chantal. He did this not so much to get her opinion. He knew she had no opinions on matters financial, other than to use his money to 'invest' in her wardrobe. He did not expect to get a judgement from her but he knew from experience that by airing both sides of the argument out loud within range of her blank face, he would arrive at the correct way to proceed.

After he had explained the broad outlines of la Fortune's proposal to her she yawned widely, placed her hand in front of her mouth hoping he would not notice, and replied, "You just do whatever you think best, my darling. I am not interested in equine matters other than they quickly get me where I wish to go. She paused a moment, as though deciding which verbal route to take, then said with an alluring look in her eyes, "Pierre, Mon Cherie. I would love to go to London with you at your next visit. I have heard the English have the most fabulous shops and fabrics just now, quite as good as the French lines."

"I think you are quite right ma cherie," replied Tremblais, not responding immediately to his wife's appeal. "I am not going to join la Fortune in his enterprise. On the other hand I love hunting on his estate and have no other opportunities to ride to hounds. I shall provide him with a token contribution, sufficient to buy goodwill and ensure continued invitations to hunt, but not so much that I am obliged to participate in decisions about his estate. And yes, ma cherie; you can accompany me to London at my next visit. I shall be going in July, six weeks from now. Thank you for helping me to make this important decision.

"How wonderful, Pierre!" she cried. She hugged and kissed him, then clasped her hands with joy. "London! I've always wanted to go shopping in London. I am sure the shops are even bigger and better than in Paris. I have only six weeks to plan and pack my wardrobe for the journey. I will have to start preparing right away."

"I hate to say this, ma cherie, but you will have to be careful with shopping. We are living through difficult times and will have to economise. We can hope the fair will be a success for me, in which case there will be less need to limit your spending. I have connections in London and know that our products are of high quality so am optimistic that good sales will materialise."

"I shall be very careful and very discreet so will not embarrass you. I shall even bargain with the English merchants so they reduce the price."

"You can try but I am not sure you will have much success. The English are very good at bargaining — not for nothing do they have the leading commercial enterprises in Europe. I hope to be able to accompany you on some of your expeditions because speaking English will help in your negotiations."

Pierre had a good grasp of English. He had learnt it originally in Québec after England had taken over the colony two decades earlier. When he became director of Sevigny Frères he had employed an English tutor, as he wished to expand the company's activities across the Channel.

"Oh, I am so excited!" repeated Chantal as she rushed upstairs. "I'm going to start preparing my armoire right away." The next few weeks were a flurry of activity for her as she sorted through her wardrobe, selecting then discarding; reselecting then packing. In the end she filled three large trunks. "I am fearful of finding myself without an essential article of clothing or toiletry while in London," she confided.

Chapter Five

London, October 1779

The seas were calm and the winds fair for the Tremblais' channel crossing from Calais. Chantal had never before been on salt water, not in a ferry boat or any other sort of bateau, and Pierre had worried slightly about her intestinal reaction. But the waves, the deep shifting colours, the gradual approach of the white cliffs excited her as if she were a mother enjoying a newborn babe. Together they spent much of the trip standing as close to the prow as the captain would allow, breathing in the salty air, the bowsprit rising and falling with the sea. The only sounds they heard were the surging swell of waves as they lapped against the hollow wood of the hull, and the creaking and flapping of stays and sails produced by the power of the wind.

After standing off Dover for several hours waiting for the tide to rise and take them in, Pierre guided Chantal ashore across the unsteady, swaying gangplank. The Custom's Official, a humourless man as were all of his breed, examined Pierre's credentials diligently. England remained at war with its North American colonies and France supported the colonies, therefore all Frenchmen were even more suspect than usual. He permitted Pierre's entry because his interests, as he repeated several times in his fluent, military English, were purely commercial. Pierre located a carriage to take them to their stopover inn, where they fell quickly to slumber, with the bed still swaying slightly for Chantal.

Next day they boarded the stage coach to London for the final day-long leg of the journey. It was a busy road, and the other passengers, none of whom knew each other, talked briefly of the weather which Pierre knew as an English obsession, then fell silent. Pierre and Chantal admired the lush, undulating chalky countryside of Kent. They passed through the market towns of Folkestone, Ashford and Maidstone, a few passengers alighting at each, more coming aboard to crowd the rough seats, the lure of London drawing them. As the sun set the coach drove through the seemingly endless row-houses of Southwark, crossed the bridge over the Thames River and entered the city of Westminster. Chantal's eyes were like a cat's, peering through the dirty coach windows, seeing the paved streets filled with young children, stray dogs and cats, horse shit everywhere and gutters filled with the stinking mix of animal and human effluent. She held her nose, crinkled her face in disgust, turned to Pierre seated next to her and said, "Pierre, the stench is awful, much worse than Paris. How uncivilised!" Then a few minutes later, she said, loudly, "Just look at the size of the bridge and the river. It amazes me. It must be the biggest in the world!"

A passenger who had joined them in Folkestone, and had remained quiet until this moment, looked over at Chantal and, shouting to be heard above the noise outside, said proudly, in broken French, "London, Madame, has overtaken Paris as the biggest city in the world, and this bridge we are crossing, Westminster, is the longest of them all. All my life London had but one bridge across the Thames but recently two more have been completed." A competitive comparison of cities followed.

The coach finally pulled in beneath the colonnade of the George Inn and deposited the tired travellers, their coachman's head being directly below the pub sign of St. George slaying the dragon. Pierre had made a reservation for seven days at the Inn, the premier travellers' residence in London. The coachman's boy struggled with Chantal's luggage, an armada's worth of 'essentials' over which she had fretted and re-fretted for weeks. "I am fearful of finding myself without an essential article of clothing or toiletry while in London," she repeated to Pierre.

The weary couple slept well in their four-poster, although, as Chantal remarked, she could have slept well on cobblestones after such a journey. Pierre was grateful that her exhaustion gave him a restful, undisturbed night. She had not risen by the time Pierre had dressed for his meeting with Sir Wilfred Montague at his office at Holborn, and he secured a coach and had his trunk of samples loaded above. The carriage moved quickly through the waking streets, Pierre hardly noticing the hullabaloo as he framed his approach for the meeting. Sir Wilfred was Tremblais' intended trading partner in London, whom Pierre had met on a previous visit to the city without then having business dealings with him, but promising to do so in the future. A resident of London, Sir Wilfred owned a large sheep farm in Yorkshire and marketed the products for sale at the Staple in Holborn - a centre for trade in raw materials of the garment guild - as was required by law. Although wool and its products were his main interest he also traded in flax and linen.

In his mid-forties, Sir Wilfred was of medium height with mournful features, dark brown hair and long sideburns with clean-shaven jaw and neck. A dense, drooping moustache that he fingered and twirled while conversing, dominated the lower half of his face, and he had drooping eyes to match.

Pierre saw that his sideburns and moustache were trimmed perfectly, his spotless clothes modern and fashionable, fitted him neatly and masked his corpulence. He had a deep, lugubrious voice and would have made an excellent funeral director if he had chosen a profession different from farming and textiles. He spent much time blowing smoke rings from his cigars towards adversaries with whom he negotiated. The rings and smoke smells, together with his moustache animation, had the intended effect of distracting them from the weighty topics under discussion.

"Welcome to England, Monsieur Tremblais," boomed Sir Wilfred. "I hope the journey was not too tiring and troublesome. Allow me to offer you an excellent cigar imported from the Spanish colony of Cuba, an island I hope one day to visit. Their women are superb, I hear, and they are said to have medicinal effects. The cigars, I mean, possibly the women too." He laughed at his joke.

"Most certainly," Pierre said, also laughing, and he took the proffered cigar and set to the business of cutting and lighting it. Once he had it lit, he attempted to blow a smoke ring towards Sir Wilfred, but managed only a vaguely pyramidal-shaped fume. "The journey went well, thank you, Sir Wilfred. Both Madame Tremblais and I feel rested after our night at the George. It is an excellent Inn."

"Yes. Its reputation is well-deserved. The owner, Sir James Derwent, is of course a member of the White's Club with me. He does everything in his power to keep the furnishings modern and up-to-date. The present building dates from the 1670's after the Great Fire destroyed the original and has been in his family over one hundred years. There was much hasty rebuilding after the fire, but they took their time with that one. And St. Paul's, naturally… "

"The architect and the builders performed excellently, in both cases," Pierre interrupted gently. "Our suite is spacious and comfortable and the furniture, impeccable." Pierre knew that Sir Wilfred would talk London all day if given the chance, so found and held the man's eye and in a business-like tone, he said, "Eh bien, I have brought samples and would like to demonstrate them to you."

"Yes, please, Tremblais. Go ahead." Sir Wilfred puffed a near-perfect smoke ring in Tremblais' direction, as its sweet aroma filled the room. Pierre watched it dissipate, the smoke snaking slowly towards the open window. He opened the trunk containing linen samples he had brought and laid them out neatly on the large oak table in Sir Wilfred's office. Though normally assured in his sales approach, he felt moisture accumulating on his palms and in his armpits. He found Sir Wilfred's supercilious style intimidating and attempted to counter it by confidently extolling the superior qualities of his products. "I want you to know, Sir Wilfred, that our flax is cultivated by hand and the roots of the plant are removed in their entirety. This technique ensures that the resulting fibres, once processed, are as long as possible, enhancing the quality of the linen fabric. In the same way, and for the same reason, our retting and scotching procedures are carried out by hand, making it easier to work with the linen through dyeing and looming, and convert it into good quality apparel. Feel for yourself. "

Sir Wilfred examined the articles carefully, turning them over and stroking them gently between his thumb and fingers to ascertain their texture and thickness while Pierre watched apprehensively. "I am doubtful, I must say, about the quality, Tremblais." Sir Wilfred declared eventually. "Coarser certainly than the best products from my own stock. You have come a long way, and so let me take some of these samples; we can use them for carpets and curtains but the quality is certainly not good enough for clothing." Sir Wilfred stroked and twirled the ends of his moustache as he spoke.

Pierre realised he was holding his breath, unsure at first how to respond to Sir Wilfred's critical comments. "I am surprised and disappointed, Sir Wilfred. I selected and brought over our best goods, knowing your astute assessment of quality. Pardon, but I believe your judgement is warped by English prejudice. In my opinion, this cambric compares with the best in Europe. Could you demonstrate the fabrics you consider of better quality?"

"I do not have samples with me but I know my fabrics, Tremblais, and have been in this business for many years. In England we do things our way, in our own time and it somehow all seems to come out right in the end." After a further few minutes examining the samples he said, "Here, this pale cream fabric you have at the bottom of the trunk is of better quality. You were concealing it from me!"

"Yes, I was," replied Pierre ironically and with relief. "You have chosen well. This fabric is used by the best couturiers in Paris. My price is only one livre per yard. How much would you like?"

"I'll take twenty-five yards, but would like it for but twenty livres."

Pierre looked at Sir Wilfred suspiciously, briefly doubting his seriousness, then made up his mind and said, "That's a deal, Sir Wilfred." He went up and shook his hand vigorously.

"I am glad we have a transaction, Tremblais," Sir Wilfred said, a fixed smile on his face. After a moment's reflection he added, "There's another thing. I would like to invite you and your wife to dinner on Friday night before you return to France. We have a mansion at Portland Place in Marylebone, at the northern outskirts, on the widest street in the city, so they tell me. All the fields and forests your eyes can feast on. Lady Jane would so like to meet you and your wife, um…"

"Chantal. Her name is Chantal. Thank you very much, Sir Wilfred. Chantal and I graciously accept."

Sir Wilfred blew one more smoke-ring of satisfaction in his direction as Pierre took his leave. Pierre, whose cigar had gone out during the negotiations, left the butt in a silver ashtray.

The next day, Pierre asked the innkeeper at the George to secure a hackney with a knowledgeable driver to take him and Chantal on a tour of the city. The man arrived on time wearing an enormous shabby blue coat and proceeded to interrogate the couple as to their plans for the 'set-down' for the day. Each man had trouble comprehending the other's accent, but by gesture and repetition Pierre understood that the price was sixpence a half mile and that 'hackney' was, as he had thought, a crude pronunciation of the word he knew to mean 'horse for hire'. Before they set off, Pierre, mindful of his coming investment in horseflesh, cast his eye over the animal that would pull them for the day. It was, by tradition, brown and stood, again as he divined by hand gestures, well above the minimum fourteen hands. The negotiations complete, the driver shouted 'Gee-O" and they were off down the hill on Red Lion Street.

The grand tour proceeded as was to be expected – a visit to the Tower of London where Chantal gasped in awe as she saw the glittering crown jewels; the crossing of London Bridge and admiration for the water cataract gushing through at its southern end. The day took a turn for the better when the driver bid them alight outside the Bedlam Hospital for Lunatics. Pierre paid the entrance fee – three pennies each – and a keeper accompanied them through the dank, urine-smelling corridors and wards. Each ward had an elevated viewing box, separated by a low wall from the ward proper, from which visitors could observe the inmates without fear of attack or injury. They were amazed, though not amused, as were other visitors nearby, to witness a dishevelled young male lunatic who believed himself to be a musket, and kept firing imagined charges through his mouth. They laughed as hard as the other visitors when another inmate, who thought he was a dog, raised his leg near a hospital pillar to pee. The keeper explained to Chantal and Pierre that having visitors laughing at the inmates benefited them because it brought light-hearted merriment to their dull lives. Chantal, who had laughed hard enough to require a sit down and several deep breaths at the peeing lunatic, must have cheered up half of Bedlam by herself.

They completed the day's tour, at Chantal's request, by visiting and admiring St. Paul's cathedral, as well as the lesser in size, though not in beauty, churches of St. Martin-in-the-Fields and St. Mary le Strand. Pierre had seen St. Paul's on a previous visit, it was hard to miss, as it almost seemed to scrape the sky, but Chantal was awed into silence by its immensity and style, and again by the spectacular beauty of the Doric columns of St. Martin's, and the quiet English baroque style of St. Mary's. Emerging from Westminster Abbey, Pierre could not restrain himself and pointed out to the hackney driver that in 1066, the year of the Conquest, the defeated King Harold and the French Conqueror William, were both crowned kings of England in the Abbey in the same year.

Knowing that their dinner appointment at Sir Wilfred's mansion was for five, Pierre practiced his usual white lie and told Chantal they had to be there by four to ensure they would not be late. Much to his surprise she completed her toiletries and preparations on time. She decided to wear an ankle-length, two-toned salmon-pink damask robe woven with exotic foliage, a matching broad-brimmed hat with a cloth rosette around the rim and pastel-coloured pointed shoes with low heels. They left early and on the way took a detour to view Tyburn, the famous place of execution. As they approached Tyburn, a huge crowd blocked their way although over their heads they could see the infamous Tyburn "Tree", a huge triangular wooden structure built in the middle of the square so that, as a symbol of justice, it could be easily seen by everyone. The coachman a regular attendee of public executions, turned his head and said to them, "We're in luck." He enquired of an older woman in the crowd as to the nature of today's event, and told Pierre and Chantal that on a good day ten criminals could be executed simultaneously on the Tree, however today there was but one eighteen year old man, orphaned and originally from Ireland, who had stolen a lady's handbag, a hanging offence. Even as he spoke, a horse cart drove by with the bedraggled thief sitting forlornly in the centre, his head on his knees, arms wrapped around his legs. The crowd bayed and screamed at the executioner to hurry up.

"Pierre, please, I don't want to see this," Chantal said, trembling and shaking her head. She removed her hat, shut her eyes, placed her hands over her ears and bent down so that her face rested on her knees, in an uncanny resemblance to the posture of the condemned criminal. To avoid witnessing the execution, Pierre ordered the coachman to proceed to their destination with all haste, but the coach was now hemmed in on all sides by other horses and carriages that had serviced the onlookers, and was unable to extricate itself from the mêlée. Responding to the impatience of the crowd, the executioner ordered the man to stand up in the cart, tied the rope around his neck and his hands behind his back. The hangman then hopped off the cart and whipped the horse yoked to it. As the cart trundled off the man fell, swung by his neck, and strangled to death in moments, convulsing as he died, while also peeing and defecating uncontrollably. The mob cheered and applauded their approval.

Pierre had seen many deaths during his years in the army and thought himself inured to it. The death of this young, anonymous man, in a cold-blooded, brutal and public manner, for a relatively minor crime of property, shocked him to the point of wordlessness. He indicated to the coachman, by hand gestures and facial expression, to proceed as quickly as possible to Sir Wilfred's mansion, which the coachman was able to do. By the time of their arrival, he had recovered his composure. Chantal, meanwhile, had neither witnessed nor heard the execution, and the event quickly passed out of her mind.

The butler was expecting them. He met them at the door, introduced himself as 'Ben' and showed them to the drawing room. The Tremblais' were familiar with capacious rooms and ornate furniture but this particular one dazzled them. Its size exceeded the whole ground floor of their house in Arras, and beautiful, but austere English-style furniture covered the floor, including tables, chairs, armchairs, of many shapes and sizes, all organised into an eye-pleasing pattern. In the centre of the room rested a fortepiano with attractively carved legs using a walnut veneer. A huge mantelpiece carved in white marble dominated one wall with large flanking windows on either side. An elaborately carved longcase clock occupied the centre of the opposite wall to them and, as they entered the room, it loudly gonged the hour of five. A veritable art gallery adorned the walls with oil paintings of portraits, landscapes and horses. One in particular, of a fine horse with its groom, caught his eye.

Sir Wilfred and Lady Jane Montague entered as they were feasting their eyes. "Welcome to Portland Place, Monsieur and Madame Tremblais. Allow me to introduce my wife, Lady Jane." A series of bows and bobs followed, and Sir Wilfred then pointed at the painting Pierre had been admiring. "Stubbs," he said, "bought it several years ago, when he first came on the market. Spent years in the country dissecting horses, so he told me. You can see how he has perfected its muscular anatomy. Remarkable! Please make yourselves comfortable. Could I offer you some excellent Spanish sherry or would you prefer a cup of tea?" Pierre acted as translator because, as he had warned her ahead of time, neither Sir Wilfred nor Lady Jane spoke any French, unusual for a man in the fabric trade, but probably a sign of his strident Britishness. Pierre took the sherry and Chantal preferred the tea.

They sat around the fireplace as Pierre described, with enthusiastic approval, their impressions of London. "We've been fortunate with our architects," replied Sir Wilfred twirling his moustache delicately. "Sir Christopher Wren, James Gibbs and Robert Adams worked wonders with our city after the fire. The Great One. Not only the buildings they designed and erected, but the streets have been paved, and lighting added for better night time security. The drainage in parts of the city remains primitive, though. More than the river can handle, I expect, and lack of restraint with the hoi-polloi."

"Yes, I noticed that," replied Chantal after Pierre had translated Sir Wilfred's words, although hoi-polloi gave him trouble. She clipped her nostrils with her thumb and index finger, while Lady Jane and Sir Wilfred laughed. Chantal added, "I observed a great many single women, alone in the streets, often dressed in colourful clothing, big hats with white plumes rising from them. That seemed strange. What were they doing there just wandering around by themselves?" Pierre knew exactly to what she referred but dutifully translated her exact words.

"We call them strumpets," replied Sir Wilfred with a knowing wink in Pierre's direction, out of Chantal's sight. "There are many in London and the commerce is popular." Pierre translated the words as, 'Ils sont des jeunes femmes qui cherchent des maris,' in other words 'he says they are just single women seeking husbands'.

"I am sure there are better ways of finding husbands than on the street," she replied loftily. "I am sure they would find them more easily if they went to church, for example." Both Sir Wilfred and Lady Jane nodded their heads and smiled wryly as Pierre translated Chantal's words.

"I see you have a fortepiano," Pierre said. "After dinner, if there is time, I can sing you a song."

"Yes, that would be lovely," replied Lady Jane. "I will accompany you."

They moved to the dining room for dinner and Lady Jane's chef had prepared a main course of top quality steak and kidney pie, mashed potatoes and swedes, not a sauce in sight, washed down with a choice of sweet Spanish sherry, cider or tea. Sadly, wine was not available because of the war, Sir Wilfred explained, although he was expecting a smuggled shipment soon. As they were eating Chantal looked at Pierre, a look that said, "Is this the best food the English can offer?" They said nothing, feigned they were enjoying the meal and emptied their plates with seeming animation.

After dinner Sir Wilfred and Pierre retired to the former's study to drink port and smoke a cigar while Lady Jane and Chantal returned to the drawing room to communicate with each other in sign language and Chantal's broken English.

Sir Wilfred and Pierre made pleasantries about the weather, a curious English habit, and then once they had settled deep in their fauteuils, cigar in one hand, port in the other Pierre asked, "What is your opinion about the political situation? I presume you have an insider's knowledge."

Sir Wilfred blew a smoke ring in Pierre's direction before replying, as if weighing his words. "You likely know we had serious riots here in London last month. They were provoked by a miserable Scottish peer called Lord Gordon, who stirred up first the Catholics, then the poor. Idiot! It would have led to a Revolution if the authorities had not firmly stamped it out. Hundreds were slaughtered and their leaders executed on the Tyburn tree. Went along myself to see them dispatched. Gordon himself is insane and should be sent to join the others at Tyburn. Fortunately our government is resolute. He will not succeed."

"There exist great social injustices in France also, Sir Wilfred. Yet with the exception of the philosophers, the people have a great respect for the king. I cannot imagine such riots occurring in our country. Do you have an opinion about the Colonies' War for Independence?"

"It's very simple. They are rebels to the rule of law and refuse to pay taxes. We must defeat their army and send their leaders too to the gallows."

"With respect, Sir Wilfred, I disagree." Pierre chose his words carefully, not wanting to antagonise his host. "I believe there is some justice on their side, though at times it may be difficult to discern. King George exceeded his authority in imposing taxes when the colonists were not represented in Parliament."

With deliberation, Sir Wilfred placed his glass of port on the table, his cigar on the nearby ashtray, twirled both sides of his moustache and responded gravely, while shaking his head, "You clearly do not understand history, power and politics, Tremblais. We, the English, established those colonies and have peopled and supported them for one hundred and seventy years. We have every right and duty to expect them to contribute to their own security."

"I fear that in your efforts to enforce payments you may lose everything. The colonists …."

"Nonsense," interrupted Sir Wilfred, reaching out again for his port and cigar, to stress the measure of his words. "The colonists are as English as I am. They are King George's subjects and owe him loyalty and fealty. We shall persuade them of this by force if need be." Sir Wilfred rose from his fauteuil to replenish his empty glass of port, as if this was the last word that

80

needed to be said on the subject. Pierre did not pursue the topic and they returned to the drawing room to find Chantal struggling to describe her millenary purchases to Lady Jane in mime. In desperation, using a quill, and much to Lady Jane's amusement, she had resorted to drawing pictures of her hats on paper. "Come now, ma chérie," Pierre said, while placing his arm around her shoulder. "I love your drawings but it is time for us to leave and get home before it gets too dark."

"What about your song, Monsieur Tremblais," Lady Jane said with a persuasive smile. "We must hear you before you go."

"Yes, of course," he replied. So Pierre sang his signature tune, Monsieur de Turenne by Jean-Baptiste Lully to Lady Jane's fortepiano accompaniment.

"You are right to travel before darkness, Tremblais," added Sir Wilfred as they left. "The streets of London are not safe at night even though we have excellent new street lights. Despite our political differences I am glad we were able to make some commercial deals. We wish you a fair journey home and hope to renew our acquaintance soon." Ben the butler appeared and led them to the front door, where a hackney was waiting. Pierre did not look back as they pulled away.

For his final day in London, on which of course it rained, Pierre visited the trade fair and found a clothing manufacturer who paid a good price to purchase the remaining five bales of the top-quality linen that had crossed the Channel with him. Meanwhile, as Pierre bartered, Chantal derived great satisfaction from a major shopping expedition to the Royal Exchange, where she picked three petticoats, a straw hat and several dresses, together with three pairs of shoes, all carried out using a beautifully decorated sedan chair for transport. On the return to The George Inn, her chaise partially scraped the ground, piled high as it was with the expensive purchases brought back to their suite. Pierre did not have occasion to accompany her, and her half-hearted attempts to negotiate a reduced price were not successful. The sample trunks that Pierre had managed to empty, she filled with her purchases and he listened ruefully as she recounted, with excitement, her plans to parade her fashionable, new hats, dresses and shoes to friends back home in Arras.

Chapter Six

October 1781

"My Maman told me you're a bastard." Alain, sitting on the school bench in the classroom next to Marcel, whispered audibly out of the corner of his mouth, his lips curling as he uttered the final word. Marcel winced, more from the force of Alain's venomous utterance than from the word itself. He did not know its meaning, so frowned, looked away and did not respond.

In the absence of a school in Vimy, the catechism class at the Church presbytery was the only learning opportunity for children, so Marie-Anne registered Marcel as a catechist at age five. Subject matter in the classroom followed the customary format; memorising by rote basic prayers such as the Our Father, Hail Mary and Creed and preparing children for the first reception of the sacraments of Confession and Holy Communion. The teachers were nuns from the nearby convent who taught children the basics of reading, writing and arithmetic.

These skills excited Marcel and at night he demonstrated them to Marie-Anne on his slate, his features and fingers coming alive as he filled the canvas with letters and numbers. He also loved drawing, and seemed to have some skill at caricature. His teacher, Sister Philomène, was a plump, warm-hearted soul who loved her pupils, especially Marcel. Under her habit she displayed an outsize nose and a small forest of hairs growing in the lower half of her face. His reproduction of her features on his slate, with both nose and hairs exaggerated in size, made Marie-Anne smile, despite herself. Though she could read some words in her missal and recognise several of the letters in the songs she sang—she could see the word 'Gloria' as she sang it— she had never been to school nor learned the elements of writing. Her brothers and father were thoroughly illiterate and could not even write their own names. In official documents they merely signed an 'X' beside their name

Marcel rushed home after school that afternoon to find Marie-Anne at the stove preparing an oxtail ragout for dinner. The complex smells filled every corner of their small home. Breathlessly, he asked her, "Maman, what does 'bastard' mean?" Until then she had told him nothing about his origins. At first she did not know how to reply. With this pointed question she now had to face, without warning, the whole perplexing problem. It was as if she had buried her affair with Pierre in the fields around their home. After an extended silence she replied, with a defensive edge to her voice, while feigning as much calm as she could muster, "Why do you ask?"

"That's what Alain called me today. It did not sound good."

Intuitively, Marie-Anne then knew which way to proceed. "Marcel, mon p'tit fils, come here. Sometimes, when children are born, their father leaves home and does not come back. That is what happened to your father and me. 'Bastard' is the name given to children whose parents are not married and whose fathers have gone away. It is also a bad name that people use to call others when they want to hurt them." As she sometimes did, Marie-Anne thought of Pierre as she spoke to Marcel.

I know what I'm telling Marcel is not the whole truth but it's better than an outright lie. Pierre, I could have told him you and I were going to get married and you were called up in the army, or even that you were killed in battle. Perhaps, though it hurts to think it, you were. I am sorry to place all the blame on you. I know I am also responsible for what happened. But I am the one living with Marcel every day, and it is I who has to deal with all his problems and questions. It is simpler for me to tell Marcel that you left, and not give him any reason. It is still my secret. When he is older I will give him more details.

"Mon p'tit Chou." She took both his hands in her hands and looked him in the eye. "You are my special child. I love you dearly and want to do the very best for you in life. There are many people who will want to hurt you, even some who will want to harm you. Sometimes it is a good idea to fight back. Other times it is better to take no notice, or even to walk away. If Alain teases you again, ignore him, or tell him you are happy being a bastard. Meantime, work hard at your lessons. The best way to fight back is to show him how well you know your work." She gave him an affectionate hug. Please don't ask me any more questions.

At night, Marie-Anne would tell Marcel stories her mother recounted to her when a child. Many were based on the fables of La Fontaine. His favourite, that he learnt by heart, was that of The Lion and the Rat in which the rat emerges from his nest in the ground to find himself between the paws of a lion. The lion deigns not to consume the rat and allows him to escape. Later the lion finds himself caught in the net of hunters. The rat gnaws through the lines of the net allowing the lion to escape. It thrilled his imagination that a tiny rat can return a favour to the lion and does something the powerful beast cannot do.

Marie-Anne sensed that her advice and reassurance might not be sufficient to help him deal with the tension at school. She knew that in schoolyard settings, petty antagonisms and minor jealousies could grow and quickly erupt into major conflicts. A trivial blow to self-esteem could have a major impact on relations. After reflecting for a few days she decided that the situation required a more long-term solution so she resolved to speak to her father. She approached him one evening after supper when he was at work in the potagerie behind the house. "Papa, is it possible, even now, for me to find a husband? I want this more for Marcel than me. He is being teased and bullied at school because he does not have a father. I want to help him."

Gabriel dug his shovel into the ground in the cabbage patch and rested on it as he replied, pensively, while nodding his head, "You are echoing my thoughts, Marie-Anne. I agree it would be better not only for Marcel to have a father, but also for you to have a husband. It is not good for a woman to be alone. You have a cousin named Hubert who lives in Arras. He is about thirty years old and is the son of my sister Catherine. She is a widow and her husband left her a big bequest when he died. I have not seen them for many years but believe Hubert is not married yet. I will invite them here and we can talk to my sister. Because he is your cousin, we would require special dispensation from the Archbishop for you to marry."

"Merci bien, Papa. I would like to meet them."

Father St. Amour wrote the letter on Gabriel's behalf.

'My dear Catherine, my dear sister,

Greetings from your family in Vimy!

You know that a few years ago my daughter Marie-Anne had a son out of wedlock. The boy, Marcel, now five years old, is a healthy youngster and has just started school.

It would be helpful if Marcel had a father and Marie-Anne a husband.
Is your Hubert still a bachelor? If so, could we meet and see if arrangements can be made for Maire- Anne and Hubert to wed?

With love and expectation I look forward to your reply.

Gabriel'

The letter delighted Catherine. Hubert had become something of a burden to her. He had refused to learn a trade, had no friends and spent his days lounging around the house. Here was a chance for him to get married and assume a normal life! She quickly responded and informed him that Hubert was still a bachelor and she was eager for him to marry Marie-Anne. She and Hubert came to Vimy for a weekend and negotiations between the two families for the marriage were quickly finalised. Catherine offered Marie-Anne a substantial dowry, payable if she survived Hubert.

When she met Hubert it took Marie-Anne just a few seconds to realise she had little attraction to him. He had untidy dirty hair, an unkempt beard and she found him coarse, clumsy and cold. He never initiated conversation, and responded to questions in monosyllables. He had a tendency to shrug his shoulders repeatedly when in conversation, as if saying, 'I don't know'. She felt she had little choice but to proceed, being swayed by Marcel's need for a father, and the possibility that he might, in due course, also benefit from the dowry. She also knew that her prospects of finding a husband if she followed conventional channels were remote.

Father St. Amour helped them make an application to the Archbishop for a dispensation for the couple to marry, despite being first cousins. In the missive he explained that Marie-Anne had a five year old son, that the identity of his father was not known, and that the family wished to legitimise Marcel's birth. He added that both families were God-fearing and he believed the couple were well-suited to each other. The Archbishop approved the application within a few weeks.

Two months later they married in St. Martin's Church in Vimy. Only family and a few close friends were present. Marie-Anne wore a plain ankle-length blue dress with long sleeves she had made herself. Head-gear consisted of a dark blue bonnet she decorated with a floral design and lace because a veil symbolised virginity so she wore no veil. The night of the wedding, Hubert moved into the Lachêne household, into the bedroom occupied hitherto by Marie-Anne and Marcel alone. As there were but two bedrooms in the house – Alexis and Monique slept in the other with their daughter Marie-Louise – Marcel now shared the room with his mother and Hubert, he on the smaller bed and with them sharing the large one.

Her experiences on their wedding night confirmed all her earlier misgivings about Hubert. He showed her no affection and had an unpleasant body odour from lack of bathing. There were no preliminaries to his sexual demands. He got into bed, climbed on top of her, thrust a few times until satisfied, and fell asleep. Subsequently she felt sore and unhappy. How different this is from you, Pierre. You were so gentle and loving. You made me feel warm, and made me want you so badly I lost my reason. I suppose that is why I am in this plight right now. She even managed a rueful smile at this last idea.

On the next occasion they made love she shut her eyes and made a forceful attempt to imagine Pierre lying on her, but so great was the contrast that she gave up.

Marcel reacted in his way to his new stepfather, seeing him as an interloper intruding on the close relationship with his mother. He could not avoid contact with him as Hubert, despite urging from Gabriel and Alexis, refused to work in the fields with the other men of the house and spent most of his day lounging around at home. He made an appearance only at the family evening meal. Listening to the muffled sounds and struggles of their love-making in the neighbouring bed at night did not make it any easier for Marcel.

His suspicions were justified in another way. A week later when Hubert and Marcel were alone in the house during the day, Hubert exposed himself while standing close to Marcel's face. "Marcel, it will make you feel good if you touch me there," he said, nodding towards his erection which he held in his hand, while shrugging his shoulders vigorously.

With a quick and emphatic, "No, I don't want to," Marcel turned around and fled. He returned home only after the rest of the family had come back. He made no mention of this incident to Marie-Anne and attempted to put it out of his mind completely. He now eschewed Hubert as much as he could.

Alexis acquired a dog from a friend who had left town and Poilu partially relieved the gloom of Marcel's life. He was a large, playful black animal that Alexis obtained to help round up sheep and cattle on la Fortune's estate. When he first sniffed Marcel, he leapt up and almost bowled him over with joy and excitement. Poilu had a long tail and he wagged it in a rotary fashion like the moving blades of a windmill. Once he had been trained, Gabriel delegated the rounding up function to Marcel and Poilu. Marcel connected immediately with the dog. Every afternoon before sundown the two entered the field and with Poilu's help, the animals were quickly herded together and penned.

Alexis showed Marcel how to throw a stick for Poilu to retrieve, explained how calling his name, scratching his back or his ears, and patting his head made him wag his tail with pleasure. He also showed Marcel how to ensure that he had enough food to eat and water to drink. In between the rounding up of sheep and cattle, he and Poilu went for long walks in the woods together, chasing each other and exploring the trails. Poilu never seemed to tire of retrieving sticks and would return each time, drop it at Marcel's feet as if asking him to throw it yet again.

Marcel loved these walks. They stirred his sense of wonder at Nature's changing seasons, at the growth of flowers and trees, and at the animal life he encountered. He brimmed with excitement when Poilu spied a squirrel or rabbit, then teased or consoled the dog when the animal disappeared up a tree or down a burrow. He even chased and barked at birds, without getting close to catching one. The swallows retaliated by flying down towards Poilu, twittering loudly and pretending they were going to strike him. They then veered off above his head before flying away. Poilu took this teasing in good spirit and it gave Marcel much cause for merriment.

Marcel followed Marie-Anne's advice regarding his lessons. He memorised his prayers quickly, learned how to spell and write, and do basic arithmetic. Sister Philoméne complimented him warmly in front of the class on his skills and alertness. This only aggravated tensions with Alain and his companions. Each time he encountered Marcel, Alain mouthed the words "bastard" or "fils de putain", contorting his mouth and face grotesquely as he did so. Marcel either ignored him or looked away. Alain also began pushing Marcel aggressively when they were physically close so that he would stumble in his stride and with difficulty, avoid sprawling on the ground. He walked away without responding to these strikes.

One afternoon after the class had been dismissed, as Marcel walked home alone, Alain and three friends leaped at him from behind a bush and brought him to the ground. All four boys kicked and pounded him, and though he fought back gamely, landing some good punches of his own, they left him beaten up on the ground, and in pain. Both eyes were swollen and his face, cut and bleeding. He had numerous bruises and cuts on his arms, legs and flanks and his knuckles were painful and bleeding. After nursing his wounds for several minutes, with no one around to help him, he slowly picked himself up off the ground and limped home, sobbing quietly.

"Mon p'tit Chou, what happened?" exclaimed Marie-Anne as he came through the door. Through his tears Marcel told his mother the story. "Alain is a bully and the only way to treat bullies is to fight back and beat them," Marie-Anne replied doggedly. "Let us talk to Grandpère, Alexis and Hubert tonight. They will suggest something."

At the evening meal, the three men decided that over the next few weeks, Alexis would coach Marcel in fighting techniques, strengthen his body and prepare him to challenge Alain to a weapon less duel.

Marcel missed classes during this period, giving time for his wounds to heal. He spent his days running in the woods, playing with Poilu and in the evening, sparring and wrestling in the living room with his uncle. Alexis showed Marcel how to anticipate and dodge punches, how to dance lightly on his feet, and how to punch solidly with his right and left fists. For training, Alexis fixed two pillows to the wall to absorb the shock of his practice blows.

As he gathered strength, Marcel surprised Alexis with his powerful punches, and Alexis even developed a bruise on his left cheek after one of Marcel's bare-fisted jabs. Monique, who had had her fair share of teasing because of her smallpox scars, added strong words of support.

During a recess on the morning he returned to school, Marcel accosted Alain. With some well-concealed trepidation he said, "Alain, just like you I have a father who left home after my birth. I have had enough of you hurting me. After class this afternoon I want to meet you in the yard behind the church for a fight."

"I will be there. I will whip you again," Alain spat back.

"Maybe, but not as easily as when your three friends held me down to let you beat me up," Marcel spoke quietly and firmly.

The two duly met that afternoon with supporters from both sides forming a ring around them. There were no rules, referees or time keepers and no nurses present to patch up wounds.

At a pre-arranged signal, the word 'Allez' shouted by one of the boys who also clapped his hands, they began slugging ferociously at each other. Alain quickly sustained a cut lip that bled profusely and Marcel a badly bruised, cut left eye that became so swollen it almost obscured his vision. Alain also used his feet, kicking Marcel hard in the shin, and later in the groin, a blow that he managed to dodge. Meanwhile, supporters of each combatant shouted cheers or jeers that were especially vocal when they saw blood.

After about four minutes Marcel gritted his teeth, looked Alain in the eye, saw that he appeared fatigued and had dropped his guard for a moment. Marcel feinted a jab with his left hand then landed a solid punch on Alain's jaw with his right fist. He fell back, hitting his head on a rock with an audible crack. Dazed, he lay on the ground for a few seconds before opening his eyes and gazing listlessly around, unable to rise. His classmates helped him to his feet and silently led him away. As he returned home, Marcel felt his heart beating with pride and relief, a feeling that wiped out the pain he felt in his bruised and bleeding eye.

He pursued his classes without further trouble from Alain and his gang.

Chapter Seven

May 1782

"Grand-père had a bad fall this morning and hurt himself. He is in my bed and cannot move." Marie-Anne greeted Marcel with these words as he returned home from school.

Marcel entered the darkened room and once his eyes adjusted to the gloom saw his grandfather stretched out motionless on the bed.

"What happened, Grand-père?"

"I woke up with a bad headache this morning ..." he whispered. Marcel noticed his handicapped speech, and saw he could gesture with his right arm but his left lay limp on the bed. "I could not go to my work in the fields. When I returned from the well with two pails of water, I fell on the floor and could not move. Now I cannot move my left arm and leg so have to stay in bed. I'm an old man now and am sure the good Lord will call me home soon."

Using his right hand Gabriel took Marcel's arm and squeezed it affectionately. "You have given me much happiness, Marcel. I did not accept you when you were born because you did not have a father. That is why we named you Marcel pierre and not Marcel Lachêne.... "

Gabriel fell back on the pillow exhausted. "Give me a drink, my boy. I'm thirsty." Marcel took the glass of water from the table and helped his grandfather take a mouthful. Half dribbled down onto the pillow, which Marcel dried, using a towel. Gabriel continued, searching for words, "You were called pierre after my son Pierre who died before you were born, though of course he is not your father. Only your mother knows his name and you will have to talk to her. I know now you are a tough and sturdy child." He pinched Marcel's cheek gently with his hand and added, "Keep up your work and prayers. I'm proud of you, dear boy.... "

"Grandpère, I'm sad you are sick. I asked Maman once about my father but she just told me that he went away."

"She is likely waiting until you are a little older and then will tell you more," Gabriel said encouragingly, but he fidgeted and looked away. "All I can say is that he is a man whom your Maman respects. For that we can be thankful."

"Thanks, Grand-père," replied Marcel with tears in his eyes. "Please get better quickly."

"I will try. Say a prayer for me."

Gabriel's condition did not improve. Three days later he developed massive swelling of his paralysed leg, over which the skin became shiny and taut, and the veins visibly swollen. Marie-Anne gave him emetics and purgatives to remove the fluid but they made him feel much worse and had no effect on his leg. The following day he developed a severe coughing spell with pain in his chest. He spat copious amounts of blood. With his family around the bed he lost consciousness and stopped breathing.

Perhaps because of his age, Marie-Anne took her father's death with surprising calm. Few peasants lived into their sixties so he had overstayed his time on earth. She knew she harboured mixed feelings about him. She respected his sturdiness and reliability, but had never forgotten, nor really forgiven, his angry reaction to her pregnancy, despite the open love he later developed and showed to Marcel. She blamed herself for these remaining resentments. When people she loved hurt her, she could not allow that hurt feeling to go away.

Much to Marie-Anne's astonishment Darel showed up at the funeral, five years after his precipitous departure from the house. She barely recognised him. He was dressed in raggedy clothes and smelled of an unpleasant mixture of dirt, smoke, sweat and alcohol. He had gained much weight and developed a sallow appearance with heavy bags under his eyes. His head and hands trembled visibly and his hair was long and wispy. Marie-Anne took pity on him and invited him home after the funeral.

"Darel, it is five years since we have seen you. Where have you been and what have you been doing?"

"Life has not been good to me, Marie-Anne." She saw that even his tongue trembled when he spoke, and his lip twitched just as it did before. "For a while I worked for a tobacconist in Givenchy-en-Gohelle but he threw me out. Said I stole tobacco which was false but what could I do? Then I worked in a tavern but the same thing happened they fired me. Said I drank and used their bottles. I would never do such a thing. The only money I get now is from begging outside church on Sundays, and I have to sleep in porches and barns at night. People are not so generous anymore. I've been arrested many times and sent to prison in Arras. Conditions there are dreadful. It is more for animals than humans. I'm now alone and have no one I can call upon for help."

"We will find a place for you. It might be easier now that Papa is gone."

Marie-Anne felt sorry for Darel. She set up a warm bath for him, gave him Gabriel's clothes to wear, and threw his old clothes into the fire because she saw they were infested with fleas. She spent that evening picking them out of her own body and clothes, one by one, and squashing them between her thumb nails. Despite their tiny size their bodies were too rigid to kill between the soft surfaces of her finger pulps. If she tried they leapt away as soon as she released her grip. She had to be quick otherwise they sprang enormous distances and disappeared from view to seek out another warm human or animal body to infest. It took her several days to dispose of all the fleas Darel had brought into the house.

She also knew it was hopeless to set no-alcohol rules for Darel and persuaded Alexis to provide him with cheap country wines in limited amounts.

Two months later Darel became seriously ill. He told Marie-Anne that he had severe cramps in his belly though when she placed the backs of her three middle fingers on his forehead he did not have a fever. She could see him unable to move or raise his right hand and forearm. His condition rapidly deteriorated, he became delirious, agitated and hallucinated, and a few days later died from mental and physical exhaustion.

They arranged a simple funeral and to save on costs, laid him to rest in the same tomb as his mother and father. Marie-Anne, Monique and Alexis were relieved they had provided Darel with some comforts in the last few months of his life.

Shortly after Grand-père's funeral, Marcel approached his mother again one evening. They were alone in the kitchen while Marie-Anne prepared the meal as the aromas from her potage filled the room. "Maman, before Grand-père died I asked him the name of my father and he told me only you knew and I must ask you. Can you tell me now?" Marcel longed not only for the identity of his father; he craved the physical sensation of a hold or a hug from one whom he could call his Papa.

Marie-Anne dreaded this moment. She had buried her brief affair with Pierre Tremblais in the depths of her heart. She knew she had promised Marcel to tell him more, but struggled to find the right words without misleading him. *I cannot betray you, Pierre, even to our son.*

It might be easiest to tell him she had been raped, but how do you explain rape to a seven-year-old boy? She also realised that telling him she had been raped was as far from the truth as she could possibly get. She recognised that Marcel knew the mechanics of conception from observation of farm animals and from their ensuing discussions. She knew also that Marcel expected her to name the person, but this she felt unwilling and unable to do. She persuaded herself that in any event, Marcel's young age meant that he could not know and understand the subtleties of an affair between an older nearly-married man and an attractive young peasant girl. She would tell him when older. The desire to forget the entire event was stronger than the desire to share her secret with her son. She decided that a few small lies that absolved all from blame were the best solution to her dilemma.

"Marcel, I told you once before that I loved your father for a short time, then he had to leave town. He lived a life of adventure and travel, came to Vimy for a brief visit and that is how I met him. He was a strong and a special man and I loved him. I do not know where he is now." She gave Marcel a hug and added, "Mon p'tit Chou: You are a brave little boy and I am proud of what you are doing in class. I know that Hubert has not always been kind to you. I thought when I married him that it would be good for you to have him in our lives. Even though he is a difficult man, I believe in the end it will benefit you. I am a peasant-woman with no education, and had to marry an unsuitable man to give my son a father. There is little I can do to pull myself up. Life is difficult for peasants in France and especially for women. Everything is expected of us and we have little choice but to do as we're told. I am doing all I can to help you do well in your life."

She released him from the hug and then placed both arms on his shoulders and looked at him intensely. "There is one other thing I have to tell you, Marcel." Marie-Anne's lip quivered ever so slightly as she uttered softly, "In about five months' time I am going to have a baby, so you will have a little brother or sister, and Marie-Louise will have a cousin." After a moment's silence she added. "It will help fill the emptiness in our lives since Grand-père died."

Marcel looked at his mother, then turned away, expressionless, but did not respond to this news. He loved and missed his grandfather and had no feelings for a baby not yet born, especially one fathered by Hubert. It reinforced the isolation he felt from his stepfather and now, also, from his mother. He sensed from the tone of his mother's voice, and the hesitation with which she gave him this information, that she herself felt dubious about the pregnancy. Despite his age Marcel realised women had little choice in the timing of pregnancy; pregnancy followed marriage as certainly as winter followed autumn One had to resign oneself and passively accept the buffetings of nature and events, much as dead leaves were swept along the road by the wind.

Marie-Anne once again employed Hélène as midwife and the pregnancy appeared to go smoothly but the deaths of Gabriel and Darel had weakened her, as had the pregnancy itself and the lack of support from Hubert. After a prolonged and painful labour the baby, a boy, was born blue and failed to breathe.

Hélène tried to revive him by squeezing his chest rhythmically to provoke breathing, but without success. Once clear the baby would not survive, Marie-Anne, sadly and tearfully, cradled the cold, blue body for few moments, then handed it back to Hélène to be taken away in a small box for burial in an anonymous grave.

Marie-Anne slept fitfully that night and next day developed a fever with an attack of "cold shivers". The following night she started vomiting and had severe pains in her abdomen.

When Hélène visited next morning she immediately knew the diagnosis: puerperal fever. It attacked women who had had multiple traumas and setbacks before and during their pregnancy. None survived this horrendous disease. She applied hot poultices to Marie-Anne's belly, gave her calomel to provoke the bowels, and laudanum to relieve pain, but her condition deteriorated rapidly.

Marie-Anne knew now she would not survive and asked Marcel to come to her bedside.

"My dearest son, my special p'tit Chou: I will soon die." She spoke quietly and Marcel had to place his ear close to her lips to hear her words. "I want you to know how much I have loved you. I had a hard life, but having you as my son made it all worthwhile for me, and I thank God for that. I know now you are strong and have many talents of your father. Live a long life and make the most of them, for his sake and mine.

"I want to give you these gifts that come from your father, and which he gave me before he left." As she spoke she pressed them into his hand, and held his hands tightly in hers which were boiling hot from the fever. "They are a neck band, a medal and a ring. I have treasured them in his memory and I am sure you will do the same. Goodbye my darling and pray for me." Goodbye Pierre, I loved you. These were her last words and thoughts. Before Marcel had a chance to respond or ask further questions she fell back unconscious and perished a few moments later.

The deaths of Gabriel, Darel, Marie-Anne, and the stillborn baby, all within the space of a few months, had a baleful effect on the survivors.

Monique and Alexis had been in their teens ten years earlier during the smallpox epidemic that had carried off Alexis' mother and brother, yet the memory of those events did not make it easier to bear their present losses. In some ways these deaths were worse because it made them feel singled out for hardships that were not being shared by friends and neighbours in the town; the smallpox epidemic affected the whole community equally, rich and poor, old and young, women and men.

Marcel, especially, felt bereft of affection. The deaths of his grandfather and mother, the two on earth who most held his love, left a large void in his life. He remembered being shown her blanched and motionless body before it was placed in the rough home-hewn casket. He placed his hand on her ice-cold forehead and then felt her stiff, unmoving hand. Her eyes were half-open but sightless. He felt numbed by the funeral in the parish church, and the casket being carried to the cemetery before disappearing forever down a gaping hole in the ground.

Hubert not only lacked sympathy but became aggressive, even brutal towards him, lashing out at the slightest transgression or disobedience. One morning he accosted Marcel, "Your mother did not want you when you were born. You made her unhappy and caused her death." He shrugged his shoulders spiritedly.

Marcel stared down at the floor, bit his lip and did not respond to this allegation.

That night Hubert made another equally clumsy attempt to assault Marcel sexually that the boy repulsed energetically.

Alexis and Monique attempted to shield him, with little effect, resulting in acrimonious and increasingly intense shouting matches. Although Monique felt protective towards Marcel, she also had a timid demeanour, so quailed in reaction to Hubert's aggressiveness. Alexis was more assertive but no match for Hubert. Marcel spent many nights crying himself to sleep. The domestic conflict and tension continued unabated till Hubert decided suddenly to return to Arras to live with his mother.

With four deaths and the departure of Hubert, quite suddenly the Lachêne home fell from nine to four individuals. One morning, shortly after Hubert's departure, and after a restless night, Marcel woke up with stomach cramps. He spent the day in bed, refused all food and the next morning felt no better. Monique invited Hélène to advise them. She made dietary changes and tried various tonics, with little effect. Marcel became visibly pale and very thin and weak.

"Marcel, you must eat," Monique and Alexis exhorted frequently. "That is the only way you will get well and strong again."

"I try," he replied dolefully, "but food gives me pain and makes me sick. I am not hungry. I do not feel like eating."

Monique prepared various dishes that she knew from past experience were favourites of his, even a special vegetable bouillon that Marie-Anne used to give him, and that she knew he loved, hoping this would stir his appetite. Cooking smells from her efforts permeated the house. Marcel pushed it away after a few perfunctory sips, provoking poorly concealed rage in Monique and Alexis.

One night he woke up screaming in terror. Monique and Alexis rushed to his bedside finding him sobbing and incoherent. After he finally settled down Monique asked anxiously, "What is wrong, Marcel?"

Through tears he responded, "I had a horrible dream. In the dream you sent me to the well to fetch water. I hauled up the pail and a man came up to me from behind. I did not know him but he was big and dirty, had a black beard and carried a gun. He grabbed me by the arms then pushed me over the wall and I fell down the well and splashed into the water. I struggled and screamed for help. I could hear the echoes from the walls of the well. Then I saw my mother looking down at me from the little circle of light at the top. She reached towards me. She touched my fingers, and then I went under and couldn't breathe."

Monique consoled him as best she could but he continued weeping for hours before falling into a restless sleep.

The following day, Father St. Amour visited the household as part of a routine pastoral visit. Monique and Alexis recounted their difficulties and the priest invited Marcel to come for a walk with him.

Marcel knew St. Amour from Sunday mass and respected his kindly demeanour and earthy common sense. He got out of bed, dressed, and the two left the house hand-in-hand.

"Marcel, I can see that you are lonely and troubled. The sisters who taught you in catechism told me how well you did. They also told me about a classmate who tormented you because you had no father."

"I loved the classes, Mon Père. It was Alain who teased and bullied me. I fought him and beat him. He did not trouble me after that."

"I can see you're a brave young fellow. Children can be cruel to each other. You are quite right. If someone torments you, you have to stand up and defend yourself. You must be careful not to start a fight you cannot win. People who do not look ahead to the results of their actions will find themselves later in big trouble.

"Marcel, I can see you were distressed by the death of your mother," St. Amour declared sympathetically.

He burst into sobs and with his hands covering his face and wiping his tears away said, "Yes, I miss Maman terribly. I loved her stories every night about the fables of La Fontaine. And my grand-père. Why did they have to die?"

"Sometimes God works in mysterious ways." St. Amour placed his arm affectionately around Marcel's shoulder as they continued walking slowly, as the dried twigs that covered the path crackled under their feet. "The loss of a loved one is an awful event. We feel bereaved and alone, as if part of oneself, like your arm or your leg, has been torn off. Not only that, but there are so many reminders of the person that is gone, the chair they used, the gifts they gave you, the stories they recounted and especially the special smells that the person may have left behind, such as in their clothing, their scent or their tobacco. That person is gone physically, but he or she is still part of our hearts and minds. It is helpful to turn these reminders into advantages. In your heart you can still talk to your Maman and listen to her talking to you. Your mother was a good woman."

"Mon Père, I loved her even though Hubert told me she did not want me when I was born." His hands still covered his face and his voice choked with tears. "But I am also angry with her. After Alain teased me about not having a father, I asked Maman to tell me about my father but she never did. It seemed like she did not even want to tell me."

"I remember meeting your mother, and Gabriel your grandfather, when she discovered she was with child with you. Hubert is quite wrong. I know with certainty that your mother wanted you and loved you from the moment she found she was with child. Both your grandfather and I myself asked her to tell us about your father but she never did. She told me she would talk to you when you were old enough. Perhaps she still meant to do so but died too soon. It is her secret. Now we can never know."

For a while Marcel and St. Amour continued on their walk silently, each deep in their own thoughts, pondering the mystery and whereabouts of the Unknown Father.

They reached a clearing and stopped to sit on a log. The afternoon sun shimmered through the trees and the leaves creating weird, unearthly colours and shadows, and jagged patches of sunlight on the forest floor. St. Amour asked, "What happened to Hubert? Did he not stay after your Maman died?"

"No, he went back to Arras to live with his mother. I *hate* that man." Marcel tightened his lips and jaw as he spat out the word.

"Hate is a strong word, Marcel. Do you really mean it?"

"Yes I do. After Maman died he used to beat me and blamed me for her death saying she never wanted me as a baby. When he first came to live with us he wanted me to touch his prick. I said no and ran away. He tried again last month. I hate him," he repeated, clenching his fists and teeth.

For a few moments St. Amour contemplated this information then said, "It sounds like he was not a good person, to say the least. I am glad he has left. He has hurt you badly in many ways and I know it will take a long time to get over that hurt, but I know that eventually you will. I swear again that your Maman strongly wanted you as a baby. Perhaps something in the future will happen to help you overcome what Hubert has done to you. I can see you are angry with him and you have every reason to be. It is anger that makes you hate him. If you could punch him you would feel better, just like you were better after you punched Alain! Obviously you cannot do that to Hubert now that he has gone, but there may be other ways you can act your anger? Perhaps what you are doing now, not eating and getting sick is a way of showing anger, but instead of hurting him you are hurting yourself?"

"That is strange. Yes, perhaps. I don't know. I don't think so. Yet I know when Alain hurt me I felt angry at him and when I beat him in a fight I felt much better! I feel angry now but have no one to fight." Marcel smiled through his tears as he thought of his fight with Alain.

"To me it makes much sense," added St. Amour, smiling back at Marcel. "If you cannot box him in real life, you can just pretend to box him. Draw a picture of him on the wall and punch him a few times!"

"I'll try, but it's not the same! I would like to box him and give him a black eye and a bloody nose. When I'm older and bigger I'll find him and do that."

"When you're older and bigger you might then find that you know yourself better so you no longer need to give him a black eye and a bloody nose!" St. Amour looked quizzically at Marcel in the eye and he smiled and nodded at the priest in reply.

They saw the sun getting low on the horizon and got up to retrace their steps back home. They emerged from the woods to a clearing near the edge of the town after the sun had set, and as Jupiter stood out brilliantly above their heads in the darkening sky. Stars were beginning to appear here and there, little points of light acting like beacons to guide a lost traveller. St. Amour pointed out the planet to Marcel and said, "Marcel, that planet is named Jupiter and is the largest in our solar system. The sun is at the centre; our earth is third, and Jupiter fifth of six planets that go around the sun. The ancient Romans called it Jupiter because he was the father of all the Roman gods. They regarded him as the source of all power and authority in the Roman world. They built large and beautiful temples to honour him. We no longer worship the god, Jupiter, the way the Romans did, but that beautiful, bright light you see in the sky is a wonderful present-day sign of God's fatherhood and wisdom."

"It is beautiful, Mon Père," agreed Marcel, shaking his head. For the first time in months he felt a sense of peace settling in his heart.

They reached Marcel's home where St. Amour said good night to the family and said he would return in two days' time.

Marcel slept more soundly that night and next morning, for the first time in weeks, he felt hungry and took a small serving of Marie-Anne's bouillon that Monique had prepared. She gave him a reassuring and appreciative hug.

St. Amour returned the following day and took Marcel for another walk.

"Marcel. Do you think your uncle Alexis and aunt Monique care about you?"

"Oh yes, Mon Père, they do. They also push me too hard to eat when I do not feel like eating."

"They push you because they are distressed about your health; they love you and want you to get better." St. Amour raised the tone of his voice on the final word. "Why not ask them not to force you. Let them know you will eat when you are ready? I know with certainty you will start eating when you want to, and when you are ready. You are a strong young man and showed it in the way you handled Alain and his friends." This struck a responsive chord in Marcel's heart.

He silently took in what the priest had told him. The congealed lump in his throat that had seemed to strangle him for weeks suddenly relaxed and tears of relief rolled down his cheeks. Until now he had lived his life with a constant feeling of obligation that he had to perform to a certain level of perfection to meet the expectations of others. He felt he could never live up to these expectations, and this gave him an endless sense of failure. St. Amour's comments made him feel in charge of his own actions. Moreover, he felt that the priest trusted him and had hope for the future.

After several minutes of silence he wiped away the tears and said, shaking his head with feeling, "I never thought of it that way, Mon Père. My uncle and aunt make me feel helpless, especially when they come at me so strongly. Then I get angry because I am letting them down. You make me feel that what happens depends on me not on them."

"That is quite right, Marcel." The priest spoke in a gentle, caring voice. "If you want to make any changes in your life you have to decide on that yourself and not rely on anyone else. And if you make a decision and something goes wrong you can only blame yourself, not anyone else. You will certainly make some bad decisions, and things will go wrong, but that is also the way you learn and acquire wisdom. Wisdom refers to the ability to make good decisions, actions that bring benefit to you, and often to others as well. It is one of the seven gifts of the Holy Spirit, and in my opinion, the one on which all the others depend. The opposite of wisdom is folly, and it surprises me how much folly men and women are capable of in the way they conduct their lives. Wisdom is meant to come with growing old but folly is no slave to age; older people can be as filled with folly as younger. People do things without considering the calamitous consequences of their actions."

Marcel did not understand all the concepts the priest described, but responded to his tone of voice. "I love you Mon Père. You are like a real father to me."

St. Amour smiled and placed his arm around Marcel's shoulder. "I can help you a little, Marcel, but remember that your real Father, not your earthly father, is in heaven, and that you talk to him every day when you say the words of the Our Father. You can continue to talk to him in your own words and I know He will help you. I believe it will also help you if you practice daily meditation based on the rosary."

By this time they had returned to the Lachêne home.

"Mon Père," Marcel said excitedly, "could you wait a minute. I want to show you something." He ran into the house to his room, burrowed under his mattress until he found the articles his mother had given him before she died, then ran out again with them in his hand.

"I want to show you this neck band, medal and ring. Maman gave them to me before she died. She said my father gave them to her and she asked me to treasure them, just as she had."

St. Amour examined them carefully then said, "I see the medal has a likeness of Our Lady and Jesus so it must celebrate a religious occasion. They are beautiful, and certainly a very special gift because they help you remember your father as well as your mother. You are fortunate to have them. Look after them and I am sure they will help give you courage."

He hugged Marcel, said goodbye and the latter ran inside. Over the next few weeks Marcel slowly resumed eating and regained his health and strength, without further prompting from Monique and Alexis.

PART TWO: 1787-1794

REVOLUTION

Chapter Eight

All Europe perceived the extremes of weather between 1783 and 1787. Winters were severe with endless days of continuous frost. Summers were hot with frequent thunderstorms during which hailstones the size of walnuts ripped through orchards and destroyed crops. Food scarcity led to price increases which led to famine and riots in which many were killed and their leaders executed. The cause of these weather excesses was unknown but keen observers such as Pierre Tremblais, Henri la Fortune and others noticed a brown dusty pall in the air, sometimes so thick it obscured the sun. The children of both Tremblais and la Fortune had developed respiratory problems, cough or asthma, from the dust.

In June, Marcel's eleventh birthday came and went with little fanfare. Still short for his age, he had an engaging smile and long untidy hair. After school one sunny spring day, he went to see Sister Philoméne, "Ma soeur, I am leaving school. My family is too poor and I have to go to work to help. I thank you for teaching me so much."

She rumpled his hair and smiled as she replied, "You've done well, Marcel. You learn quickly and I love teaching you. I am glad to hear you will help support your uncle and aunt. I will pray for you."

He next approached Adolphe Girouette, still the manager of la Fortune's estate. Girouette worked out of a small dusty office in the barn. Marcel rapped firmly on the door.

"Come in," a loud voice responded from within.

Marcel entered and found Girouette lounging in the chair, with his feet, covered by heavy, muddy farmer's boots on the table. Windowless, the small room was dense with fumes from his cigar. Without rising, he brusquely asked, "What do you want?"

Marcel knew Girouette by repute and had prepared his piece. "Monsieur Girouette, I have worked as a shepherd for four years, know I've done well, and want a change. I have been watching Rita with her foal, Angelique. Last week Angelique roamed into another field away from Rita and I helped her find her mother again. I love horses and especially love Angelique. I want to work in the stables."

Girouette scanned his puny size then replied gruffly, with seeming disinterest. "A horse will blow you over if it neighs. What else are you good for?"

"I can do anything, Monsieur. I can run, I am strong and can fight. I want to learn all about horses." Marcel spoke with assurance and decided it would not be wise to tell Girouette that he could also read and write. Not only was this not needed for a stablehand; his presumptuous attitude would antagonise the manager.

The boy's spunkiness struck a resonant chord in Girouette. "Are you not the bastard son of Marie-Anne Lachêne who died in childbirth a few years ago? She bailed out your family before you were born when you were all threatened with eviction. She had a strong, cussed mind. I'd like to have popped her cherry but someone else got in there first. Who's your Dad?"

"I do not know my Papa. She never told me. She never told anyone." Marcel's insides roiled at Girouette's aggressive interrogation but he managed to keep a bland exterior.

"No matter. Some visitor at the chateau or perhaps our Count himself must have got her, or bought her. Sold herself cheap, I bet. You look like her, especially your mouth and lips. Alright, I will take you on as a stablehand. Five sous each day and you must be here from sunrise to sunset, every day except Sunday."

Girouette showed Marcel his responsibilities there and then. They were basic, repetitive and nothing to be frightened of. He had to muck out the stables and place the horse shit in piles so it could mature into manure. It was also his job to ensure the horses were well fed and watered, and kept clean and well-groomed. There were ten horses in the stable and he quickly got to know them all so did not mind his minuscule pay. He also loved his Sundays, when, accompanied by Poilu, he would go for long hikes in the fields and woods around the town. The highest point of Vimy ridge became his favourite haunt. Trees had been cleared around that area and he loved standing on its rocky peak to view the fields and villages of the Douai plain.

While tending the horses one afternoon, Marcel saw Monsieur la Fortune entering the stable accompanied by a tall stranger. Each carried a musket. The day was warm and sunny. Full, fleecy clouds covered the sky like broken pieces of a puzzle on a deep blue background, and a gentle breeze moved them slowly and silently to the east as they gradually changed their wondrous shapes.

"Marcel, get Bonneau and Marquisse ready immediately. Monsieur Pierre Tremblais and I are going hunting," ordered la Fortune loudly.

"Yes, sir, right away, sir," replied Marcel, as he set to work placing bridles and saddles on the selected horses. As the two trotted off, Marcel saw that Pierre handled his professionally, and appeared elegant and comfortable in the saddle.

On their return two hours later, after dismounting, Monsieur la Fortune went off to speak to Adolphe Girouette, leaving Marcel alone with Pierre Tremblais. He noticed Marcel's baggy clothes, untidy long hair, and his bright, brown eyes, widely spaced, and a slightly protuberant nose for his age. He liked the way the angles of his mouth turned up as if he had a perpetual smile. "Do you like your job in the stable, young boy?"

"Oh, yes sir, I love it. I love the horses and I especially love Rita and her little foal Angelique."

"I heard Monsieur la Fortune call you Marcel. Is that your name?"

"That is correct, Sir."

Tremblais smiled broadly, "It seems the horses like you too, Marcel. I watched them as you were getting them ready for our ride. Did you know you have to talk to horses, they get to know your voice, which can help calm them, and they can even understand some words?"

"I talk to them sometimes, Sir, but I did not know they can understand words."

"Well, you try that with Rita. Next time you give her water, or take her out for exercise, say "water" or "trot". If you repeat that many times she will quickly learn what you mean. Each horse has a name. When you approach a horse, always call it by its name. It will later recognise both its name and your voice so when you call, it will come to you, especially if you give it a treat, like a handful of hay. Horses are sensitive creatures. They can also let you know when they need something and they know quickly when you are pleased or angry with them. You have to watch them carefully. If you talk firmly to a horse it will look you straight in the eye and you know it is listening to you. When you hear a horse neighing, you know it is happy, letting you know where it is, or just saying thank you."

Marcel felt enthralled with the idea of communicating with a horse and said excitedly, "What must I look for to find out what a horse needs?"

"You have to watch how a horse acts. They are built to eat almost constantly, and must have plenty of exercise. If a horse does not get enough to eat it will bolt its feed and may get sick. If it does not get enough exercise it will start pacing and get restless. When you see it acting like that you know you have to do something to make it better. If horses are kept in stables they need exercise at least once a day and food twice a day. After an outing a horse gets sweaty, so on return you must take off its saddle and take it for a short walk to dry out. Only then do you let it drink its fill. If you let it drink too soon after heavy exercise it may get a sickness called colic. Then you have to nurse it till it recovers. Do you know how to lift a horse's hoof?"

"No Sir, I do not. Please will you show me?" Marcel saw Pierre beaming with pleasure.

Using one of Rita's front legs, Pierre showed Marcel how to lift the hoof. He placed his shoulder adjacent to the horse's shoulder, and starting above the knee ran his hand gently down the leg towards the hoof. On reaching the fetlock he squeezed it gently, and with his shoulder gave the horse's shoulder a gentle nudge towards the other front leg, shifting its weight towards that leg. Rita obediently raised the hoof of the leg he had stroked.

"Now you try it while I am watching, Marcel."

After several tries he persuaded Rita to raise both of her front legs.

"See how easy it is! Don't try that on the hind legs until you are bigger and stronger," Pierre said with a smile, patting Marcel on the shoulder. "Horse kicks are painful, even dangerous."

"Oh thank you Sir," replied Marcel with enthusiasm. "I love watching Rita and Angelique together, nudging each other, and the foal drinking her milk. Rita looks after her baby very well!"

"Yes, Rita is a beautiful horse. I love her chestnut colour and the white heart on her forehead. Bonneau, the horse I rode today with Monsieur la Fortune is a sturdy, strong Arabian breed. He can gallop really fast. I had no trouble staying ahead of la Fortune who rode Marquisse!"

Pierre and Marcel walked over to Bonneau's stable together and Pierre allowed Bonneau to sniff the back of his left hand, while repeating his name. While doing so Marcel noticed his deformed hand. The fingers were curled over like a claw and Pierre appeared unable to move, straighten or use them.

"Do you live near here, Marcel?" He realised he felt a bond with this young boy who was, like him, charmed by horses.

"Yes I live in the town, Sir, with my uncle Alexis, his wife, Monique, their girl, Marie-Louise, and best of all is our dog Poilu. He comes with me and helps me look after the sheep and cattle."

"Do not your mother and father live at home?"

Marcel stumbled when he replied, "M-m-my Maman died when I was seven. I never knew my real f-father who left home when I was little. My uncle and aunt are good to me but I especially like Father St. Amour from the church. He's become like a father to me. I got sick and he helped me get better. Our family is very poor and I have to work."

Pierre took a ten-sous coin out of his tunic pocket and pressed it into Marcel's hand.

"Here is a small present for you Marcel. Buy yourself and your family a meal. I am pleased Father St. Amour is looking after you. We all need a father, or someone who acts like one. I like the way you look after horses. They seem happy when they see you. You are a brave young man." He gave Marcel another affectionate slap on the shoulder. At that point they heard a nightingale singing its melodious song, and Pierre added, raising his finger to his ear, "Is that bird song not beautiful, Marcel?"

"It sure is lovely, Sir. Thank you. It is very good of you, Sir. You are very kind."

When he returned home that night, Marcel gave Monique and Alexis an excited and detailed account of his meeting and exchange with Monsieur Pierre Tremblais. He described all he had learnt about horses and mentioned also the strange deformity he had noticed in Pierre's hand.

La Fortune had invited Pierre alone without Chantal, his wife, for two reasons: firstly because they were to go hunting, an activity of no interest to Chantal, and also because la Fortune had planned a lunch party the following day to honour Maximilien Robespierre, a bachelor. It would not have been appropriate to have a small luncheon with Robespierre the only man without a wife.

When Pierre arrived at the chateau with la Fortune, he searched diligently for Marie-Anne, examining each of the women servants carefully as they appeared. Even though over ten years had passed, he knew he would recognise her immediately. How would they react when they caught each other's eyes? Memories came flooding back. Where are you now, ma chérie? I would so love to see your cheery face again, feel your warmth and softness, and hear your teasing voice! I think of you often.

That night Pierre slept in the same room and bed he had occupied on his earlier visit, the night he seduced Marie-Anne. He slept fitfully and dreamt he saw her in an open doorway dressed in a beautiful full-length white dress, smiling silently at him. She held up her arms as if to embrace him and he smiled and opened his arms in response. She then lowered her arms, turned around and disappeared into the house, leaving him feeling abandoned. He woke up puzzled and unhappy.

Maximillien Robespierre was a young lawyer from Arras becoming well known in the region for defending difficult cases, especially with poor clients not able to afford normal legal fees. Monsieur la Fortune had sought Robespierre's legal advice on a complex issue involving a land dispute with a neighbour and had been very satisfied with the outcome. He thought that a lunch party with an opportunity to meet an illustrious traveller and entrepreneur would be an appropriate way to express his appreciation.

Robespierre arrived on horseback on schedule at eleven in the morning and Marcel met him at the gate of the stables. "Are you the stablehand, young man?" asked Robespierre.

"Yes I am, Monsieur," replied Marcel. "I will care for your horse today."

"Here are five sous for your trouble. His name is Roulette and if you speak to him nicely he is obedient." Giving Marcel the coin he added, "Make sure you give him plenty of water and hay. He does not need exercise for now."

"Oh, thank you, Monsieur." Robespierre then walked to the front door of the Chateau where Monsieur and Madame la Fortune greeted him and introduced him to Pierre Tremblais. Robespierre came from a respectable and prosperous middle class family. The oldest of four children, his mother had died during childbirth at the age of twenty-nine. His father subsequently disappeared and the children were raised by relatives.

"Monsieur Robespierre," la Fortune spoke loudly, placing his right arm on Robespierre's shoulder, and with his left gesturing towards Pierre. "Allow me to introduce you to Monsieur Pierre Tremblais. Monsieur Tremblais is Director of Sévigny Frères, the leading linen and textile enterprise in Arras. He is a retired general in the Army and fought in the Battle of New France." Turning to Tremblais he added, "Monsieur Robespierre is a lawyer from Arras and a graduate of the College Louis le Grand in Paris. He has given me excellent legal advice, so far, and I fully expect this to continue. Messieurs Tremblais and Robespierre, please meet my wife, Madame Madeleine la Fortune."

"I am glad to meet you both," replied Madame la Fortune. "Monsieur Tremblais, how is Madame? I have good memories of our talk in Arras. Please offer her my best wishes."

"She is well, thank you, Madame, I shall do that."

"I am interested to hear about your experiences in Québec, Monsieur Tremblais," said Robespierre, pronouncing each word distinctly. "Is there any possibility that France will recover her territories in North America?" Pierre assessed this young notary even as he began to describe his service abroad, nearly as tall as Pierre himself, and who listened with pinched expressionless features. The receding forehead, sharp, straight nose, narrow lips and jutting jaw gave his head an odd angular structure, almost cat-like in appearance.

"There is no possibility whatsoever, in my opinion. We had our chance during the American War of Independence against les Anglais. I believe I am not exaggerating when I say that the Colonies would not have won their war had it not been for the support that France provided. It was the French fleet that won the crucial naval Battle of the Chesapeake and prevented the English army from receiving reinforcements, giving the Colonies' army its victory. The remarkable thing is that France received nothing in return. We could have insisted the Colonies allow us to retake New France, but they refused to permit this. The result of the war is that our country is bankrupt, and all we have is the satisfaction of defeating England."

"Why did we make that unfair agreement with the Colonies?"

"That is a good question, Monsieur Robespierre, and I do not know the whole answer, but …"

"Well, surely you have some views on the matter that are better informed than most, having spent time there fighting for France in Québec?" Robespierre interrupted with a tart edge to his voice.

"Why, yes. In my view we wanted, in part, to avenge the loss of New France by defeating England. However, the Colonies had a greater fear of French than of English control of Canada. They also wished to take control of that country themselves. They attacked Canada intending to make it the fourteenth state. An army of colonists led by Benedict Arnold actually invaded Québec but were incapable of wresting the city from the English. The English had made a pact with the French-speaking Canadians. In return for their support of England against the invasion, they were offered freedom of language and religion. As a result of this collaboration between the English army and the Canadians, the invasion failed and Canada remains an English colony today." Pierre hesitated a moment and looked intently at each of his listeners to maintain their attention.

"It is interesting that Canadians fought on both sides in the Colonies' fight against England," he continued. "Most sided with England but a substantial number fought with the colonists. Another reason why the Canadians did not support the Colonies is they believed that England would be victorious, just as they were against us in the Seven Years War, and did not wish to be on the losing side yet again."

"How do you foresee the Thirteen Colonies, the United States of America as they now call themselves, developing from the political perspective?" enquired Robespierre.

"They have a strong sense of freedom and a spirit of independence. They also see the English control in Canada as a threat. I believe they will bide their time and eventually take over Canada by force and turn it into the fourteenth state. In my opinion, they will be less generous to the Canadians and to the French language than are the English.

"Because I lived in Canada for so long I retained my interest in the country and returned to visit it two years ago. I befriended two young lay Canadian leaders, Joseph Papineau, a lawyer, and Fleury Mesplet, a journalist. They, and others, are determined to maintain French language and culture in North America. If they succeed, it will be due to their own efforts, not from any help they received from their former motherland."

Pierre's discourse on the politics of North America was interrupted by the maid who entered offering to replenish their glasses. Monsieur and Madame la Fortune all had more of la Fortune's excellent Champagne Henri Abelé, bottled in Reims in 1782. Robespierre declined the champagne and drank only a light red wine diluted with water.

After their glasses had been refilled, Pierre turned to Robespierre and said, "Monsieur Robespierre, your reputation has preceded you. I read about your success in securing the release from prison of the Englishwoman, Marie Somerville from St. Omer. I commend you for your defence in her case because we know she was treated abominably in prison. However we have serious and increasing problems here in France. What are your opinions about these?"

"You are correct. We have major social and political problems," Robespierre said gravely, emphasising the word 'major'. "As you know, there have been riots and strikes in Paris and elsewhere over the poor harvests and price of bread and the authorities executed the leaders. The country faces bankruptcy. There are great inequities between the rich and the poor. The king attempted to make the rich nobles pay more taxes but they refused, and he proved incapable of using his power to force them. The king cannot even control expenses of his own household. Queen Marie-Antoinette spends money as if it is spouting out of the fountains in the Gardens of Versailles. I do not accept the ruling of the Court that found her free of guilt in the necklace controversy. She loves expensive jewellery more than she loves her children. The necklace has never been traced but I believe she hid it somewhere, probably buried it in the capacious gardens of the palace."

"I do not care about her love of jewellery," replied Pierre. "To me, her main fault is she is an Austrian woman who has no loyalty to France. She has strong opinions but is fickle, and her influence on the king causes him to vacillate. The country desperately needs firm leadership and all it is getting is irresolution. I believe we should… "

"Well, I do care about her jewellery," interrupted Madame la Fortune, uncharacteristically. "The poor woman has been grossly maligned by her critics. I believe she was innocent in the necklace controversy. Moreover, she dresses beautifully, sets the fashion for the world and has even presented the king with a son and heir!"

Pierre and Robespierre nodded and smiled indulgently. Monsieur la Fortune replied, "You are likely quite right, ma chérie, but those matters do not concern whether her political influence on the king is good or otherwise for France."

"I agree with you, Monsieur Tremblais, that King Louis is providing poor leadership to France." Robespierre replied to Pierre's last comment. He chose not to argue with Madame la Fortune on the queen's guilt or otherwise in the necklace issue. Pierre widened his eyes with surprise at the apparent concordance in their views. He had learnt how to conceal his opinions. "Political power is centred in the king's hands," Robespierre continued, "and he has been unwilling to share decision-making with the people who are seething with anger against him, the nobles and the Church. Anyone who petitions for change is served with a 'lettre de cachet' and sent to the Bastille."

"The problems appear serious, Monsieur Robespierre," replied Pierre affably. He sensed his political perspective was different from that of Robespierre and had no wish to cause conflict at a small dinner party. "What do you think the solutions might be?"

"I had the good fortune to meet Jean-Jacques Rousseau in Paris not long before he died, and his memory remains to me a source of joy and pride. Like him, it is my desire to work hard for the benefit of the poor and the virtuous in our country even, if needed, at the price of my early death. Rousseau believed that society itself is the source of evil and corruption. I believe that public virtue can be imposed by force, that power must be transferred to the people and France must become a republic to reach its full potential. I believe the country is ready and ripe for change."

For a few moments both la Fortune and Pierre maintained a shocked silence, broken finally by la Fortune. "I believe you exaggerate the gravity of the problems, Monsieur Robespierre. France has had a king for over one thousand years. He has the support of a powerful nobility and church, and even the peasants revere him. It is only a segment of the bourgeoisie who desire such drastic transformation. The church especially has influence in every village in the country. It would never agree to dethrone the king."

"The Church is divided like the head of the Hydra, Monsieur la Fortune. Most of the Bishops live in luxury and contribute little to the public good. They have no interest in change. A few bishops and most priests in the parishes are aware of the grave injustices in the system. Unfortunately this group has little influence on the direction the church will take. Church leaders will likely side with the king and nobility and suffer with them in consequence."

"I cannot agree with you, Monsieur Robespierre," said Pierre emphatically. "I am a Catholic at heart even though I no longer practice my religion. The Church has certainly committed great historical wrongs for which it has never made amends. Consider the Crusades, the Inquisition, and the immoral acts of some of its priests. At times I am sure that Our Lord and Father in Heaven must shake His head in despair at the actions of some of His representatives here on earth. As such the Church is an easy target for non-believers such as you. But overall it has been a force for good in the world, as shown by its support for music and the arts, its many undertakings on behalf of the poor and the destitute, its pursuit of peace between nations, and its emphasis on the benefits of virtue and charity in human activity. It would be a sad day for our country if the regime weakened its power."

At that point the maid re-entered to refill the glasses of Pierre, and Monsieur and Madame la Fortune with champagne. Robespierre had not touched his glass of diluted wine.

"Nor will you get much support for your changes from the nobility, Monsieur Robespierre," continued la Fortune, clenching his fists, as the maid left. "I agree the king is a weakling who is under the pernicious influence of the queen. Nevertheless, we have a strong feeling of loyalty to him and his office. We nobles are the ones who have made all the sacrifices and pay more than our share in taxes. We have supplied many leaders and soldiers to the army, and through our stewardship of the land we make a huge contribution to the economy. Meanwhile the peasants and the so-called bourgeoisie sit on their backsides and draw all the benefits of our work."

"You have to realise, Monsieur la Fortune that many in the nobility also believe that change must come," replied Robespierre gravely, jabbing his finger at the count. "The Marquis de La Fayette, for example, returned to France from helping the United States' fight for freedom, and he wishes now to bring these same ideals to France. The Comte de Mirabeau is another member of the aristocracy who supports constitutional change. Democracy, when it comes, will permit each citizen, women as much as men, to contribute their talents and their work to benefit the whole country. We must emulate the revolution of the American colonies. I have corresponded with Mr. Benjamin Franklin, their representative in Paris, and been impressed with his scientific knowledge and political guile. Incidentally, it is Mr. Franklin who informed me that the gigantic eruption of a volcano on the island of Iceland is the cause of the red dust in the air and the extreme weather changes in Europe over the last few years."

"I too have perceived the dust in the air," replied la Fortune. "My youngest daughter develops severe coughing spells on those days. I did not know the cause was a volcanic eruption. Mr. Franklin is clearly a savant of the first order. To get back to our topic, do you believe that change can come peacefully, Monsieur Robespierre, or do you think there will be violence?"

"It would be good if it could come peacefully, but I believe the king and his advisors are too entrenched in their beliefs and practices to make the radical changes required. I believe much blood will flow."

"I strongly disagree with you, Robespierre, that violence is inevitable. The king himself has acknowledged that change must come. He has appointed talented money-men such as Jacques Necker and Charles de Calonne to positions of power and urged them to bring order to the country's finances."

"You forget my dear la Fortune, that the two gentlemen you mention uncovered serious problems of corruption and unfair taxation. They resigned or were fired because they were incapable of effecting any changes. The peasants and middle classes are seething with fury."

Pierre broke in, "I have heard some philosophers calling for an end to the death penalty, even for crimes such as murder and treason. What is your opinion on that matter, Monsieur Robespierre?"

Robespierre replied without hesitation, "As a young man I could not harm an animal. I had some birds as pets and cried when one of them died. But my views have progressed and matured as I have grown older. Two years ago when appointed as judge in Arras, we found a man guilty of murder. It was my responsibility to sentence him to death. For days I wrestled with this decision. I decided eventually that the law had to be followed, and it was in the public interest that he be executed, so I signed the death warrant and the criminal lost his head. I have no feeling of regret or guilt about that decision. Criminals cause unhappiness in others and must be condemned. On the other hand, virtue brings happiness just as the sun produces light. In a revolutionary setting, there will be those who will vote against change. If they persist in their view, they must be eliminated. The peoples' decision is paramount."

"You have strong views about social and political issues, Monsieur Robespierre. I hope it never happens that you are appointed to a position of power."

"We shall see, Monsieur Tremblais," replied Robespierre quietly, but with an ironic smile and a deepening tone of voice. "It all depends on events that unfold in France over the next few years."

113

Chapter Nine

Arras, Spring 1789

Charles Cavigneau returned home from the tavern late one Saturday night and staggered shakily up the staircase. The bed rocked and creaked noisily as he demanded satisfaction from Pauline, his wife. Charles was a sot but because he confined his drinking to weekends, it did not affect his job. When drunk he became irascible and required little provocation to strike Pauline or the children. There were two levels to the Cavigneau house. The ground floor consisted of two rooms, a large communal living room and small kitchen. One large bedroom covered the whole upper floor. He and Pauline slept in one bed, two boys in another and three girls in the third bed. Both levels of the house were carpet-less.

Aged in his mid-forties, he had spent his entire working life in a textile plant in Arras. With a greying beard, sallow, gaunt expression he looked older than his years. Although not tall he had a stocky muscular build, as muscular as a draught horse bred for strength, with sharp eyes and a loud opinionated voice used frequently to impose his will. He lived with his family that included Pauline and five children, Clementine, Demy, Veronique, Odette and Benjamin, aged thirteen, eleven, nine, eight and five respectively. The family lived in a drab, back-to-back terraced house close to the five-hundred-year old gothic cathedral. Beautiful and imposing from afar and also in its interior, from close up the cathedral appeared cold and austere, attributes it transferred to people cast in its shadow.

Pauline had a secret, unexpressed admiration for her eldest daughter Clementine's fearless and outgoing nature, qualities she felt she herself lacked. Nicknamed "Fossette" because of a large dimple in her left cheek, Clementine was a lively, engaging girl with a ready smile and long auburn-coloured hair braided into a pony tail. She attended a convent school close to the cathedral.

One day in the winter, Clementine, who had been uncharacteristically gloomy of late, came home, her face grim and expressionless. "What's wrong?" asked her mother with little sympathy.

"Sister Sixta whipped my fingers." She displayed the badly bruised knuckles of her right hand. "I hate her and I hate the school." She burst into tears.

"You have to learn how to read and write. I know you learn easily, much easier than I ever did. If you sit quietly and follow the teacher, you would not get into trouble."

"I try. It makes no difference. Sister Sixta has favourites and I am not one of them."

"I will talk to Papa and we will try to make another arrangement," replied Pauline.

Charles and Pauline visited the school to see Sister Sixta who told them about her disobedience and her tendency to talk and distract others in the class. Sister believed the punishment was justified and would repeat it if necessary. After considering the matter, Charles allowed Clementine to drop out of school but decided to administer his own thrashing – four strokes on her bare bum with a stiff, wet cane – to ensure she did not take advantage of the situation. Though embittered by the double punishment, Clementine felt relief to be out of the regimentation of school and helped her mother with the housekeeping and the care of young Benjamin.

Clementine led the group in street games, deciding which ones were played, and each participant's role. Her favourite game was Escargot, a variant of hopscotch that could be played competitively and they marked out the spiral-shaped course with chalk on the cobblestones in the street. She generally won these games but there would be squabbles about honesty if she lost. Because she lived in close quarters with adults, she was mature beyond her years.

She developed a fancy for Stéphane, a neighbourhood boy who had an infectious smile and a red béret. Many men and boys wore bérets but this was the first time she had seen a red one. She fell in love first with the béret and then, by extension, with the attractive young face on whose head it perched.

"Where did you get that awful cap?" she asked Stéphane with a smile after she had won yet another game of Escargot.

"My uncle gave it to my dad but it is too small for him so I wear it," he replied, smiling with satisfaction at her back-handed compliment. She resisted the temptation to grab the béret from his head and run off with it, but Stephane sensed her impulse and instinctively placed his hand over the béret to keep it in place.

"Let's go and pester Monsieur Plouffe," she said, changing the subject with a giggle.

Pierre Plouffe ran a small tobacconist store on the street. He sold everything connected with smoking, including pipes, tobacco, matches, snuff, cleaners, ashtrays and even some expensive cigars. Pipes were the main item and they covered the shelves in all shapes and sizes, made of clay, porcelain, and different varieties of wood. The store was arranged impeccably with every article in its proper, permanent place. Monsieur Plouffe had an ample belly and a large red nose that unsteadily supported half-moon spectacles. Childless himself, he disliked children with a vengeance. On the way to the store, Clementine and Stéphane met her brother Demy.

"Come join us, Squinty," said Clementine without stopping her stride. "Stéphane and I are going to torment Monsieur Plouffe."

Demy joined them wordlessly. She knew that he tended to ingratiate himself with his peers. The second child in his family, Demy had been baptised "Denny" but the priest writing out the name in the logbook wrote an 'm' instead of two 'n's'. Pauline decided she preferred Demy to Denny, so Demy he became. At six months' old, his mother had noticed his lazy left eye. He could look directly into her eyes with his right eye but his left eye gazed way over to the side in another direction. As if to conceal this deformity, he had a tendency to shut and screw up his eyes frequently, especially when nervous, which happened often. He never looked anyone in the eye. His friends gave him the nickname of 'Squinty', which did little to instil confidence.

They quickly reached the store which Fossette entered alone and she began, with feigned respect, "Monsieur Plouffe, my father asked me to… "

"Be off with you, you rascal," he yelled, grabbing, then waving his cane and running her out of the store. In the commotion his spectacles fell on the floor, then under his shoes, smashing the frame and lenses.

As they emerged, Stéphane and Demy were standing at the entrance. Stéphane seized a clay pipe and the three children ran off laughing in opposite directions, Stéphane taking care to drop the pipe a short distance from the shop in full view of M. Plouffe. "I will get you, you enfants térribles. I'll report you to your parents and to the police," he shouted as they disappeared down the street. They knew that being short-sighted without his spectacles, he did not recognise them. They heard nothing more about the event.

Visible signs of Fossette's adolescence developed a few months later. Charles accosted her loudly one evening.

"Clementine. I see you are becoming a woman. I warn you that if you come with child, you will leave this house."

From hearing her parents in bed at night, and from street talk with other children, she knew exactly what pregnancy involved, and responded meekly, "Yes, Papa."

She had decided in any case she did not want to get pregnant, not so much because of fear of her father or of being ejected from the home she found it more significant that a pregnancy would be physically inconvenient, would create a hole in her life at her young age, and hinder her aim of escaping the rut of daily existence. She also had no intention of letting the decision not to get pregnant interfere with her enjoyment of the company of boys, and of contact with them.

A few evenings later, she led Stéphane to a recess between the flying buttresses of the cathedral. There they enjoyed their first kiss. Even more exciting for Fossette was she got to handle and playfully wear the red béret.

Charles Cavigneau worked for Sevigny Frères, the linen factory that the family had built up over several generations. A smart-looking stone building, the factory occupied a city block to the west of the cathedral. Separation of the flax-fibres took place on the ground floor of the building, while workers on the second floor turned the fibre into linen of many different hues. The manufacture of fine quality batiste and cambric took place in a small reserved area. The factory employed over fifty workers making it one of the largest in the city.

Pierre Tremblais was the owner of the Company. The textile industry in Arras had gone through a period of decline during the late eighteenth century because of competition from Flanders and England. Sevigny Frères had kept going with difficulty. In the spring of 1790, the manager died and the following day Pierre called Charles to his office, a large room occupying the corner of the building on the second floor, overlooking streets in two directions. Ornate Louis Quinze furniture, including a large desk in the centre, filled the floor space. The powerful and sweet smell of cigars wafted through the air like smoke curling up from a chimney on a windless day. As Charles entered the office, its size and ornamentation overwhelmed him. He had never seen such ostentation and felt intimidated.

After the opening pleasantries Pierre said, "Charles, I have been impressed with your work and initiative and you get along well with other hirelings. Our company is in difficulties because the country is bankrupt. People have no money so do not buy new clothes. Company earnings have gone down but expenses have stayed the same. I am inviting you to be the new manager but cannot increase your wage. Some workers will have to be fired and those that remain will have to work harder. Are you able to take on this position?"

Charles dropped his head and eyes for a few moments, and then replied questioningly, "Monsieur Tremblais: you put me in a difficult position. The workers are my friends. I drink and play cards with them. You are inviting me to throw some of them out on the street so they will have nothing?"

"We live in troubled times, even though there are some hopeful signs. The king has recalled the Estates General in Versailles, for the first time in one hundred and fifty years I am told, to develop some sort of new Constitution that may help resolve the country's vast economic problems. But I cannot wait that long. If we cannot reduce our expenses very soon, we will go bankrupt and that would be the end for us all. I have to be hard on the few so that I can be kind to the many. I cannot give you a better wage now, but if my plan succeeds, and if the politicians resolve their conflicts and the economy improves, I could give you a raise next year."

Charles turned away as he pondered his dilemma. "Are you making any sacrifices yourself, Monsieur Tremblais?" he asked.

"I could regard that question as impertinent," he replied sharply. "I could fire you for even posing it but I'll respond honestly. I have sold all but one of my horses and no longer hunt. I have placed my wife on a personal spending budget. Not an easy matter because she has something of Marie-Antoinette in her when it comes to clothing and jewellery. Do you have any other questions?"

"I will, if you will allow, think about it till tomorrow," replied Charles, ignoring the sarcasm.

"Remember there are other workers interested in this position. If you do not take it, you may find yourself in the firing line in the future. I repeat I shall do whatever is required to ensure the company survives."

"Then I accept the position on your terms," replied Charles, feeling coerced and cornered. "My life and that of my family is important to me. I shall do what needs to be done."

The following day Pierre called a meeting of all the workers. He held the meeting in the main work area, big enough to accommodate all fifty workers. The men stood or sat around the furniture, tables, chairs and giant looms while Pierre himself stood on a small dais near the front entrance so he could be seen and heard by all. He announced Charles' position as the new manager, reported that the company faced difficulties and stated that firm measures, including firing unproductive workers, were required to rectify the situation. Other than anxious and subdued cries of "Oh, No!" the assembled workers did not respond to this shocking information The rebelliousness of the revolutionary elites had yet to percolate down to the common man and woman in the street.

Over the next few weeks, in regular consultation with Pierre, Charles dismissed several workers in the company. Amongst them were erstwhile friends and neighbours who wept or yelled at him as he fired them. He called Gaspard, one of his former drinking companions into his small windowless office on the ground floor, "Gaspard, as you know the company is in trouble and may go bankrupt. In discussion with Monsieur Tremblais we have to terminate your employment from today."

"Charles," he replied angrily, with pursed lips, "I thought you were a buddy of mine. I have a wife and six children. How will I feed and clothe them?"

"Times are tough for us all, Gaspard. You may find another job."

"You know as well as I do, Charles, that none exists. We will end up in the poorhouse, perhaps even on the streets. Let that motto be on your gravestone, you god-forsaken pig!"

Charles did not respond and rose from his chair to hustle Gaspard out of the door.

He had to remind himself regularly that, "it is them or me." Surprisingly, with his new responsibilities, Charles mellowed at home. He no longer came home drunk on weekend nights and his short temper and imperiousness were less in evidence.

A year later, in the spring of 1791, the political situation in Paris had stabilised. The National Assembly brought out the Declaration of the Rights of Man, and worked on creating a new constitution, with the king as a constitutional monarch. The Revolution had run its course; its ideals had been accomplished. News of these developments was published in the Arras newspaper and pinned on the bulletin board at the Mairie. Pierre belonged to the Girondins Club of Arras, a political group with branches throughout the country that had worked for years to accomplish these goals.

Charles knocked on Pierre's door late one Friday evening.

"Come in."

"I would like to speak with you," said Charles respectfully as he entered.

"What is it?" asked Pierre, crossing his arms and frowning.

"I would like to discuss with you my role in the company."

"Go ahead."

"When I took on the position of manager a year ago, you said that when the political and economic situation stabilised you would raise my wage. I believe we are there now."

"Things have improved but we have not arrived yet. The king has yet to sign the new constitution. The Jacobins are screaming that we Girondins, who run the country, are betraying the Revolution. Two years ago I voted in support of Robespierre as Arras representative to the National Assembly in Versailles, a decision I seriously regret. He has now become leader of the Jacobin group who are determined to take over the country and eliminate all opposition including the king and us Girondins. A lot more blood could be shed which would have a huge impact on the economy. We need to wait another year."

"You are not true to your promises," Charles said sharply. "At a big cost of the respect and friendship of my co-workers, I have carried out your orders. I have met my end of the deal. I expect you to meet yours."

"You may leave if you wish. We will have no trouble finding a replacement."

Charles clutched the armrest of the chair in frustration. He knew that Pierre spoke the truth, but felt it unjust that he had broken a promise. He got up and walked out without a farewell.

He was silent at the dinner table that night.

"What is wrong Charles?" asked Pauline.

"I want to leave Sevigny Frères but have nowhere else to go."

Pauline leaned over and gripped Charles's hand.

"You have done well at Tremblais' place. He is well-known in Arras as a tough businessman. That is why his business has not collapsed like many others. You must stay and hope that next year you get what you deserve."

"Pierre thinks only of himself but pretends he thinks of others," added Charles bitterly. "At heart he is a ruthless dictator. Things are better in France but he gives the excuse that they may deteriorate again."

"I think he may be right," replied Pauline. "My friend Joanne works as a maid for the Robespierre family on the rue Saumon. Joanne says that both Maximilien and Augustin, his brother, are angry that the Girondins are supporting the king. When they visited from Paris last week they said the king should be executed and France become a republic. They have strong voices and much influence. If Robespierre and the Jacobins take over there will be many more problems."

"I disagree," replied Charles firmly. "The king, in combination with the Girondins, is more than a match for the Jacobins."

"Robespierre is a man who knows what he wants." Pauline knew that her inside information had more value than Charles' suppositions. "I know him only from what Joanne tells me. Do not sell him short. He is ruthless. Here is another strange thing, Charles. Women support Robespierre strongly despite him behaving like a tyrant. It is because he preaches that women equal men in all respects. Yet he has neither a wife nor a woman in his life. Joanne would do anything for him. Not only that, she trusts him completely. He always pays her on time and if she does extra work for him, he pays her more than is due. I believe it likely that he will take over the country."

"Last year Pierre told me his wife loves clothing and jewellery like Marie-Antoinette," Charles replied with a sneer, ignoring Pauline's comments about Robespierre. "Because of weakness and vacillation, the king is unable to cut the queen's spending. Women whose husbands have money love to spend. If that is their custom in good times, they do not change when times are hard. Pierre's wife is like a spoilt child used to its comforts and toys. He uses his authority over us workers but is not able to use it over her and we all suffer as a consequence."

"I do not know Madame Tremblais but I have heard it said that she is a jealous woman who trusts no one and rarely lets him out of her sight. Such women do not know the word 'sacrifice'."

"I shall stay where I am at Sévigny Frères. Pierre said I can leave if I wish. I will not give him that satisfaction."

Pauline rose from her chair, went over to Charles, kissed him on the forehead and gave him a hug.

"Although you often drive me crazy, I still love you."

Another year passed. In spring 1792 Charles decided to approach Pierre again about a wage increase. Pauline had predicted correctly that the political and economic situation would deteriorate. The king and queen and their two children had been caught attempting to flee the country. The Revolutionaries, now under Jacobin control, proclaimed a new Constitution and put the king on trial for his life. Political uncertainty causes economic instability. Sevigny Frères faced bankruptcy.

The meeting with Pierre took a very different course from their previous meetings. When he entered the office there was an empty bottle of wine and a half-empty glass on the desk. A stale smell of wine permeated the office. Pierre appeared irritable and fidgeted visibly. Charles quickly realised his appeal for a wage increase was a lost cause and did not pursue it. He knew of Pierre's political interests and leanings and suspected these must be the cause of his discomfort. He decided to discreetly enquire after Madame Tremblais' health.

"She is very well. Very well," Pierre repeated, with ironic emphasis. "I do not know what to do about her. I give her almost everything she asks for, more than she needs. But she remains dissatisfied. Here we are in the midst of an earth-shaking Revolution, where no one is certain whether they will be arrested and executed, and all she worries about is her appearance and what the neighbours might think. The world seems to pass her by. It is as if she lives on her own little planet separate from the rest of us. She is not an affectionate woman although she does not refuse my needs. Now I escape into wine but it does not do much good either. Just helps me forget. In the past the business kept me going but now it is in chaos, together with the country. I would like to be in your shoes with not a care in the world!"

"Monsieur Tremblais, you mock me! I do have a wife who cares for me, but I too once used wine to ease my problems! It is only when you asked me to be manager that I stopped. The extra responsibility you placed on my shoulders gave me a desire to prove myself. I have you to thank for that."

"I thank you for what you have done for Sevigny Frères. It has helped us survive until now and I believe we can keep going for a few months longer. But soon enough we will both be out of work. Who knows what happens then?

"Even religion gives us little solace," Pierre went on. He did not look at Charles. It was as if he was speaking to himself. "The Convention has closed cathedrals and churches and forced priests and bishops to make an oath of loyalty to revolutionary principles. Last week a group of tricoteuses, together with some men, and led by that brute Girouette invaded a convent with cudgels. They first disrobed then fustigated the nuns. Priests are threatened with banishment to the Bagne of Toulon, or even execution, if they refuse to take the oath of loyalty. Many have left the country and some, especially those representing the Sulpician Order, have gone to England with the idea of immigrating to Canada.

Charles listened intently to Pierre's musings but decided not to interrupt.

"The Government has introduced a new calendar. Called The Revolutionary Calendar, it replaces the old Gregorian. It will cause chaos and place an extra nail in the coffin of the church." Pierre doubted that Charles knew anything about the calendar so decided to inform him. "The months and days are being abolished. There will be twelve renamed months and each month will have three, ten day decadi which will replace the weeks. The tenth decadi will replace Sunday as a day of rest, but religious ceremony is banned. Marriages can take place only on the tenth decadi and the official is a bureaucrat, not a priest. These changes will destroy the Church. You cannot imagine the confusion this will cause in daily life. There will be many who will be unable or unwilling to learn the names of the new months and days."

"It is obvious we are in the midst of a real Revolution, the beginning of a new era in history," replied Charles with feeling. "The gendarmes entered the cathedral last week. They tore down the ancient sculptures and works of art and fired musket bullets breaking up the irreplaceable stained-glass windows. It is criminal. What is more, it is officially approved. What does the Church do that brings such anger and persecution upon itself?"

"That is an excellent question Charles. I have read and thought about it for years. The Enlightenment philosophers were almost all against the Church although Diderot reconciled on his deathbed. Though raised in the Church I no longer practice religion. There is, of course, no simple answer to your question. There are historical, political, moral, and emotional reasons. There is much jealousy of the Church's power, influence and riches. Many priests and bishops misuse their authority, judge people wrongly, so they see their leaders as hypocrites and react with anger. What's happening now is extreme and worse than the worst of the Church's sins."

"It seems you have led a full and adventurous life?" Charles asked.

"That is true. As a young man I joined the army and they sent me to New France. I fought in the Battle of Québec, which of course we lost. I had nothing when I returned to France. Meeting my wife and her family helped me find my feet, by allowing me to rebuild Sevigny Frères. Now it is all crashing down around me. Despite our serious difficulties I am not about to desert my wife. I have much for which to be thankful to her."

The light faded as the sun set. Pierre got up, went around the desk and gave Charles a warm handshake. "I thank you again for your help over the past two years. Without your contribution the Company would already have sunk. Offer my best wishes to Madame and your family. I shall keep you informed of Company affairs."

Charles left the office and the building with a feeling that combined relief and bewilderment; relief that for the first time he had established a constructive relationship with Pierre and bewilderment about Pierre's profound pessimism. He felt sufficiently assured to know that even if Sevigny Frères collapsed, he himself had learned enough as a manager to know that another opportunity would come his way.

As he turned the corner and approached his front door, he saw a couple standing in the shadows in passionate embrace. He looked more closely and recognised his daughter Clementine with Stéphane. With clenched fists and pursed lips he went up to them and said,

"Stéphane, will you let go of my daughter. Clementine, you will come home with me immediately. "Stéphane turned, punched Charles in the face and ran off. Charles fell back on the cobblestones but managed to avoid cracking his head. Clementine rushed up to help him up and supported him as he hobbled to their front door. A large bruise formed on his left eye and face while Pauline dabbed it with cold water.

"Clementine, you have to stop seeing that boy. He is a good-for-nothing lout who is just using you," Charles shouted.

"That is not true Papa," she exclaimed. "I have known him for two years and I like him. We have much fun together."

"You are a child, Clementine. I have told you, if you come with child you leave this house. It will ruin your life forever."

"I know all about coming with child, Papa, and have no intention of letting that happen," she retorted. "I know what has to be done to avoid that. I can look after myself and am no longer a girl!"

"I order you to stop seeing Stéphane. He is an aggressive scoundrel." Pointing to his face Charles added, "Look what he has done to me."

"I am truly sorry about that Papa. It should never have happened. I will stop seeing him for one week and then decide what to do."

This is what Clementine told her father but in her mind she had already decided to see Stéphane again, even before the promised week had elapsed. She would obviously have to be very discreet, and choose her times and places carefully.

After several days the swelling subsided and her father returned to work. Clementine went to Stéphane's house and waited until he emerged. Their eyes caught and without saying a word she invited him to follow her. She led him to a secluded spot behind a shrub under a buttress of the cathedral, where they embraced. "Stéphane, they want me to stop seeing you."

"I suppose I should not have punched him. I did it on impulse. He is an old man. But he should not have accosted me like that."

"It is folly for us to embrace right outside our home. No matter, it is done. He will get over it. I want to continue seeing you. Let us meet here every afternoon." With that agreed they lay down on the grass. She held and touched him affectionately. She loved the way he ran his fingers gently through her hair.

Pauline and Charles and a small group of like-minded friends attended a clandestine Christmas Nativity Mass in the home of Catherine Lachêne. It was the fifth day of the month of Nivose, Year II of The Revolutionary Calendar (25th December 1793). Now almost seventy years old, Catherine had grey hair and walked with a stoop, but her eyes were sharp and her brain alert. Before the Revolution, Catherine had been a leading member of the Cathedral parish and, after closure of the churches, took it upon herself to organise services using underground non-juring priests, those who had not taken the oath of allegiance to the Revolutionary regime, and who had remained loyal to the Pope. Her husband had died many years previously and left her a substantial inheritance. She had had one son, Hubert, who married a young farm girl called Marie-Anne in Vimy, the daughter of her brother, Gabriel. Marie-Anne had an illegitimate son from an earlier liaison whom Hubert adopted as his own. Hubert returned to Arras after Marie-Anne's death to live with his mother.

At the end of the service Catherine approached Charles. "I have not seen you for some months. How have you been?"

"Other than some back trouble I have been well. I lost my job at Sevigny Frères when the company went bankrupt but quickly found a new one in a wool tannery. It is a good job once you get used to the sickening smells. Pauline and I live our lives quietly. We try to adjust to all the changes taking place. I no longer have an interest in politics. I just try to earn enough to place food on our table for Pauline and the children. And what about yourself, Catherine?"

"My son Hubert died last month. He'd been ill for some months with an intestinal condition and suffered greatly." Catherine frowned and fidgeted as she replied. After a moment's silence she added, while lowering her voice, "I am guilty to admit it but I was actually relieved by his death. I could not bear to see him suffer and the doctors were no help. Now I too try to live quietly, the only way to survive these troubling times. What about your children?"

"All five are well," he replied, guardedly. "Clementine had a good-for-nothing beau last year but fortunately I managed to terminate that. She now helps her mother with the younger children. She's a mischievous girl and always getting into trouble. Demy is a worry too. Timid, does not say much. A stubborn nervous tic affects his face and eyes. He is not strong and does not act like a man. He should have been a girl. I do not know what will become of him."

"Sorry to hear that Charles. I cannot do much to help Demy but if you think it would be useful I would be happy to talk with Clementine."

"That is kind of you Catherine. I will see how it goes and let you know."

"Very best Christmas greetings to you Charles."

"Same to you, Catherine."

On the first decadi in the month of Pluviose, Year II (7th February 1794), the Revolutionaries in the Arras area, led by the mayor, Joseph le Bon, held a Cult of Reason ceremony in the cathedral. Le Bon had been ordained a priest in his mid-twenties but two years later he joined the revolutionaries, left the priesthood, got married and was elected Mayor of Arras. He made an odd, long, rambling sermon of sorts extolling the virtues of science and knowledge as the new deity. An army band performed martial music to accompany the ceremonies, and these included the first performance in Arras of a newly composed piece by Rouget de Lisle, "Chant de guerre pour l'armée du Rhin", later renamed "La Marseillaise." At the height of the ceremony, an attractive young Arrasienne entered the cathedral dressed splendidly in a long white chiffon dress with a white, woollen ankle-length coat. A garland of imitation red roses covered her head and her blonde hair rested lazily over her shoulders. She wore a tricolour sash made of silk and led a procession to the altar then walked up the steps to the pulpit raising her arms in jubilation, and giving a radiant smile to encourage admiration from the large congregation who applauded enthusiastically.

The Reign of Terror began gathering pace. The city of Arras acquired a new guillotine and Mayor le Bon ordered it to be placed on an elevated scaffold in the centre of La Petite Place. Every morning a notice appeared on the wall of La Mairie giving the time of the execution and the names of the day's victims. A crieur publique, the town crier, and his wife walked the streets, she ringing the bell and he shouting the execution announcements. As soon as the crieur publique passed down their street Joanne, Pauline's neighbour, would gather up her knitting and hurry to La Petite Place to witness the spectacle and share the excitement with the other tricoteuses. Pauline informed Joanne she had no interest in a commentary on the proceedings.

Clementine had not stopped seeing Stéphane. At one of their trysts in the month of Floréal (May), Clementine saw that Stéphane had developed a bad cough and he failed to appear at their next meeting three days later. She walked past his home but saw no sign of activity. Most of the doors and windows were shuttered and the remainder had their curtains drawn. Clementine became increasingly restless and withdrawn over the next few days, unable to sleep, and when she could contain herself no longer, she approached Pauline tearfully, "I have been lying to you, Maman. I have continued to see Stéphane secretly despite my promise to stop. Now he is sick. I am very troubled and don't know what to do."

"You are a stupid girl, Clementine. Your father and I told you to stop seeing him because he had a bad influence on you."

"That is not true Maman," she wailed through tears. "I liked him, cared for him and I needed him. He was not a bad boy. He had a kind heart even though I know he hurt Papa without meaning to. He did not harm me."

"I will have to tell your father. He will not be pleased."

Pauline gave Charles the news when he returned home from work that evening. "Clementine, I ordered you to stop seeing Stéphane," Charles shouted in shocked disbelief. "How can you disobey me so shamelessly?"

By this time Clementine had recovered her pluck and replied firmly, "Papa, I loved Stéphane even though you disapproved of him, even though he hurt you. I knew if I told you, you would disapprove so I did not tell you. I hoped you would accept him in time."

Charles responded by striking Clementine in the face with his open hand causing her to sprawl on the floor. She got up holding her face, red and burning from the slap, and without crying, glared at her father, and with curled lips said, "If you ever do that to me again I am leaving home even if it means I end up living on the street!"

Pauline looked at Charles then at Clementine but said nothing. For a few moments Charles remained silent then said through clenched teeth, "Let us go and visit Stéphane's house, see what is going on, and end this affair."

Clementine accompanied her parents and they discovered that Stéphane had pneumonia. A physician visited him daily and treated him by attaching leeches to the chest wall to promote bleeding, and by giving him a combination of emetics and laxatives. Although expected to recover he also had a high risk of death.

"Why did this have to happen?" Clementine cried, after they returned home.

"Be calm," Pauline replied crossly. "I cannot understand why you did not tell us earlier?"

"I knew you disapproved and would have tried to stop us from seeing each other," Clementine declared. "There was no other way, Maman."

"We will wait and see what happens when he recovers. If you listened to your father this would not have happened. Papa and I will meet with his parents again and see if we can work out an arrangement.

Stéphane did not recover. Weakened by the medical treatments he received, he died three days later.

On a cold, dull and damp day during the month of Germinal, Year II (March 1794) as Father St. Amour finished his dinner of vegetable broth and bread, eaten in solitude, he heard a knock on the door.

Monsieur and Madame la Fortune stood on his doorstep. He recognised Madame who attended Mass occasionally, sometimes paid her tithe, and otherwise played little part in the activities of the parish. St. Amour had never met Monsieur la Fortune but well knew of his reputation as a heartless autocrat.

Both were dressed simply. Monsieur wore loose-fitting culottes and a black coat that clearly did not belong to him. Madame wore a brown ankle-length wide skirt with a plain coat. She had a bonnet pulled over her head with only her face visible. They both wore poorly fitted clogs. If the priest had not known them, he would have thought them peasants visiting from a neighbouring community. He noted that Madame trembled visibly and that Monsieur cowered beside his wife, as if a beggar.

St. Amour welcomed them as best he could. The room was ice-cold because of the widespread fuel shortage, and one dim candle provided light, causing their gaunt faces to flicker between light and shadow. To keep warm, the visitors kept their coats and shoes on.

"It is good to see you, Monsieur and Madame la Fortune. Come in. What can I do for you?"

"We came to seek your advice and possibly your help, Father St. Amour," ventured Monsieur la Fortune as they sat down. St. Amour recognised an exaggerated meek and respectful attitude. "We are desperate. My estate is in chaos. Adolphe Girouette, my manager has left and joined the revolutionaries and I cannot find field workers. The government has confiscated my harvest and the sheep, cattle and horses are starving. I know I have not been an active member of your parish and trust you will not hold this against me. You are a well-respected member of the community and have connections with Church and Civil authorities in Arras and Paris. We are here to request your assistance in persuading the government to return our harvest, or at least pay us a reasonable sum for it. In return we will offer you a percentage." St. Amour noticed a pleading and obsequious tone coloured his voice, as if he thought that debasing himself would increase the likelihood of obtaining the priest's support.

"You misjudge me seriously," St. Amour replied. "Whatever influence I had with either Church or Civil authorities is now gone. The Church is being heavily persecuted. Although some priests, such as Joseph Le Bon, have supported the excesses of the Revolution, many more have been exiled or even executed. Sunday, our holy day of rest has been abolished by the new calendar, and no one knows when to celebrate their birthdays and anniversaries. As a result church attendance has fallen precipitously. Even if I had political connections, I would not support your proposal with the aim of obtaining a reward."

An icy silence pervaded the room. Madame La Fortune broke the hush by changing the subject. "We are fearful of what is going on in France; it is bad enough for them to guillotine the king. Now the poor queen has also lost her head. I cannot conceive such brutality. Evil pervades their souls. The horror has spread to the people. Crowds of women seat themselves around the scaffold and applaud when each severed head is displayed on a spike. Between executions they while their time away by chattering and knitting. They call them "les tricoteuses."

"I fear we have yet to see the worst of it, Madame la Fortune," St. Amour replied. "Joseph Le Bon was ordained a priest four years ago. Two years later he met Robespierre and under his influence, he left the priesthood, got married, and is now Mayor of Arras at the age of twenty-eight. Le Bon has already committed barbaric excesses and he is only at the start of his term of office. Violence breeds violence. It will stop only when the perpetrators themselves are eliminated, but who is brave enough to do that? Young Charlotte Corday made a valiant effort by assassinating Marat, but she lost her head within days and the savagery continues. They even executed that great woman, Olympe de Gouges. For years she fought for the rights of women, and attacked slavery and capital punishment. Our government leaders are butchers."

"Madame La Fortune and I thought of fleeing the country but we knew we would then lose all our possessions. We also considered the disaster that befell the king and queen when they attempted to flee, were recognised and captured at the border and marched back to Paris in disgrace. I believe that this event, more than any other assured their execution. We know that to be caught would guarantee the loss of our heads."

"Besides, we have our young daughters to consider," added Madame La Fortune, her voice and lips quivering with anxiety. "We confine them in the chateau as much as possible. We have heard dreadful stories about attacks and raping of young aristocratic women in Paris and elsewhere. It is said that when a soldier has raped a virgin who is an aristocrat, it is looked upon as a special badge of honour by his unit."

"Despite the claims of the revolutionaries that they represent the people, the people have no power," replied St. Amour. "Peace will come only when the revolutionaries devour each other."

"Because of the shortage of workers, my wife and I are even obliged to work in our own garden, planting seeds, watering the vegetables and picking them when ripe," la Fortune confided mournfully. "You can imagine that respectable people like us are not used to this type of labour, especially at my age and state of health. My back aches painfully after an hour using a shovel. Until two months ago, we had the assistance of a young boy from the village called Marcel. Then he suddenly disappeared without a word. He must have been called up in the army, or perhaps even killed. These days people seem to come from nowhere, then disappear again into the void."

"I know Marcel well," countered the priest. "He is alive and healthy. He is in hiding to avoid being called up by the army. Because of the war the authorities are rounding up every able-bodied young man they can find. If found he would be executed as a deserter. I too am at risk for concealing him. Because he is in hiding, he is not available to lighten your gardening load at present," he added with an almost imperceptible smile. The priest felt a twinge of guilt from the pleasure he derived from the image of la Fortune labouring in the garden like a peasant.

"Of course we understand, Father St. Amour," replied la Fortune. "Let him know we valued his help and he is welcome back when he is able."

"I regret my inability to assist you in your conflict with the authorities. With this government you cannot win by confrontation, or even by trying to circumvent them. My recommendation is that you keep out of their way until the heat has passed, even if this means you have to work your own fields." St. Amour hesitated a moment as he again smiled secretly to himself. He then continued, "In the end you may be left without your possessions, but hopefully, and most importantly, you get to keep your heads."

"We thank you for your advice and kindness, Reverend Father," Madame la Fortune replied. "We are poorly equipped to deal with these violent and unpredictable times but shall try to heed your counsel."

Chapter Ten

Vimy, 15 Floréal, Year II (5th May 1794)

Vimy appeared to be the picture of tranquility on this lovely spring day. Sunny and windless, the aroma of wild rose blossoms filled the air. Nesting birds covered the trees twittering excitedly to each other and in the distant fields, sheep bleated and cattle lowed. The only human sounds came from the fields where both men and women were sowing seasonal crops, chattering amicably in muted words, the sounds of their voices wafting through the village on the gentle breeze. Another peaceful day dawned in this beautiful corner of France.

About mid-morning, a group of six armed soldiers from Arras, led by Adolphe Girouette, marched into Vimy and immediately made their way to St Martin's Church, the spire being visible from anywhere in the town. Using the butts of their muskets, they pounded heavily on the door, Girouette shouting repeatedly, "Open the door, Priest! Open the door!" Getting no response, they began efforts to break it down using bricks and stones that edged the flower garden near the entrance to the church.

Father St. Amour approached them from the neighbouring presbytery, limping because of pain in a knee joint. "What do you seek, young men? If you wish to enter the church to pray I have the key right here." St. Amour well knew that prayer was furthest from their minds. He judged that a gentle reminder about the purpose of a church would not be inopportune, despite their obviously aggressive intentions. He recognised Girouette as the former manager on Monsieur la Fortune's estate.

Girouette addressed St. Amour loudly, his face flushed with fury, "This church is henceforth the property of the state. Open the bloody door, priest, and give us the key. I, we hereby demand you sign an oath of loyalty to the Republic. Now! Here and now."

"My first loyalty is to God, and this church belongs to the people of this parish," St. Amour replied quietly.

"Then you are under arrest for sedition and for crimes against the State. You will accompany us back to Arras immediately."

"My door has always been open to the people of this town. I have gone out of my way to assist them in their trials and tribulations. What evidence do you have for my crimes?"

"You can argue your case before the Revolutionary Tribunal," replied Girouette, his voice choking with anger, spittle flying through the air as he shouted.

He snatched the key from St. Amour's hands, unlocked the door and the group entered the church. The men proceeded to break open the tabernacle, threw the sacred vessels on the floor and desecrated the consecrated hosts, as the horrified priest watched helplessly. Two of the group then grabbed the aging man, one holding onto each arm and frog-marched him twelve kilometers back to Arras. During the silent march, and despite rough handling by the soldiers, St. Amour contemplated his situation. I supported the original aims of the Revolution, the need for justice, equality and tolerance. I did not anticipate that extremists would take over and spread brutality. Now I am its victim. I knew this could happen yet hoped it would not. I only hope that Marcel remains secure and safe in his cave.

The Revolution did not begin this way, nor was it meant to go down this path. Increasingly bloody extremism followed the accession of Robespierre and the Jacobins in late 1792, with the execution of King Louis XVI in January and Queen Marie-Antoinette in October of 1793. Robespierre orchestrated the Reign of Terror that followed, and tens of thousands of men and women were sent to the guillotine, a daily public spectacle in many cities. The Terror had no kinship with justice; the good were dispatched with the bad, quickly and efficiently.

St. Amour arrived in Arras exhausted and in pain at the end of his forced march from Vimy. His captors threw him into an underground, dingy cell that stank of human excrement. He slumped onto the stone floor as the guards clanged, and then locked the prison gate. It took ten to fifteen minutes for his eyes to adjust to the gloom and for his bruised body to recover at least partly from the march. He may have passed out.

He looked around the cell and saw no furniture other than four narrow cots covered with one blanket each and no mattress. One corner, close to an outlet drain, contained a small overflowing bucket that served as a latrine for the inmates. It clearly was the source of the noxious odours that permeated the cell.

"Father André St. Amour, welcome to the Chateau de Versailles!" St. Amour sat up, surprised to hear his name, blinked a few times to ensure he was awake then recognised Father Charles Baréz from the neighbouring town of Givenchy-en-Gohelle. He rose slowly from the floor, smiled at Baréz's incongruous humour, and weakly shook his hand. The men behind him came into focus.

Barez made sure his eyes were holding the old man's, which took a moment, then he continued, "Allow me to introduce my fellow, shall we say, outlaws. This is Monsieur Antoine du Moulin whose crime is that he belongs to an ancient aristocratic family." He indicated a man with an erect posture and ordinary, but very clean clothing. And here we have Monsieur Pierre Tremblais, charged with crimes against the state for belonging to the Girondins. Girouette arrested me yesterday outside my church and marched me here with his armed militia, just like you were today. I have been charged with sedition because one of my parishioners alleged, falsely of course, that I preached an anti-revolutionary sermon." Turning to Pierre and du Moulin he added, "Messieurs, this is Father St. Amour, parish priest at Vimy."

"Despite this dark setting I am pleased to meet you, Father St. Amour." Pierre Tremblais embraced St. Amour. "I have visited Vimy on a number of occasions and love the Chateau, the town and the environs. I believe we are all to be arraigned before Le Bon and his Revolutionary Tribunal tomorrow morning," Pierre continued in an uncharacteristic sombre, monotonous voice, his shoulders slumped. "We have five minutes to present our case and are permitted neither witnesses nor legal representation."

"You can see and smell the comforts that surround us in the cell, St. Amour," added Barez. "Twice daily, morning and evening, they bring us an unidentifiable slop they call food, and each of us is allowed a bowlful. We have no cutlery. If the authorities do not execute us we would soon die of inhumanity."

Word about St. Amour's arrest and his march to prison in Arras spread rapidly through Vimy. Despite his allegedly lenient attitude on moral matters, most members of the parish, even the starched traditionalists, regarded him with affection. They were universally outraged by his arrest. All knew that, now that they had seized him, execution followed, inevitably and quickly, so Alexis and his friend Grégoire decided to travel to the prison immediately and attempt to rescue him. Alexis had a friend who had joined the army, stationed in Arras. The friend, in turn, had contacts amongst the prison staff. With their help they were able to gain access to him in his cell in the bowels of the building.

"How did you find me?" St Amour asked with astonishment as he recognised and embraced Alexis when the guard opened the gate.

"I know people who know people here," replied Alexis, vaguely. "What can we do to get you out of this foul den? It smells worse than an abattoir," he added, while crinkling his face at the putrid odours.

"Likely nothing. Our hearing before the Revolutionary Tribunal is tomorrow morning and I suspect we will all be directed rapidly to the guillotine. Allow me to introduce my fellow-felons, Father Charles Baréz, Antoine du Moulin and Pierre Tremblais. Messieurs, this is Alexis Lachêne, an exemplary member of my parish."

"Glad to meet you all despite this awful locale. Mon Père, could we not appear at the Tribunal as witnesses in your support?" asked Alexis.

"We are not permitted witnesses, and in any event this would be dangerous for you," replied Pierre. "We have to conduct our own defence and we have but five minutes to do so. There is little hope. The country is cradled in fear and perceives conspirators or enemies everywhere, even when there are none. Whether or not we contest the allegations will make little difference. Our fate is sealed. We can only hope that our deaths and the deaths of many thousands of other innocents will bring the country to its senses. Meanwhile, the dead king's brothers, and the armies they lead outside the borders of France, are not helping by threatening words and postures."

"You are dead wrong," cried du Moulin. "The only language this regime understands is force. We need a powerful army to invade France from the outside, eliminate the revolutionary leaders, restore order in the country, and place the king's young son on the throne, if the poor wretch is still alive."

"I do not believe that restoring the monarchy would restore order in the country," replied Pierre. "The Revolution has gone too far. Louis XVI and the regime he represented made too many missteps, caused too much suffering and injustice. In my opinion the country will never again accept a monarchy, even a king without power. But these times are turbulent. A heavy wind, almost a hurricane, is blowing. Anything could happen."

After a brief silence, Alexis brought them back to their current situation. "None of this helps us with your present predicament. Grégoire and I came here to see if we could assist Father St. Amour in any way but it appears there is little we can do."

"I appreciate your gesture but your conclusion is correct," replied the priest.

"I have an idea," said Grégoire excitedly. "Father St. Amour, why do you and I not exchange clothes now, and you walk out of the prison as if you were me? I will take your place on the guillotine row. I am young and have no one who depends on me so my life does not count for much."

"Grégoire, you deserve to be canonised as a saint and a martyr, even for making that offer," St. Amour replied without hesitation. "Of course I cannot accept it. Even if by good fortune I managed to evade the guards and escape from the prison, as soon as the authorities discover what happened, as they

134

assuredly will, they will hound me down, and in the end two lives, not only one, will be lost. I deeply appreciate your generous offer, but must refuse it."

After embracing the four prisoners, Alexis and Grégoire took their leave from the prison, emerged gloomily into the daylight and walked back to Vimy. Occasionally one or the other would stop to relieve themselves in the bushes beside the road, and they would say out loud the thoughts that had been building up in their heads. "I have much respect for St Amour," Alexis ventured. "His death will be a huge loss to Vimy. It would have been better if he had signed the oath of allegiance."

"St. Amour follows his own creed," replied Grégoire and then added, with an edge of bitterness in his voice, "whereas Pierre Tremblais follows no creed. My oldest brother, Thomas, worked for Sevigny Frères, the factory that Tremblais owned in Arras. Two years ago Tremblais fired Thomas for no reason. He and his family have been destitute ever since. Perhaps Tremblais, at least, deserves what's coming to him."

After their visitors had left, St. Amour said, "They took a big risk in coming to see us. Both Alexis and Grégoire have a generous spirit but it is folly to visit condemned men in prison. They will be fortunate if they are not arrested on the road back to Vimy."

"I have come to know the town quite well, Mon Père," said Pierre. "Before the Revolution I visited it a number of times at the invitation of Monsieur la Fortune of the Chateau. Poor man, the authorities also arrested him last week. We are all about to die!" As Pierre spoke the priest gazed into his eyes. Their brown colour, wide spacing and slightly protuberant character had a certain familiarity, yet he knew he had never met this man before.

"I think you are right, Pierre," replied St. Amour, nodding. "Under the benevolent guidance of our friend and representative, Maximilien Robespierre, the Revolutionary Tribunals have a reputation for ruthlessness. They will listen, without hearing, to our defence, and immediately send us to the guillotine. The situation has become especially bad here in Arras, compared to other parts of the country, since Joseph le Bon became mayor. He laughs and applauds after an execution, then boasts to his friends about how many people he has "shortened" that day. Cutting off the heads of priests and aristocrats gives him special satisfaction and brings him more joy than drinking a glass of wine."

His three listeners stared at him incredulously.

"I know of a situation where he demanded sex from a woman to save her husband then executed them both the next day," St. Amour continued. "The mother of another victim calls him 'ce prêtre infernal'. His evil acts betray the irony of his name. The Revolution began with the noble ideals of Liberty,

Equality and Fraternity and I supported it strongly. It has degenerated into a chaotic mess where vengeful personal scores are settled by execution, all, allegedly, in the name of Liberty and the will of the people."

"It is a curious fact, or so I have noticed, that we live our lives as if we believe we will never die," replied Pierre, in a quiet and intense voice. "It is only when we face the prospect of imminent death that we begin to think about the meaning of life. As a young man in the French army in Québec, I faced death many times, yet continued to believe it could never happen to me. I was fortunate. Many of my friends were killed, including our leader the Marquis de Montcalm. The revolutionaries are right that there are many injustices in our society but they are not resolving them expeditiously. In fact, they are now making them much worse. I believe there is life after death, where such injustices are corrected."

"You are very perceptive—" began St. Amour.

"You are both talking nonsense," interrupted du Moulin. "Life is like a game of roulette. There is no way of predicting the winning or losing number. If you're in the wrong place at the wrong time, the bullet or, these days, the executioner's blade will strike you, and you are gone, forever. What is the end of your story? Where do you see signs there is life after death?"

"I understand your difficulty," replied St. Amour calmly. "Your body, and things around you, you can see with your eyes, perceive with your other senses. Your Soul, you cannot see, hear, touch or smell. This does not mean it does not exist. When I make a decision to do this, or do that, it is my Will that is speaking, and my Will is part of my Soul. Free Will is a fundamental part of our humanity. It makes us different from all other animals."

"Your so-called Free Will is just part of your imagination," replied du Moulin. "We are all victims of our emotions, our circumstances, and our backgrounds. If you had Free Will you would not be here, in this dungeon, facing an awful death tomorrow. You would have chosen to retire, to sign the oath of allegiance, or leave the country."

"You are right in one respect, but wrong in another, Monsieur du Moulin," replied St. Amour respectfully. "For me, I have chosen to be here, even though it outwardly may seem a foolish and destructive decision. I have no wish to desert my parishioners by retiring or emigrating, and cannot, in conscience, sign the oath of allegiance to a regime that spreads death and destruction. I am taking a stand in the hope, and expectation, that I am making a small but essential contribution to changing the system."

"I admire your idealism, Father St. Amour, but disagree with your premise of Free Will. It is pretence, perhaps even an excuse to justify your present unfortunate circumstances. I certainly had no control over my arrest and imprisonment. I had a "du" in front of my name, my only crime. I am bitter and angry, yet helpless in the face of such crazy injustice." Pierre Tremblais and Baréz both nodded in agreement as they listened to their distressed fellow inmate.

"I know we have a Soul and Free Will," said Pierre. "My crime was my political association with the Girondins Club in Arras, and I could have chosen not to be a member. With the ascendancy of the Jacobins, the Girondins in Paris and around the country are now being rounded up. Although raised in a religious setting I lost my faith when in the army. The army's killing philosophy does not mesh well with religion and spirituality. At heart though, I still have faith." The imminence of death and the wise, comforting words of Father St. Amour forced Pierre to reflect on his own words. He turned to St. Amour and asked, "Mon Père, would you hear my confession, likely my last one?"

"Why, yes of course. Let us talk here quietly in the corner of the cell."

"As a young man in the Army I visited prostitutes on many occasions," Pierre whispered, as he began his confession. "On one occasion shortly before my marriage during a visit to Vimy, I deflowered a beautiful innocent, and willing, farm girl. Since my marriage to Chantal I have been faithful despite many temptations to stray. I have also committed the sin of greed in my business dealings. For these sins I am heartily sorry."

"Christ gave His disciples the power to forgive sins on His behalf, and knowing of your fidelity and sincerity, I forgive you. As Penance you will recite the Act of Contrition. Go in Peace." The priest made the sign of the cross, Pierre smiled at him, and at that serendipitous instant, St. Amour knew he was speaking to Marcel's father. The eyes of Pierre Tremblais were the eyes of Marcel pierre! They had the same brown colour, wide spacing, and the same focused concentration. They even had the same slightly hooked nose. Marie-Anne, Marcel's mother, was the young farm girl whom he had seduced and Pierre Tremblais, Marcel's Unknown Father!

After completing the confessional rites, St. Amour reached out and placed his arm around Pierre's shoulder. "Pierre, I believe I know your farm girl friend. Her name was Marie-Anne, and she had a son called Marcel. I recognise your eyes in his." He paused a moment, and sadness replaced the excitement in his voice. "I have to tell you, Pierre, Marie-Anne died in childbirth a few years ago."

Pierre hugged St. Amour and wept in shocked disbelief. "That is incredible, Reverend Father! I loved Marie-Anne and cared for her even though I went with her but once. I never forgot her. It breaks my heart to think that Marie-Anne is now dead, and I am shocked, though not surprised, to hear she bore me a son." He recovered some of his composure, and then said, "I feel bad that I caused her suffering. She was a good and gentle woman who did not deserve unhappiness. Oh, my God, I would love to have met Marcel!"

"There is no need for you to feel guilty," replied St. Amour, patting Pierre on the shoulder. "Marie-Anne loved your son and cared for him very well." He went on to tell Pierre about Marcel's schooling, the deaths of his grandfather and uncles, the marriage to Hubert and then the death of Marie-Anne and Marcel's ill-treatment at the hands of his stepfather. He included Marcel's illness in the tale and how he himself had attempted to fill the manly void in Marcel's life. He told Pierre that Marcel now comported as a sturdy young man who previously had obtained a job as stablehand on la Fortune's farm, but was now in hiding to avoid being conscripted into the army.

"It must have been Marcel that I met when I went riding and hunting with la Fortune." Pierre said excitedly. "It was my son who cared for my horse! It is remarkable. It gives me much consolation to know now that I met him, even without the knowledge at the time that he was my son. I remember him telling me that you were like a father to him, Mon Père. As an ex-army officer I am disappointed that he is avoiding army duties. Yet I loved the way he cared for the horses. He appeared to be such an eager youngster and seemed to learn quickly what they needed."

"That sums him up very well," replied the priest. "Even though you met him briefly, it appears you understood him. He loves animals and hated the idea of killing someone even in battle. He once showed me a medal, chain and ring given him by Marie-Anne. She gave it to him on her deathbed. Marcel told me that Marie-Anne said you gave it to her."

Pierre wept again. "That is correct. I gave it to her in part to thank her for her love and in part as a memento. They were minted for me at my birth and baptism. It is an enormous consolation for me to know that Marcel now owns them. I have passed something on to him and his children and can now die contentedly!"

"There is one other thing I must tell you, Pierre. Marie-Anne never told anyone that you were Marcel's father. We all tried, all without success. I believe she saw it as a betrayal of a secret between the two of you."

"I did not request that she tell no one about us, but obviously that has simplified my life, so I must be grateful to her. I am just sorry it became a problem for you all. You must have become like a father to him. I feel bad I let her down in that way, although at the time I felt she desired me as much as I desired her. It is good to know that Marcel is now a sympathique young man. Perhaps goodness and benefit will yet come out of our recklessness. I do

138

not know how to express my gratitude for all that you have done for him and for Marie-Anne. There is so little I can do in return when we have but a day or two to live!"

"It really was not difficult. I loved Marcel and the family, and thought I could help them. I neither need nor ask for anything in return. It makes me happy that I have come to know you before our deaths."

"I cannot believe I am crying here like a child. I have not done this since my childhood. My own father would beat me with a strap if I cried, always a man, even at five years old."

"Pierre, it is not bad to cry. You have just made an astounding discovery, that you have a son, a love-child, you never knew existed. You know he owns a gift you gave his mother in love. You know he is a strong child who will spread your seed. All this on the day before your death! You are entitled to shed tears. Even your father would permit this!"

Early the following morning, the four men faced the Prosecutors on the Revolutionary Tribunal, presided over by Joseph Le Bon. Pierre saw his small blue eyes, his short stature and his large bulbous nose. On each side stood two gendarmes armed with muskets, pistols and truncheons. Le Bon acted as both prosecutor and judge. Each prisoner entered with a guard on either side and the guard marched them into the prisoners' witness box with wrists shackled behind them. Le Bon read out the allegations and gave each of the accused men five minutes to state their defence. On completion of their evidence they stood aside to make way for the next defendant.

"Monsieur le Président," Pierre began in his defence, addressing Le Bon and speaking gravely while choosing his words carefully, "I supported the original aims of the Revolution to bring Liberty, Equality and Justice to our burdened country. I took part in the election that sent Citizen Robespierre to Versailles as our representative to the National Convention. As a young man I fought in the Army in North America defending our country's interests against England and suffered severe hunger and privation after the defeat of Québec. On my return to France I settled in Arras, joined the firm of Sévigny Frères and have built up a successful enterprise that has provided employment and sustenance to over fifty Citizens of the Republic."

Pierre was silent for a few moments to secure the full attention of the Tribunal for his next words. "I plead not guilty to the charge of conspiring to bring down the Republic. I have no desire to destroy any member of the Government. Therefore, in accordance with the principal of justice on which this Republic was founded, I ask that I be granted my freedom." Le Bon's face remained cold and expressionless as the gendarme hustled him back to the prisoners' box.

Antoine du Moulin harangued the Tribunal with a defence that over the centuries the nobility had contributed to the country's wealth out of all proportion to their numbers and they should be allowed to continue doing this as before. After two minutes the prosecutor tried unsuccessfully to silence him, and then ordered the gendarmes to return him forcibly to the prisoner's box. Fathers St. Amour and Baréz emphasised their commitment to peace and charity. St Amour stated that he strongly supported the original objectives of the revolution. He found the injustices of society grossly unfair, and believed that tolerance and hard work for the communal good were the way forward for the country. "I cannot sign the oath of loyalty because the State is suppressing the Church's charitable role in society," he concluded gravely, while staring into the eyes of the prosecutor.

Le Bon gave his decision immediately Baréz had completed his defence and intoned, 'I find you all guilty as charged. St. Amour, I have evidence you resisted arrest and that you were tardy in the march from Vimy to Arras. Not signing the oath of allegiance is a treasonable offence. Tremblais, Baréz and du Moulin, you are all found guilty of treason for plotting against the state. You are all sentenced to beheading on the guillotine at 14.00 today."

"Monsieur le President," Pierre replied without prompting from Le Bon, "I wish to appeal your decision to the National Convention. I believe the Constitution of the Republic permits this action." Le Bon laughed loudly and all present at the hearing emulated his guffaw. He ignored Pierre's request and ordered the gendarmes to return all four men to their cells in preparation for their execution.

Pierre felt inwardly composed while being tied to the bascule board. His mind went back to that unfortunate eighteen year boy he had seen hanged at Tyburn in London, fourteen years previously. "Now I am going the same way, based on equally unfair laws. Justice in Europe is a farce," he thought bitterly. He contemplated the highs and lows of his life and relived the moment of ecstasy he experienced with Marie-Anne at the Chateau in Vimy, thoughts and feelings now all reactivated by his talk with St. Amour. He felt relief that part of himself would live on in Marcel. For a brief second he heard the execution blade as it slid down the tracks towards his neck and felt shock but no pain as it sliced cleanly through the tissues of his neck. For a few seconds he remained aware after his head had been severed, as it lay in a basket below the guillotine. The executioner noticed a fleeting smile flicker over his eyes and lips. "Marie-Anne, I love you!" He lost consciousness and expired.

Du Moulin, Baréz and St. Amour embraced and consoled each other while the executioner guillotined Tremblais. Du Moulin did not speak as he mounted the scaffold but tears streamed down his face and all heard him wailing softly. When his turn came, Baréz stated quietly and firmly to the assembled tricoteuses that he had been falsely accused and did not oppose the regime. "I support the government in its efforts to provide food and shelter for the poor."

"Get on the Board," screamed the mob in reply.

St Amour was the last of the group to mount the scaffold. He turned to the large crowd of tricoteuses and said in a loud voice filled with power and passion, "I speak for my friends when I say we are not guilty of these so-called crimes. Slaughtering innocents will not solve the regime's problems any better than slaughtering innocent children solved Herod's problem after Jesus' birth. I pray for the day when this abomination can be destroyed… " He nodded and gestured towards the guillotine.

Les tricoteuses interrupted his speech and shouted, "Shut up, shut up, get on the board and we will see who gets destroyed!" The executioner duly carried out his obligations to the satisfaction of the crowd. Joseph le Bon watched the proceedings from an open window overlooking La Petite Place, and gave a satisfied smirk as the executioner 'shortened' the body of the last one of this latest pack of traitors.

At that instant an inexplicable shudder coursed through the body of eighteen year old Marcel pierre, as he lay on his straw-bed in a cave near Vimy.

PART THREE: 1794-1803

IDENTITY

Chapter Eleven

Spring Year II (1794)

Marcel was hiding in a cave on the eastern slopes of Vimy ridge, about a thirty minute walk from the town. The cave consisted more of a rocky overhang, but with a shovel, he managed to deepen and enlarge it. He built a frame over the entrance using dead logs and branches, and used a cut-up sack cloth as a door, but the wind still whistled through. The cave floor was stony and uneven, and the air damp and mouldy. Dried leaves and straw spread over the ground in the corner served as a bed and clothes as pillow. With his ragged clothes, unshaven face and his long hair hanging untidily over his shoulders, he was dirty and unkempt and for lack of washing, he emitted a disagreeable body odour. He would pass as a tramp or a beggar on the streets of any city.

Early in the year, before being led away to his wrongful death, St. Amour had warned Marcel that officials representing the Army were passing through Northern France recruiting able-bodied young men. Despite the dangers facing the country from hostile armies, Marcel felt alienated by the revolutionary excesses, and chose to go into hiding to avoid being drafted. From a young age, Marie-Anne had imprinted on his mind the sacredness of life, and the thought of killing another man, even with the protection of the passions and legalities of war, repelled him. He decided to go underground.

Alexis visited him every few days to bring food, tools and other essentials. Water came from a nearby spring. The cave provided some protection from the rain, but if wind and weather came from the east, he got soaked. He spent mornings cautiously wandering the woods gathering edible berries and fruit but could not light a smoky fire because of the danger of detection. By offering leaves from a plane tree, he made friends with a family of rabbits and they provided genial, even playful companionship. As long as Alexis brought him sufficient nourishment, he chose not to slaughter them for food. Periodically he caught sight of foxes, wild boar and hares but they gave him and he gave them a wide berth.

At times, the monotony and solitude preyed on his mind and he became gloomy to the point of suicide. They say it's wrong but if I die now who will remember me? Whom have I touched? What is the point of going on? I lost my mother and my father deserted me. Losing a parent so young forced him to grow up quickly. His uncle and aunt, though good to him, would not miss him for long if he died. In fact it would simplify their lives. What is the easiest way to kill myself? A large branch extended from an oak tree near the entrance to the cave, just beyond his outstretched hand. It would be simple to stand on a stump, throw a rope over the branch, tie a loop around his neck and leap off into release.

"What will Alexis do when he finds my body?" he said aloud, as if talking to himself would help clarify his mind. "What will he do with my body?" he repeated. "If the military police discover he has been concealing me to avoid the draft, he will be executed." Strangely, it was the thought of Alexis finding his unsightly, discoloured corpse, and the problem his uncle would have in disposing of it secretly, that persuaded him not to make the attempt.

Later he went for a long walk. He felt guilt now that he had even contemplated suicide, also relief and strength that he had refused that route. In killing himself he was only passing on his problems to others, in particular his uncle. Marcel resolved to go on, accept the challenges and consequences that came from hiding in the cave. "I shall live. For myself. For my mother. For my Unknown Father."

The enemy soon became boredom, not the Revolutionaries who were trying to track him down. Each day became a struggle to keep mind and body active. He recalled that while working at the Chateau, he had on occasion been in la Fortune's office and saw beautifully carved figurines on his desk. He knew that carvers used linden wood for this purpose, and as he found a linden tree nearby, he decided to try his hand at wood carving. Alexis brought him a saw, knife, chisel and mallet and though the results of his carvings were modest, both the project and the product gave him satisfaction. He began with a simple figure, a sheep standing motionless in a meadow, and then fashioned Poilu as if the dog was chasing a hare. A horse on its hind legs rearing up towards the stars became his favourite representation. Marcel spent hours ensuring its features were expressive, that the body parts and muscles were proportionate and that the angles of the joints were correct. About the length of his hand from the wrist to the tip of his middle finger, he was proud of this sculpture and displayed it on a small rocky ledge near the entrance to the cave.

Although he could be soaked by rain, his cave also gave him a superb vantage point to view nature's changing elements. Because it faced east he witnessed spectacular sunrises, especially following rainy days or nights, when the air would be moist and clouds would adopt jagged yet symmetrical shapes, with iridescent red and yellow colours tinted by the rising orb.

Slowly, as the days became weeks, and the weeks, months, the solitude and silence became a stimulus for meditation. St. Amour had taught him the elements of prayerful contemplation and he spent hours outside the cave seated on a small stool he had fashioned from broken branches. The enforced isolation deepened his understanding of himself and his relationship with God. He recalled St Amour preaching about the noble aspirations of the Desert Fathers, Christian ascetics who chose to live a life of prayer and solitude in the Egyptian desert during the dying days of the Roman Empire. Each morning, he read the Bible that Alexis had brought him and tried to focus on pleasing God and carrying out His Will in all things.

At his next visit, Alexis brought Marcel the news about St. Amour's arrest, imprisonment and execution, and the abortive attempt to aid or rescue him.

Marcel felt as if a musket had blown out his heart. "That is dreadful," he said, shaking his head so vigorously that his long hair flew about his shoulders. He placed both arms around his midriff. "It is outrageous that they can kill a good and innocent man. I loved him dearly. The land is ruled by villains. What can we do?"

"Nothing at present," Alexis said quickly, placing a hand on his nephew's shoulder. "If you raise your head to protest they will lop it off. Best to keep out of the way until the present leaders are removed. Hopefully this will happen soon. The war is going better for us. If, when, we win, the country may stop shaking."

The two sat side by side on a log outside the cave, gazing at the vistas visible between the undulating trees. Two crows flew by, squawking loudly at each other. "I want to assassinate le Bon," cried Marcel, his voice passionate with fury, punching his right fist in the palm of his left hand. For a moment he forgot his non-violent convictions. "How is it possible that people like him, pervaded by evil, get positions of power? Doubtless because they shout the loudest, are the most devious and seem to know what they want. They have no other redeeming qualities," he added, answering his own question.

"It is true that he is the cause of our problems in Arras," said Alexis. "Because of him there are more executions here than in all the other towns of the Department combined. But if you kill him, you too will die and accomplish nothing. It is best to wait. Le Bon is getting to the end of a long rope and will eventually strangle himself with it."

"I admire Father St. Amour for staying at his church and caring for his parish, knowing that he courted arrest and execution." Marcel raised his head and eyes to the sky as if talking to the priest. "Here I am running away and hiding from the same problems. It makes me feel bad, yet he encouraged me to hide and avoid the draft. He, too, believed that killing was evil, even in wartime. I would have been useless in the army, likely shot by my own before being shot by the enemy. St. Amour helped others before looking after himself. He should be canonised as a martyr and a saint. Meanwhile, what is happening at the Chateau?" he enquired.

"They arrested la Fortune last week and executed him along with St. Amour and a group of eight men. They included Pierre Tremblais, an ex-army officer, Father Baréz the parish priest at Givenchy-en-Gohelle, and a nobleman by the name of Antoine du Moulin. I met them during my visit to the prison with Grégoire. Tremblais was apparently a friend of la Fortune and visited him at the Chateau for hunting expeditions in pre-revolutionary days. Politically he belonged with the Girondins."

"Oh, I remember meeting him when I worked in the stables, a real gentleman, so tall and good-looking." Marcel's eyes glittered as he recalled his half-hour meeting, alone with Tremblais. He remembered also his deformed hand. "I liked him and he taught me so much about horses. I remember telling you and Monique about him when I got home. It is a tragedy that he too has been executed. What about Madame and the two girls?"

"As far as I know Madame la Fortune is still at the Chateau. But she is in grave danger now that Monsieur is gone. The situation is especially bad because Adolphe Girouette has joined the Revolutionary Gendarmes. It was he who arrested and imprisoned St. Amour. I expect he will now have Madame la Fortune in his sights. She is an arrogant woman whom no one loves much. If she had any sense, she would flee across the border with her children."

Despite their distress about the political situation and Marcel's impoverished circumstances, they chuckled as they reminisced about Marie-Anne and how she entertained the family by mimicking Madame la Fortune's accent, haughty demeanour and speaking style. Marcel tried to emulate his mother's characterisation of Madame la Fortune, with such little success that Alexis broke into gales of laughter.

That night, after Alexis had left, Marcel gazed up to the skies and recognised Jupiter. Shining brightly above him with a white warm glow, it appeared quite unlike the twinkling spots of light caused by stars that covered the night sky. To the west he saw the crescent moon, with the rest of its disc outlined like a darkened mirror. Observing Jupiter reminded Marcel of his illness many years before when he had gone for long walks and talks with St. Amour.

He sat down on his rough stool and gazed into the darkness of the night to meditate. In the distance, towards the town, he perceived points of light from fires and lanterns that glimmered like stars. Marcel pondered the unsuccessful efforts to discover the identity of his birth-father from his mother, and this ignorance still preyed on him. Although traumatised by the execution of St. Amour and Tremblais, these noxious events also instilled a vicarious sense of constancy, even resolution, in his attitude and provided a paradoxical hope for the future. The violence of their deaths seemed a sign that something special would be required of him for what remained of his life. Not sure yet of what this consisted, nor whether or how it could be found, it forced on him a sense of resolve and purpose, a sense of personal destiny.

He knew this would require hard work and sacrifice. Marcel had lost almost everyone he had treasured in his life, father, mother, and now the man he loved who had become like a father to him. He valued the fact his uncle kept him alive in his present penurious circumstances, but had no desire to follow Alexis' bleak and tedious lifestyle.

His affection for Father St. Amour and the trauma of his death acted as a spur that would help him accomplish the aims he would set for himself. By his actions, the priest had displayed a life-path that he himself became determined now to follow, and thus avenge the fact and manner of his death. It would avenge also the bitterness he felt because of ignorance about his own background.

For a moment, a nightingale interrupted is reveries. He listened to its song and shook his head with awe. Despite the cruelty of humans there is still such beauty on this earth.

He wondered if he had a calling to the priesthood. Marcel loved his God and in becoming a priest he could emulate St. Amour and would be in a position to improve the lot of others, just as he had. He knew priests took vows of poverty, obedience and chastity and did not view poverty as a problem; he was penniless anyway. Obedience he thought he could handle because he easily accepted the opinions and decisions of people whom he respected. Marcel expected difficulty from authorities he did not respect, both within and outside the Church. Dealing with these would require humility of which he knew he was capable.

However, keeping the vow of chastity would be difficult. Every night he struggled with sexual thoughts and temptations and felt unsure whether he could manage these in the celibate life of a priest, even with God's help. In any event, Marcel decided he wanted children. He wanted to leave a legacy and even allowed himself the grandiose thought of founding a dynasty. If ever I have children, I swear I will not desert them as I was deserted. He aspired to holiness but this did not require being a priest. He could achieve this as a lay person through works of charity in his daily life. As he retired to his straw-bed that night, and covered himself with his winter coat, he had a sense of relief about these thoughts and commitments, nebulous as they were. Even though Marcel had made no firm decisions, and felt grief about St. Amour's death, he felt a burden had been lifted from his soul.

Three days later Alexis returned with the next basket of food, and smiled with excitement as he gave Marcel the latest news items. "Girouette and his gang ransacked the Chateau yesterday but Madame la Fortune and the children had gone. They destroyed almost everything and would have raped and killed Madame and the girls if they had been there. She must have escaped just in time. Meanwhile the army has won a battle and pushed the Austrians out of France."

"It is good that she got away and I'm glad to hear that we seem to be winning the war. I am getting tired of the cold and loneliness of my cave." He then asked gloomily, because he knew what the response would be, "When will it be possible for me to return to Vimy?"

"We will have to wait till the war ends. Whether it is victory or defeat, they will stop seeking conscripts." Despite his profound discomforts, Marcel decided, on the advice of Alexis, to remain in the cave.

That night, unable to sleep, he hatched a plan to avenge the deaths of St Amour, Tremblais and la Fortune. Although Girouette now spent much of his time with his revolutionary friends in Arras, Marcel knew he kept his home, wife and family in Vimy. For a brief moment he contemplated assassinating Girouette, but much as he hated him, could not persuade himself to act on this plan. Apart from his objection to killing, the risk of being caught was too great, and this would defeat its whole purpose. So he plotted an alternate scheme. Knowing that Girouette had a chicken run in his backyard, Marcel decided to raid the run. Assuredly not as dramatic an act as assassination, discovery was much less likely, and robbery would still provide the satisfaction of reprisal. Moreover, chickens would give him a few days' worth of much-needed nourishment. He knew this plan was inconsistent with a commitment to charity but decided to proceed anyway to satisfy his strong need for retribution.

The weather proved ideal the following night. A dense cloud cover hid the moon and stars, providing extra darkness, while a breeze in the trees served to muffle sound. After midnight, with a large, used flour bag in hand,

150

he crept down the hill towards the town and made his way to Girouette's house. Stealthily he skirted the area to ensure there were no guard dogs or late-night revellers about and, if possible, to determine the exact location of the chicken run. He also noted with satisfaction, through the shadows, that the wooden shutters in the house were closed.

A thick cedar hedge encircled the backyard and in the far corner he found a garden gate with a latch but no lock. He lifted the latch and pushed gently on the gate which, to his dismay, squeaked noisily as it opened. He stopped and listened for a few moments, his heart beating wildly, to ensure that no one had been disturbed, then entered the garden, and saw the blurred silhouette of the chicken run behind the garden gate. Using his hands, he groped the length of the cage to determine the placement of its door, found the latch that he disconnected, and entered the run. Disturbed by his entry, the hens clucked and mumbled quietly and this enabled Marcel to locate them. With both hands he grabbed one, tucked it under his arm, then opened the flour bag and stuffed it in. Using the same technique he added two more until the bag could hold no more. Muffled clucks of protest emanated from the bag but fortunately, he knew that poultry are not noisy in darkness. He closed the bag, carried it out of the run, closed the door of the run and the garden gate, swung the bag over his back and returned quietly to his cave where he immediately wrung the necks of the three birds. With the winds of both fatigue and satisfaction in his sails, Marcel slept well that night.

Two months later, Alexis brought him the news that Robespierre had been guillotined and le Bon banished as Mayor of Arras. Marcel wanted to know the details of Robespierre's fall, and Alexis told him that Robespierre's colleagues, beginning to realise they were likely next on his execution list, combined to defeat him on the floor of the National Assembly. Within hours, they arrested him, tried and condemned him to death. He tried to avoid the guillotine by shooting himself, but succeeded only in shattering his jaw bone which his gaoler roughly bandaged up. The next day, before tying him to the bascule board, the executioner ripped the bandages off his neck and jaw to ensure they did not interfere with the efficacy of the guillotine.

Marcel returned home to Vimy that night. He gazed at himself in the mirror with astonishment and scarcely recognised the image, the long dirty hair, thick bushy beard, and tired, gaunt eyes. His cheeks were sunken and bones exposed by weight loss. After a cold-water wash, Monique cut his hair and beard in a stylish manner, keeping a small moustache and goatee beard to make his features look older. He cleaned and cut his grime-filled nails. Getting a new set of clothes proved more difficult because he had no money. For the moment he used his old peasant garments but made sure they were clean and neat. That night, for the first time in six months, he slept in a warm dry bed.

Next day Marcel went to the tobacconist and bought an oak wood pipe. Smoking a pipe, he believed, would make him look and feel more mature. The queasy feeling caused by inhaling tobacco smoke took days to fade.

Marcel's eighteenth birthday had come and gone two months previously. On that day, a gentle rain had pattered down on his small cave-dwelling and he had spent the time just inside its mouth on the wooden stool with his back leaning against a cold rock. Despite the uncomfortable wetness, he had found the unique aromas and quiet, dripping water exhilarating, and it reinforced his sense of mission. Though he had grown old by a day, he felt he had matured by a year. He had had much time for reflection during his six months' isolation. The traumas in his life caused him to feel apart, even alienated from his peers. He could read and write and knew from his life as a stable boy on la Fortune's estate that he had the capacity for hard work of good quality.

Two years previously while working on the Estate, he had developed a passion for a seventeen year old shepherdess called Thérèse. She had bright blue eyes, long dark hair, lovely pink cheeks and an upturned nose. At the time she rebuffed his advances without explanation. Eventually his passions had cooled. Now that he had escaped his cave-prison, he renewed his search for her, yet procrastinated for fear of being rejected again. It is strange that I am confident when learning at school or doing work on the estate, yet so unsure of myself with girls.

The state had taken over the Chateau and its grounds, or what remained of them after the invasion by Girouette and his henchmen. The authorities planned to subdivide the estate into smaller parcels of land and auction them off at modest prices. Marcel longed to have property and own horses but had no resources and no prospects. Despite taking over the chateaux and estates of the émigrés, and appropriating many of the Church's properties, the regime remained bankrupt and inflation was rampant. At his age, without assets, he saw no prospect of obtaining credit from a moneylender.

With the help of Alexis, he managed to get a job caring for horses in the remnants of the estate's stables. The manager, a local notable by the name of Hébert Pichot, could not offer him a wage but agreed to reimburse him periodically with flour and vegetables from the estate. He quickly fitted into the job and also with other the workers, some of whom he remembered from his schooldays. He felt at home with horses around him.

Several weeks after starting the job, he met Thérèse in the street. With a smile and a shine in her eyes she asked where he had been. "I've been avoiding trouble by keeping out of the way. I am now working on the farm." He smiled guardedly in reply. "And you?"

"Oh, I am engaged to be married to Damien Pichot, the son of Hébert. They called him up in the army and he has not returned. I do not know where he is. He cannot write and might even be dead." She smiled demurely while looking deeply into his eyes, and after a brief silence asked, "Do you like the farm and the horses?"

"Yes, I love it and love them," he replied with feeling. "They are such affectionate animals. You can make friends with them. Years ago I worked with a mare called Rita who had a foal. Rita is gone but the foal is now a sturdy mare called Virago. I can talk to her and she understands. Horses seem to have all the good qualities of people and none of the bad. We need to copy them more. I do not get paid. They just give me some food. What are you doing now?"

"I work looking after the young children of Madame Delisle. They give me one franc a day. It does not buy much but helps the family a little."

Marcel admired her young features and engaging smile but did not know how to broach the invitation to see her again. He not only feared another rebuff; he felt a lustful passion just beneath the surface and knew it could spin out of control. He believed it wrong to indulge in intimacy outside marriage. It was best to avoid closeness. He perceived a pleading look in Thérèse's eyes but ignored this, said goodbye quickly and went home.

That night he dreamt of being a country squire on a large property with Thérèse as his mistress. In the dream, his oldest son became seriously ill and Marcel saw himself galloping on horseback through the forest trails near Vimy in an abortive attempt to get help to save the boy. He felt depressed and drained when he woke up and noticed also a small damp patch in the centre of his blanket. I should not have rejected Thérèse yesterday. Next chance I get I'm going to seize her!

Chapter Twelve

Thermidor Year II August 1794

Catherine Lachêne returned home late one afternoon from the market with two baskets of groceries, and almost tripped over what first appeared to be a large log of wood. It had been a hot, sultry day and she perspired from her exertions. She put down the bags down on the doorstep and wedged them against each other to ensure they did not fall over and disgorge their contents in the street. When she stooped and looked more closely, she saw the so-called log as the torso and legs of a man lying on the cobblestones. His head and upper body lay in an alcove beside the house and were veiled by the gloom of the gathering dusk. She did not recognise him and noticed he was dressed in raggedy clothes, clearly a beggar. His cheek bones stood out prominently and his body looked emaciated. Poor man. How did he come to be here? Likely seeking shelter in this exposed and pitiless city.

"What's wrong? Can I help you?" she asked, placing her hand on his shoulder.

"I'm thirsty. I'm hungry," he replied, barely audible.

She placed the backs of her three middle fingers on his forehead and sensed it felt hot and moist. He shivered violently despite the warm weather. She lifted his hand and said, "Come with me. I live next door. I will look after you."

"I am sick and weak. I cannot get up. I cannot walk."

At that point Charles Cavigneau passed by and recognised Catherine. She explained the situation to him and he lifted the pauper by his shoulders and dragged him into Catherine's home, dropping him just inside the front door. She lifted the beggar's head and tried to give him water, but this led to a fit of coughing and retching. She rolled him over onto his side, placed a pillow under his head and tried to make his breathing more comfortable. By this time he was breathing heavily and no longer responded to stimuli.

Charles, who had remained to the side in case Catherine needed him again, disappeared in an unsuccessful attempt to find a doctor and by the time he returned, the man had stopped breathing. His limbs went limp and his body cold in death. Inspection of his clothes and pockets revealed a few sous clearly given him as a beggar, but no other identification. He appeared of short stature, shorter even than Catherine, herself not tall, and his legs bowed outwardly in symmetrical fashion with further deformities in his feet and boots. Charles left again to get the municipal funeral cart and as the hirelings placed the corpse on the cart, Catherine gave them some coins so he could be given a pauper's burial in a common grave the next day. She would report his death to the municipal office but knew they would take no action unless he could be identified, or unless the death came from unnatural causes, unlikely in his case.

Despite her cheery and generous nature, the beggar's death within her own home had a baleful effect on Catherine. The dead man was so young, much younger than she! Although she felt healthy, her knees and hips were painful when she walked any distance and she knew that at her age a serious illness could develop easily and quickly. She decided to speak with Father Claude Ladouceur, a non-juring priest, one who had not signed the oath of loyalty to the Revolutionary regime, whom she knew. A young man, not yet thirty, Ladouceur belonged to the Sulpician order of priests. They were a teaching community and had been heavily persecuted during the Reign of Terror. She found him at his home, a one-room poorly furnished apartment, dressed in casual clothes, without clerical collar, as if he were a day-labourer. She also admired his handsome features, straight nose, ready smile and a bright glint in his eyes. Before she had time to utter a word he said passionately, "Catherine, have you heard. Robespierre's been executed and Le Bon recalled to Paris! Perhaps they will now give us some peace!" He embraced her excitedly.

"What a relief!" she replied. She then wagged her finger at the priest, as if age and wisdom enabled her to foretell the future. "We still must wait to see what effect this has on the cursed Terror, if any. My long life has taught me patience. Predict something with confidence, and the opposite will surely happen. Perhaps greater villains will take their places."

"I am sure you are wise to be prudent, Catherine. But I, I am optimistic. The next few days will provide a sign of where things are going. Now, forgive me, it is you who came to me, to talk to me, not me to you. Please sit down. This stool is the only chair I have." He waved his arm in the direction of the stool. "What did you come to see me about? How can I help?"

Catherine sat slowly down on the stool, her knees giving her a jolt of pain, and went on to tell the priest about the dying beggar she found outside her house. "His sad, premature death made me think that perhaps I have not long to live. My husband left me a large inheritance when he died, and I have looked after it carefully by living simply. Until now, today, I have told no one about its existence. My only son, Hubert, died last year."

"Oh, I am so sorry to hear that Catherine," interposed the priest sympathetically.

"It was a relief for him and for me," Catherine continued quietly. "He suffered much. I should not say this, but he caused me much suffering too. Many years ago, with my approval, he married a young farm girl in Vimy called Marie-Anne and they had one child who died at birth, when she died also." She paused a moment as she dabbed a tear trickling down her cheek, then continued, "Marie-Anne had an illegitimate son called Marcel, from a previous liaison, but the family were never able to determine from her the name and identity of the father. Although I have not heard from him for some years, I believe Marcel is still alive, and know he used to be a God-fearing child. Hubert did not like him but, I have to admit, even as his mother, Hubert was a difficult man and I suspect he may have been jealous, as many men would be in his situation. I would like you to write to Marcel on my behalf and offer him my inheritance. I shall tell you what to write."

"What a remarkable story, Catherine," replied Ladouceur. "I shall do that with pleasure. I have a priest-colleague who like me is non-juried. He lives in Arras but since St. Amour's execution, he visits Vimy regularly to minister to the people there. Would you like me to make some enquiries through him to see if Marcel is still alive and still God-fearing?"

"That would be kind of you Claude. Please do not say anything about the inheritance."

"No, of course not."

Seven days later Ladouceur reported to Catherine that Marcel was still alive and had started attending Mass again, although for the previous six months he had vanished without explanation. Catherine dictated the wording of the letter to Ladouceur and employed a letter-carrier to deliver it to Marcel. She paid the letter-carrier in advance according to the distance he needed to travel.

Marcel was at the table having lunch with Monique and Alexis when the carrier delivered the letter. He left it on the table next to his plate until he completed the meal, frequently glancing at it, trying to determine who the author might be. It keenly kindled his curiosity as he had never before received a letter. At the end of the meal, with a sense of excitement, he took it over to the window to open and read it.

The envelope bore the name "Marcel pierre" scratched in clear, cursive letters. The enclosed missive had been written on behalf of his great aunt

Catherine Lachêne, his grandfather Gabriel, Lachêne's sister, and the mother of Hubert, his step-father.

'Mon Cher Marcel,

I am giving you the sad news that my son Hubert died six months ago from natural causes. Because of the political disturbances, I have not been able to communicate this information to you earlier.

He continued to live with me after his return to Arras from Vimy but suffered increasingly poor health, and the doctors only made things worse with their useless treatments. His death was a relief for him and for me.

I myself am at the advanced age of seventy-two. My health is not good and at my age you never know when serious problems will occur.

I live alone but manage with the help of a very kind neighbour.

You may not know that when Hubert married Marie-Anne, your mother, he promised her a bride price if she survived him. The bride price consisted of five hundred louis d'or. By living a simple life, I have been able to keep the coins well hidden from the prying eyes of the tax collector.

Hubert never remarried and I have no other descendants. The coins are yours when you have time to collect them.

I hope you are surviving the turmoil of these trying times.

I look forward to seeing you again, my dear Marcel, and offer you all my affection.

Tante Catherine Lachêne'

He felt shock as he pored over Catherine's note. His hands dropped and he flopped down in the chair. When he recovered his strength he took the letter to his room, re-read it a few more times, and then lay down on his bed to contemplate the situation. For the whole of his life he had been near-penniless and could not grasp the concept of one louis d'or, let alone five hundred, or what that sum meant in goods. Although he had worked with horses for much of his life, he did not know the value of one horse. Because he never conceived himself as having enough money to buy one, he had no interest in finding out their cost. He remembered his mother telling him, when she married Hubert, "my marriage to Hubert might help you one day," or some words to that effect. She obviously knew something then that he did not know.

Over the years since she died, he had become increasingly resentful towards her because of her refusal to tell him anything about his father, and because of her marriage to Hubert, whom he detested. Marcel now felt guilty about harbouring these thoughts. He could do nothing about knowing the identity of his father but now, at least, he would get some restitution for all he had suffered as a result of her marriage. He offered up a silent prayer of thanksgiving to Marie-Anne, wherever her soul might be, for her far-sightedness, and an apology for his feelings of disgruntlement.

At the supper table that night Alexis asked, "Marcel, you are very quiet; I saw you got a letter from Arras today. Was it bad news?"

Marcel beamed a broad smile and shook his head. He had not learnt yet how to hide his feelings. He also did not know how to reply, because he was not yet ready to divulge the letter's contents. "No, it was just a note from a friend," he lied, but kept on smiling.

Monique was more perceptive and said, while looking straight into Marcel's eyes, "You smile as if you have just won a great reward. It must be a very generous friend."

Marcel fidgeted uneasily at Monique's accurate insight. He kept on smiling, shook his head again and looked down at the plate to indicate he would say no more on the topic. Monique and Alexis looked at each other, shook their heads and frowned with frustration. Marcel left the table and returned to his room as soon as the meal had been completed.

He slept little that night. Should I refuse the money? What have I done to deserve it? If I take it what do I do with it? Where do I keep it? What do I tell Alexis and Monique? Must I give them some? They have been very good to me. I would never have survived all that time in the cave without their help. Preoccupation with these thoughts and questions increased his restlessness and insomnia.

As dawn broke, he made his decisions. At first opportunity he would talk privately to Alexis and give him the letter's details. Also, he would go and visit his great aunt Catherine in Arras. In his mind he had not yet decided to accept the gold coins so did not have to confront the issue of what to do with them. Having made up his mind he relaxed and fell into a deep sleep from which he did not awaken until mid-morning.

Seated at table smoking their pipes that evening, while Monique prepared the meal, Marcel told Alexis about the letter. "What do you think I should do, Alexis?"

Alexis shook his head with amazement, while exhaling smoke through pursed lips. "I could tell last night at supper that you had a secret. It is incredible that anyone has money in these times of hardship! I remember grand-père and Marie-Anne talking about a bride-price before she got married but when Hubert left in anger, I thought we would hear nothing more. It is good of tante Catherine. Will you share some of it with me?" he added with an ironic smile.

"I am not even sure whether to accept it," Marcel replied as he took a deep puff on his pipe. He knew Alexis would never accept money from him, so smiled, without responding directly to Alexis' question. "I will go and speak to tante Catherine."

A light drizzle fell the next morning as he set out to walk to Arras, using a protective parapluie he had borrowed from Monique. The rain did little to dampen his feeling of expectancy. Along the way, the sun emerged and a rainbow formed a huge arc in the eastern sky, stretching from horizon to horizon. A secondary rainbow added to the spectacular colours. He stopped to admire their wondrous hues, while sniffing the unique and earthy aromas released by raindrops. The wind had dropped and he was surrounded by silence and beauty. He continued his journey and stepped lightly and quickly as if a burden had been lifted from his shoulders. Although he had tried hard to forget his mother's wedding, he dimly recalled seeing Catherine that day. Yet he retained fond memories of his grand-père and knowing that Catherine was grand-père's sister kindled his curiosity to see her again. He arrived at his great aunt's house and with a feeling of anxious expectancy, rang the bell.

"Tante Catherine! I am Marcel," he cried as she opened the door.

"My dear boy," she replied as they embraced with both smiles and tears on the doorstep. "Come in. How you have changed! You were just a young boy when I last saw you! You seem so thin. Let me give you some hot cider with cinnamon and some gateaux I prepared this morning."

"That would be great, ma tante," he replied, as his stomach rumbled in anticipation.

She bustled in the kitchen preparing the platter, singing a joyful Latin hymn as she did so, "Laudate omnes gentes, laudate dominum... " Sing praises, all you people, sing praises to the Lord. Marcel smiled to himself with pleasure as he listened.

"Tell me what you've been doing," she said happily as she presented him with a tray of luscious-looking gateaux. The odour of the cinnamon and cider mingled with that of the sweet-smelling gateaux and caused Marcel's mouth to water. The long walk had made him ravenous. Between mouthfuls of patisserie he brought Catherine up-to-date on his activities, his illness after Hubert's departure, his work with horses, and his life in the cave. The more he spoke the more silent Catherine became. She shook her head sadly when he told her about Father St. Amour's disappearance and death.

"The situation is calmer now that Robespierre and Le Bon have gone and that is why I wrote to you with Father Ladouceur's help," she said, with a cheery smile. "I really would like you to meet him, and the Cavigneau family. Tell you what. I shall arrange a dinner for them. Can you stay the night?"

"Of course, I would love to. It is kind of you to offer me the louis d'or, ma tante. I am not sure whether to accept it. I have done nothing to deserve it."

"Écoute, Marcel. With the death of Hubert and his baby son I have no descendants, so as Hubert's stepson and my brother's grandson, you are my nearest relative. Family are vital to me and you, you are family. It is my wish that you should have it. I believe you will use it wisely and well."

Marcel, blushing slightly, said, "In that case, I accept it. When hiding in the cave I did much thinking and praying, and now have ideas about what to do with my life. I will indeed use it wisely and well. Je promis," he gave Catherine a thank-you hug and then helped himself to the last remaining gateau, licking his fingers clean to savour every crumb.

That night Marcel met Ladouceur, with Charles, Pauline and their five children. Catherine had prepared a fish stew with salads and artichokes, and another mountain of gateaux in an effort to satisfy six hungry young stomachs. Clementine quickly caught Marcel's attention. He discerned her dark complexion, long, auburn-tinted hair and sad, downcast eyes, and especially delighted in the prominent dimple in her right cheek. She wore a dark-blue ankle-length gown with close fitting sleeves. The low neckline was trimmed with beautifully crocheted lace. As the odd person out in the group he was the centre of attention for the evening, and the company wanted to know in detail the story of his six month sanctuary in a cave. All applauded his raid on Girouette's chicken run. "I would have killed him but you did the next-best thing," said Charles, nodding his head approvingly.

Marcel frequently caught Clementine's eyes during the evening but no words were uttered between them, though he saw her listening attentively to his story. He saw her silence and forlorn demeanour and had a powerful urge to hug and console her.

Early next morning Charles and Pauline appeared alone on the doorstep, wanting to speak with Catherine and Marcel. In a grave tone Charles said, "Marcel, Catherine knows that Clementine has been very unhappy since the death of Stéphane two months ago. Despite being her friend he was full of mischief. Clementine met you last night and wants to see you again." Marcel blushed again, a happy blush. "Catherine has given us a good report about you. We know that you never knew your father but that does not trouble us. We believe Clementine is old enough to settle down. Having a home, a husband, and above all some children would be a both a distraction and a blessing for her." He paused a few seconds then ended with a peremptory question, "Would you marry her?"

Marcel listened with increasing apprehension to Charles' solemn speech. He had only just met Clementine and her family. Although he liked her, he felt his youth and inexperience rendered him ill-equipped for marriage. Marriage might solve her problem, as Charles had put it, but what would it do for him? He then thought about his secret sexual passions and unfulfilled desires. Perhaps marrying Clementine will solve a problem for me too? He decided to delay his reply.

"I am not sure Monsieur. She seemed very quiet and troubled last night."

"She has yet to surmount Stéphane's death," Charles said quickly in her defence. "She sparkled when he was alive. In fact, they used to get up to pranks together. My wife and I considered him a bad influence. Do you not agree, Pauline?"

"Yes that is correct, Charles," his wife replied quietly and dutifully.

"To make it easier for you we would like to offer you a bride price of two hundred francs, to be delivered on your wedding day." Once again Marcel felt overcome and for a few moments, speechless. Eventually he turned to Catherine and asked, "What do you think, tante Catherine?"

"I know both Clementine and the family well, Marcel. Clementine has not been herself since Stéphane's death. She is normally a high-spirited girl and I believe her good humour will return. I do not agree with Charles that Stéphane had a bad influence on her. Clementine knows her own mind and made her own bed in that affair." She turned and looked at Charles guiltily after the last statement.

"Catherine may be right," Charles conceded, quietly. "Clementine has not always been obedient and respectful towards Pauline and me. We have been patient with her and she has learnt some lessons from her romance with Stéphane. She is now, we believe, ready for marriage and will make a right and proper wife for you."

"I will have to return to Vimy and talk with my uncle Alexis about this," replied Marcel uncertainly. "He and his wife Monique have been like father and mother to me. I wish to seek their opinion."

"That is fine, Marcel." Charles said, nodding his head. "Let us know your decision."

"Marcel, could you come back and visit us next week?" Catherine enquired.

"Yes, I shall." He smiled at Catherine, Charles and Pauline in turn, then said au revoir and kissed each on both cheeks.

Marcel returned to Vimy slowly, thinking through key decisions along the way. It seemed as though the complex puzzle of his life, based on the nebulous ideas about his future while hiding in the cave, were suddenly fitting into place. The inheritance, the visit to his great aunt, meeting Clementine and her family, the bride price offer that seemed a partial recompense for the abuse he had suffered at Hubert's hands. He felt as if fate, or perhaps God Himself, had intervened in his life and was bearing him forward on the crest of a wave.

It was during this walk, about halfway home, just as a man on horseback galloped past him that he decided what he would do with the money and with his life. "I love horses," he said aloud, talking to the trees and surrounding countryside, as the gallop sounds receded into the distance, "I will marry Clementine and together we will create a horse farm. I have never dreamed of this before because I could not imagine owning one horse, let alone a farm. It is incredible the change from a few weeks ago when I hid in a cave like a fugitive, cold, hungry, penniless. Now I have a clear plan for my life!"

He contemplated other changes he would need to make. If he had any hope of digging himself out of his status in life he would also have to work on his accent. The way a man spoke French marked his origins like a stamp. He still spoke the regional picard patois like a peasant. His wedding to Clementine and acquisition of new friends and family in Arras would help him work on this change.

He arrived home with a spring in his step, repeating Catherine's hymn of joy. There would be no need to ask or even discuss these matters with Alexis. He might pretend to do so, but in the end would just inform him, as politely as possible. "Marcel! What's wrong? Are you crazy singing Latin hymns?" Alexis cried as he walked through the door. He had never before heard Marcel singing.

"I had a good visit with Tante Catherine. And I have found myself a wife!" He went on to tell Monique and Alexis about the visit, leaving out no details other than his horse farm plans.

"It sounds good, but what are you going to do with the money?" Alexis enquired.

"I want to buy a horse. I do not know yet what to do with what's left over."

"What do you want to buy a horse for? It's just going to bring trouble. Where will you keep it? Where will you get food for it? 'Oo will look after it?"

Marcel detected envy in this barrage of questions. He loved and respected his uncle and had no wish to alienate him. "I cannot answer right now. It is all but a dream. I have a desire to make something of my life. What is happening now is giving me a chance to get out of this cage in which we are trapped. It is strange, we struggle from one day to the next, from one meal to the next, and without realising we have so little control over events. Our poverty makes us helpless and resigned. On top of that we have tyrants like King Louis, Le Bon or Girouette ordering us about. I want to grasp the opportunity with both hands. Whatever I do, Alexis, I want you and Monique to be part of my life. I can never repay you for what you have done for me. I would not be alive if it had not been for you. You looked after me when I became sick and nearly died after Maman's death, and later when I hid in the cave. You have been the father I never had! I want you to help me look after the horse!"

Alexis smiled appreciatively. "You are right. You can help me get out of the cage as well. I did not know that our lives were such a trap. We get so used to it that we stop thinking how wrong it is. With the Revolution now over perhaps we will become freer." After a moment's reflective silence he added, "I will help you look after your horse, Marcel!"

They embraced affectionately and sat down to have their evening meal.

The following decadi, the day of rest that replaced Sunday in the revolutionary calendar, Marcel and Alexis walked to Arras together. They spoke little during the two-hour walk as Marcel was lost in thought about Clementine and the horse farm he planned, while Alexis never squandered his breath needlessly on words. As they neared the city Alexis asked, "Marcel, tell me more about the Cavigneau family."

"I have met them but once, at my last visit. I could see that Charles was a determined man, a man who knows and gets what he wants in life. He works as a floor manager in a tannery. Before that he worked as a manager for Pierre Tremblais in his textile firm. As you know all too well, all commerce suffered greatly during the Revolution. His wife Pauline is pleasant and keen to please everyone, especially her husband. They have, let me see, five children, the oldest of whom is Clementine who is beautiful and has sad but alluring eyes. They told me she still mourns a young man who died suddenly two months ago. Our Aunt Catherine, whom I respect, likes the family and she considers Clementine and I are well suited. The second son is called Demy and he has a nervous tic and cannot look at you."

"I have my doubts, Marcel. It seems they are at a different level from us peasants. When it comes to family, friends and especially wives and husbands, we must keep to our own level."

With more heat than he intended Marcel replied, "Tante Catherine is our family because she is your father's sister, yet she is friends with the Cavigneaus and wishes me to marry Clementine. There is no rule that states you have to remain forever at the level at which you were born. Though I was born to a métayer family I have no wish to remain one and will do everything possible to escape from that trap!" Alexis remained silent in response to Marcel's salvo.

On arrival at Catherine's home she greeted them affectionately with hugs and kisses on both cheeks. "I am so glad you have come. Alexis, you have not aged a day since I saw you twelve years ago at Marie-Anne and Hubert's wedding! "

"Looking after Marcel has kept me young," he replied, with an ironic smile.

"I am sure that was not an easy task," she replied in mock sympathy, while glancing smilingly at Marcel. "You both must be hungry. Marcel emptied my garde-manger last week," she added laughingly, "but I have replenished it to prepare for your arrival. Let me serve you coffee and tartelettes before our guests arrive."

Clementine, with her parents, brothers and sisters came to visit that evening. Marcel observed that Charles behaved differently compared to his previous visit. Then he appeared polite and effusive; today he strutted around as if, as the oldest man in the party, he owned them all. After the introductions, Charles immediately accosted Alexis, "Glad to meet you, mon ami. What is your métier?"

"I just work as a métayer in the fields around Vimy," replied Alexis, lowering his head and eyes.

Charles pulled back his head, as if trying to add a few inches to his height. "That seems not only boring, but also a dead-end job. Have you not put together funds to purchase your own property?"

"That is not my ambition, no. Times have made it difficult in the country and on the land the last few years."

"The Government is taking over the estates of the émigrés and of the Church, sub-dividing them and selling them off at very reasonable prices. This is the ideal time to get a little plot of your own."

"I am content with what I do. It is easy to get into trouble when you own or buy land and I wish to avoid that."

"If you want changes you have to fight for them. Obviously that is not important for you. Progress would never happen if you were in charge."

"That is probably true," replied Alexis weakly, while clenching his fists so tightly that his nails scratched the palms of his hands. Charles frowned, shook his head disapprovingly, and moved on to talk to Catherine.

Meanwhile Clementine said little. She attempted to engage Marcel and although they smiled pleasantly at each other, their conversation was necessarily brief and superficial. They both would have liked time alone together, but this was not allowed. They knew that parents took responsibility

164

for decisions about the marriages of their children and actively discouraged communication between prospective partners. In their present circumstances she had little choice but to accede.

Clementine liked the little she saw of Marcel. Lean and above-average in height, he had sharp, widely-spaced and slightly protuberant eyes, a slightly angled nose and a mature bearing. She liked his smile, his well-cut hair, moustache and beard, which were auburn-tinged like hers, and found his sweet smell of tobacco smoke seductive. Marcel, in turn, liked what he saw in Clementine, who was definitely more cheerful than she had been the previous week. Even though they could not converse personally, their eyes engaged frequently and conveyed an abundance of feeling. Their situations were, to be sure, very different, Marcel an orphan, with Alexis his acting parent, she with both parents, keen to be actively involved in decisions about her marriage.

The party ended amicably, all thanking Catherine for her tasteful hospitality. Alexis overcame his aversion and managed a polite au revoir and handshake with Charles. Both he and Marcel spent the night in Catherine's house while planning to walk back to Vimy early next morning. As Catherine cleaned up the dishes she felt delight at having brought Clementine and Marcel together. She saw the tension between Alexis and Charles and shook her head at Charles' arrogant attitude. She knew Alexis would likely now oppose the marriage between Clementine and Marcel but expected the latter to be forceful enough to overcome his uncle's opposition.

On the road back to Vimy, it did not take long for Alexis to register his opinions, using uncharacteristically strong language.

"Marcel, Clementine is not the right woman for you. She is young and frivolous. Her father holds his nose in the air. I do not like him and I do not like them. You must break it off!"

Marcel felt a twinge in the pit of his stomach and his palms became sweaty. "You are wrong Alexis. She is a nice girl and I like the family. I agree Charles appeared haughty last night but he is not always like that. To me he seems a generous man."

"You're as interested in the money, as in her, Marcel, I'm thinking," Alexis said, beginning to get angry. "They have offered you a bride price and that is it. I do not think the girl is worth it."

"I am sorry you say that Alexis. Obviously I do not know Clementine well yet. Neither of us knows her. In fact I will not know her until I marry her. I do like what I have seen. As to the family and the money, that has nothing to do with it. I am marrying Clementine, not the family. I respect tante Catherine and her opinion and she also belongs to our family. Obviously

I would like you to support me, and if you cannot, I would like you at least to understand. In the end it is my life and my decision."

"I am disappointed in you Marcel." The two completed the rest of their journey in defensive silence.

Although they continued to live under the same roof, it took many weeks for Marcel and Alexis to resume an amicable relationship. Initially their only communication concerned basic business and home-running topics. Alexis used as few words as possible and never looked Marcel in the eye. Marcel spent as little time as possible at home. When not doing his job in the stables at the estate, he planned his own home. He continued to receive nothing for his services but this no longer bothered him.

The government had taken over Monsieur la Fortune's estate, and subdivided it into numerous five to ten-hectare lots. He met with tante Catherine at his next visit to Arras, arranged to receive part of his inheritance and used it to purchase a ten-hectare plot. Situated to the north-west of Vimy, it ironically included the cave on the ridge where he had spent six months in hiding. He stopped working in the stables, walked the land intensively and planned how each part would be used. The plot lacked any edifice so he planned to build a home. To build it, he would employ a professional builder, whilst himself acting as the builder's assistant, thus learning how to construct while saving on expenses.

Every second or third decadi, Marcel walked to Arras and stayed two nights and a day with tante Catherine. Using her home as a base, he visited Clementine and her family. He never spent time alone with his fiancée - if they went for walks, Pauline or Charles, or one of the younger children, accompanied them. They were permitted only to hold hands but found subtle ways of communicating feelings, using fingers and thumbs for caresses, eye contact and facial expressions. On one occasion when chaperoned by her sister Véronique, the latter met a friend and while distracted Clementine turned excitedly to Marcel and said, "Come Marcel, let's go. Véronique has gone off. I know a place where we can hide and kiss!"

"No, Clementine," replied Marcel soberly. "I prefer to stay with the rules. We will only regret it if we take risks."

"Why, you old fogey! Come on. Come quick with me." She pulled his arm, but Marcel held back. Eventually Véronique caught up with them and that ended Clementine's attempted escapade.

To make it a surprise he told her nothing about the plot of land and the home he was building. When she asked where they would live after the wedding he replied vaguely, "Somewhere in Vimy, we will see," then changed the subject.

The wedding took place one year later, during the month of Thermidor Year III (August 1795). To meet the new government requirements concerning marriage, they held a brief civil event before the magistrate early in the morning. The family then retired to the Church of Saint-Jean-Baptiste on the rue Wacquez-Glasson that had been desecrated but not destroyed by the revolutionaries. Here, for them, the real ceremony took place. Father Ladouceur celebrated a nuptial mass attended by a small group of family and friends. It was a muted affair. Although the anti-religious vitriol of the Reign of Terror had subsided, censorious laws were still in place and they exercised care by inviting only immediate family members and also banning music, a sacrifice because Catherine loved music and instilled this love in Clementine and Marcel. Clementine wore a plain white ankle-length dress with close-fitting sleeves extending down to the wrists, and Marcel an ill-fitting dark suit and blue cravat given him by tante Catherine. The suit had belonged originally to her husband, a large man, so the tunic could easily have accommodated another individual in addition to Marcel within its ample cloth. Catherine stitched up the lower end of the breeches so its legs would not extend below the ankles. Moreover, the suit had gathered a myriad of moth holes during many years' of disuse and smelt strongly of camphor. "You smell like you've been sitting in a clothes closet for a few years, Marcel," Clementine teased laughingly as they emerged from the church. Alexis, having realised that Marcel would not be dissuaded from marrying Clementine, gave the couple his patriarchal blessing with forced grace.

Following the ceremony the company retired to Catherine's house, as it was larger than that of the Cavigneau's. Ladouceur gave an entertaining speech in which he facetiously compared Clementine's youth and beauty with Marcel's inelegance and stodginess. "This is a good sign," he concluded with a wicked smile. "Opposites attract each other so it means they are going to have a happy marriage."

For reasons of security and economy they spent their wedding night in a spare bedroom at Catherine's home rather than at an inn. Marcel felt apprehension. He knew what he had to do but had no idea how to get there. He was aware of the basics of female anatomy from seeing his young cousin in the nude, but knew no details. He had had no experience and no instruction from teachers, parents or peers, but knew he had to undress and get an erection.

The undressing part went easily. Not so the erection. Never before had he had trouble getting his member to rise but tonight, when most needed, it refused to budge, despite tender and aggressive manipulations by himself and Clementine. The bed was narrow and had a deep furrow down its centre, from the top to the foot. Essentially it had space for only one person and that within the furrow. Moreover it creaked and groaned with the slightest movement. Eventually, without success, they fell asleep exhausted, packed in the middle of the furrow like two ripe peaches wedged in a small carton. When he awoke next morning his member appeared in full bloom and the marriage was quickly consummated to their mutual satisfaction.

Marcel then realised Clementine was not a virgin. "Have you been with a man before?" he asked quietly. "Yes, I have," she whispered. "I was impulsive when young. I'm sorry Marcel." After a moment's silence she asked, "Have you been with a girl?"

"No, I have not but for me it happened easily. Although I thought a lot about girls I also felt scared of them so kept away. I had this idea, I suppose it's a little crazy, that girls were like angels, holy, up there on a stand, and boys could not, and should not, touch them. It probably comes from my catechism class where we were taught all about Mary and her holiness. We had to respect and be like her. That's likely why I had trouble last night."

"Marcel, do you mind I am not a virgin?" Clementine clung anxiously to his arm. For a few moments he pondered the question. He realised he had become very fond of this lively young woman, so open and cheery, so wild and different from himself!

"Clementine, I will not let it bother me. You are beautiful and I love your sparkling eyes. I love you like you are and for what you are. You are helping to bring me out of myself. I need you!"

"I love you too Marcel but I understand if you are disappointed in me! I did the best I could and will make up for it in other ways." She hugged and caressed him. Almost against his wishes his penis responded again and what remained of his discontent drowned in an ocean of passion. When they finally emerged around midday they found tante Catherine seated anxiously in her armchair overlooking the street. "How are you, my dear girl, are you all right?"

"No, I am terrible, ma tante," replied Clementine glumly. "Last night Marcel hurt me and took something away from me that is very precious. I am finished with him and am going to leave him." She spoke in a quiet grave voice and her face appeared the picture of seriousness. Marcel meanwhile felt embarrassed and fidgeted uncomfortably, gazed at the ceiling, unsure where Clementine was heading.

"Oh, you poor darling. You must be patient. Men can be very rough, especially the first time." She glared sternly at Marcel, and he looked at Clementine while shaking his head helplessly. "Just be patient," Catherine added, "I am sure you can work it all out. Just talk to him and ask him to be gentle."

"No, ma tante, it is too late. I have packed my case and today I am going back to live with Maman and Papa." At that point she could contain her mirth no longer and burst out laughing. "I am just teasing you, ma tante; we had a wonderful night. Marcel and I are off to Vimy today."

Tante Catherine then also burst out laughing. "You little imp. I really believed you. I've known you a long time and should have realised you were deceiving me. Let me give you some lunch and then you can go." The day before the wedding Marcel had purchased a calèche and horse from a market in Arras. He made Clementine wait at tante Catherine's house while he went to fetch them at the home of the seller.

"What have you done, Marcel!" she gasped when she saw the calèche outside the front door.

"I've bought a small farm near Vimy and this will help us move around. The horse's name is Alouette. She is well-trained and just five years old. "

"But where will we live?"

"There is a small cave on the farm at Vimy ridge, the same one I lived in for six months two years ago. We will live in the cave."

"Marcel, that is impossible. Where will I store my clothes?"

"You can pack them all in a pile in the corner."

Marcel smiled enigmatically and saw Clementine giving him a suspicious sideways glance. An hour later they drove through Vimy to Marcel's farm and stopped at the house that he had built.

"Marcel, did you make that?"

"Yes, I did. For you. "

"It is beautiful! It is even better than a cave!" She hugged and kissed him.

Marcel tied up Alouette, unloaded suitcases from the calèche and settled in the house while Clementine rearranged the furniture that, in her opinion, he had misplaced in the rooms. Marcel introduced Alouette to the stable and ensured she had sufficient hay and water in the trough.

Chapter Thirteen

Vendemiaire Year VI (September 1797)

The house Marcel built prior to Clementine's arrival contained but three rooms, a bedroom, a large sitting room and a kitchen. The front of the house faced south so the sitting and bedrooms could absorb the maximum volume of sunshine. At the rear it also included a stable, abutting the house, with an inner door connecting it to the kitchen enabling Marcel to attend to the horse without leaving the house. A horizontal slit across the middle of the outer door ensured the horse could view the outside world from the interior when the upper half of the door was open. Building materials for the house consisted of stone obtained from a nearby quarry, mortar and thatch for the roof.

Together, Marcel and Clementine spent much time planning the next stages of the farm development. They complemented each other well. Marcel knew his long-term objectives and Clementine had the practical common sense and concern with detail that ensured each element of the project was completed and functioned according to design. Although she could not ride and did not have Marcel's passion for horses, she had a visual imagination and a practical mindset and provided Marcel with many ideas to facilitate the smooth running of the building schemes. They planned also to expand the size of the house once children were born.

No stream flowed through the property so a well to provide drinking water was their first vital project. For this, Marcel employed two young men from the village who dug a hole ten metres deep to reach the water table. The sides of the well were lined with brick that rose to waist level at its top end, and he built a wooden canopy over the mouth to house a bucket and pulley system for drawing water. He painted the roof of the canopy bright green and ordered its sides covered by beautifully carved pine wood lattice to ensure that the water did not attract birds and animals. Water taken from the well was cool and clear and had a clean, refreshing flavour. He also made a decision about a name for the farm. He loved trees and because of two prominent and mature maples that were close to the entrance, he decided to name it Les Érables.

A large ten-stable barn became their next major task. Situated fifty metres behind their house Marcel used oak wood slats for both walls and roof with two levels to the barn, the lower being stables to house the horses and the upper a hayloft accessed by ladder from ground level. The front of the barn had a large, arched doorway facing the road, big enough to allow a riderless horse to pass through comfortably and at Clementine's suggestion, they painted the double-doors of the archway a bright red colour. On the far side of the barn, Marcel built a trough and pulley system so that hay could be raised mechanically into the loft from a wagon on the road below. Above each stable he built a trap door making it a simple matter to feed the horse by throwing hay through the floor of the loft into the stable below. Each stable had a trough that he kept well filled with water.

Marcel decided to make the Andalusian horse his specialty. Bred originally in Spain, Andalusians were sturdy animals popular with riders. They could be used as work horses and even trained to do dressage.

Soon enough, the farm was ready for animals. Marcel knew he would get the best deal at the regional farmer's market in Arras. Leaving early one morning with Alouette he rode quickly to leave plenty of time to inspect the horses he planned to buy, and negotiate a price with the vendor. Good quality was essential but Marcel had no desire to pay a large sum for it. The chances of making such a deal were best if he waited until later in the day. He tied up Alouette and ambled slowly around the market grounds, studying both the animals and owners carefully from a distance. He saw a pair of horses, a mare and a stallion, both Andalusians, which appeared strong, sturdy, and spotless. He saw the owner became restless and attempted, seemingly without success, to engage passers-by. An hour later the horses were still there so he went to the vendor, introduced himself, and said, "Your 'orses look nervous and flustered. Is there something wrong with them?"

"There is nothing wrong with them," he replied with a sneer. "Perhaps they just need exercise."

"What are you asking for them?"

"Two hundred and fifty for the mare and two for the stallion."

"I'll give you three hundred cash for them both."

"Monsieur: I'll take three fifty but three is not reasonable. They are a clean and healthy pair and will be good for breeding."

"I am not so sure about that. Look, the stallion's hooves have not been properly trimmed and the mare's mane is unkempt. Three is all they are worth. Take it or I am off."

Reluctantly the vendor accepted three hundred and Marcel, riding Alouette, led his two newly-purchased horses back to his farm with a feeling of quiet satisfaction. He had a sense of excitement about the inauguration of his new and very different lifestyle.

Two years after their wedding Clementine gave birth to a baby son. They named him Louis-Marcel to commemorate the ten-year-old King Louis XVII, young son of the executed monarch, who had disappeared and likely died in prison from starvation and abuse at the height of the Reign of Terror. His whereabouts were never traced and his body never found.

Baby Louis-Marcel brought a new dimension into the relationship between Marcel and Clementine. She bustled about feeding and caring for the baby, endlessly. Marcel felt neglected and became increasingly frustrated. At first he dealt with this in sulky silence but then, as nothing changed, he broached the topic. "Clementine, you fuss about the baby so much. Can you not leave him alone and let him cry himself to sleep rather than feed him the moment he opens his mouth?"

"If a baby cries that means it needs something, usually food. I cannot leave him to cry when he is hungry. He will not stop. He will be an unhappy baby. I can no longer attend to your every need. In some things you will now have to look after yourself."

"I do not have the time," he replied, now with an edge to his voice. "There is so much to do on the farm. I cannot neglect it."

Clementine's face flushed with anger. "The work I do here is just as important as yours," she said loudly. "I cook and keep house for us both. The baby is yours just as much as it is mine. I am still weakened by poor health from childbirth. I work in this house for you from morning to night. I cannot do all this alone." By this point her voice had crescendoed to a shriek so Marcel covered his ears and left the room, leaving her sobbing on the bed. For the next two days they avoided each other while Marcel slept alone in another room.

The passage of time seemed to cool the force of their feelings. After feeding the baby one evening and placing him in his crib, she took Marcel's hand, drew him towards her body, embraced him, and said, "Marcel, I am sorry I got angry. I know I have been more moody than usual. There have been many changes in my life in the last year, especially the birth of our baby. It takes time to get used to them."

"I too am sorry. At times I am demanding and impetuous," Marcel responded affectionately, while embracing her. "I shall try to be patient and help you with the baby. Most times I am filled with energy and ambition, but I can get melancholic and want to go away and be alone and don't want to speak to anyone. Fortunately it does not stay with me for long. I've been like that for a few years."

"We both seem to be outsiders," she replied. "I have always been easily excited, much to my mother's dismay. When I became angry she locked me up in my room. She would even push my head into a bucket of cold water, thinking this would calm me down but it only made things worse. I would get so enraged that I could no longer speak and would just sob uncontrollably. My soft, toy dog became my only companion. His name was 'Flouffe'. I remember once when I was about six years old, my mother and I were on the street outside our house. It was midsummer and hot so I sat down on the stones and took off my shoes. I had Flouffe with me and hugged him tight on my chest. My mother tried to force me to put my shoes back on but I refused and just sat on the ground. I think she must have been with child so could not bend over. She tried to compel me, so screamed at me from above, while I stubbornly stayed sitting and crying on the ground. I don't know how long we carried on like that, the two of us. It seemed like hours but perhaps only a few seconds. A man, a stranger, came by and asked about the cause of the commotion. My mother told him angrily I was a naughty, disobedient child who would not put her shoes on and that I *had* to put my shoes on. I just continued sitting on the street, wailing loudly. The man bent down, took my hand in his and said, 'Come with me little girl. I'll take you and your Maman to my house and we'll see if we can find a nice biscuit and a sweet juice for you to drink.'

"You know what happened then? I stopped crying, put on my own shoes, got up from the ground, hugged the man's legs - I was so little! - and then walked off quietly with Maman! It's amazing what a little kindness can do. I did not get much as a child."

Marcel listened silently as he contemplated this anecdote. "That is a striking story, ma petite chérie," he finally replied, squeezing her hand and forgetting his own frustrations. "You were fortunate to meet a Good Samaritan in the street. They are rare in our savage world."

Clementine's story reminded him of his own rough childhood. A father who abandoned him, a mother who, though loving and affectionate, died when young, which also led him to feel abandoned, being bullied at school, a stepfather who abused him. Six months living in a damp cave, cold and hungry. Hearing Clementine's story provided a supportive bond and made him determined to be protective towards her.

The end of the Reign of Terror signalled the start of many changes in the country. Local and regional elections were held, the financial situation stabilised, land redistributed, and relations with the Church moved towards an uneasy truce. The government also confirmed the use of the revolutionary calendar in perpetuity. The new Mayor of Arras appointed Adolphe Girouette chief of the regional police force, and the government named a juried priest, one who had signed the oath of loyalty to the regime, as curé of the parish of Vimy. His name was Father Jean Lepire. The church itself had been badly damaged during the revolutionary excesses, but Marcel, together with others, volunteered to assist in its repair and reconstruction.

In his early thirties, Lepire had a balding head and rotund figure. He closely followed the external dictates of his calling but possessed a pompous, verbose attitude in which he expatiated at length, and with apparent expertise, on topics about which he knew nothing. He insisted on supervising the workers repairing the church despite being a dilettante in matters concerning construction. There were numerous conflicts and delays and Marcel, regardless of his dislike for Lepire's boastful and self-centered attitude, used his talents as a conciliator to ensure completion of the task. It took the volunteer parishioners almost two years to do the work and return the church to its former glory.

Even as he worked diligently on the church, Marcel continued to expand the farm. He knew he needed a sturdy wooden and post fence around the property with an additional fence down the centre to separate one field for animals and the other to grow feed, so solicited his uncle for assistance. "Alexis, I need your help to make fences on the farm. I can draw the plans and get the materials but I need help with construction. It will take us about six months."

"What do you want to do that for?" replied Alexis, his voice becoming louder. "You have a farm, a barn and four horses. Is that not enough?"

"I plan to buy more horses to breed them. I'll pay you for your help." Marcel knew immediately he had made a mistake offering Alexis money and tried to salvage the situation. "I would like you to help me with the fence," he added. "In return I will give you a horse. You may keep it in our barn." Alexis stretched out his hand and smiled with pleasure. "I accept, Marcel. I too have a secret love for horses but have never indulged the thought of owning one because of its impossibility. I wish Marie-Anne could see now what you are doing. She would be proud of her son!" Marcel looked intensely at Alexis, and for a moment was speechless. Alexis rarely gave compliments so Marcel felt pleased that he recognised his accomplishments.

"Thank you, Mon Oncle. I have done my best. Yes, I badly grieved her death. Even though I am now married, I think of her often and miss her. I would like her to have met Clementine." Then remembering that both Marie-

Anne and Clementine had more than a small stubborn streak to their dispositions he added, "But I believe they would have quarrelled." He had a picture in his mind of Clementine in an argument with Marie-Anne, and shouting at her in the same way as she had shouted at him. He shook his head sadly.

"Your Maman was certainly headstrong, Marcel," replied Alexis. 1 am sure you are correct they would have argued."

"Alexis. Did she ever say anything to you about my father? Do you have any ideas regarding his name?"

"She never said anything to anyone about that, Marcel. I remember your grand-père trying hard to persuade her to tell us but she never did. She herself chose "pierre", your family name, because I had a brother called Pierre who died in the smallpox epidemic before you were born, so that does not help us much. I will tell you what my own opinion is. Your mother worked at the estate of Monsieur la Fortune before you were born. I believe something happened there. It may have been la Fortune himself or it may have been someone else like another worker or a visitor. It is so long ago now. I do not think we can ever find out. Why let it bother you?"

"It is important. No, Alexis, not important, it is vital for me to know." Marcel spoke quietly but with passion, measuring every word. "It may be hard for you to understand because you know the name of your father, so cannot conceive why it is essential knowledge to someone who does not know. Part of knowing who I am is to know where I come from. Not knowing makes me feel incomplete, as if half my soul is a blank, and does not exist. I also have a secret hatred towards him for abandoning me, but this does not stop me from wanting to find out who he is. Perhaps the very fact of not being able to find out provokes my desperate desire to know. I realise that this is without reason, but still cannot accept not to know. Besides, I dislike the 'pierre' in my name. I never knew my uncle Pierre so it means nothing to me. The fact that it is always written with a small 'p' is a constant reminder about being born a bastard."

"What you say is a mystery to me, Marcel," replied Alexis, shaking his head. "If I was in your shoes I would just forget about it and get on with my life. No one can solve all the problems they might have. It is like war. If you cannot win the war you should not start the battle."

"You do not give me much encouragement Alexis. Yet somehow I feel I can win this war, even though I have few weapons at present."

Marcel then remembered the silver medal, chain and ring that Marie-Anne had given him before she died. His father had given them to her. Other than his life and very existence, this was the only link with his father. Could he use these gifts to track him down? He would go home and examine them more closely. Perhaps there were tiny markings on them to indicate their provenance. Why have I never thought about doing this before? The discussion with Alexis had provoked the idea. He did have a weapon after all, admittedly a small one.

He said nothing to Alexis about these thoughts. Alexis had no idea about the existence of the gifts given him by Marie-Anne. Next day, during a quiet moment, he took out the medal, chain and ring from their hiding place and examined them carefully in the sunlight. The medal had a circular form and was about two centimeters in diameter. One surface had an imprint of the Holy Family, with Mary holding the baby Jesus and Joseph at her side. The obverse had a floral design. The medal, as well as the chain and the ring, each had the word argent inscribed on them and the year 1740 inscribed on the medal. After deliberation, he concluded that the three articles had been struck simultaneously to celebrate an important occasion, likely of a religious nature, which took place in 1740.

1740? I am sure it will answer my question.

Chapter Fourteen

11 Nivose, Year IX

Charles Cavigneau robustly popped the cork and poured the champagne, a Dom Pérignon bottled in 1788. He filled eight glasses, and called for a toast. When everyone in the salon had a glass in their hand, he said cheerfully, holding up his glass, "Bonne année! Bon nouvel siècle! I wonder what the new century will bring to our tragic country and this crazy world." They clinked each of their glasses and Maxime Béthune, after sipping his with quiet confidence, put down his glass and then groomed the sideburns of his right cheek with the middle three fingers of his right hand, all the while holding his right elbow in his left hand.

The eleventh day of Nivose, year IX, was a meaningless date in the new Revolutionary calendar. But for Pauline and Charles, and others who continued to use the beloved old Gregorian calendar, it was the first day of January 1800, the start of a new year and a new century. To honour the occasion they arranged a small clandestine party to which they invited Clementine and Marcel, with two-year old Louis-Marcel, Father Jean Lepire, who arrived at the party wearing casual clothes with no external signs of being a cleric, Catherine Lachêne, and Maxime and Brigitte Béthune. After drinking the new century in, and because Pauline and Charles had no servants, Pauline, Brigitte, Catherine and Clementine retired to the kitchen, with little Louis-Marcel toddling behind them, to finalise the meal preparation. Even he savoured the Dom Pérignon. Clementine dipped her little finger into her glass and inserted it in his mouth. Louis-Marcel sucked the finger wet with champagne and screwed up his mouth and face, seemingly with relish, much to the amusement of the company.

The owner of the tannery factory at which Charles worked, Maxime, in his late fifties, came from a prosperous family. Like many others in his class, he had survived the revolutionary turmoil by dressing and living modestly and keeping his opinions to himself. Of medium height and with a muscular build, his features were bracketed by those long, brown, curly sideburns. Brigitte, a motherly, engaging woman who talked well with her hands, had borne him six children. The three survivors were now all grown-up.

177

Because of the need to provide warm clothes and boots for the troops, the tannery business prospered during the seemingly endless revolutionary wars. Charles had worked there since the bankruptcy of Pierre Tremblais' textile business, becoming manager and working closely with Maxime. In response to Charles' pondering of what the future nineteenth century would reveal, Maxime said, "I know exactly what the new century will bring, Charles; more wars, more destruction and more chaos. Perhaps I should not complain. I know our business has benefited from the political turmoil. Perhaps I should even feel bad about profiting from the misfortune of others. But I don't. We can but console ourselves that we were not the cause of the turmoil," he added, while continuing to stroke his sideburns.

Charles's eyes narrowed and he pursed his lips, "I do not see a problem with making money during wars. If the politicians and generals are stupid enough to start a war, they must be prepared to pay for their adventures. Soldiers have to be armed, fed and clothed, and if the government is willing to pay, I am willing to provide the matériel." He pronounced these words with an air of finality as though nothing more needed to be said on the topic.

There were a few moments of silence, broken by Marcel. "With respect, Charles, I disagree with you. To me, there is no such thing as a fair and just war. In my opinion war always does more harm than good, even to the victors, who often commit outrageous acts of pillage and rape. If enough men refused to fight, and if enough people refused to offer matériel, the generals would quickly make peace. By doing business with them you are encouraging and rewarding the warmongers."

"There you go again with your fanciful ideals, Marcel," replied Charles airily. "It is easy for you to say that, when you never have to make a decision. If you had a business, and the army needed your product, would you refuse to sell it to them because you disapproved of war? I think not," he added, replying to his own question.

Marcel's eyes sparkled with conviction as he replied, "It is true that because of my youth I have not been in that situation, but if I did find myself there then yes, I would refuse to sell matériel to the generals. I would stand true to my principles even if I lost business or they arrested me for my beliefs." Lepire nodded his head approvingly at Marcel's strong moral stand, while Maxime and Charles shook their heads in disbelief, Charles merely adding, "We shall see. Soon enough you will get a chance to test your convictions."

At that point Pauline tinkled the cow bell kept on a ledge near the door between the kitchen and salon calling them to the dining room for dinner. They moved with alacrity as the aromas from the kitchen had kindled their appetites. With Catherine and Clementine's help, Pauline had prepared a celebratory 'New-Century' meal consisting of potage aux legumes, gigot d'agneau à l'ail, with haricots vert amandine and pommes de terre farcie au fromage. Special home-made patisseries topped the meal. The company raved about her culinary skills.

Towards the end of the meal, Charles leaned over towards Maxime, seated at the head of the table, and asked, "What do you think of our new consul?" He spoke in subdued tones as if he suspected the secret police had their ears to the keyhole. As closet royalists, they knew they had to express political opinions with strictly guarded restraint.

"Bonaparte is certainly an able general," replied Maxime, equally softly. "There is not a battle he has not won. He has opened our eyes to the wonders of ancient Egypt. Now he has chosen, no, forced upon us a career in politics, and I consider good generals make bad statesmen. I doubt we will see much Fraternity and Equality, let alone Liberty, despite his claims to be true to the ideals of the Revolution."

"Perhaps he will bring peace and order to the country after the tumultuous past ten years," Charles ventured cautiously.

"That would surprise me. With his military background and expertise we may see wars and destruction continue for a while yet." Maxime stroked his sideburns as he spoke.

"Did any of you attend the royalist demonstration yesterday?" Catherine enquired.

"No, I did not and would not," Béthune replied immediately. "I know they broke it up ruthlessly. Girouette and his henchmen from the military police used guns and machetes and many were seriously injured. Louis XVI's younger brother Stanislaus, who is exiled in Russia at present is wasting his time if he thinks he will be invited back to rule France."

"That Girouette is a strange man." Marcel chose his words carefully. Like Girouette, Marcel came from Vimy and had had several encounters with him, all unpleasant, in his short life. "Before the Revolution Girouette managed the estate of Monsieur la Fortune near Vimy," he continued. "In those days he certainly was a Louis XVI royalist. During the Revolution he became an ardent revolutionary and arrested hundreds of alleged royalists, including his former master, many of whom ended up on the scaffold. Now he is a Bonapartist up to his gills. His name is apt."

Charles smiled and nodded his agreement. He then turned to Lepire and asked, "How is the Church managing the changes?"

"It is a disaster," he replied, throwing his arms into the air, and then bringing them to rest again across his ample belly. "Many priests have left the ministry, joined the revolutionaries and got married, and some even exiled or executed. I struggle in my parish, from morning until night, to bring The Lord's Word to the people but get no help. Some even hinder me. A parishioner stopped me after Mass last week and said my sermons were too long and I talk too much about myself in them. That is not true. I preach the word of God, pure and simple. My sermons may be long but the Bible also is long and detailed. I preach only what the Church teaches. I follow the rules closely in all things, unlike many priests who make rules as they go along to suit the convenience of their parishioners. Perhaps persecution will remove such rabble in the Church and help it return to its original simplicity. That is my wish and prayer."

"I believe you are being optimistic when you say that persecution will remove the rabble," replied Maxime, refilling his own glass with champagne as though this would stimulate his tongue to new heights of sagacity. "There are too many with a vested interest in maintaining the status quo. When peace returns to the country and the Church's position is re-established, I believe the same abuses will recur. Even though new bishops will be appointed they will fall into the same traps as the ones who have gone. They have too many comforts and there is no one to tweak their ears and say, 'Listen to what Marie-Jeanne, sitting in the back pew in the church, is saying'."

"I believe you are wrong," replied Lepire firmly. "The Church is an ancient organisation with traditions and dogmas built up over centuries and these must be preserved. I know these dogmas well, having learnt them all when I attended the seminary. I follow the teachings closely, both in my personal life and in my preaching. I know the Church cannot change these principles to suit any passing fad."

"You men are all up in the clouds with your theories about what's wrong with the Church." Catherine interrupted Lepire heatedly, like a water-kettle on a fire that had just exceeded its boiling point. She wagged her finger at the three men who had been loudly proclaiming their opinions. "I am your Marie-Jeanne sitting in the back pew of the church. Religion is not about principles and dogmas and sermons. It is about charity, generosity and love of every person to one another. It is about the relationship each of us has, through prayer and meditation, with God. You can have all the theories and principles you like. If people don't show love and charity towards each other in everyday life, your theories count for nothing. The story of our country during the last few years, even before the Revolution when the Church remained powerful, shows a striking lack of charity. The Church is failing in its mission if it does not promote love."

The room hushed in response to this unaccustomed and vehement declaration from Catherine. The men she assailed glanced at each other guiltily, unable to deny the truth of what she had said. Eventually Lepire, not used to being either interrupted or contradicted, broke the silence, saying, almost meekly, "What you say, Catherine is accurate. I agree that the Church, and all of Christianity, has failed miserably in getting that basic message out to its people. I see Christians from different countries killing each other in war! Jesus told his disciples at the Last Supper, 'by this love you have for one another, everyone will know that you are my disciples.' Surrounded as we are by a wave of fratricidal wars, it seems we have not learned much in eighteen hundred... "

"It is men, not women who fail to practice the virtue of charity." Catherine interrupted Lepire yet again and warming to her theme, added, "It is men who rule the countries of Europe, who make decisions about war and slaughter and impose these decisions on the world! If only women could be released from the bonds that bind them to childbirth! They would then be free to devote their lives to pursuing professions, including that of governing others. I believe we could teach men something about... "

"I disagree strongly with you," interrupted both Maxime and Charles together and loudly. Charles looked at his employer respectfully who then continued alone, "Women do not have a lock on charity. I have seen many examples of women who lack charity at home. If they ever got into government they would equal men in ferocity and selfishness! We already have examples such as that virgin Queen Elizabeth in England and the decadent Empress Catherine in Russia. Neither treated their enemies gently or charitably. Both executed their opponents!"

"I continue to believe that women have more natural charity and generosity than men," responded Catherine firmly. "Perhaps it is by force of circumstances, the need to bear and raise children, who then demand and obtain our care. Neither of the women rulers you mentioned bore and raised children, so lacked experience in this domain. Moreover, they had to compete in a state contest where the rules were set by men. In any event, other than the codes of chastity followed by nuns in convents, there is little we can do to liberate women from childbearing," she concluded, resignedly.

"The points you raise are nonetheless true, Catherine," said Lepire, wagging his finger at her as if he was the arbiter of the accuracy of her moral opinions. "I can tell you with authority that the rules of charity apply equally to men and women. We are all at fault in not applying them consistently. Even I am at fault at times. I believe our rulers, whether men or women, are not reflecting the beliefs and practices of their subjects. Perhaps that must be our lesson for the nineteenth century that is now unfolding — we must make ourselves heard!" He punched his fist on the table for emphasis, folded his arms across his chest and looked around the group as if the last word had been spoken.

"I agree with Catherine," Marcel ventured quietly, ignoring Lepire's sermonising. ''Women do have more natural charity than men. Because of having to bear children they are tied to the hearth and the home. I foresee a time when women are given rights equal to those of men, which our Revolution proposed but never practised. All it needs then is to find a way to control when a woman comes with child; they will then be free to become involved in governing. Europe will be a better place when that happens."

"I doubt that will happen," replied Maxime, shaking his head and smiling cynically. "Even if women do take over from men, charity or no charity, I believe they will commit the same sins as men, or worse. To quote an ancient but apt cliché, 'Plus ça change, plus c'est la même chose!'"

"I see little hope for either France or the world," replied Charles, his mouth twisted into a cynical smile. "While spouting about how much they do for the country and the people our political leaders look after themselves, their pockets and their families, in that order. Bonaparte will be like a shooting star. For a brief moment he will dazzle the sky then he will fizzle out and burn into ash, taking the rest of us with him!"

On that pessimistic note, with a 'new century' kiss on both cheeks, and a grand merci to Pauline and her helpers for the feast they had prepared, the company bid each other goodnight. Maxime and Brigitte, Lepire and Catherine returned to their respective homes in Arras while Clementine, Marcel and Louis-Marcel spent the night with Pauline and Charles, planning to return to Vimy early next day.

Several months later Catherine became troubled about her health. She had fleeting pains in her chest and stomach that disrupted her daily routine. Her hips and knees were especially painful when she walked. For a while she could only hobble around using a cane, but then her symptoms became so bad she took to her bed and, as she lived alone, employed a young neighbourhood girl called Louise as her maid. Her physician, Dr Jean-Paul Poirier, the most reputable physician in Arras, made frequent visits.

On his third visit one week later she clutched her stomach and said, "Doctor, I have a constant colic in my stomach. My bowels will not move even when I struggle and strain. Yet other days I seem to run every five minutes. I pass so much wind that sometimes I feel I am going to take off into the air like a bird."

"Dear Madame, I gave you calomel powder last week that contains mercury. It is a chemical that stimulates the bowel. Have you been using the powder?"

"Yes but it did not work so I took double the dose and that's when I started running."

"That is dangerous, Madame. Mercury is a poison when taken to excess. You must not use more than the amount I prescribe. You will have to stop using it now, and allow the body to dispose of the excess. I will return next week."

"I shall suffer if I have no medicine," she said plaintively.

"I cannot give you more medicine until what you have taken is out of your system," Dr Poirier replied firmly.

For the next three days her bowels refused to move and this caused her to feel irritable and dejected. She spent much of her day on the chamber pot — a special outsize one to accommodate her ample behind, rimmed with fabric for comfort. On the fourth day she managed to expel a small dry pellet.

"Louise, Louise, Halleluiah! Halleluiah! Deo Gratias!" she sang whilst stamping her cane on the floor joyfully to the rhythm of her melody. "It must be a gift from heaven. Dr Poirier will be so proud of me when I present him with my creation, produced, moreover, without the need for medical intervention. I cannot wait to see him again."

"That is excellent Madame," replied Louise. "Dr Poirier will indeed be pleased. I shall place it in a separate pot to show him when he comes."

At that point Catherine emitted a loud fart. "That is a good sign, Madame," said Louise encouragingly. "It shows your body is ridding itself of gases and poisons.' Meanwhile she opened the window to ensure the gases did not contaminate herself and the house.

Catherine displayed her dropping to Dr Poirier at his next visit.

"That is excellent, Catherine," he said encouragingly. "You show every sign of recovery, but we do not want to push it too quickly."

The doctor reminded himself that Catherine remained one of the few patients who could afford his visits at full rates, so he did not wish to hurry her recovery. He thought of giving her castor oil, knowing this would act quickly, but decided its foul flavour might cause her to seek medical attention elsewhere, so he said simply, "We have to work slowly with the body's natural defences. I will give you a special almond oil mixture, an emollient that has a pleasant flavour. It will act as a gentle bowel stimulant and also a lubricant. I order you to take one tablespoonful at night before retiring. No more, no less. I shall return to see you again in two days' time. And make sure you conserve all your ca-ca for me to view." Dr Poirier knew that it gave Catherine much satisfaction to create and exhibit her oeuvres.

"Yes of course, Doctor. I will do that with pleasure."

Within a week Catherine recovered her bowel function, amply so, but her condition deteriorated in other ways. She lost her appetite, lost weight and her abdomen and legs began to swell. At his next visit Dr Poirier noticed the whites of her eyes had a yellow tinge. "I regret to say you have developed jaundice, Madame. It is a serious omen."

"Does that mean I'll die? If it does, I am ready. I have made my peace with God."

"That is correct, Madame. Jaundice carries a serious prognosis. I would strongly recommend applying leeches to your abdomen. Although not a cure they remove poisons from the body and promote recovery."

"Thank you Doctor, but no," Catherine replied without hesitation. "My husband's doctors treated him with bleeding and leeches and thereby helped him travel more speedily into the next world. Although ready to die, I have no wish to hasten the process."

"You disappoint me, Madame. I urge you to reconsider your decision while you have time. Doctors have been using leeches with benefit for thousands of years. You are rejecting the wisdom of medical tradition!"

"To me it does not make sense. Blood is necessary for strength and for life. Removing blood causes weakness and death. I saw what happened to my husband. I am happy to take your pills and your potions but will not part with my blood!"

"I see you are stubborn and set in your ways so have to accept your decision," replied the doctor, shaking his head with disapproval, and crossing his arms. "Perhaps you will reconsider when your condition deteriorates."

"I can assure you that that is my final decision and I will not change my mind."

Four months later during the summer month of Thermidor, Clementine and Marcel got news that Catherine had died in her sleep. Clementine was in the late stages of pregnancy and had had three miscarriages since the birth of Louis-Marcel. Despite this, she and Marcel left immediately for Arras with four-year-old Louis-Marcel to attend the funeral.

Because the magnificent 12th century Gothic cathedral of Arras had become a pile of rubble, destroyed by enthusiastic revolutionaries, the family held Catherine's funeral in St. Jean-Baptiste-Church, the one in which Clementine and Marcel were married.

184

"How have you been?" Pauline questioned Clementine after the funeral. Her critical eyes searched her daughter from head to foot. "I see you are with child again at last."

"I have been fine," responded Clementine icily, ignoring her mother's tart comment about the pregnancy. She had not told her mother about the miscarriages since Louis-Marcel's birth, and had no intention of doing so now. She then added, "Marcel and I have little Louis-Marcel. I love my Marcel who is good to me. He is building a horse farm called Les Érables and is planning to breed them."

Clementine felt ill at ease, as if under interrogation from her mother. The memory of her head being plunged into a pail of cold water as a child came back to her. "Please do not question me, Maman. I am getting along well," she added, pursing her lips.

"I only wanted to know how you are. There is no need to get vexed." Pauline almost sang these words, a sign of her own growing irritation.

"You still treat me as if I'm a child. I am now a married woman with a child of my own. Can you not understand?" Clementine clenched her fists for emphasis.

"I suppose that is true. It takes time for mothers to accustom themselves to the fact that their daughters grow up. If you have daughters you will find this out yourself." Pauline glared at her daughter.

"You were hard on me when I was a child. I got much punishment and little praise." A tear trickled down Clementine's cheek but she did not weep.

"You were not an easy girl. You always had ideas of your own and wanted your own way." Clementine noticed that her mother had a way of talking like her father in his absence, using the same peremptory language, sometimes even the same words. Yet in his presence she invariably bent like a broken branch to his will.

"Is that bad? It is usual for children to be active and lively. They don't need to be punished for everything they do." Clementine's lower lip quivered as she remembered her chastisements.

"Clementine; I did my best for you." Pauline raised her voice to ensure that Clementine heard each word. "I felt accablée when you were young. I had five children, a demanding husband, and our lives were shattered by the chaotic political events. I am sure I made mistakes. We all do, and for that I am sorry. We cannot live our lives over again."

"I suppose that is true," Clementine replied, reluctantly accepting her mother's apology. "I will try to understand. I still go into rages and shout at Marcel when he does something wrong. Perhaps what you are telling me will give me more patience and serenity. Meanwhile, I am sad that Catherine has

185

left us. I loved that woman and believe she loved and understood me. As a child I often visited her to get away from the agitation at home and without saying a word, she would caress and console me. She became like a cherished grandmother to me and gave me the care I never received at home."

Pauline digested this information then replied simply, "I loved her too. She was a strong woman who knew her own mind!" After another brief interval she added, with a note of envy in her voice, "She had a simple life with but one child and a husband who had money and died young, giving her freedom and a large inheritance. Few women are so fortunate. It is easy to be generous and caring under those conditions."

"You are very unfair, Maman," replied Clementine heatedly. "She may have had only one child but Hubert was a troubled man who assaulted her many times and nearly killed her once. Catherine felt relieved when he married Marie-Anne, Marcel's mother, and sorry when he returned home after Marie-Anne's death. She never talked about these troubles but I saw what happened. Many times Hubert hurt me badly when we were in the house alone. He did things to me that I cannot repeat to anyone. I hated him and am glad he died." Pauline did not want to hear any more and to emphasise the point, she placed her hands over her ears and quickly walked away.

Clementine and Marcel returned to Vimy in their calèche next day. She went into labour shortly after arrival, this being provoked by the jolting of the vehicle on rough, unpaved roads, and gave birth to another boy whom they named Jean-Baptiste. Premature, he was tiny and had to be nurtured carefully. The following day Marcel registered the birth at the Mairie and went into a cold sweat of fury when he saw the clerk writing the family name "pierre", with a lower case "p". As if struck by lightning he decided, at that instant, to formally and legally change his name. When he thought about it he realised the idea had been fermenting in his mind for months if not years. He cringed inwardly when addressed as 'Monsieur pierre'. It is bizarre. Why did it take so long for me to get this idea?

He accosted Clementine as soon as he arrived home. "Clementine, I am changing my name," he said vehemently. "I flinch every time I see or hear the name 'pierre.' It was the last straw to see the clerk writing 'Jean-Baptiste pierre' in the log book. The name 'pierre' means nothing to me. They say I had an uncle called Pierre and that I was named after him. I never knew him because he died before my birth, The Lachêne family brought me up and Lachêne was my mother's name but by calling me 'pierre' they disowned me, even more so by writing the name with a small 'p'. At heart I am ashamed of my background. This name, and the way it is written, reminds me forever of my obscure origins!"

186

Clementine face fell hearing Marcel's unaccustomed passion. "I have never heard of anyone changing their name. Is that possible?"

"I've not heard of it either but I am going to the Mairie to find out."

"So what name will you chose?"

"I hate the new calendar," replied Marcel, still speaking strongly. "We have used it now for ten years and I continue to find it offensive. The decadi is not a holy day like Sunday is meant to be. I never know which day to celebrate our birthdays and anniversaries and forget the names and the correct order of the months. I get mixed up when I make appointments with people.

"I was born in the month of June so 'Juin' will be my new name," he went on, dropping his voice and speaking gravely. "I want to be called Marcel Juin. 'Juin' in my name will be an everlasting reminder of the old calendar, of its Christian character, and the month of my birth. It will be my protest against the revolutionary calendar and all it represents. It will enable us, through our children and the children they have, to found a new line of descendants!"

"That sounds fine and noble, Marcel, but it will also be strange," Clementine replied thoughtfully. "I too will have to change my name. Again. Born Clementine Cavigneau, I then became Clementine pierre, and now I will have to become Clementine Juin. It is clearly important to you so I will support you, and I like the name Juin. June reminds me of the spring, of warmth, flowers and love. I also like the idea of protesting against the calendar although I suspect the government will not take too much notice," she added, with a smile.

"I could not care less about them," he replied angrily. "They have caused more than enough disruption in our lives. It will give me satisfaction even if they take no notice. I am going back to the Mairie. I am going through with this even if I have to pay."

"That shows you are really serious," she added with a knowing stare that Marcel pretended not to see.

Marcel got up early next morning, trimmed his beard, brushed his hair neatly and put on his best suit. Though it was late summer he felt a cool, refreshing dampness in the air as he rode to the Mairie where he tied up his horse. As the first client of the day he found the clerk sitting at the other side of the desk in an office beside the entrance hall, rubbing sleep out of his eyes. It was the same clerk with whom he had registered Jean-Baptiste's name a few days earlier but the clerk showed no signs of recognising Marcel. Many people came through everyday sitting in that chair and they all looked much the same. His face expressionless, the clerk wore a dark grey chemise with long sleeves and brown breeches.

"I demand information about changing my name," Marcel said loudly, causing the clerk to start in his chair.

"Quoi, Monsieur? Please repeat what you've just said?" the clerk asked tremulously. Marcel observed the young man pinching himself.

"I have decided to change my family name. I want to know how to do this."

At last the clerk felt more on his home territory. "There is no form or certificate available for a person to change his name. It cannot be done," he replied authoritatively.

"Are you telling me it cannot be done just because there is no form or certificate?"

"That is correct, Monsieur. If I do not have a form or certificate to complete, then an act cannot be undertaken." The clerk spoke in a monotonous tone of voice as if he had rehearsed that refrain many times in his life.

"That is unacceptable. I want to see the mayor."

"He is not here today, Monsieur. You will have to come back tomorrow."

Inwardly Marcel seethed with frustration, his hands were moist and he clenched his fists firmly. With outward self-disciplined calm he replied, "Thank you, I shall return in the morning."

He felt more composed with the passage of twenty-four hours and a refreshing night's sleep. He realised that if he seriously wished to pursue the name change, he would need to adopt a more expedient approach.

"Monsieur le Maire," he addressed the mayor respectfully. "I am not satisfied with my given family name of 'pierre.' I wish to change it. I request your advice on how to proceed with that act."

"That is a strange request," the mayor replied with an air of self-importance. "Women change their names and take on their husband's family name when they marry but I have never heard of a man wanting to change his name. Why do you want to change it?"

"I have my own good reasons. It would not seem necessary for you to know. It should be sufficient that it is my wish."

"It makes no difference," the mayor replied curtly. "In my opinion, according to the law, it is not possible for a man to change his name. Perhaps you should go and see a notary. He might know if there is a way. I cannot help you."

There were no notaries in Vimy. From the mayor's office he found the name of a Maître Augustin Gibet in Arras and rode off to see him. Maître Gibet received him in an office lined with legal tomes, on the second floor of a building overlooking La Petite Place. The scaffolding and guillotine were still in place in the square but public executions now were much rarer than during the Reign of Terror. Only convicted criminals, not political opponents, were its victims. The window gave Maître Gibet an excellent vantage point from which to view these bloody events.

Dressed formally, the notary would have preferred to highlight his authority and expertise by wearing a wig, but because wigs symbolised the decadence of the ancien regime, they were outlawed. To compensate for this sartorial omission, he sat in a large, elevated chair with a huge desk between himself and the client. Two large picture windows situated directly behind him framed his seat; this arrangement ensured daylight would shine into the face and eyes of those before him, enabling him to view changing expressions and give him a window into their motives and character.

With his legal background, the notary knew there were only two reasons why people came to seek his advice: fear or anger. He wondered about the reason in this, his first client for the day.

"What is the problem?" he asked solemnly.

"Monsieur le Maître, I have come to see you because I wish to change my family name. I never knew my father. They gave me the name of 'pierre' at my birth. It means nothing to me. I wish to drop it and adopt 'Juin' as my family name. Can you advise me how to accomplish this?"

"It is possible, but it is difficult, and there has to be good reason," Maître Gibet intoned, with gravitas in his voice. "I had a client once who bore the family name of 'le Con' and understandably he wished to drop that name. The legal process is time-consuming and therefore costly. I can also inform you that under the directorship of our esteemed First Consul, Napoleon Bonaparte, the legal system in France is right now being totally revised. It is possible that the new Code, when it is published, will simplify the process. If you wish, we can wait until the new guidelines are available and I will inform you of the result. I expect this to be in the near future."

"That will suit me very well," replied Marcel, feeling at last that he was making progress, though he remained concerned about the expense and the time it might take. "The matter is urgent but can wait a short time. You mentioned it would be costly. Can you give me an estimate?"

"It will be at least one thousand francs," the notary replied firmly.

Marcel drew in his breath sharply. "Can you not give me a better rate?" he enquired.

By this time Maître Gibet had appraised both the motivation and the financial assets of his client. "I regret there is no better rate. That is my minimum fee. It could well be more, depending on the circumstances, the time taken to prepare the documents and the procedures required.

Furthermore I will require the thousand francs immediately, before I proceed with the work. If it transpires that I am able to complete the work in less time, I shall reimburse you."

Dropping his eyes to the floor for a moment, which did not go unnoticed, Marcel battled with the reluctance to part with his money on the one hand and, on the other, his passionate desire for a new identity. He had come this far and could not now turn back.

"We can proceed, Monsieur le Maître. Inform me when the new Code is published. I do not have the money with me and will have to return."

"Certainly Monsieur," replied the notary with a self-satisfied smile. "I shall proceed with my enquiries as soon as I have the funds in hand, and will contact you when the new Code is published."

Six months later a letter carrier delivered an envelope to Marcel pierre. He saw it had been sealed with the official waxed red stamp of Maître Gibet in Arras. The enclosed letter requested he see the notary at his earliest convenience. He galloped off to Arras the next day.

"I have good news for you, Monsieur pierre," stated the notary when Marcel sat down after the opening pleasantries. "Book I of the new Code Napoleon has been published. This book concerns the civil rights of persons. Title I deals with the enjoyment and privation of civil rights such as birth and marriage. Chapter VI considers amendments of acts of a civil nature. The matter of changing personal names can be viewed as coming under that heading. In brief, it gives the commissioner of government, such as our mayor, the authority to go before the Tribunal, and request a name change. You will have to swear an affidavit in my presence and I will present it to the mayor and Tribunal. You will be present and may be called to give evidence as a witness."

Marcel had no knowledge of legal terminology, but he caught the drift of the notary's explanation. "I will do whatever is necessary."

Maître Gibet prepared the required documents and set a court date. Marcel had never before attended a hearing, and to relieve any apprehension, the notary explained the process in detail, including what would be expected of him. Marcel's case was the first scheduled for the day and he saw other litigants lined up in seats along the wall outside the court room awaiting their turn. In the presence of Marcel, Maître Gibet submitted the change of name to the Tribunal, and the Tribunal Chair, a judge, cross-examined him. Marcel noticed his long grey hair, pince-nez and his cultivated mournful expression.

"Monsieur pierre," the judge intoned in response to Maître Gibet's presentation, "A new Code has been enacted by the First Consul that permits a citizen to change his name. However there still needs to be justification. The law is firm on this point and we have to respect the law, otherwise every other citizen would be dropping by to change his name, which would create chaos in our courts."

The judge knew the legal significance of the small 'p' in pierre, and Marcel knew the judge knew, but was affecting ignorance. Marcel had not wanted to go into details about his reasons, but also knew that if he failed to provide any, his request could be refused.

"Monsieur le Juge, my father abandoned my mother before my birth and I never knew him. My mother's family were named Lachêne, and she died when I was young. They gave me the name 'pierre.' I do not know why and do not like the name. I like the name 'Juin' because June is the month of spring and celebration so desire to adopt it as my family name."

"I see from your birth notice that you were born during the month of June in the old calendar. Is that another reason why you chose June as your name?"

"No, that is not so, Monsieur le Juge," Marcel lied, looking the judge in the eye. "The reasons are as I gave you." Marcel thought if he admitted any affinity with the old calendar, his request might be turned down.

"Right," concluded the judge solemnly. "I accept and approve your application for a change of name."

So Marcel pierre became Marcel Juin.

PART FOUR: EXPANSION, CONTRACTION.

1803-1812

Chapter Fifteen

Germinal Year XI (April 1803)

Monsieur Pierre Plouffe tidied up his tobacconist store before closing for the day. He always enjoyed these few moments after the last customer had left, when silence reigned and he was alone. He sat down in a comfortable arm-chair near the counter, took some deep breaths, relished the sweet tobacco aromas permeating the air and then closed his eyes to relax. After a few minutes he rose, saw it was getting dark and as the store contained but one window, he lit a candle and unlocked the drawer under the counter that contained the metal money box to tally his take for that day.

Suddenly the door burst open and two masked men entered, one carrying a knife and the other a baton. "Hand over all your money," growled one, his voice muffled by the mask.

Monsieur Plouffe put his hands above his head and retreated into a corner, indicating with his eyes the location of the drawer and money box. One of the burglars lifted the box onto the desk, opened it and emptied its contents into a bag he carried. Meanwhile, the second burglar forced Plouffe to sit on a chair while he blindfolded him, stuffed a cloth into his mouth and tied his arms and legs to the chair, which Plouffe did not resist. They walked out quietly with their loot.

Before being blindfolded, Plouffe noticed that the burglar tying him to the chair had brown eyes and a severe squint. He knew only one other person with these features. Demy Cavigneau, one of his customers, had been in that morning with a friend to purchase smoking supplies. He had never liked Demy Cavigneau, or any of his family for that matter, not at all. Demy belonged to the gang of children, led by his sister Clementine, who used to torment him many years previously. The deformity of Demy's eyes was ugly and offensive, and this somehow went along with him being a criminal. Now was his chance to get even with Demy and whole Cavigneau family. Monsieur Plouffe easily persuaded himself that the muffled voice of the second burglar sounded like that of the friend and that the two had come to the store that morning to check it out, prior to a burglary.

He struggled to free himself. Although middle-aged, overweight and not strong, he eventually managed to dislodge and spit out the cloth, which enabled him to breathe more easily. Despite cries for help, no one came to his aid. Plouffe became increasingly sweaty and frustrated and eventually gave up wriggling to wait. He knew that darkness had set in and that his wife expected him home and he hoped she would send someone to look for him before he expired. About thirty minutes later, although it seemed like hours to the immobilised Monsieur Plouffe, he heard the door open.

"Monsieur Plouffe, are you there?" He recognised the voice of a neighbour.

"Yes, I am here in the corner, tied to a chair and cannot move or see. I've just been robbed. They took all my money. Call the gendarmes!" The neighbour removed the blindfold, released his bonds and helped Monsieur Plouffe return home.

Shortly after sunrise the following morning came a loud knock at the door of the Cavigneau home. Still dressed in her nightclothes, Pauline opened the door and saw two gendarmes led by Girouette, now head of police in Arras, looking resplendent in his uniform and cocked hat. She spied his crooked nose, scarred face and absent front teeth.

"Is Demy Cavigneau here?" he shouted peremptorily.

"What do you want of him?" she replied quietly.

"I want to speak to him."

"What about?"

"Madame that is none of your business. I order you to bring him to the door immediately," replied Girouette, still shouting.

Pauline went to get Demy, who had been asleep but woke up with the commotion. He came to the door, half-dressed and rubbing his eyes.

"Are you Demy Cavigneau?" Girouette asked loudly.

"Yes, I am," replied Demy with a yawn.

"You are under arrest for burglary of Monsieur Plouffe's smoke shop last evening." The two gendarmes grabbed Demy's arms and tied them behind his back. He struggled but they soon overpowered him.

"C'est des conneries! I was nowhere near Monsieur Plouffe's shop last night. I visited the house of my friend Richard," he yelled as they tied him firmly.

"Just tell that to the judge," Girouette sniggered in reply. "He is sure to believe you."

Without waiting for him to change into his day clothes, Girouette and his assistant, one on either side, each gripping an arm firmly, marched Demy

196

forcibly to prison, pummelling and pushing him, even kicking him, when they thought he moved too slowly.

"What could have happened?" Pauline asked in an agitated voice, as the threesome disappeared down the road.

"I do not know," replied Charles. "Let us go to Richard's home and talk to him." They arrived just as Richard too was marched down the street from his home, a gendarme on each side of him, hands tied behind his back, loudly protesting.

The trial of Demy and Richard took place the following week at the Palais de Justice in Arras. Judge Maurice Genereux, a middle-aged survivor of the Terror, presided. Overweight and plethoric, he smoked heavily using tobacco he purchased at Plouffe's store. The prosecutor had discovered a witness, a woman named Celeste Bourdelle, who had allegedly seen Demy and Richard emerge from Plouffe's store on the evening of the crime. The defendants were not permitted legal representation. A crowd packed the small courtroom for the hearing with the families of both Demy and Richard present.

Pierre Plouffe, the first to testify, stated with conviction that he recognised Demy's eyes because of their colour and squint and he knew Richard's voice. He had no doubt they were the burglars who had invaded his store because they had entered the shop that very morning to purchase some items. They obviously came to scout out the store prior to the burglary. Despite their disguise he recognised them.

Girouette testified that both individuals had resisted arrest and force had to be used to restrain them and march them to prison. Demy used a sacrilegious oath at the time of his arrest, consistent with criminal intent and guilt. He had inspected their rooms and had not found the loot but this could be because they had spent it or hidden it. In his opinion the law had to be followed to the letter and, for a crime of that gravity, he recommended the criminals be deported or sent to the galleys.

Celeste Bourdelle then testified. Obviously overweight, she wore a long red and blue dress with a low neckline extending to just above the nipples. Her lips and cheeks were well rouged. Long curly dark hair extended down to her mid-back and on top of her hair sat a large, broad-brimmed hat sprouting a huge white plume. Each of her ear lobes contained a large, circular, silver earring and on her left wrist were several bangles that jangled loudly when she moved her arm, sounding like the tympani of an orchestra. Her cheap perfume filled the court room as if fogged on a cold morning. As she sat down in the witness box, a slit appeared in her dress that exposed her thighs covered by a tight black stocking.

"Mademoiselle Bourdelle," intoned the judge, "Can you tell us what you saw outside Monsieur Plouffe's store last week?"

"Certainly, Monsieur le Juge. I was walking the street close to the door of his shop. Suddenly the door opened and two young men came out. Both wore masks and one carried a bag. They both tore off their masks then ran off." Mademoiselle Bourdelle smiled and then winked at the judge, while moving her shoulders and breasts seductively.

"Mademoiselle, did you recognise those two men?"

"Yes, Monsieur le Juge. They are seated right over there." She pointed in the direction of the prisoner's box where Demy and Richard were seated. The bangles jangled as she raised her arm.

"Thank you, Mademoiselle. That is very helpful. You may step down now." Judge Genereux indicated with his head that Bourdelle could return to her seat. He nodded and gave her a knowing smile.

Both Demy and Richard testified and they were cross-examined by the judge. The two looked haggard from their week in prison. Their baggy, black and white striped prison garb did not help their case. Each testified independently that they spent part of the evening on which the burglary had occurred in Richard's room and then went for a stroll before returning home. Each admitted they had been at the store during the morning to purchase smoking supplies but strongly denied responsibility for the burglary. They invited the authorities to inspect their rooms to locate the money.

In his verdict, given immediately, Judge Genereux found both Demy and Richard guilty. He accepted the testimony of Pierre Plouffe, a respected shop owner and Adolphe Girouette, police chief, both upright citizens, above that of two irresponsible young men. Above all he accepted the evidence of highly trustworthy Mademoiselle Bourdelle who not only saw the two men emerging from Pierre Plouffe's shop while walking the street, but recognised them in the Prisoner's Box. The fact the money could not be found simply meant the two had hidden it well after the theft with the intention of retrieving it later. He sentenced them to ten years confinement in the Bagne of Toulon, the prison-hulk in the Bay of Toulon famous for providing rowers to the French Mediterranean fleet during the reigns of Louis XIV and XV.

As Pauline left the court room she saw Celeste Bourdelle enter, without knocking, the private chambers of Judge Genereux.

Pauline and Charles were devastated by these events. They had had their difficulties with Demy — when young he often needed to be caned for disobedience, refusing to do his chores and he sometimes got involved in fights at school, especially when called names about his deformity. He lied but had never stolen and seemed to settle down during his twenties, especially after developing a friendship with Richard. The two had had escapades with drinking but the gendarmes had not been involved. Both had started work as floor cleaners at the tannery where Charles worked. Being sent to Bagne of Toulon was, in effect, a sentence of death. Few returned.

They realised the trial was a farce but without a lawyer to advise them felt helpless to overturn the decision. The next day Charles went to see Pierre Plouffe at his store. "Pierre, my son strongly denies the charges," he told Monsieur Plouffe firmly. "He is not a liar and has never stolen. I am here to ask you to withdraw the allegations against him. Moreover, he does not have any cash. How can he steal a large sum yet not have the money?"

Pierre Plouffe's hands trembled. His face, already plethoric, became even redder and beads of sweat gleamed on his brow. "Tell me, Monsieur Cavigneau, how would you like to be threatened with assault and with death, tied to a chair, unable to breathe, and have all your money stolen? I know Demy and recognised his eyes and Richard's voice. Both Demy and your daughter Clementine tormented me in the past. They have their just desserts. Ten years on Satan's ship will put them right."

"Monsieur Plouffe," Charles tried to be respectful but Plouffe caught an undertone of irritation. "Have you considered the possibility that you may be wrong? That they may not have committed this crime? In that event, there are still a pair of men out there, at large, seeking their next victims? Would it not be wise to spend time and trouble finding the real culprits to make sure this does not happen again?"

"Monsieur Cavigneau. I have nothing more to say. The matter is closed." Plouffe got up, walked to the door, and hustled Charles out.

Chapter Sixteen

Vimy, Thermidor Year XI (Summer 1803)

"Louis-Marcel," his father said one morning, speaking at his didactic best. "I want to tell you something about horses. You must look closely to see how a horse acts. You learn much from watching them. They are built to eat almost constantly, and must have plenty of exercise. If a horse does not get enough to eat it will bolt its feed and may get sick. When you see a horse acting like that you know you have to do something to make it feel better. When you hear a horse neighing, you know it is happy, or letting you know where it is, or just saying thank you." While speaking he had a flashback to his brief meeting with Pierre Tremblais when, as a boy of eleven working as a stablehand on Monsieur la Fortune's estate, Pierre had instructed him in the proper care of horses. Louis-Marcel was not quite six years old, Jean-Baptiste three and Clementine six months' pregnant with their third child.

"Yes, Papa, I already know all that." Louis-Marcel gazed up at his father in wide-eyed wonder. ``I've heard you talking to other people. But I want to learn how to ride. I'm old enough now."

Marcel furrowed his brow and stared at his son incredulously, secretly proud of his son's cheeky confidence. He smiled then looked at the puny height of the boy and knew he could not even reach the stirrup without assistance. "Ça va. But I will have to help you get up in the saddle. You can ride Senorita. She is gentle and not easily frightened."

They placed the bridle, reins and saddle on Senorita and Marcel lifted his son onto the horse before leading her around the property, holding the reins as he walked to make sure Senorita did not bolt, while Louis-Marcel sat perched on her back like a king, smiling from ear to ear with pleasure.

"If you want your horse to move, you shake the reins and dig your heels into her stomach. If you want the horse to slow down or stop, you pull the reins in towards you. Always be gentle with the horse. Did you know that you have to talk to horses, that they get to know your voice, which can help to calm them, and they can even understand some words?" Marcel loved instructing his son in the minutiae of horse care.

"You did very well, mon fils," he added, helping his son dismount. Patting him on his shoulder he said, "Next time we will tie Senorita up near the gate. You can climb onto the top and get on her back from the gate."

"Yes, I would love to Papa! Can we do that tomorrow?" exclaimed Louis-Marcel, looking up with an excited smile and admiring eyes.

"All right, we'll see," Marcel replied. He took delight in his son's eagerness and thought that feigning uncertainty would stimulate his enthusiasm even further. He knew that Louis-Marcel shared the tendency of many children to push their good fortune to its limit.

Marcel loved his horses. They were exercised and groomed every day and the farrier visited regularly to ensure their hooves were kept in top shape. He had passed on his love to Louis-Marcel who followed his father around the property, helping with the feeding and the grooming, soaking up knowledge about horses as easily as a two-year old child picks up language.

The day after their equine discussion, Marcel tied Senorita to a post near the gate and Louis-Marcel climbed the gate and transferred to the saddle. Meanwhile Marcel mounted Macario, a five year-old gelding, and together they circled the property at a slow walk. Near the end, as they were approaching the house with Louis-Marcel following his father on Senorita, Macario emitted a loud, prolonged fart.

Louis-Marcel burst into uncontrolled laughter. His body went limp, lost control and promptly fell off Senorita. On hitting the ground he heard a crack, felt a burning pain in his right forearm and burst into tears. Senorita, realising she no longer had a rider, turned around and sniffed Louis-Marcel's ear as if asking, Are you hurt? This tickled Louis-Marcel's neck, forcing him to laugh through his tears.

Meanwhile Marcel turned Macario around, jumped off when he reached Louis-Marcel, saw his forearm bent at an angle, and realised he had broken a bone in the fall. He quickly tied the two horses onto nearby fence posts and carried his sobbing son back to the house where Clementine attempted to console him.

There were as yet no doctors in Vimy. Marcel had no medical knowledge or expertise, but being a practical man, he knew instinctively what had to be done. He remembered that Clementine had a small quantity of powdered laudanum left over from her last childbirth. He fetched it, dissolved a small quantity of the powder in water and gave the potion to Louis-Marcel to drink. He then went to his small workshop in the barn and prepared three pieces of wood that he judged were the length and width of Louis-Marcel's arm and forearm. He planed and sanded the ends so there were no splinters or sharp edges, took a bed sheet out of the closet and using a pair of scissors, cut and prepared several, long thin strips of material.

"Clementine," he ordered when he returned, "Hold Louis-Marcel still and try to comfort him. I have to straighten and secure his bones. It will be painful." By this time the laudanum had begun to have an effect and Marcel saw his son's eyes drooping. The boy nevertheless winced and screamed as Marcel manipulated the bent bones in his forearm.

Clementine attempted to control the agitated child, while she herself gritted her teeth and shut her eyes, using her sense of touch to hold and console him. "You will be fine, mon cher petit garçon," she said. "Just bite your teeth hard. I know it is painful but it will soon be over. I know you love Senorita, and she loves you too, just like Maman and Papa. When you get better you will be able to ride her again!"

"Yes I would love that," replied Louis-Marcel through his tears. "She is a beautiful horse. The pain is awful!"

Meanwhile Marcel pulled hard on Louis-Marcel's wrist and elbow to separate the broken bones, hearing them crackle and crunch as he did this. He adjusted them carefully so they were in approximate alignment, and then fitted the three pieces of wood, one to the arm above the elbow and the others on either side of the forearm down to the hand. He wrapped the strips of material, firmly locking the arm to the wood to prevent any movement of the elbow and wrist joints. Clementine and Marcel then embraced the sobbing child, placed his arm in a makeshift sling and left the splint in place for several weeks allowing the bones to heal.

Every night over the next few weeks, Marcel made a point of going to Louis-Marcel's room at bedtime to recount the La Fontaine's fables that his mother had told him when young. He had purchased a book of the fables but many he knew from memory, particularly the story of The Lion and the Rat that his mother had told him. Louis-Marcel loved these night-time stories and gazed in wide-eyed admiration at his father's face as the story unfolded, even though he might have heard it many times before. His broken bones quickly repaired.

Three months later Clementine gave birth to their third child, a daughter. Marcel thought he recognised his mother's eyes and features in the baby's face so called her Marie-Anne in her memory and Father Lepire baptised her as such next day. It thrilled Clementine to have a baby daughter who would become a companion for her, and Marcel to have a child that carried his mother's name. He imagined her growing up to become as resourceful and capable as her grandmother. Together, he and Clementine composed a letter to Pauline and Charles inviting them to visit them in the spring when the weather warmed up, to see their new grandchild.

"Pauline!" Charles cried as she entered the house from the back garden where she had been tending vegetables in her potagerie. "It is three months since we received the invitation to visit Clementine in Vimy. Much has happened, both there and here. She and Marcel now have three children and he has built up what seems a great horse farm. Let them know we are coming next week," he ordered.

Her hands were covered with dirt which had also got under her finger nails. She poured water from a jug into a basin and washed her hands as best she could, then wiped them dry with a cloth. "Yes, I would like that," she replied meekly. "It is sad our grandchildren are so far away. I would like to see more of them."

Pauline had had an elementary education so, using a pencil, she scratched out a note, folded it and gave it to the son of a neighbour to deliver by foot to Clementine and Marcel in Vimy. She knew Marcel would pay the boy on delivery according to time and distance covered. The following week Pauline and Charles rented a horse and buggy to make the trip, carried out on a lovely spring day. The two families embraced on arrival and Pauline cooed and cuddled her newest grandchild.

Marcel showed his father-in-law around the farm and Charles fell in love with the horses. He admired the cleanliness, and even found pleasure in the acrid smell of the stables. Though he had little knowledge and experience of horses he could tell when a horse looked contented and well cared for.

"You have done an excellent job, Marcel. Does the farm pay for itself?"

"It required much capital to set up. I use the stallion to breed and have made some money from selling foals. I rent out horses for specific purposes and am training geldings for dressage. That too will bring in some income. One has to watch expenses of course. Most of the feed is grown on the farm and I hire young men and women from the village for the harvest, and it is beginning to pay for itself. What about yourselves? I hear there have been serious problems with Demy."

"Yes, poor Demy was a real tragedy," Charles replied, shaking his head sadly while also clenching his fists, as he recounted the story of Demy's arrest, conviction and sentencing. "He told lies sometimes, but never stole. He did not commit the crime. Those two ass-holes Plouffe and Girouette accused him falsely and they got this hooker to testify that she saw them emerging from Plouffe's shop. The trial was a mockery of justice. He's gone now and we will likely never see him again."

"I liked Demy." Marcel said. He reflected back on his encounters with Demy's mischievous nature when he first met Clementine and the Cavigneau family. "I knew he felt bad about his eye-deformity and that got him into trouble. In the end it destroyed him only because he resembled someone else."

"Demy disappointed me," replied Charles. "He had a weak will and did not act like a man. He seemed like a leaf, just drifting in the wind.

"What about your change of name, Marcel?" Charles asked, changing the subject. "It puzzles us."

"It's a long story, Charles. You know I never knew my father and they gave me the name 'pierre' at birth. Despite all my efforts I could not find out the name of my real father. The republican calendar became the last straw. I hated it and all it symbolised. I thought to myself: why don't I change my name to 'Juin', the month of my birth? It would have double value: demonstrate I owe nothing to my paternal roots, and show that I oppose the new regime and all it represents. Moreover, both Clementine and I love the warmth and joy of the month of June."

"That all seems reasonable, though our glorious regime is unlikely to see the style of your opposition." He looked at Marcel to see if he saw the sarcastic note of his comment, and Marcel nodded and smiled back in acknowledgement. "If you took a gun and tried to shoot a member of the government, or if you published tracts criticising them, then they would take notice," Charles added.

"You are right, but it still gives me small satisfaction. It has not stopped my desire to know the identity of my father. But I suppose there is now no way I can find that out. He is likely long dead, or if alive, has little desire to know me."

"Did you know our government is likely bringing back the old calendar? The new one caused so much chaos that many, even bureaucrats, stopped using it. The government is like a spinning top, it changes its mind so frequently."

"Yes, I heard that would happen. It makes no difference to me or my decision. I like my new name and will continue to use it."

Charles changed the subject again and asked, "How is that good-for-nothing uncle of yours?"

Marcel briefly clenched his teeth and then replied, seemingly coolly, "Alexis is well, thank you Charles. I believe you judge him too harshly. He's an old fogey with little ambition, but has been a loyal friend to me. If it had not been for him and Monique I would not be alive today."

"Perhaps," replied Charles doubtfully. "I respect men who are strong and enterprising. Look what you have built up here around you," he added as he stretched out both arms towards Marcel's farm and twirled around on his feet. "What has Alexis accomplished? He can barely feed his wife and child."

By that time Charles and Marcel had returned to the house and found Pauline and Clementine admiring baby Marie-Anne's engaging smiles. All four adults joined in the gurgling interaction with her.

Next morning Pauline and Charles were sitting on a bench outside the house watching young Louis-Marcel and Jean-Baptiste playing in the sand. The game suddenly turned ugly when Jean-Baptiste destroyed a castle that Louis-Marcel had built. Louis-Marcel grabbed a stick and slapped Jean-Baptiste over the head, making him scream in pain. Charles leaped up from his seat, took the stick, grabbed Louis-Marcel's arm, and whacked him six solid strokes on his behind, leading him also to burst into tears.

"That will teach you to hurt your little brother!" he said vehemently.

Clementine and Marcel emerged from the house to find out the cause of the commotion. "Papa, I will not have you touching my son," she screamed at her father. "You did enough damage to me as a child." Meanwhile Marcel tried to console both children, and Pauline remained seated looking glum and expressionless, staring ahead and avoiding eye contact.

"Let me explain, Clementine," said Charles with feigned patience in his voice. "Louis-Marcel hurt Jean-Baptiste needlessly. I merely gave him just punishment. Next time he will think twice about hurting his little brother. Thrashing a child who has done wrong does not harm the child. It makes them think. It is like a lesson so they will behave better next time. Besides, everyone ..."

"The fact that everyone does it does not make it right," Clementine interrupted, still shouting, glaring at her father. "There are other ways of chastising children without laying hands on them. It is not right for a big person to use strength to hurt a small person. My life is scarred by the way you treated me." She began sobbing, and flung herself into Marcel's arms.

Pauline remained seated like a sphinx, staring uncomfortably at the trees swaying in the wind. Charles sat down again in puzzled silence; the children had stopped crying, looked with bewilderment at the agitated adults around them, and then amicably resumed their game in the sand.

Clementine's tears slowly subsided and she went to sit next to her father. "Do you not understand, Papa?" she gestured emphatically. "People hurt other people but it does not solve any problems. It makes those who are injured bitter and they want to strike back. So they do strike back and more people get hurt. It goes around and around like a circle. It is stupid and futile."

"I am not persuaded," Charles replied firmly. "Look at those two lovely boys playing happily in the sand. A few minutes ago they were fighting. Now they are best friends again. People can fight, and they can make up and become friends again. There is no rule that says that if you fight you will make an enemy for life."

"Papa," she repeated angrily. "I am scarred for life by the punishment I received from you and Maman. It was excessive in relation to my so-called misdeeds. I remember Maman pushing my head into a pail of cold water and threatening to drown me. That is a brutish thing to do to a young child. I have bitterness that does not go away. I get angry easily and say hurtful things without meaning to. I am making poor Marcel miserable because of this."

Marcel had been listening to this exchange intently and, until this point, without a word. "There is much truth in what Clemmie is saying," he said calmly and firmly. "Charles, no one beat me during my childhood, though I was harmed in other ways. Striking a child is wrong because it teaches them that thrashing is an acceptable way for people to solve their problems. Jesus did not strike back when they scourged him, and when Peter cut off the ear of the soldier who arrested him, he repaired the ear and told Peter to put away his sword.

"Clementine is combative," Marcel added, in a matter-of-fact tone of voice. "She is easily angered and although she does not attack me or the children, she says things that hurt and then is sorry afterwards. When she accuses me falsely of doing things, I get angry and strike out, sometimes even slap her. Our lives have not been easy. She is quite right when she says this is because of the way you treated her when a child."

As Marcel chastised him verbally, Charles' expression became darker. The corners of his mouth drooped, his head bowed, and his eyes went blank, staring vacantly into the middle distance as he kept his silence.

Pauline, seated next to him, saw this, placed her hand on his arm and said, "I have always cared for you and loved you Charles. We had difficult children and we did our best for them. I see nothing wrong with punishing children when they do something bad. I did not strike them myself but I supported you when you beat them. It is unfair of you to blame Charles for your difficulties, Clementine and Marcel. You have to accept the results of your decisions. I love Charles. He hurts me and even beats me sometimes, but that does not change my love and respect for him. I accept his decisions even when they go against my will. We never argue."

"You have spoken well, Pauline", said Charles, emerging suddenly from his slouch. "Clementine, you were a mischievous girl and needed a firm hand. I do not regret anything I did."

"It is a matter of balance and fairness," said Marcel. "It is possible that an occasional thrashing does no permanent harm to a child but when it is excessive in relation to the wrong committed, and especially if the child does not comprehend, it can do much damage. Besides, Clemmie, though you were badly hurt as a child you have grown into an elegant and intelligent woman, an affectionate wife and a loving mother."

Clementine went over and embraced Marcel. "Thank you for your support, Mon Cheri," she said tearfully. "It means much to me." Feeling reassured by Marcel's support she turned to her parents and added, "Even if you do not understand or apologise I'm glad I spoke my mind. I may have seemed 'mischievous', as you say, but inwardly I was brittle, unhappy and easily hurt."

"You were also a difficult and disobedient child," replied her mother, holding firmly onto Charles' arm. "Parents know best what is good for their children. We did what we thought was right. If we harmed you we are sorry. That was not our intention. You seem to have found a man who loves and cares about you, despite your many faults, so perhaps you will find the happiness you seek!"

As the sun sank low on the horizon, Pauline and Charles excused themselves to get home before dark. With dutiful pecks on the cheeks of Marcel and Clementine they left to return home in their buggy.

They sat glumly side-by-side for the first part of the trip, Charles still smarting from the berating he received from Clementine and Marcel, watching the hedgerows slipping by, and the cattle and sheep grazing in the fields beyond. The late afternoon sun cast long shadows from the trees, and they saw their own shadows, and that of the horse and buggy moving along in the ditch as it travelled on the bumpy road to Arras. Charles eventually broke the silence. "They are a strange couple, those two. I know of no one else who does not strike their children if they do something wrong. A father must assert his authority to show who is master, just as a political leader does in a country. If not, the child, just like the people of their leader, will take advantage of the father. I could never put up with that."

"Not only that," agreed Pauline, "it is Clementine, not Marcel, who makes those decisions. Marcel meekly accepts whatever Clementine decides. That is not normal. The husband is the head of the family. It is the duty of the wife to follow what the husband has ordained."

"Agreed. Imagine, in our family, if we had to wait for you to make a decision. No action would ever take place."

The buggy ambled along slowly for another few hundred metres, when Charles said, "Did you see that Marcel has an odd resemblance to Pierre Tremblais? It is ten years now since he was guillotined so I do not have a clear recollection of his appearance, but Marcel has the same look in his eyes and shape of his nose, the same timbre in his voice and hair colour. Even seems to use the same words sometimes. If he had long sideburns and no beard they would be like father and son."

"No I did not notice anything. I did not know Tremblais well like you did. In any case there are many people who resemble each other. There is a woman in Arras who has a similar appearance to our neighbour, Joanne. Both women have the same height and build, and even walk the same way. From a distance it is easy to mistake one for the other, as I have done, but they are not related."

"Yes, you are right, Pauline. I knew Tremblais well as my boss. He certainly left no doubt as to who controlled the business. Strange to say, I remember him telling me that he could not control his wife's spending and this became the main reason his business went bankrupt. It seems like he was in charge in his business but not in charge at home. I could never put up with that."

Pauline did not respond to this statement, and the two continued home in silence.

In the late autumn of Year XVI (November 1805), Clementine became depressed on discovering she was pregnant yet again. Including four miscarriages between the live children, this became her eighth pregnancy. This time she did not miscarry. Without telling Marcel she tried to induce an abortion. She had heard that tying a corset firmly around the lower abdomen, taking a laxative and then doing vigorous exercise would have that effect. Nothing happened. Once she felt the child's movements, and above all following his birth, she quickly came to love him like the others. Clementine's fourth child was born before Marie-Anne reached her third birthday. They named him François, after the 16th century king of France, famous as a patron of the Arts, and builder of the Palace of Fontainebleau.

One evening, once all the children were settled, Clementine approached Marcel. "Mon Cheri, I need help with the children. It is hard to care for four of them. I get exhausted and irritable and yell at them. Could we employ a nanny?"

"That is not necessary, Clementine," he quickly replied. "We do not have enough money. You are a strong and good mother. I will help you. I love singing lullabies to the children at bedtime and tucking them in for the night and they seem to like it too. I am no good at cooking but can help you wash dishes and clean the house."

"You have promised that before and nothing changes," Clementine spoke more loudly and there was an angry edge to her voice. Marcel sensed a gathering storm. "You always tell me you will help and never do. I am getting tired of empty gestures."

"This time it will be different," replied Marcel, though he knew there was truth in her allegation. "I know it is difficult with three children and a baby."

"You are deceiving me," she screamed. "You are a harpagon. You do anything to save a penny, even if it destroys your wife's health and your own happiness. You do not think of anyone or anything other than your own self and your own pocketbook. You are mean and selfish." By this point her face became flushed, eyes bulged and the veins stood out in her forehead and neck.

"Clemmie, darling—"

"Don't 'darling' me! It is not the first time I've asked you for something special. You always say no, or you will think about it and nothing ever happens. I cannot stand it any longer. I hate you!" Clementine fled from the room in tears.

Anger and frustration surged in Marcel's heart; instinctively he wanted to shout back, "You are unfair and wrong, Clementine! I do mean it when I say I will help you! Don't scream at me as if I am a child or an idiot!" He felt his heart pounding and sweat pouring into his armpits. He went out into the open air hoping the breeze would calm his troubled spirit, and then decided to go for a walk up the ridge. He quickly calmed down in the fresh hillside air and gloomily pondered his situation. When I get back should I follow her into the bedroom and say sorry? Should I keep quiet and just hug her? Should I say and do nothing and wait till she calms down? He knew from past experience that this could take days, and during that time there would be a wall of stony silence between them. He also knew that if he got angry, as he had on similar occasions in the past, there would be an ugly scene in which he could hurt her.

When he returned home he found her lying on her bed, head in the pillow, sobbing quietly. He removed his tunic, pantaloons and shoes and lay down on the bed beside her, his arm around her waist. Her tears slowly subsided. As he held her he warmed towards her and his desires were stirred. In his mind he thought, what better way to settle a quarrel than to make love?

Clementine replied to this unspoken thought, "No Marcel. I have no feeling for you at present. I am still too hurt. I have to want to make love to you, and I do not want you."

Frustrated, Marcel thought, shall I force myself on her? It will satisfy me but what will it do for her? It may make her even angrier. He contemplated letting go to get off the bed and put his clothes back on when she added in a quietly firm tone of voice,

"There is another thing I want to tell you Marcel. I want no more children. I have enough love for the four that I've got. If I have any more, I fear I may not love them. It will damage both them and me. There is only one way to do it and that is for you to withdraw before you complete the act of love so your seed does not enter me. Are you able to do that?"

"I do not like the idea. It sounds wrong to me. It is certainly incomplete and may disappoint us both. I will think about it."

Clementine replied with thinly disguised scorn, "There you go again, 'I will think about it'. You never do, and nothing changes. If you do not wish to do that I will stop making love to you altogether. Which would you prefer?"

Marcel briefly pondered the implications of living a chaste existence. "I will withdraw, as you propose," he replied, reluctantly. Once again I am compromising my principles, he thought to himself sadly. I know when I am aux abois.

Shortly after her third birthday Marie-Anne took ill. It started with a sleepless night and next day she refused all food and could barely sip and swallow warm water, wailing endlessly, "Ma gorge me fait mal, my throat is sore."

Clementine saw her neck swollen and her body hot to the touch. The child looked miserable and spent the day sobbing silently, drooling saliva as swallowing caused her severe throat pain.

When they peered into her mouth they saw whitish scales at the back of her throat. Marcel called in Dr. Vincent Cadieux, an enthusiastic young man who had graduated the previous year in Paris and then opened a practice in Vimy — the first doctor ever to do so.

"I am afraid your child has diphtheria, Madame," he confided after his examination. "It is a serious condition especially in young children. I have had several cases the last few days. An epidemic, I fear, is brewing. Keep her warm, give her this medicine and try to give her sips of warm milk with a little sugar dissolved in it. Keep her apart from the other children. I will come and see her again in two days' time."

Marie-Anne's condition deteriorated rapidly. That night she started coughing, each cough being accompanied by painful, tearful spasms, and her breathing became noisy and strained. With the painful inflammation of her throat her weeping became progressively more pathetic.

"Maman, Papa, my throat is sore. Please make it better!" she repeated again and again, tears streaming down her soft, red cheeks.

"Yes my sweetheart, we are doing all we can," Clementine replied as she squeezed her hand lovingly, while tears of helplessness and sympathy flowed down both her and Marcel's cheeks.

Marcel and Clementine spent the night at her bedside, alternating with each other, supporting her by holding her hand and wiping her face with a cool damp cloth for comfort, but because of the pain and the cough, the unfortunate child became increasingly restless and could not sleep. Her forehead felt hot and moist but the cloth seemed to give some relief. All night long the flickering candle created eerie and ominous shadows on the wall.

Next morning during a severe coughing spell her throat blocked up completely and she could not breathe. For a few moments she struggled unsuccessfully to inhale, her chest heaving with each attempt, but the efforts became fainter and fainter. Her skin turned blue, she lost consciousness and within a short time she suffocated to death.

Marcel shook her little body and squeezed her chest frantically but got no response; she went limp in his hands. He and Clementine clung to each other, wailing helplessly, gazing at the lifeless little corpse, whilst Louis-Marcel and Jean-Baptiste looked on in puzzled silence, and baby François cried in the background in seeming sympathy.

Both Clementine and Marcel had had experience of deaths in their families, but the loss of a three-year-old child and only daughter, was quite new. Marcel thought it is understandable when an older person dies. They have had their life, and death is its natural and expected conclusion. Young men die in war, young woman die in childbirth, but the death of an innocent, young loving child in a brutish manner is a travesty of justice. In the midst of their grief they could see no good side to the loss of their beloved child.

At the funeral, Father Lepire, without a touch or a hug, tried clumsily to reassure them. "Your lovely little Marie-Anne is now an angel in heaven. Just think of her up there with Jesus, Mary and the saints, interceding for you in your prayers. I believe, no, I know, she is now contented and happy, no longer suffering the trials of life. Get down on your knees and thank God that you still have three healthy children you can give your love to." For an instant Clementine and Marcel were silent in response to these well-meaning but nonetheless cold, comfortless words. At length Marcel ventured a reply,

211

quietly but with an angry undertone. "Father, at a time like this we do not need a sermon. We need sympathy and support."

"And that is why I am asking you to think of your little one happily in heaven, with her soul resting in peace." He joined his hands together and placed them next to his right ear, as if to signify sleep and tranquillity. "I know what you are going through. Yes, I have not had children, but I have lost both my parents and a sister and it gave me great consolation to think of them as saints in communion with God. I am counselling you to do the same."

"We will do our best," replied Marcel acidly, glaring at the priest. Without the customary au revoir, Mon Père, he placed his arm around Clementine's waist and guided her away.

For weeks Clementine was inconsolable. She had loved her Marie-Anne, who had already grown into a cheerful and engaging little girl with endearing qualities that she, Clementine, had lacked as a child. She now clung to her three-month old François, afraid that if she let him out of her sight he too, would die. Her nights were restless with endless pictures of Marie-Anne's cheery little face, in both her waking and her sleeping hours. Yet in company Clementine could appear outwardly cheerful. Monique and Alexis came to express their condolences the evening after the funeral but Clementine dismissed their efforts with an ironic laugh, "It is nothing," she said, the smile on her face quivering as though about to fall off. Waving her arms in the air, she laughed again then said, "Come in and sit down. Let me offer you a glass of wine, or milk. I might even have some coffee if the army or the English have not stolen it. There are thieves everywhere and things disappear, especially things you need and love dearly. It is best to stop loving, and then you won't be disappointed when objects vanish. Marcel says I'm crazy, I must accept God's Will, but I know what's right and no one will tell me what to do." Clementine spoke excitedly and clenched her fists for emphasis, all the while maintaining the strained smile.

For a moment Marcel, Monique and Alexis looked at each other silently with puzzled expressions, and then Marcel said, "Clementine, no one is stealing things from you. I never said you were crazy. I know we have coffee because I saw it there this morning. I will prepare it for our guests."

"Yes, you do that and I will look after them." Clementine continued to smile, but Marcel did not leave the room as she went on, "Monique, have you ever loved, and then lost something?" Without waiting for a reply she went on, answering her own question, "Yes, it is cruel. No, not cruel, it is diabolic. There are people out there who take pleasure in stealing things you love. You must not love; you must not hate. You must keep your distance and remain aloof, like nuns in a convent. That way you avoid pain and avoid going crazy. Do you hear me? Do you hear what I am saying?"

Monique shook her head helplessly. "I don't know. I don't know what to say, Clementine."

"Well I am just telling you and you just listen." Clementine waved her finger in Monique's face. "Do not get attached to anyone or anything. It will only be taken from you and you will be hurt. You must put up your hand like this and say 'No'!" She raised her right hand to demonstrate the gesture. Then, all of a sudden, she fell with her face on her knees and sobbed loudly, a sound from deep within.

Marcel went to sit next to her, placed his hand on her back and said, "Clementine, Ma Cherie, you and I have both lost something precious. We cannot change that. We still have each other and we still have our three boys. Our lives will go on, must go on. With time we will accustom ourselves to the twin holes in our hearts and may even find ways to fill them. We must look to each other, to our children and to others such as Monique and Alexis here to help us."

"I feel so bad," replied Clementine through her tears. "As if I have done something wrong and am being punished, perhaps because I did not care for Marie-Anne well enough and so she got sick and died."

"Clementine, you loved her and cared for her," Marcel said emphatically. "You did not cause her death. She got an awful, awful disease. Almost all families lose young children to diseases, to diphtheria or whooping cough. Like them we must place that behind us and get on with the business of bringing up the survivors. In your heart you are angry that God took your beautiful child away, and it seems brutal because we do not understand. Even though you did nothing wrong you feel guilty so you are punishing yourself. Sometimes when you are angry about something you feel better if you bang your fist into a cushion, or even give someone a black eye. Just as long as it is not me!" he added with a smile.

Through her tears Clementine smiled in sympathy at this thought and grasping his hand said, "I sometimes do have the desire to bash you. Pressure builds up inside then I explode like a volcano and set fires around me. It has been like that since I was a little girl. I suppose I am weak-willed. When I love someone I love them with all of me. It is the same when I hate them. I cannot hide my emotions — they all hang out like washing on a line, so everyone can see. It is as if a storm is raging inside me and Marie-Anne's death has brought it out." Marcel, Monique and Alexis listened to this outpouring of feeling in thoughtful silence. Monique and Alexis were not accustomed to men and women talking about their personal sentiments but listened respectfully to Clementine's earnest intensity.

Marcel knew exactly the feelings behind Clementine's outpouring, having been on the receiving end of many of her emotional storms. He knew also that though she demanded much, she also gave much. While continuing to hold her hand he eventually broke the silence. "I know I do not always make things easy for you. I have my own demons boiling inside that cause tension." He turned to Monique and Alexis. "Remember when I became sick when my mother died? I became angry too and had stomach pains, could not eat. I could have died! Our parish priest, Father St. Amour, helped me realise I had control over my own destiny. Little Marie-Anne's death has brought all that back to me, especially as she is my mother's namesake."

"You are right, Marcel," Alexis said. "You were very stubborn; Monique and I were afraid you would die and tried to force you to eat with no success." This discussion of their experiences of death helped Clementine speak more easily about her own life. "I have had but one person die that I knew well, my friend Stéphane, when I was seventeen. It came as a huge shock and meeting you, Marcel, helped me surmount that setback. Calamity is sometimes followed by a providential event that helps bear the burden of the misfortune, don't you find? Perhaps something similar will happen now and there is hope for us still."

"Perhaps there is," agreed Marcel, relief in his voice. Squeezing her hand he added, "If you tie yourself too tightly to the past, you cannot contend with the future. I believe there is meaning and opportunity in adversity but it may take time to know what that might be." He fell silent, his gaze fixed ahead as though looking for that opportunity. Monique and Alexis, wordlessly catching each other's eyes, used the break in the heavy talk to excuse themselves and return home. Clementine and Marcel put the three boys to bed then retired themselves, comforting each other with long, tender hugs as they dropped off to sleep.

Early on the morning of the 11th day of Nivose XVI (1st January 1806) a clerk nailed an announcement on the notice board at the Mairie in Vimy. It said simply, without giving a date:

NOTICE
AS FROM TODAY
ALL GOVERNMENT BUSINESS WILL BE CONDUCTED
USING THE GREGORIAN CALENDAR ONLY

No reasons were given and no mention made of abolishing the Revolutionary calendar. As he knocked the last nail of the notice into the board the clerk struck his thumb hard with the hammer and yelled, "MERDE! MERDE! SALE OUTIL!" His voice carried through to the neighbouring streets causing a crowd to collect around the Mairie. In a fit of fury he threw the hammer and it flew through the ground floor window of an office at the Mairie, shattering the glass. Alexis happened to walk by, read the notice and said to the clerk with a smile, "I understand your frustration at the government for once again changing its policies but surely that is not a good enough reason to break a window at the Mairie."

"Foutre le camp," the clerk replied angrily, waving his hand at Alexis to piss off.

Still smiling with satisfaction at the clerk's torments, Alexis immediately went to visit Marcel, meeting him on the road outside his house. "Have you heard the news? We are going back to the old calendar! Are you changing your name back to pierre?" Grinning teasingly he slapped Marcel on the back, causing him to take a step forward.

"I have buried the name pierre with my father and his ancestors, wherever they are," replied Marcel, speaking loudly and ignoring the chance to banter with his uncle. "They have caused me too much grief. I no longer wish to know who they are, or where they came from. They can burn, I am satisfied with my new name. Once people get used to it, I've found, they accept me. The name Juin gives me joy." After a moment's silence he added grimly, "The government can do what it likes with the cursed calendar. It has given me enough trouble in my life. Governments have no concerns with the needs of individuals. Politicians just consider themselves, their families and their friends, and of course power — power to control the lives of others, whatever the cost to the country and its citizens. Not only that, but they enrich themselves while ruining others. It was this more than anything else that cost Louis his throne and his head. If he and the queen had shared the pain of his people they would still be with us today." He spoke so strongly that droplets of saliva flew through the air. Some lodged on his beard and glistened in the sun.

Alexis responded quietly, "To me you still seem angry, despite what you say about joy. You must lie back and resign yourself to what you cannot change. You act like a person who thinks he can get rid of fog by waving his arms forcefully and shouting insults. Fog dissolves only when the sun rises and burns it away. Wait for the sun to rise, Marcel. You cannot control when that happens but you know it is going to… "

"You sound like Father Lepire with your sermons. Talk, talk, talk. Words slip out of your mouth like rain drops off a bird's back. Keep out of it, please, and let me deal with this matter in my own way." With that Marcel turned and stormed into the house, leaving Alexis in the road, shaking his head.

Twelve months had passed since little Marie-Anne's funeral. François, now aged fifteen months, waddled through the house, getting into trouble for touching things when told to leave them alone, dropping and breaking fragile glassware in the kitchen. His two older brothers found they could avoid discipline by blaming him.

As for Clementine, she slouched around gloomily, did minimal house work and neglected her appearance. Marcel felt in a constant state of poorly-concealed anger. At the slightest provocation he yelled at Clementine and the children and sometimes even had to restrain himself from beating them. He spent as much of his day as possible on the farm fussing about his horses and going for long rides in the countryside. The wind in his face, the aromas in his nostrils and the exercise would distract him from the domestic turmoil, briefly invigorating his spirits.

Every Sunday morning the family would attend Mass together. They mouthed the prayers, but for much of the service Clementine and Marcel struggled to quieten the boys. Even attendance at communion became an indifferent experience. One Sunday after Mass, they went to the cemetery and prayed beside Marie-Anne's gravesite, a small mound of dried earth with a white unlabelled cross in place of a headstone.

That night, after the last of the children had settled to sleep, Marcel went to sit beside Clementine and placed his arm around her shoulder. "Clemmie; we cannot go on like this. You are unhappy and sorrowing for Marie-Anne. I too am unhappy and angry because in your affliction, you give me no affection. At times, I confess, I even imagine going with other women. The occasion has arisen, yes, but I have not yielded. It would solve my problem, but only briefly, and it would do nothing for you." He looked over at her, but could read nothing in her face, even as images of their early lovemaking crowded his thoughts. He went on. "As you know I do not care much for Father Lepire, yet he said something in his sermon this morning that struck a chord. 'It is', he said, 'part of the sin of pride to hold on to a hurt'. We are all subject to wounds by others. It is wrong to hold on to these wounds and nurse them as a way of avenging the one who caused the hurt. But you are deceiving yourself. You believe you are hurting the other but in effect you are hurting yourself."

216

"Remember that you are not the only one who needs affection," Clementine retorted, "always making promises you quickly forget and nothing changes. You are holding me now but how often do you do that? I cannot make love as if I am a doll. My feelings have to be stirred and they are stirred by holding, touching and affection. You think that because I am a woman, I will remain forever faithful to you, but you are wrong Marcel. Like you, I have a great need for love. If I do not get it from you I will get it somewhere else."

Marcel was speechless. How can this woman, my faithful wife of nine years, say she can break her marital vows? Do those sacred words uttered at our wedding mean nothing to her? How can she even contemplate such an action? What would it do to my reputation in the community if it came out that she made herself available to any man needing some light diversion? Eventually he replied firmly, "Clementine, you will do no such thing. You are a wife and a mother. Your husband and your children come first. You could not betray me like that. I would become a laughingstock… "

"Marcel, did you not say that you had occasion to be unfaithful, though you did not yield?" Clementine interrupted with a sharp edge in her voice. "Is there one rule for husbands and another for wives?"

"It is different for husbands and wives," replied Marcel trying hard to appear reasonable. "A wife's place is in the home, caring for her family. A husband does have a place in the family, to make decisions and provide discipline. He also has an important task outside, to work and provide a home, food and clothing for his wife and children. Because of this division of interest it is less harmful for a husband to stray than for a wife. It is still wrong, but it is less wrong. A husband can be unfaithful, but still remain loyal, even loving, to his wife. It is like a physical release, because his emotions are not involved."

Clementine shook her head sadly, "You are playing games with words, Marcel. I am deeply disappointed in you. Women are physically weaker than men, and because they carry and bear kids, they have to care for them, so cannot escape the home to earn a living. This does not mean they have any less value in God's eyes, nor does it mean that different rules apply for men and women, or that we should not respect what each brings to the family. I do not know how you can say emotions are not involved when you make love. They are always involved."

"I disagree with you," Marcel retorted, trying to be forceful yet realising he was losing the argument. "Different rules do apply because men and women have different responsibilities within the family. This does not mean that I do not respect you and your contribution. I suppose you are right, though, that emotions are almost always implicated, unless one goes with a prostitute."

"I know I have not been an easy person to live with, Marcel, and for that I am sorry. But I have to say this, firmly. I would be not only disappointed, but angry, if you were unfaithful to me, and hope it does not come to that. Perhaps we can both try to be more affectionate."

This discussion took place while they were seated together on the couch, and Marcel felt increasingly aroused as the conversation progressed. He held and stroked her affectionately as Clementine said, looking into his eyes, "While we have been talking Marcel, I have made a decision, in which I will use my power as a woman. I would like another baby. I know that feeling another life inside me, more than anything else, will help me overcome Marie-Anne's death."

Marcel smiled and replied, "And I shall use my power as a man, and say 'yes, my darling'." He took her hand, stood up and added, "Let's get to bed quickly before either of us changes our minds."

Nine months later Clementine gave birth to another daughter, whom they called Charlotte.

Chapter Seventeen

Vimy, Spring 1807

Marcel rose early on this dull, grey spring morning. Little Charlotte at six months of age gurgled with delight as she took the nipple for her first feed of the day while Marcel helped dress and feed the older children. He had finally understood Clementine's need for help with domestic chores but had not yet found his way to the kitchen to assist with meal preparation.

He heard a commotion outside, peered between the curtains of the living room window and saw two mysterious visitors arriving at Les Érables on horseback. They appeared distinguished, with one being the obvious leader because of his superior bearing and attire. He appeared to be around thirty years of age, was of medium height, had neatly trimmed sideburns, and wore a smart-looking cocked hat. Both were dressed in army regalia bedecked with colourful ribbons and prominent epaulettes. They tied up their horses and marched in step to the front door.

"I am Colonel Michel le Grand," declared the leader, when Marcel came to the door. "My aide here is Sergeant Jean Patois. I am head of the Dragoons of General François-Étienne Kellerman in the Imperial Army. Allow me to get straight to the point. The Army has a great need for horses of good quality and I have been authorised to procure them; recent battles especially that of Austerlitz cut a huge swathe through our best breeds. General Kellerman realised the horses used at Austerlitz were too young and weak and he has ordered us to obtain more mature ones, especially horses that are powerful and able to move quickly. We have exhausted our regular suppliers so are widening our search. You have a reputation in this community for breeding and training strong horses. I would like to inspect your stables."

For a few moments Marcel struggled with his conscience, as le Grand looked at him quizzically. I oppose war and, at great personal cost, hid in a cave for six months to avoid conscription. I told Charles and Maxime six years ago I would never personally profit from war by selling matériel to the army. They jeered me and said I would never live up to that promise! What will happen if I refuse? At best, they will impound my horses, without payment. At worst, they'll arrest and imprison me for failing to help the war effort. What would then happen to my farm and family? Marcel gazed towards the stables and heard a mare whinny sorrowfully. He foresaw the awful battleground deaths they would meet. Legs broken, stomachs impaled, muzzles shot off.

Marcel shuddered inwardly at these developments, quickly made his decision and replied with enforced grace, "Of course, Colonel le Grand. Come along with me and I will show you my horses." As they walked towards the stables, Marcel explained, with the little enthusiasm he could muster, "At present I have twelve horses. These include two foals, six mares, three geldings and one stallion. I look after them carefully and train them to be both sturdy and fast. You must remember they have been prepared for a life in agriculture or transport. They would require much additional training for warfare."

Le Grand appeared not to be listening, his head slowly turning as though surveying a battlefield. But he had heard every word. "I understand that," he said, still not looking Marcel in the eye. "I can assure you we have specialised programs that prepare them for battle. Both the Emperor and General Kellerman now believe that a highly trained cavalry is imperative for battle success. A well-timed cavalry charge strikes terror into the enemy's infantry." Marcel showed his visitors the stables, where Le Grand inspected the horses carefully, particularly the condition of their teeth and hooves, and the size and strength of their hindquarters. He appeared satisfied.

"We would like to purchase the three geldings and a mare. What is your price?"

"One hundred gold francs for each of the geldings and eighty for the mare," replied Marcel without a moment's hesitation. He knew his horses were of top-grade quality and the price he could obtain at the market in Arras.

"That is far in excess of their value," replied le Grand tersely, turning now to look directly at Marcel. "We are willing to pay a maximum of fifty for each of them. Total two hundred. You would be doing well. If this does not suit you I will arrange for an army group to come and procure them. Ultima ratio, you know the rule: Might is Right. You will then get far less for them. What is your decision?"

It is now Marcel's turn to survey his beloved equine enterprise, as the grey skies began to drizzle gently. When his eyes alighted on the horses whose fate he was about to decide, he gave the proud creatures a look of sympathy, almost apology, then replied, "I love these animals and tend them carefully. The thought of them being used for warfare appalls me but you give me little choice. I have to accept your two hundred."

"I can see you are a wise man. I agree with your sensitivities about battle slaughter. Remember that far more men than horses die in battle, and their deaths are even more gruesome. The course of history hinges on success in warfare. The Emperor's highest goal is to defeat la perfide Albion, and he is prepared to make any sacrifice to accomplish that aim. And he will succeed whatever the cost!" Le Grand spoke forcefully and to emphasise the point, he punched the fist of his right hand into the palm of his left hand.

"There is also a cost, and a much larger one, in defeat," replied Marcel quietly. "Has the Emperor considered that possibility? A moment ago you complimented me on being a wise man. Even though you were, forgive me, being sarcastic, I believe you are correct. I know when I am beaten and will retire, hopefully with some grace, before I have to grovel in the dirt. The Emperor has won many battles and is at the height of his power and fame. A wise man would retreat when he is ahead, pursue peace and solidify his accomplishments."

"With respect, Monsieur Juin, you are quite wrong. The Emperor is a born warrior. His presence on the battlefield is worth one hundred thousand men and ten thousand horses. In ten years he has not lost a battle. There is absolutely no doubt he will win this one also."

"Other than opening up the secrets of Egypt and its ancient culture, I am not certain how you see his campaign in that country a success, or the naval battle of Trafalgar. In my opinion they were both serious losses."

"It is correct that England still controls the seas and that is our weakness. But her success depends also on commerce. The Emperor now controls most of Europe. Preventing the sale of English goods in Europe will cause commercial chaos in that country, and force its eventual capitulation. What is your opinion, Sergeant Patois?"

"I totally agree with you, Mon Colonel," the sergeant replied deferentially in his regional patois. "The Emperor is a great man and a great general. He knows what he's doing. I've complete confidence in him as do all my pals in the army."

"There you have an objective opinion from a man in the ranks, Monsieur Juin," replied le Grand with authority. He then added, while raising the palms of his hands, "What more could you need?"

Warming to his theme Sergeant Patois added, "All the chaps in our company admire our Emperor and are willing to die on the battlefield to serve his cause."

"I do not know much about England," replied Marcel doubtfully. He felt intimidated by this confrontation with imperial might, in the form of two imposing-looking representatives, but decided to venture a different perspective. "I suspect England will build on its strengths and fight with determination. You must remember also that large numbers of our compatriots are in England supporting the English cause."

"Traitors they are, to a man," snapped le Grand, with venom in his voice. "If I could lay hands on them I would execute them all. Here in France, we are making great sacrifices for the glory of our country. There our co-citizens do everything to undermine and defeat us. It is outrageous."

"I agree," echoed Patois. "Just wait an' see. The English will poop in their pants and run when they meet La Grande Armée on the battlefield!"

In his heart Marcel felt overwhelming sympathy with the "traitors" in England. As a young man he had fled conscription. The thought of killing a man, even in anger, shocked him. He deeply regretted parting with his horses and he felt guilt, bordering on disgust that he had not lived up to his principles of not profiting from the war, even though the profit was minimal. The probable loss of his farm, his family, perhaps even his life weighed heavily in his decision but he had no wish to incur the wrath of a senior delegate of the Imperial Army. There came a time when one had to compromise principles with unassailable power. He decided that any further discussion or resistance to the deal was pointless, and as the drizzle had turned into a light rain he changed the subject, "Let us proceed with our arrangement. When will you require the horses?"

"We will take them right away," replied le Grand without hesitation. "They will accompany us back to the barracks in Arras where they will start war and battle training tomorrow. I will report the purchase to our office and you will be reimbursed within a month."

"Those am good horses," stated Sergeant Patois with copycat authority in his voice. "I'm going to take this one for meself," he added, pointing to the mare. "She's stronger than this old nag I've got 'ere."

Marcel placed bridles on the four selected horses and watched sadly as they followed the horses of Colonel le Grand and Sergeant Patois out of the gate and on the road to Arras. I know my poor steeds won't last long in the army. Likely be gunned or speared in their first battle and die lingering, painful deaths. He shook his head, pursed his lips and returned indoors to complete his domestic tasks.

PART FIVE: REVELATION

1813-1840

Chapter Eighteen

Early in the spring of 1813, a man limped into Vimy on the rough country road from the east. The fruit trees were in full bloom and their sweet scent perfused the countryside. It being late afternoon the air felt cool and refreshing. In his late thirties, and normally a neat man, his journey had converted him into someone whose beard and hair looked like places where birds could nest. The wanderer wore old army clothes that were dirty and torn, and boots that had as many holes as a sieve, yet a bleu-blanc-rouge cockade stuck out of his breast pocket. Although of medium height he had a thin, almost emaciated appearance. Once a decorated officer who had looked down on the lower ranks, he now looked as if he would be at home on the streets. According to his story he was one of the few soldiers from Napoleon's army who had managed to find his way back to France following the disastrous invasion of Russia the previous autumn.

He had survived by living off the land, begging or stealing along the way, and on occasion offering his manly services, sometimes without permission, to lonely or isolated women, in return for a warm meal or a bed for the night. Many soldiers returning to France from Russia chose to walk in groups for mutual support but he chose to walk alone, calculating that this would increase his chances of survival. He had no idea what to do once he reached France, though there were savings in a bank in Paris, if he could get there. The once-mighty imperial army no longer existed so he had no prospect of getting back his army position and income.

Upon reaching Vimy, he went straight to the tavern, surmising it to be the place where he would most likely obtain local information and perhaps find a generous soul who would pay for his drinks or even provide a meal and free bed for the night. Called Le Cheval Blanc the tavern had a large black porcelain plaque hanging above the entrance with a figure of a white horse, one front and one back leg elevated, as if trotting. The tobacco smoke and alcohol fumes that pervaded the airless space overwhelmed him as he opened the door. Once his eyes adjusted to the gloom, he spied a table in the corner where two men were seated, and sat down at the vacant chair with them.

"Can I join you? My name is Raymond. Raymond Batarse."

"I am Robert and own the smoke shop in the town and my friend here is Alain. He is the carpenter. You look like you have been travelling. Where do you come from?" The stranger's unusual accent had given him away.

"Oh, I have just dropped in from Moscow."

"From where?" the two exclaimed in unison.

"From Moscow," he repeated coolly. At this point the hubbub of conversation in the tavern dropped and the tinkling of glasses disappeared. All strained to hear the stranger's story. "I fought in the imperial army during the invasion of Russia," he continued, gazing intently at the crowd in the room. "The invasion was not successful. The army is no more. I am not certain what happened to our Emperor — he has no experience of defeat." Silence pervaded the group as they pondered this information. They had heard that La Grande Armée invaded Russia in 1812 but news of La Grande Débâcle had yet to reach Vimy.

"How did you arrive in Vimy?" asked Robert, with curiosity and deference in his voice. Despite Raymond Batarse's shabby and dishevelled appearance, Robert and Alain sensed their visitor was accustomed to authority.

"How else than on my feet?" Batarse began to enjoy his role of informant of dramatic historical events to these naïve commoners. He gave a self-satisfied smile as he added, "My horse died on the retreat from Moscow and public transportation no longer exists. In any event I am without gelt. I slept in barns along the way and when food was not available I caught, cooked and consumed rats, of which there were plenty. A combination of cold and starvation has killed most of the soldiers returning from Russia. The pitiless cold I conquered by sleeping, uninvited, in barns. I would not recommend rats as plat du jour for this tavern, but they provide basic nourishment in emergencies. I received some help from Polish peasants along the way. They have little love for Russians and supported the Emperor's invasion. The Prussians and Germans are different. They are jerks, hate anything French and it did not help that I spoke no German. I kept out of their way as much as possible. When death is close you learn the art of survival. I did not have to resort to killing and eating my fellow human beings, but would have done that if I'd had to."

Robert and Alain listened to this tale in silence, their mouths and eyes agape with shock at the French defeat.

"What are you going to do now? I see your left ear is missing," Alain said eventually.

"A son-of-a-bitch Cossack shot it off during the retreat from Moscow. Just a thumbnail distance to the middle and my brain would have been goulash. Luckily it healed without inflammation so did not affect my march home. As to what I'm going to do, that is a good question. I have army savings at a bank in Paris so that is where I am headed first. After that I do not know."

"Where do you come from? Do you not have family? I am puzzled by the way you speak. You obviously are not from these parts."

"You are perceptive, Monsieur Alain, and you are correct. I come from everywhere and I come from nowhere. The army is great training for any young man who wishes to learn a language, collaborate with others and learn discipline. It also teaches you how to slaughter but that is another story, although I never had difficulty acquiring that particular skill. Any man who gets killed in warfare likely deserves to die because it is a sign of a weak will. That is why I admire our Emperor. He brought France out of the chaos of the Revolution and wrought many changes, despite being attacked and vilified by all, from the Pope to the King of England. He has survived many battles and endless assassination attempts. Now, he has been subjected to a terrible defeat, but I have no doubt he will recover and restore glory to this country. I would follow him to hell, if needed."

Robert and Alain shook their heads in wonder at Raymond's story of valour and adventure, and his assured manner of speaking. During the Reign of Terror twenty years previously Alain had once travelled to Arras, less than twelve kilometres away, to witness some executions. Otherwise their lives had been limited to the confines of Vimy.

"If you have nowhere else to go, why do you not come and settle in Vimy?" Robert asked, looking down and bowing his head. "It is but a small town that serves the surrounding agricultural region. Our best-known citizen is Marcel Juin. He owns the farm Les Érables that supplied quality horses to —"

"I disagree with Robert about Juin and his horses," Alain interrupted, recalling the childhood event when Marcel beat him up. "He is a jerk full of his own self-importance. His horses are like glorified asses."

"I do not wish to get involved in a debate about the merits of a horse farm operation even if its success is apparent rather than real," replied Batarse, diplomatically. "What are the possibilities if I settled here?"

"You could buy a farm or a business," Robert said. Then his eyes lit up. "Ah! Monsieur Tricheur died last month. He owned a business that supplied equipment to the farms and his business may be for sale. Yes. We could introduce you to his wife who is now the owner. On the outside she is an amiable woman but can also be hard, sometimes even tricky. Actually, we could take you to meet her tomorrow."

"That all sounds worth considering, but you are moving too fast for me," Batarse said. "Look at me, I look like a tramp and as yet have no money. If you could provide me with a bath, some clothes, a bed for the night and a small loan, I shall get the carriage to Paris tomorrow, access my funds, and return next week. Meantime, let Madame Tricheur know that someone is interested to buy her husband's business. This is most kind. I would not mind another drink, if there is room on the table for more."

When he thought about it, Batarse liked the idea of settling in an out-of-the-way place such as Vimy. He had no wish to remain a soldier and felt afraid of being charged as a deserter if his whereabouts became known. Making his home in Vimy would be akin to going underground to avoid being discovered and charged. When Robert invited Raymond to his home, there to provide him with clean clothes, help to trim his hair and his beard, and enough money to board the Paris coach in Arras the next day, he accepted.

As promised, Raymond Batarse returned to Vimy the following week. He had travelled to Paris in the comfort of a carriage, retrieved his bank deposits and spent a few days shopping for clothing and other accoutrements befitting a man with ambitions in the world of business. Robert had indeed arranged a meeting with Madame Tricheur and this occurred shortly after his return. He prepared for the meeting by dressing in well-fitting but casual clothes. He wished to present himself to Madame as a man of modest but dependable means, and knew he had to keep his language clean.

He found himself facing a woman dressed in black clothes of mourning, features plain and without makeup or perfume. A full-length prominent portrait of her husband, looking sombre and dressed in his Sunday best, rested on the table beside her. He knew he had to approach her tactfully. "Madame Tricheur, I am profoundly sorry to hear about the recent death of your husband. Allow me to offer you my deeply felt condolences." Batarse spoke with assurance and affected feeling. In her mid-forties, Madame had been married to Monsieur Tricheur for over twenty years. Devoted to him, she had raised their five children while he built up the business. While in a barn attending the needs of one of his clients, he had stepped on a rusty nail that had penetrated his shoe. The wound was superficial and appeared to heal, but two weeks later he developed lockjaw and after a short illness died a painful death.

She bowed her head and wept. Raymond thought if he played his cards carefully in their negotiations, he might secure more than just the business. "Madame, I came to see you to discuss my possible purchase of your husband's business." Raymond spoke with apparent sympathy. "It seems that now is not the time to discuss this matter. I shall return on another day when you are more composed. I am staying at the tavern until I have purchased permanent accommodation."

"You are very kind, Monsieur Batarse," she replied between sobs. "Life is not generous. You work hard, make sacrifices, then die after a small injury. They say your reward is in heaven but that is hard to believe, but, if there is a heaven, he must be there. Monsieur was a good husband, father and provider. Meanwhile I am now alone and have to live on this pitiless earth, raise our children and provide food and shelter for them. It would be easier if I married again. Our country is not generous with widows, but what man wants a forty-five-year-old woman with five young children?"

"What can I say, Madame?" said Raymond with well-feigned affection. "I believe you still have resources you can rely on. Perhaps you just need time to discover what they are. I have no wish to impose myself on you when you are grieving your dear departed husband. Clearly you are still much attached to his memory."

"Monsieur, you still have told me little about yourself. Where do you come from? Do you have a wife and family?"

"I have no attachments. I fought in the Imperial Army for twelve years. I have travelled all over Europe and it is not possible to develop family bonds when one is moving constantly. I am now no longer a soldier and am seeking to establish a home. Although I have been in Vimy but a short while, I like the town and the region and wish to remain here."

Madame Tricheur looked at Raymond Batarse doubtfully, but he remained purposely remote and expressionless. "All right, Monsieur. I shall communicate with you in a few days' time and we can then carry this matter further. I am not disappointed to have met you."

"And me also. Au revoir, Madame."

Three days later, Madame Tricheur sent for Raymond Batarse to discuss the sale of her late husband's business. They agreed upon a price and sealed the deal. In the interval Madame Tricheur had spoken to Robert and Alain about Raymond and had discovered that the sum of their knowledge coincided with hers — nothing more, nothing less. Raymond Batarse had the required funds in hand to purchase the business and for the moment, that was the main issue for her.

In the two years following his arrival in Vimy, Batarse made great strides, after the many strides he had taken to get there. After purchasing the farm implement business, he bought a large house on the southern outskirts of the town, on the far side from the ridge. Local citizens recognised and responded to his entrepreneurship so the business prospered. Northern France had a wet spring in 1815 causing turmoil in the towns as troops, both French and foreign, swept through, travelling either towards, or away from, Paris. Heavy army traffic on roads built for pedestrians, horses and the occasional carriage rendered them almost impassable. Local citizens were agitated by these changes. Families were expected to billet soldiers for the night without recompense for cost and inconvenience.

Raymond Batarse knew how to turn adversity into opportunity. Having spent many years in the army he knew the needs and protocols of regiments. He used his French army connections to ensure they paid him well for billeting, but was less successful with the foreign armies that passed through on their way to Paris, and had to take the abuse alongside other citizens of the town.

Though he received the abuse of foreign strangers, Batarse's good looks and affluence, and status as a single man were the subject of praises at dinner tables throughout Vimy. Families with eligible young women among them sought him out as a prospective husband. Josette and Jeanine, two non-identical twin daughters of a local peasant, each considered themselves eligible. At different times Batarse led the pair on, and both were enticed to his bedroom. Despite her initial interest, Madame Tricheur did not respond to his overtures, and he quickly gave up on her.

Batarse knew what he wanted from a wife. Dalliance of course, but perhaps even more important he sought a woman with status, someone who could further his business and political goals. He heard from Madame Tricheur that the mayor of Arras had an eligible twenty year old daughter named Adélaïde so he galloped off to the city and called on the mayor at the Hôtel de Ville. After introducing himself, Batarse came quickly to the point. "Monsieur le Maire. I come to seek the hand of your lovely daughter Adélaïde in marriage. Let me tell you something about myself. I spent over ten years in the Imperial army and was invalided out because of a serious head wound in which I lost my ear." Batarse turned his head and displayed his missing left ear to the mayor. "I have settled now in Vimy and have purchased and built up a successful business selling farm implements. I offer a dowry of one thousand francs."

The mayor's eyes lit up as he replied, "That's an interesting proposal, Monsieur Batarse. Tell me more about yourself."

"Like most people you are likely wondering about my accent. I lost my parents when young, and neighbours raised me. They came from afar and I speak like they did. At seventeen I joined the army as a simple private. I worked hard and rose to the level of lieutenant. If it had not been for my critical head injury I would now be a general. Two years ago I bought the business from Madame Tricheur and have built it up. You may speak to Madame Tricheur. She can vouch for my character and honesty."

"That is kind of you, Monsieur Batarse. I shall make some enquiries. Come and see me again in a week."

Madame Tricheur confirmed the account that Batarse gave of himself so at his visit a week later, he and the mayor finalised the terms of the betrothal. At this rencontre Batarse also met Adélaïde and noticed her pretty, demure face with rounded features and hair made up in a bun. Loose clothing extending up to her neck concealed her breast contours. She bowed her head while meeting him and looked at him merely by raising her eyes. She did not smile and other than ritual formalities, said little. The wedding was scheduled to take place in Arras in three months' time, the late summer of 1815.

During the engagement Batarse continued to meet and spend the night with either Josette or Jeanine. A week before the wedding he sent a message to their father informing them that he was getting married in Arras and would not be seeing Josette or Jeanine again. A major family spat ensued in which each blamed the other for the rejection by Batarse, while their father screamed at them both. In the fight, Josette badly scratched Jeanine's face and Jeanine bit Josette's forearm causing a large bruise, to all of which Raymond Batarse assumed total indifference.

In the late summer of 1815, shortly after his wedding, Batarse paid his first business visit to Les Érables. He had learnt much about Marcel and his farm from town talk, about his fine-quality horses that he provided to the army, his ideal family who had connections with good families in Arras, and not least, about his position as a respected member of the parish. He tied up his horse near the front gate as Marcel walked towards him from the house, and they met and shook hands under the maple tree. The day was cool and the sky overcast.

"Good day, Monsieur Juin," he said pleasantly. "My name is Raymond Batarse. I am the owner of the farm implement business, bought it from Madame Tricheur after the old man died. I am here to interest you in our new equipment."

"I've heard much about you, Monsieur Batarse. Not much happens in this town without it getting about," replied Marcel quietly. From what he knew about Raymond Batarse, he had neither a philosophical nor a personal attraction to him and he was suspicious also about his curious accent. He knew many of the regional accents of France but this one sounded unlike any he had heard before. He decided to play along with Raymond's approach and keep his distance.

"I am here to introduce you to a new type of plough. It comes from Rotherham in England. We have not been able to purchase it until now because of the wars. I hate to say it but the best farming inventions come from England. Now that the trade blockade has been lifted, we are able to buy the best and most modern equipment from across the channel. The leading edge of the plough is made of iron so it is both sharper and lighter than the wooden ploughs we used previously and it also lasts much longer. It slices through the ground like a keen guillotine blade through the neck. I have one at my house if you wish to see it." Raymond spoke with assurance and conviction, as if he had had years of experience in agriculture, although he had never in his life used a plough, and knew nothing about farming.

"How many horses are required to pull it?" Marcel asked.

"I am told but one, but this is something you may have to try out."

"It sounds very interesting. I shall come and see it," replied Marcel while smiling half-heartedly and shrugging his shoulders.

At that point they heard loud neighing and snorting emanating from a field behind the barn and moved over to investigate. It appeared that the stallion had briefly escaped from his pen, and was loudly protesting his recapture by the two stable hands, and forcible return to the enclosure.

Batarse studied this scene and then said, "To change the subject, Juin, have you heard that the emperor has abdicated and given himself up to the English? They are sending him to exile on the tiny island of St. Helena in the South Atlantic Ocean to make sure he can never escape again. How dreadful! Poor man! He will not survive long in such isolation, even if the English do not poison him. I fought in the Imperial Army for many years and was one of the few to return from Russia alive. Napoleon is a great man and an excellent general, one of the greatest who has ever lived. I shall miss him."

The wind rustled through the maples above and some dead leaves rained down on them. "I have little attachment to The Revolution or to Napoleon," Marcel replied with terse conviction. "I am a royalist and approve the Bourbon restoration The Emperor was a great general but where have his victories led France? Nowhere but death, destruction and ruin."

"I am surprised to hear you say that, Monsieur Juin. You provided the Imperial Army with excellent horses, and I believe you made quite a profit out of that business."

Marcel winced. "I had no choice in the matter," he replied curtly. "The army commissioners arrived here, liked my horses, and demanded I provide them to the army."

"And of course they refused to pay you," replied Raymond with a sarcastic smile. "You could have declined and continued to just live on your small, country horse farm."

"The monetary aspect played no part in my decision, Batarse." Marcel tried, with little success, to avoid sounding defensive. "The army offered me a certain amount and I had no choice but to accept. They offered much less than their value on the open market. Nevertheless, I am proud of my horses and pleased they were found acceptable to the army."

"I note your principles have their limits," Raymond replied icily.

"I have my principles and they stay with me in matters of importance," Marcel replied firmly, looking Raymond in the eye. "The matter of how I make my decisions is not your affair so you may keep those opinions to yourself." Marcel then asked calmly, "I am interested in your accent. Where do you come from?"

Raymond Batarse had been asked this question many times since his arrival in Vimy and now had a prepared answer. "I came to France as a young man and joined the Imperial army where of course I did much traveling. I learnt French in the army and that accounts for my accent."

"That does not answer the question of where you come from. What language did you learn at your mother's knee?"

"A moment ago you told me that a question of mine concerning your decisions was not my affair. I am now giving you the same reply. It is not your affair."

Marcel remained silent for a moment and a puzzled expression crossed his features. "I have no wish to interfere but to me, where a person comes from is not only a matter of interest but a source of pride."

"It is easy for you to say that," Raymond Batarse retorted, his lips pinched with bitterness. "You come from these parts. You have your whole bloody family around you, a mother, father, brothers and sisters. I envy people like you. You are comfortable — you have stability and security. You know everyone in the area, because you've always lived here. I had no family to protect me when I was young. I had to struggle, raise myself. Until I entered the army I had nothing. In the army, I found I belonged. I found a wonderful ésprit de corps until the Russian debacle. I chose to remain in Vimy after my return from Russia, now have a home, wife and a business with security. As to my origins, I prefer to keep that to myself." Marcel fidgeted uncomfortably in response to Raymond's tirade and said nothing. For a moment the two men looked past each other silently.

Eventually, Marcel said, "I think I understand, Monsieur Batarse. I shall not pursue the point. Every person has their secrets and they are entitled to keep them."

"I came here to interest you in some farm tools, and perhaps make a sale. It appears we have drifted on to other topics. No matter. Come and see me at my house if you wish to see the plough. If not, I shall visit you another time. Au revoir, Marcel Juin."

"Au revoir, Raymond Batarse." They shook hands coldly. Raymond mounted his horse and cantered off. Marcel observed it as a powerful Arabian-type stallion and that Batarse handled it very professionally, suggesting he had been in the cavalry rather than the infantry. Marcel then wandered thoughtfully back towards the house. He paused beside the large maple tree which, like his children, was now much closer to the sky than when he had first moved onto this land. Much time had passed since he last pondered his family roots. Leaning his back against the solid tree trunk and looking up into the sparse foliage, he let his thoughts travel. He was now close to forty and Batarse's outburst had lit embers in his heart that had been dormant for years. Like Raymond Batarse, he never talked about his origins. He kept them a secret because he was ashamed about his illegitimacy. There were still some in the community from his generation who knew about it, but they respected him for his accomplishments and so did not talk. There were others who, if they knew, would not hesitate to use this knowledge against him and he was not prepared to take a chance on that. He was interested in local politics and had decided to enter the contest for the office of mayor of Vimy, an appointment made by the regional prefect. The position held much power in the local arena. The mayor held responsibility for policies and decisions related to health, education and policing. He knew he would enjoy a position of authority, and having this power would compensate for the lack of direction, the aimlessness and deficiencies of his childhood. The position carried modest pay and could be for life if he avoided conviction for fraud or a criminal offence, but if his dark origins become known he stood no chance of being nominated. To secure the position he would have to maintain the façade, as he had done successfully all these years, of normalcy and legitimacy.

He remembered how his talks with Father St. Amour helped him as a child. Now, he had no one with whom to talk about these issues. Clementine knew his family history but to her it was a non-issue. She accepted him as he was, with his frailties and questionable origins, so there was no point in discussing these concerns with her. Besides, he felt once again frustrated with her. She had been devoting much time and energy to the children, especially seven-year old Charlotte who was sickly and had a bad cough. He felt neglected at home, a problem magnified by lack of intimacy.

I wish I had the courage to have an affair!

He could not talk to Father Lepire. That man was no match for St.Amour, not un homme sympathique. Full of his own self-importance, he liked the sound of his own voice and had little grasp of human weakness. Unlike St. Amour he had no capacity to listen. Uncle Alexis knew more than anyone, but for him it also was a non-issue. Although he understood Marcel and knew him well, he lacked verbal fluency and would have difficulty giving advice, or even support. Meantime, he saw the stallion had stopped protesting his confinement but the rustle of the wind in the leaves and the faint sounds of cows lowing in the distance suddenly became audible, and then faded again as he fell back into reverie.

It was not only the matter of being illegitimate. He had no choice but to accept that immutable fact. He did not know the identity of his father and had no means of finding out but knew he would be more at ease with himself if he had this knowledge. As a child he remembered questioning his mother unsuccessfully and still felt bitter that she told him nothing. Time often relieved such agitation, true, but could he ever come to terms with these issues? The whinny of a horse broke in on him, he recognised the mare as one close to foaling, and he pushed himself off the trunk and headed towards his present life, to his family. He saw Clementine come to the door as he walked towards the house. Clearly agitated, her eyes sought him out and she waved him over. He ran to her. Something was wrong with one of the children. He felt it even before she said it.

"Charlotte has coughed up blood." she said through tears, her voice trembling with agitation. "She had a fit of coughing, and then brought up the blood. I am so worried. I cannot bear the thought of losing another child, another daughter. You must do something!"

Marcel swept past and entered Charlotte's room. The afternoon sun came streaming in to the small but bright room as it faced west. Charlotte lay on her side, under the covers on the small bed, her pale face expressionless and long dark hair splayed about the pillow. Marcel saw streaks of blood on the blanket.

"What is it? What happened, ma petite?"

"My throat itches. I cannot stop coughing and am bleeding. I feel weak."

Marcel placed the back of his hand on the child's forehead and noticed it felt warm and sweaty. "We will call Doctor Cadieux," he quickly decided. "I've heard he has new techniques. I shall get him right away."

Dr Vincent Cadieux had been away and arrived three days later to see Charlotte. He brought with him a black bag containing medical instruments and emergency drugs. Short in stature, he had brown penetrating eyes and straight black hair that extended down to his shoulders with long sideburns but no moustache. Although his bedside manner appeared curt he kept abreast of advances in medical knowledge and techniques. He carried out his examination using a curious device. Made of solid wood and about twenty centimetres long, it had the shape of an ear trumpet, with flared ends.

"I attended a doctor's meeting in Paris last week and heard a presentation by Dr René Laënnec who invented this device which is called a stethoscope," the doctor explained to Clementine and Marcel as he showed them the instrument. "When I place one end on the patient's chest and my ear at the other, it enables me to hear the sounds created by the heart and the lungs." The doctor placed the stethoscope on his ear to demonstrate the technique. "Although expensive, I immediately purchased one. The sounds one hears may be normal or they may indicate pathology."

At the conclusion of his examination, Dr Cadieux gravely gave his conclusion. "Your daughter has phthisis. She has râles in her lungs that are typical of that condition. Her situation is serious and the prognosis, I'm sorry to say is not good. I have the following recommendations. You must give her plenty of air, leave the window open at night and encourage her to take ten deep breaths three times a day at the window so she can fill her lungs with fresh air. Give her a good diet with plenty of beef and chicken flesh. I also recommend that she suck a clove of garlic continuously during the day, if she chews and swallows it, so much the better. Finally, give her a teaspoonful of this tincture three times a day. I shall come and visit her again in a week's time."

"I do not know if I can live through this," Clementine said tearfully after the doctor's departure. "I have yet to overcome little Marie-Anne's death and now this!"

Marcel attempted to console her. "It appears that God is testing us like He tested Job. We have to follow Doctor Cadieux's orders and pray for the strength to overcome this trial. We will ask Father Lepire to come and bless Charlotte with Holy Water."

"Pain such as this makes me doubt my faith," Clementine replied. "If God is so good why does He allow unbearable suffering?"

"It is hard to understand." Although Marcel himself felt doubts about God's goodness in this situation, he tried to reassure Clementine. "Pain and suffering goes with being human and God Himself suffered horribly through Jesus on the cross. Seeing one's beloved children get sick and die is even harder to bear than physical pain. It is fortunate our three boys are healthy. We shall do all the doctor suggests and offer up Masses for Charlotte's recovery. We can do no more."

Marcel and Clementine hugged each other tearfully.

They followed every detail of Dr Cadieux's prescription while Charlotte spent all day in bed, rising only for her toilet needs and her fresh air prescription. She appeared pale and had lost weight so Clementine garnished her meals, providing small palatable portions. They could not persuade her to suck cloves of raw garlic so Clementine used the herb liberally in dishes she prepared, to such an extent that its spicy aroma pervaded the home. She spent many nights at Charlotte's bedside, comforting her, telling her stories and attempting to cheer her up.

Lepire visited at the invitation of Marcel. Despite Marcel's opinion of him as a man, the priest carried the spirit of God within him, and Charlotte needed it now. However, the holy man carried out the required blessings in such a mechanical manner that Marcel doubted the prayers would be heard, despite Lepire's assertion on his departure, "I know the Lord will hear my blessing and help the sick child."

Doctor Cadieux came regularly to ensure they followed his orders. Each visit he examined her chest using his stethoscope. While doing so he closed his eyes to better concentrate and hear the sounds emanating from Charlotte's chest. The family watched his serious features in awe as he did so, convinced the instrument had magical curative properties.

For some weeks Charlotte continued coughing up streaks of blood after which the bleeding stopped and she slowly began to regain her appetite, weight and strength, moved about more and went outside for short walks. Her cough gradually subsided.

The family offered up prayers of thanks that her life had been spared and her health restored. Clementine and Marcel suspected that the power of Cadieux's stethoscope rather than Lepire's blessings wrought her recovery. Relief at Charlotte's improvement seemed also to have a beneficial effect on their relationship. Mutual affection returned and they were able to make love frequently with pleasure and satisfaction.

Chapter Nineteen

Arras, Late Summer 1816

Charles Cavigneau, now in his late sixties, was feeling his age. Overweight—he liked his food, always had, his hips and knees were painful and he had difficulty walking. Trifling events irritated him and he had a tendency to be somnolent, dropping off to sleep several times a day while seated in an armchair, head on his chest, snoring loudly. Pains arose in his chest, especially when he went for walks or became emotional or angry.

He and Pauline were sitting quietly having their evening meal, his portion twice that of his wife's, herself not a small woman, when they heard a gentle rap at the door. Charles rose slowly from his chair, shuffled across the room, opened it and saw a scraggly, dishevelled young man, of short stature with a bushy, unkempt beard, standing on the threshold. He immediately assumed this was a vagrant or a beggar asking for alms and was about to send him away angrily when, with a second look, he saw the eyes had a familiar squint. After a brief silence, followed by the shock of recognition, he exclaimed, "Demy!" Father and son burst into tears and hugged each other, with Pauline joining them when she heard the commotion at the door.

"We thought you were dead!" exclaimed Charles. "No one comes back from the Bagne of Toulon. How did you survive?"

Demy did not reply at once. Charles and Pauline saw that his lips and hands trembled and he struggled to find his words. They knew that because of his squint, he had a tendency to focus his eyes anywhere but towards the person to whom he spoke. This problem now appeared much worse and not only his eyes, but his mind focused elsewhere. "Come, sit down and calm yourself," his mother said with deep affection, her eyes still filled with tears.

"I do not like talking about it," replied Demy once seated, his eyes darting between objects in the room, his voice monotonous and barely audible. Words came haltingly, like droplets of water emerging sporadically from a leaky faucet. "I will just say this. We were treated like slaves. I have a number branded on my back – 568152. They didn't call us by name they called us by a number. Worked and punished, punished and worked. Starved, eating our own lice. Every day, someone died. Richard, Richard died from fever shortly after we arrived. I survived only because I met a priest, Père André, sent there because he had opposed the revolution and bonapartism. Through him, I came to God, to Faith and, eventually, to Love. Because of him, that wonderful priest, I learnt to endure suffering, by keeping quiet and hiding, forcing myself to eat the awful food. Père André died, painfully, from the dysentery." Demy stopped talking, while grief overtook his face. He drew a hand across it, as though wiping something off, started to talk, gave up, then started again.

"We were chained to the floor. Only one man ever escaped, helped by a prostitute, a few years before I arrived, a man called Eugéne François Vidocq. He was in the Bagne for theft and impersonating a nun. They say he came from here in Arras. Then the fever found me too. A guard, an older man who had survived the fever himself, took pity on me and brought me garlic herbs he grew in his garden. As the priest had asked me to, I survived. After ten years, after the end of my sentence, I asked for release but had to wait for the political situation here to settle. When I walked off the hulk, I kissed the soil in thanksgiving, ate the dirt that had stuck to my lips. I had no money, so I walked to the nearest church, and the priest there heard me out and gave me enough to take the coach to Arras, to you. Here I am."

Charles and Pauline who had listened speechlessly to this woeful tale, looked at each other, and Pauline shed fresh tears of both joy at having her son back, and sorrow, mixed with fury, at the ordeal he had undergone. Charles shook his head incredulously, and then said, "I know that man Vidocq. He used to live just around the corner here on the Rue du Mirroir-de-Venise. Believe it or not the Emperor appointed him Head of the Sûreté Nationale. From the Bagne of Toulon to Head of the National Police Force! Not many have accomplished that leap!"

They waited for Demy to speak again. "What happened to Plouffe and Girouette?" he asked.

"Plouffe? Girouette? Well, they both came to a bad end," replied Charles. "Plouffe died suddenly about four, no five years ago. His wife found him in the shop late in the day after it closed. When he did not come home she went to look for him. His head had fallen into the money box, so he died while counting the day's take. Girouette, they executed last year, shortly after Louis XVIII came to power. He became chief of police in Arras and there were many rumours about ill treatment of female suspects in prison, but nothing could be proven. Then one day, the Superintendent caught him assaulting a woman prisoner, in gaol for stealing a loaf of bread for her starving children, and they dragged him off. She later died. They arraigned him in Court and many witnesses and victims of his previous attacks came forward. He thought he might escape by swearing allegiance to the new king, Louis XVIII—this after he had previously sworn allegiance to Louis XVI, the Revolutionaries and Bonaparte. This time it did not work. They found him guilty and sent him to the guillotine."

"I am not disappointed," said Demy with bitterness, "I still have nightmares about those two. The town is better off without them." A rage passed over his features, tightening them.

His mother saw it. "My poor boy, I still cannot believe you are home!" Pauline went over to his chair and hugged him. "Let me prepare a hot bath for you and you can have some of your father's clean clothes. Meanwhile, I can prepare a potage for you."

"Yes, I would like that. Very much, Maman," he replied, with a weak but warm smile. "Potage."

Over the next few weeks Demy regained some weight, though he remained distant and lethargic. When addressed he would respond after long delays, sometimes unrelated to the topic being discussed. In the middle of one night, with the house at its most peaceful, he suddenly let out a piercing scream. Pauline rushed to his room and found him bolt upright in bed, eyes wide open, flailing his arms as if defending himself from attack, staring, and then pointing into the corner of the room as if someone were there, yet he was alone.

"What is it, mon fils? What is wrong?" she asked anxiously.

"Go away! Stop it! Stop it! I can't stand it!" he shouted, his body shaking violently, sweat pouring off his brow like tears of wine flowing down the inside of a glass.

"Demy, Demy, it is your Maman here with you, protecting you. No one will harm you!"

She placed her arm around his shoulder but he threw it off, shouting again, "Leave me alone! Go away! It is morning. The sun has risen. The wake-up gong is clanging. The call up for breakfast. Cold porridge. Awful coffee. The guards are shouting and cracking whips, screaming at the prisoners to hurry up."

"Demy, darling! No one will hurt you," Pauline cried. "You are home in Arras with your family. You are no longer on the hulk at Toulon. We will look after you!"

He ignored her, seemed not even to see her and continued crying out loudly. His agitation gradually subsided and he fell back on his bed, exhausted. She wiped the perspiration off his face, tucked him in and went back to her bed, trembling violently.

Demy woke up late next morning, feeling worn-out. He remembered being terrified during the night, though none of the details.

Charles slept in a room on the remote side of the house and had not heard the commotion. He shook his head in disbelief when Pauline recounted the events. "He must snap out of it," he said curtly. "What's happened has happened. You cannot change the past."

Pauline said nothing. She knew an argument would follow even a reasonable explanation. She felt a deep tenderness for her eldest son and the ordeal he had undergone, and said a silent prayer of thanksgiving that, after she had given him up for dead, he was now home. She intended to console and nurse him back to health. It shocked but did not surprise her that she needed to protect him even from her husband. Under his mother's ministrations, Demy slowly recovered a little weight and strength. He remained listless and frightened easily. An unexpected sound, especially a knock on the front door, would make him start, clutch the armrest or table, then sweat and tremble. A door rap would remind him of the gendarmes arriving at the house twelve years earlier to arrest him. He slept poorly and had several more night terrors.

Inwardly, he felt a conflict. The experiences on the Bagne at Toulon were still fresh in his mind, the physical pains that accompanied lashings, the skin eruptions that followed and the profound weakness and aching that went with various fevers. There he felt constant hunger with the desire and search for food an endless preoccupation. He experienced death on an almost daily basis, usually fellow convicts who were publicly executed for minor misdemeanours or attempts to escape, died of starvation or disease, or who just gave up. The hard realities of living in such a macabre environment somehow forced his survival. He knew also that he had a healthy modicum of good fortune, such as meeting Père André and the guard who provided the life-saving garlic. How is it possible that on the hulk at Toulon, I had the will to survive, surrounded by such suffering, yet here at home with warmth and comfort, I have given up? Yet, here he was back home, in a warm, nourishing environment, and unable to function, as though he could not let go the traumas of life in the penal colony, as though some force made him relive them every day, despite the comforts of home.

He became conscious of a volcano of anger welling within him, yet felt unable to express, or even channel it. Bizarrely, he also felt guilt. You only feel guilt when you do something wrong, he told himself. But what wrong had he committed? He had not even stolen the money from Plouffe's shop, the alleged crime for which they sent him to the Bagne. Why do I feel guilty? Then he thought of the gruesome deaths of Richard, Père André, and other

241

fellow convicts. Why is it that I have survived, and they did not? I should have gone with them. I have done nothing to merit survival. I feel bad that I am alive, eating, drinking, having a warm bed at night, and them? They died painful, miserable deaths, are buried in unknown graves, and have no one to grieve them. "I must join them," he repeated loudly to himself.

One evening Charles told his son brusquely, "Why do you not go out and get yourself a job?"

"I cannot Papa. I am scared of people. I am scared of everything," Demy said. The small spark he had had in his voice on arrival home now seemed to have left him.

"Sitting around the house being pampered by your mother does not seem to do much good either." Demy sensed the irritation in Charles' voice.

Listening to this dialogue Pauline could contain herself no longer. "Charles, stop this!" she shouted, bursting into tears. "The boy is sick. Can you not see! He has been through hell on earth. Life on the hulk has seared his soul, especially knowing he did not commit the robbery!" For a few moments Charles remained speechless. During their many years together Pauline had never once shouted at him in anger. He made the decisions and set the tone of their marriage, and she meekly complied.

"That boy must get off his arse, get out of the house and find work," he said loudly, pointing his finger at Demy. "If he cannot do that then send him to the asylum in Amiens. Perhaps meeting the other crazies there will teach him about life!" With fists clenched he left the room. Meanwhile, Demy curled up on the couch, saying nothing, lying on his side with arms clutched around his knees, eyes blinking. He had heard much shouting and bullying on the Bagne. Now back home, the same pattern repeated itself. Pauline went to sit on the couch beside him and placed her hand on his shoulder. "What is it we can do for you?"

"I do not know Maman. I feel weak and scared and cannot make decisions. For years I fought just to stay alive. Now I have no fight left in me. I just want to be left alone. It would have been better if I had been killed, or died from fever. I am good to no one."

"Demy! Listen, I love you. You are still young and your life is not over. Your strength and faith has helped you through this far. That strength and faith has not gone, it is still there, a vital part of you. You just need more time to rest and recover. I shall ask Dr Poirier to examine you and see if he can suggest a tonic that would bring back your energy. He is the best doctor in Arras. Do not concern yourself with what Papa says. He likes to have his own way, but when he knows it won't happen, he accepts and waits. We have been together nearly forty years, I know him well. On the outside he appears gruff and curt but if you scratch hard there is a soft heart inside." She smiled weakly, not entirely convinced by her own description of her husband.

Demy also smiled at this incongruous allusion. "I am thankful for what you are trying to do for me, Maman," he replied. "You help lessen my load. I would be glad to see Dr Poirier."

Dr Jean-Paul Poirier visited next day and after his examination said, speaking to both Pauline and Demy, "You have a condition known as hysterie nerveuse. It usually occurs in young females but I have seen it in males as well. It is commonly the result of unpleasant events and experiences. Sometimes it corrects itself over time, but the condition can last a life time, though that is rare. I know it is expensive, but I consider the best treatment is to take the waters at a maison de santé such as exists in the village of Spa, in the Ardennes Hills. You and the family can reflect on that. In any event I shall provide you with tonic medicine, a tisane de quinquinna. You will take a full tablespoonful in the morning and the evening. It has a bitter taste. If you follow this with a glass of sweet wine you will not perceive the bitterness as much. I also want you to rest during the day, and go for a brisk walk every afternoon. Finally, you must eat plenty of meat, bread and green vegetables. I want you to get some flesh to cover those skinny bones! I shall visit you again next week."

"We cannot afford for you to take the waters in Spa," Pauline said after the doctor's departure. Demy had already come to the same conclusion, and he nodded in agreement to his mother. "We will follow his other advice and hope that is sufficient."

Over the next few weeks Demy did gain some weight, but otherwise there were few changes in his condition. He continued to be listless and to have unprovoked attacks of fear during the day, during which he would breathe heavily, his heart would pound and he would sweat profusely. Most unpleasantly, he continued to have frequent nightmares when he would unknowingly scream in terror and re-experience the horrors of the Bagne. It would take Pauline almost to dawn to settle him down, but she remained patient and supportive. Charles, on the other hand, saw Demy's condition as weakness and to avoid confrontations, gave him a wide berth. Dr Poirier visited frequently and changed the tonic but there was little visible progress. Charles grumbled angrily about the cost of the doctor's visits with little evidence of progress.

Late one Sunday morning, a few months later, early in the spring of 1817, Pauline entered Demy's room and found him sitting shirtless before an open window, with the sun streaming in. It was early spring and the air dispersed a cold bite. Demy's head flopped forward on his chest. "What's wrong? Do you not feel well, mon fils?" she asked anxiously. Demy raised his head slowly, his face expressionless, and said in a monotonous tone, "I thought during the night, Maman. One other thing helped me survive the Bagne. For a while we were forced to work in a wooded area around the Armory in Toulon, clearing trees. Horses helped move the logs. Poor things, the guards flogged them even more than they did us prisoners. I became fond of a horse called Bonita. She gave me the only affection that I had after Richard and Père André died. I said goodbye to her sadly. She likely is dead now. A few days ago Papa mentioned that Marcel had a horse farm near Vimy. Would it be possible for us to visit the farm? I would like to see the horses."

"I shall speak to Papa. I am sure it will be possible. We have not seen them in a long time."

"Yes, I would like to see Clementine, Marcel and the children again," said Charles when Pauline approached him. "I do not know why he would want to see horses. They are only good for transport and warfare. I am not sure I can make the trip in my present condition, with my pains and discomfort, but you cannot go alone with Demy. I shall make arrangements for us to go to Vimy next week."

The next week Charles rented a horse and trap and the three made the trip on a sun-filled day.

"Look at that beautiful copse of huge plane trees," Pauline said with forced animation, speaking to no one in particular. "They must be hundreds of years old."

"Yes," replied Charles curtly without turning around. Demy did not even raise his eyes to look at the trees. Pauline made another, equally unsuccessful attempt to engage her husband and son in conversation and thereafter, they completed the rest of the journey in silence. The trio arrived at Vimy late in the morning. Not having heard about his return from the Bagne, and not recognising him until they were told, Clementine and Marcel were overjoyed to see Demy again. They showered him with kisses and hugs, to which he responded with a wan smile.

"When did you return? How did you survive?" asked Clementine. She continued, "You look so pale and so thin, Demy. It must have been awful. We are so glad to see you again!" Demy again smiled weakly but did not reply.

"He has been very ill since his return," explained Pauline. "He saw Dr Poirier who gave him tonics. So far, they've not helped much. We can no longer afford the cost of his visits. Dr Poirier recommended water treatment at Spa but we cannot afford that either. Last week Demy told us he wanted to see your horses so that is why we are here. Of course, we also wanted to see you and visit our grandchildren."

"Great," replied Marcel. "Let us have lunch, and then I'll take Demy to the stables."

Throughout the meal Demy only spoke when directly addressed, and even then as briefly as he could. But Marcel saw his mood change as they walked on the trail to the stables. "What got you interested in horses, Demy?" Marcel asked.

"I worked with a horse called Bonita at Toulon," Demy replied. "After all my human friends had died she became the closest thing to a friend I had. I treated her gently so she was very faithful."

This was the most he had said all day, talking almost at a trot, and Marcel kept up the pace. "Horses really are, once they trust you," he said, with feeling. They entered the stable and Marcel watched Demy as he approached each horse. He saw him making soft cooing noises with his arm stretched out, calling out the horse's name and allowing it to sniff the back of his hand. Then he bent down to collect some hay from the floor of the stable and offered it to each horse in the palm of his hand. One neighed gratefully in response, while Demy gently rubbed its forehead with appreciation.

"You seem to have a way with horses, Demy," said Marcel. Demy nodded in agreement, all modesty set aside. Then he surprised Marcel by asking, directly, "Could I stay here and help you look after them?"

"I would like that Demy. I am impressed with the way you handle the horses. Let us talk with your parents and see if we can work out an arrangement."

Pauline and Charles were pleased and silently relieved at the plan for Demy to remain in Vimy at Les Érables. Marcel asked Charles to send him ten francs a month to help defray some of the expenses of keeping Demy clothed and fed, to which Charles readily agreed.

Pauline and Charles had barely entered the buggy to return home when he accosted her, "Well, it is not a paying job but at least he is out of our house. Ten francs a month is not much to pay for that advantage." Pauline noticed but did not reply to the cutting tone in his voice. Her lower lip protruded but her face remained otherwise expressionless. She turned and saw her son speaking with his new employer. She waved but Demy did not see her. She and her surly husband completed the rest of the journey in stony silence.

Next day Marcel took Demy on a tour around the farm. The horses he had already met. Marcel showed him the chicken run and sheep, the animal pastures and the potagerie maintained by Clementine. The sun shone on a beautiful spring day, wildflowers covered the meadows, birds were nesting and singing lustily and a flock of sparrows murmured in the hedgerows. At the end of the tour they returned to the stables where Marcel said, "What do you know about the care of horses, Demy, the daily routines of the stables?"

"Just a little," he replied, without looking at Marcel.

"It means keeping them well fed and watered, and making sure they have plenty of exercise, at least thirty minutes daily. They also have to be kept clean and well brushed. Most important is the care of their hooves. Inspect them each day and remove stones, dirt and other objects that get lodged there. Twice a day, morning and evening, you will muck out the stables. Horses eat constantly hence produce a large amount of manure. Place it in this heap outside the stable. Later we use it as fertilizer in the fields."

From his experience with horses at Toulon, Demy knew only that horses had to be fed and watered. The constant attendance to the health and cleanliness of a horse was a whole new arena of knowledge that he felt keen to gain. "Show me how to do that?" he asked, frequently. Patient with him, Marcel saw he needed only one demonstration. He showed Demy how to brush a horse's coat, comb its mane and lift each of its legs to remove objects from the hoof. Demy saw the purpose in the grooming. "It will help me get to know the horse better and make it trust me," he told Marcel.

"Correct. The more a horse likes and trusts you, the more it will follow your lead and your orders." As they were walking back to the house Marcel asked, "Demy, can you tell me about the Bagne?" Demy remained silent for a moment, felt his heart beginning to palpate and sweat forming on his brow. "I do not wish to talk about it. Things were bad, very bad. No one lives long on the Bagne."

"I can see you know how to handle horses." Marcel sensed Demy's reaction then added quietly, "They are such powerful and proud beasts. Human civilization would never have accomplished what it has without their assistance. It saddens me to see them mistreated and slaughtered in war. Without horses it would take weeks, if not months, to travel from one end of France to the other. They are essential also for ploughing fields and sowing crops. Without them, how would we produce enough food for our people?"

Demy did not respond. Reference to the Bagne had caused him to shut out Marcel's equine musings. Quite suddenly he saw himself back on the hulk, a guard screaming at him while whipping his back. He cowered down and began to shake and whimper, "Go away, stop beating me. I'm doing all I can."

Marcel placed his arm on Demy's shoulder and asked reassuringly, "What is wrong, my dear brother?" Demy threw Marcel's arm off his shoulder and said, glaring at him angrily "Don't touch me. You're hurting me."

"Don't yell at me. I have no wish to hurt you," Marcel said loudly. After a moment's silence he added quietly, "I've been through rough times myself and know what it is like to feel pain. We cannot purge painful memories from our minds, but must not allow them to fester. We have to learn to rise above them."

"I have lived in hell on earth." Demy spoke through his teeth, sweating profusely, as if, at that very moment, he was living through the fire of the Bagne. "We were not people, we were animals, lower than slaves. When you are treated like an animal you become one, even if you were not one before."

"I think I understand, Demy. I have been impressed how well you treat our horses and learn as quickly as a young child learns a language. You have a natural flair, especially the fact you have had so little experience. I am pleased you are here to help us, and I believe it will benefit you as well.

"Demy, I would like to recite you a poem. It is a fable called 'The Lion and the Rat' by the great poet Jean de la Fontaine. My mother taught me the poem when I was a boy. Here it is.

'It's well to please all people when you can;
There's none so small but one his aid might need.
Here are two fables if you give good heed,
Will prove the truth to any honest man.

A rat in quite a foolish way,
Crept from his hole between a lion's paws;
The king of animals showed on that day
His royalty, and never snapped his jaws.
The kindness was repaid;
Yet, who'd have thought a lion might need aid
From a poor rat?

Soon after that
The lion in the forest brake,
In their strong snares the hunters take;
In vain his roars, his frenzy, and his rage.
But Mr. Rat runs up; a mesh or two
Nibbles, and lets the lion through

Patience and length of time sever,
What empty wrath could never.'

Marcel remained silent for a few moments after completing his poem to allow its message to sink in. "I think I get it," Demy replied eventually. "Even if I am small and weak I have strengths. Being angry does not solve problems and being patient often does."

"Absolutely correct," replied Marcel with a broad grin. "Let's go and have supper."

Demy smiled in response and his agitation gradually subsided as they ambled slowly back to the house. He remained silent and pensive throughout the evening meal. The four children were noisy and playful as ever and were chastised by Clementine, but the family commotion did not seem to affect Demy. It was as if he had a wall around him, shutting out the world. She attempted, without success, to engage him in light conversation. Marcel remained content to lessen the pressure by ignoring him. Yet he also felt a certain apprehension about Demy's unpredictable behaviour, and the possibility that he might lash out at one of the children, or hurt himself but not the horses. He knew he could never harm them.

Chapter Twenty

The St. Lawrence River, Canada, Spring 1796

Following a rough Atlantic crossing of more than a month, the fleet of five English frigates entered the river named the St. Lawrence by Jacques Cartier in the sixteenth century. They were the first ships in after break-up of the winter freeze. Large chunks of blue-white ice, some the size of small hills, were still adrift in the St. Lawrence River. The ships' captains carefully avoided collisions with the biggest of them, not an easy task as the ships were heading into both the westerly winds and the river's current. Tacking, sometimes abruptly, for two days, all five arrived below the citadel at Quebec, on the cliffs at a narrow point in the river, and anchored safely. Several hundred prospective settlers divided evenly among the five frigates disembarked, some to remain in the city others to carry on. Calm now, the city had seen more than its fair share of conflict, the last only twenty years earlier when the Americans had attempted to capture it. Unlike the English, twenty years before, the Americans failed to breach the walled city. The ships remained in Québec a long week, waiting for the ice to clear further upstream and then sailed in a line up to Montréal, where all the remaining passengers disembarked. Among them was Father Claude Ladouceur, formerly a resident of Arras, now around thirty years of age.

Apart from the sailing itself, Ladouceur's struggle to reach Canada had been long and eventful. Shortly after the wedding of Clementine and Marcel in August, 1795, he had decided to leave his native France, for how long he did not know. The memory of The Reign of Terror and persecution of priests was still fresh in his mind, and he remained fearful of his security as he had refused to sign the oath of allegiance to the Republican regime. Besides, he was aware that many priests of his Sulpician order had fled to Canada before him. He would find them there and wait out the threat. Once he had made the decision, he informed only Catherine Lachêne, Pauline and Charles Cavigneau and one fellow priest of his intentions. Yes, he was sorrowed to be leaving, but he fully intended returning to France once the political situation stabilised. And so one morning before the sun had risen, he left Arras quietly on a rented horse heading for the channel seaport of Boulogne-sur-Mer. Once there he quickly connected with other priests and refugees from the Revolution whose intentions matched his own. Together they purchased a large rowboat and one dark night, with the sea relatively calm, they set off from a beach at nearby Wimereux to cross the Channel. The group landed on a pebble beach near Folkestone early next morning, cold, wet and exhausted. To their utter dismay an English sentry immediately arrested them all and imprisoned them as spies.

Ladouceur had papers confirming his priestly status, but papers were easily forged and not readily believed. For several weeks - he counted twenty-two sunrises—he remained in prison, awaiting investigation of his case. Just when beginning to slide into despair and his prayers seemingly futile, the authorities allowed him to present his papers to Bishop Douglass, Vicar Apostolic in London, for confirmation. The next day, quicker than he could have hoped for, word came through his cell door that the Bishop confirmed their authenticity and they reluctantly set him free, with the proviso that he report to the police weekly. For months he lived with a community of hundreds of émigré French priests, all supported by the English government, until at last he secured permission to emigrate to Canada. Ladouceur spent the winter in London learning English and left for North America in April of 1796.

On arrival at the dock in Montréal, Ladouceur left the ship and stood on the cobblestoned quay and waited until the chaos of disembarkation had died down to a gentler rhythm. The weather that morning was cold and clear, with patches of unmelted snow still lining the streets. There had been overnight rain and he breathed in the air of this vast new land, filling his lungs with its fresh woody aroma. Looking north, he discerned from the number of visible steeples in the skyline that, as he had been told, Montréal was a substantial, growing city, already populated by many thousands. Some he had met on the ship from Quebec, and they reassured him that although the English had won Nouvelle France a generation earlier—one of the older men had been a boy when Montréal fell, bloodlessly—French was still the language of the street, and even some of the English in their counting houses spoke it, although their accent hurt your ears. Turning to gaze at the river, Ladouceur saw on the south side only a sparsely inhabited shoreline. The Indians lived there, in a place whose name he had not been able to pronounce. He was anxious to see un vrai sauvage. He had only heard of them from returning priests who had been on missions to bring these godless people into the arms of St. Peter. For a moment, as the bustle of the docks began to swell again with the arrival of a ship from London, he went back over the journey that had brought him here. Had he been wise to allow his fear, alloyed with his resurgent sense of adventure, to make such a drastic decision? He would know better, he told himself, when he had been here a few days, Checking in his shoulder bag, Ladouceur retrieved the instructions and letters of introduction he had been given in France to present to the Father Superior of the seminary. Turning back, he began the short walk to the rue Notre Dame. In the distance, at the foot of the long dead volcano known as Mont Royal, he could see the twin towers of the Fort de la Montagne, once a mission to Christianize les sauvages, now a peasant commune.

As he turned onto Rue Notre Dame, Ladouceur paused again to take in the massive stone structure before him. The Séminaire St. Sulpice stood solid and imposing, already over a century old. Ladouceur read the time on the square clock, with its prominent roman numerals, near the top of the tower. It had taken him most of the day to get here and dusk was setting in. Soon it would be Vespers. He went up to the front door of the Séminaire, pulled the door-bell handle and heard a loud ding-dong sound coming from the interior as if echoing from the inside of a church. A young man, dressed simply in lay clothing, came to the door and Ladouceur introduced himself and asked to see the Father Superior, Gabriel-Jean Brassier. Brassier had been assigned to Canada a full forty years earlier, and had built a reputation as a humble and discreet man, always concerned about his pastoral responsibilities.

After a minute or two, there was the sound of feet moving along a corridor. Ladouceur expected the young man to re-emerge, but Brassier himself appeared in a black soutane with a girdle around his middle and a rectangular white tab tucked into the front of his collar, and set out towards him across the entrance lobby. Ladouceur had time to take in his unattractive but kindly features, the diffident smile and the greying hair combed back down to his shoulders with a bald patch above his forehead, clearly a man of humble confidence. Brassier invited Ladouceur to sit down in a simple chair while the latter explained his background and arrival in Montréal whilst Brassier remained standing. As Ladouceur completed his story, Brassier gave him a firm pat on the shoulder, "I am so glad you have come. The political disturbances have made us desperately short of priests. We have lots of work for you, believe me. I also want you to meet Monsieur Joseph Papineau," Brassier added with fervour, "our leading Canadian citizen. He has an excellent education in both land-surveying and the law, went into politics, and has represented a Montréal riding in the House of Assembly since 1792. It is entirely because of his influence and the force of his character and arguments that proceedings of the debates in the House are now recorded in both French and English. A group of powerful English-speaking politicians and merchants wished them to be recorded in English alone. He does much work for the

Séminaire and gives us good rates. We have invited him with his lovely wife Rosalie to lunch here on Saturday. Perhaps you would like to join us?" Brassier smiled as he mentioned Rosalie.

"Thank you, Reverend Father," replied Ladouceur, thrilled at being so welcomed, rising now and giving the Father a small bow. "That would give me great pleasure." Brassier gave him a nod in return and summoned the young man to show Ladouceur to the small bare cell that would be his living quarters for the duration of his stay in Montréal. The cell, at most ten feet square, was furnished with a bed, table, chair and a small drape-less window. A crucifix above the head of the bed adorned the otherwise bare white walls.

"I am pleased to meet you both, Monsieur and Madame Papineau," Ladouceur said after the introductions. "Father Superior has told me much about your accomplishments." Both in their early to mid-forties, Joseph Papineau had a medium stature, stolid build, penetrating eyes and curved, pointed nose, and Madame, attractive, clear features with dress a la mode. Ladouceur saw Madame eyeing him admiringly making him conscious of his youth and good looks.

"I did what I had to do, what had to be done," replied Papineau firmly. "If you don't fight for your rights, no one else will. I came from a poor background and know what it is to be cold and hungry. I learnt to use my wits at an early age and learned also the value of hard work."

"Joseph and I married nearly twenty years ago," added Madame Papineau. "We have four children, three boys and a daughter, all healthy and doing well. Our family is important to us both."

Ladouceur drew in his breath with admiration for this warm-hearted couple who had struggled through the myriad of political and social changes that occurred during their generation, and come out on top. Nodding his head with approval, he said, "I can see it has not been easy for you. I am full of respect for someone who has started with nothing and built a successful life."

"Joseph took a lead role amongst Canadians," added Madame Papineau, speaking in a resolute and authoritative voice. "And I supported him strongly. Yet his heart is not in politics. He has too many other interests, such as business, land surveying and real estate, and of course his family."

Papineau nodded in agreement and added, raising his right arm to point in a westerly direction, "It is my aim in due course to purchase a property in La Petite Nation area on the Ottawa River about sixty miles west of Montreal, and there establish an Estate. It is a lovely part of the country with rivers, mountains and waterfalls."

Brassier invited them to be seated for lunch and a lay man servant, the same young man who had opened the door to Ladouceur on his arrival, brought the meal and wine, serving each of the guests and replenishing the glasses.

As they sat down Papineau asked, "Ladouceur, some ten years ago we had the visit here in Montreal of a Monsieur Pierre Tremblais, a businessman from France, from your city of Arras, I believe, in textiles. I got to know him well and had some dealings with him. A real gentleman and a good businessman. What happened to him?"

"That is a tragic story," replied Ladouceur. "I knew Tremblais well as my close friend Charles Cavigneau worked for him in his linen factory, the best in the city. The Revolutionaries executed him two years ago. He belonged to a political group called the Girondins and when Robespierre and the Jacobins took over the country, they purged all the Girondins, not only in Paris but in the whole country. Thousands were murdered including such innocent and great individuals as Antoine Lavoisier and Olympe de Gouges."

"How awful. What monsters they are. I have to say, that whether we like it or not the Revolution is a remarkable historical event that had huge repercussions even here in Canada," replied Papineau. "At the outset we Canadians strongly supported it, especially the call for liberty and democracy, much to the dismay of the English authorities. The English, as I'm sure you know, take a dim view of angry rebels. However when they executed King Louis we turned resolutely against the Revolutionaries. Within minutes, just like that," he added, flicking his fingers. "At heart we are Royalists, so now we support King George and our English administration. This fact strengthened our arguments when it came to getting our language rights." Papineau called the servant over and asked for his wine glass to be refilled. He then cleaned out the ash in the bowl of his pipe, getting up to empty the ash in a nearby wastepaper basket.

"And what about Queen Marie-Antoinette and her unfortunate children?" asked Madame Papineau, her mouth contorted with ire. "They executed her and killed the young dauphin in prison. 'Monster' is a modest word to describe the magnitude of their malice. They have Satan in their souls!"

"Madame Papineau," exclaimed Ladouceur in reply, raising and gesturing with his arms enthusiastically, "I agree with you and that is why I am here! There are signs that the situation may be easing in France but there is still a long way to go. I am excited about being in Canada. What an extraordinary experiment to see whether French Catholics and English Protestants can live together. After the vicious religious wars of the last few centuries it will be a test of Christian charity and patience, if nothing else. Perhaps the new-found English talent for tolerance will assist this collaboration."

"I see you are still a young idealist, Père Ladouceur," replied Joseph Papineau with a paternalistic smile and a gesture of his hands. "I am not so sanguine. The merchants here in Montréal are refugees from the United States. They are extreme English chauvinists, and are few but powerful. They have little tolerance, want more power and are more stubborn than oxen. We Canadians will have to fight for our rights. Fortunately we have the numbers, our numbers will grow quickly and we will use them! Curiously, I see our English colonial status as protective of our culture. If we became a state, the Americans would swallow us up in no time."

"I may be an idealist but I am also a rebel," replied Ladouceur with a smile, looking guiltily in the direction of his Superior, who nodded but did not respond. He had not told Brassier that he had left Arras secretly without the knowledge or permission of his superiors. With the administrative chaos of the Church in France, he hoped his disappearance would not be missed, at least not too quickly.

"That is of little concern," replied Papineau. "In one sense we are all rebels in North America, the English, the French and the Americans. Even the Indians, though they came here a long time before we did. So you will feel much at home."

By this time the lunch had been completed and Monsieur and Madame Papineau rose to leave. "I am pleased to have met you, Ladouceur," Monsieur concluded. "I am sure you will be an excellent addition to the meagre numbers of Sulpicians in Canada. We hope you will achieve success in all your undertakings. Au revoir."

"Au revoir, Père Ladouceur," added Madame Papineau embracing him with a broad smile and looking at his handsome features with admiration, "I too am pleased to have met you. I can see you are a very talented young man and have no doubt your ministry will be a success."

Ladouceur remained in Montréal for two years, working in city parishes under Brassier's supervision and teaching at the Séminaire when invited. During this period he became friendly with a number of his parishioners including particularly a Monsieur Thomas and Madame Laure Coupé. In their mid-thirties, Thomas worked as a fur trader with the North West Company. Laure had borne five children three of whom had survived infancy. The couple had attended and enjoyed Ladouceur's services and sermons and met him at church functions. They invited him to lunch in their home one Saturday in the summer of 1797. Ladouceur walked the half-mile distance from the Séminaire to their house, a two-storey wood-panelled home surrounded by a large well-maintained and fenced flower garden. A gardener tilled the soil and he bid bonjour to him as he walked up to the front door.

"Welcome to our home," said Laure as she opened the door with a smile, Thomas standing next to her at the entrance. "May we call you Claude?"

"Why, yes of course," Claude replied also with a broad smile. Thomas had a tall, lean frame, well-trimmed beard and moustache and friendly open demeanour. Laure wore a long ankle-length grey and white skirt with tight-fitting red and white jacket and low neckline. Her dark, curly hair extended down to well below her shoulders. He perceived also her attractive, lively features. Claude wore a plain black suit with a clerical collar.

Laure flicked her hair out of her eyes with her hand and then threw her head back seductively while saying, "You seem to have settled down well in Montréal, Claude. Both Thomas and I enjoy your sermons on Sundays. They give us much to think about. You speak so well and so clearly. It must have taken many years of training. And you preach without notes. How do you remember what to say?"

"Thank you kindly. It is easy because I speak from the heart. Yes, I love the city. It has much to offer. People are so hospitable."

"That is true," replied Thomas firmly. "When you live in an isolated community you have to collaborate otherwise you sink without trace. Our fur business depends heavily on collaboration. Our voyageurs spend months in canoes on the lakes and rivers of Canada trading with Indian tribes. We get some ass-holes amongst the voyageurs but they do not last long. They leave or get croaked."

Claude's mouth dropped open at Thomas' blunt language and he saw Laure looking at him intently as she asked, "Why did you leave France? Do you have family?"

"I was born and raised in Amiens where my family still resides. My ministry was in nearby Arras and I had a wide circle of friends there and felt sadness to say farewell to them. I left because of the political situation and sought adventure, and chose Canada because of language and culture."

"How interesting," replied Laure with fervour. "I would love to visit France but am sure that will never happen because of the endless wars. I'll just have to depend on enchanting stories from interesting travellers like you." Laure again smiled at Claude, who saw her lips quivering slightly and eyes glistening, while he felt a moistening of the palms of his hands and armpits.

"Personally, I have no desire to go to France," Thomas countered emphatically, almost angrily. "France treated us Canadians shamefully after the Conquest. The Revolution has shown they are just a bunch of shits. We'll make our own way in the world. So far England has treated us well, likely because it needs us to buck the United States. We can only hope that continues."

Thomas' spirited intervention gave Laure a few seconds to collect herself so she announced that lunch was ready to be served. They retired to the dining room and a maid-servant attended them for the meal during which conversation was prosaic.

As Claude left the house to walk back to the Séminaire, his heart palpitated with anxiety. Until now I've been able to govern my passions. I like this woman Laure, and she seems to like me. I hope and pray that temptation does not overpower me!

A week later a sealed letter arrived for Claude at the Séminaire St. Sulpice. He took it to open in the privacy of his cell and read,

'Dear Claude,

It made me happy to meet you for lunch last week. You seem such a calm and cultivated person while I am surrounded by philistines! I wish to get to know you better.

Thomas is away on business in Quebec next week and the children are at school. Could you come for lunch say on Tuesday? You need not reply to this note as I know it is difficult for you to communicate quietly. If you come, you come. If you cannot, I will understand.
With all my affection
Laure.'

Claude lay down on his bed to ponder his choices. As a teenager he had struggled with sexual issues, yet at the time these were only of a personal nature. Educated in a boys-only school, and later in the seminary, he had little contact with girls other than his siblings. The oldest of six children from a devout Catholic family, it had been expected of him from an early age that he would be destined for the priesthood. He longed and prayed for sanctity and believed he found it, or at least its general direction, during his long training in the seminary, and eventually secured control over his passions. Because of the disruption of Church administration during the Revolution, he performed his priestly functions in Arras in relative isolation with little overseeing, and from the responses received, he knew he performed them well. Yet here a totally new situation presented itself. He knew if he sought advice from his superior he would be told not to visit Laure under any circumstances. Yet he had a strong urge to taste what had been forbidden. He thought of Adam in the Garden of Eden. He still had a few days to make his decision and reminded himself that one of his reasons for coming to Canada was to seek adventure. This could be an adventure as none other!

Claude arrived at Laure's home at noon the following Tuesday. After closing the door they fell into each other's arms and Claude quickly felt his rising sexual urges, strongly stimulated by Laure's affectionate caressing. After several minutes Claude gently disengaged and said, "Laure, before anything happens we must do some talking so we know what we are getting into. I am a priest and have made a lifelong vow of chastity that I had every intention of keeping when made. You are a well and happily married woman with children. If what we are planning to do came out in the open it would be an unmitigated calamity for us both."

"I realise that, Claude," replied Laure tearfully. "My marriage is not happy as you think. Thomas is away a lot. He shows me little affection, even on his return from long trips. I am as cold as a fish when I go with him. I strongly suspect he has at least one mistress. I no longer love him, if I ever did! I want you!"

"I am touched by what you say, Laure," replied Claude. "But I cannot be a substitute for your husband. I cannot, and will not give up my priesthood. Too much of my devotion and my life's energy has been put into it. Moreover, I actually love what I do! It gives me huge satisfaction helping people find their God and their way in life. It would be hypocritical for me to have one life in public and another in private. I could not do it, even assuming we could have an extended affair in this small city without it being discovered!"

Laure remained silent for some moments pondering Claude's words. "I love my children but have little desire to remain with Thomas. I understand your calling to the priesthood and know you do it well, as I've told you. I understand the disastrous results if we were discovered, for me as much as for you. I care for you. You are gentle and thoughtful, so different from other men I know! And you are so good-looking. I cannot believe that a pretty girl never snagged you before you took your priestly vows; if only we could have met when we were younger. I wish the Church would change the rule that priests cannot marry! Claude," she added, speaking slowly and firmly, enunciating each word, "There is one thing you can do that will help me stay with Thomas and live without you. Give me your child! That way a piece of you will remain with me always. When I hold and caress your child I will see and feel you!" Laure looked firmly into Claude's eyes.

He felt as if a cannon ball had hit his gut. Throughout my life, despite much temptation, I have tried not to think of myself making love to a woman.

Even less have I thought of myself as a father to a baby! "Laure. You shock me! I care for you deeply and wish to love you. I feel love for you! I love your eyes, your mouth, and the warmth of your hugs and caresses. How can we make love once, or twice, to have a baby, and then not see each other again?"

"It will be hard for us both, Claude," Laure continued to speak fervently. But it will be less hard than saying goodbye now and never seeing you again. It will also be less hard than seeing you often, which my heart wants me to do, and our affair then coming out in the open as will certainly happen, with all its fateful consequences!"

"I think you are right, Laure," mused Claude. "Another big question bothers me. If you do come with child what will you tell it about its father? I have seen so many children, and grown-up people that do not know who their fathers are and are unhappy about this."

"I will just pretend that Thomas is its father," she replied without hesitation. The child will have brothers and sisters. All will seem to have the same father."

"I do not like that, Laure," replied Claude firmly. "I would like you to tell the child the truth."

Laure paused a long time before replying, "At a certain age, when it is old enough, I will do that Claude, for you." She added with a smile.

During the discussion about these practical matters, Claude's urges had cooled. Now that all issues had been resolved, he felt them rising again and they kissed and embraced passionately. Laure then got up, took Claude's hand and led him to the bedroom where, under her direction, they consummated their love.

As Claude walked back later to his cell in the Séminaire, slowly through the lonely streets of Montreal, he shook his head with disbelief at what he had done. I have broken my vow of chastity. I feel guilt, yes, and will have to confess. Yet I also have a keen sense of satisfaction and accomplishment. I feel a completed man now that I have tasted sexual ecstasy! I would never have thought I could have done that. Laure is a remarkable woman. I wish I could possess her. Thomas is a fortunate man even if he does not know it. Claude went to confess his sin of adultery to his superior, Father Brassier. He thought Brassier would be shocked, perhaps even excommunicate him. In the confessional however, Brassier remained serene as if he had heard this story many times before. When Claude assured him this would not happen again, he gave him absolution and applied an appropriate penance.

For the next few weeks he saw nothing of Laure but she remained in his mind almost constantly. About three months after their tryst she came to the church where he had said Mass that Sunday. After the service, as they were leaving the church he saw her smiling, nodding her head at him and secretly giving him the "thumbs-up" sign. He smiled quietly in response.

In the summer of 1798 Brassier had a stroke that paralysed his right side rendering him unable to speak. He died one month later. Jean-Henri-Auguste Roux succeeded Brassier as Superior of the Séminaire St. Sulpice. Roux had fled France for Switzerland in 1791, and three years later went to England, then on to Canada. Shortly after Brassier's death, a large group of French aristocrats led by Joseph-Geneviéve, Comte de Puisaye arrived in Montréal with the intention of settling permanently in Canada. The English Government had decided to send them on to Upper Canada in the region around the town of York where they would be given tracts of land to farm as pioneers and be a bulwark against any attempted takeover of the area by the United States. The Government hoped it would be the first of a large-scale immigration of French émigrés to Upper Canada. Roux asked Claude if he would like to accompany the group to York and Upper Canada as their pastor and he readily accepted. By this time he had resigned himself to not continuing any relationship with Laure. He knew that she had gone through a pregnancy and given birth to a daughter. Shortly before his departure he met Laure and Thomas after Mass one Sunday and briefly coddled the baby whom Laure had called Claudine. He looked at the baby's brown eyes and dark hair, like his, and shook his head. I am overwhelmed! This is my own girl, part of me. I am so proud. O God! I thank you for your goodness in sending Laure to me!

Claude met de Puisaye on one of the small barques that transported the group up river to Lake Ontario. He perceived de Puisaye's sharp aristocratic bearing and dress, high forehead, small mouth and widely spaced eyes. Claude told him about his flight from France three years previously and recounted some of his activities since arrival. "How did you come to leave France?" Claude asked in reply.

"Before the Revolution I was a lieutenant in the army and through marriage in 1788, I acquired a large property in Normandy," de Puisaye replied. "A year later they elected me to the Estates General that met in Versailles in 1789. I played an active role representing the Second Estate, the aristocracy, in the initial deliberations. My politics is liberal so I tried, with some success, to work with liberal elements in the Third Estate, the ordinary people. When the extremist Jacobins took over I vanished from Paris, became a counter-revolutionary and joined a royalist army in Normandy. The English supplied us with money and equipment... "

"The Jacobins must have loved you for that," Claude interjected ironically.

De Puisaye smiled, nodded and then continued. "I left for England in 1794 with a plan to raise an army of émigrés to invade France and hopefully start a general insurrection. In June and again in September the following year, we crossed over to Normandy with an English fleet. Our numbers were paltry compared to what we had been promised and on both occasions I had men under my command who subverted my orders so we were defeated with much loss of life. The French were more brutal than bears. They executed prisoners on the spot, no questions, no trial. They blamed me for the defeats and even falsely accused me of cowardice for leaving the army and returning to England before the end of the battle. I could never do such a thing. I did this only to return essential documents and reports concerning the invasion. Nevertheless King Louis forced me to resign. I had no future in France, or with the émigrés in England. In addition my wife Louise had died and I had no attachments other than my faithful servant Susanna, so decided to come to Canada with my supporters and here I am!"

"I suspect your invasion was doomed from the start," replied Claude, speaking in a serious, reassuring tone. "Especially if you lacked the army you had been promised. The French army is galvanised and more determined than a hungry wolf. Though I cannot understand why, perhaps it is fear; the army seems to have the support of many peasants. Why did you choose an isolated, wilderness spot like York in Upper Canada rather than come to Quebec or Montreal?"

"There is a good reason. We are all aristocrats from good families in France. Many can trace their ancestry back to the Middle Ages. We consider ourselves superior to Canadians in Lower Canada who are descendants of peasants and poor people, even from prostitutes sent out by King Louis XIV from Normandy, Brittany and Paris. These women were known as Les Petites Filles du Roi. They were the dregs of French society. Our association with Canadians would not have worked. The social differences were too wide and there would have been too much friction. I am looking forward to starting a new life in Upper Canada, building a home and starting a farm, just like a pioneer," added de Puisaye, his eyes bright with enthusiasm. Here in North America there is no history to drown us, as in Europe!"

Looking closely at de Puisaye, in a rare cynical moment, Claude replied, "Something else will likely happen to submerge you. This is a rough country that brings unexpected surprises, including drownings, especially when you are tilling new soil."

"That is exactly what we will be doing when we reach York," he said smiling at Claude's jeu de mots, and rubbing his hands with satisfaction, while ignoring Claude's pessimistic prophesies. "But I am optimistic. The English Government has been supportive and I'm told the farmland around York is fertile and the climate much milder than Montréal."

"We can but hope and pray," replied Claude, thinking it appropriate to end the conversation on a spiritual, and positive note. In his heart he suspected there would be many drenchings, perhaps even drownings amongst the new settlers. They seemed to him poorly prepared for an adventure in a god-forsaken wilderness.

The barques sailed up the St. Lawrence River and entered Lake Ontario, anchoring briefly at the small village of Kingston. Its most prominent feature was the spire of the newly built St George's church but de Puisaye spied, with nostalgia, the ruins of the Fort Frontenac, now partly rebuilt and called the Tête de Bois Barracks. A naval depot, headquarters of the Provincial Marine was sited at Point Frederick at the east end of the town. The fleet of small ships then continued their voyage along the north shore of Lake Ontario and arrived at York on a dull, overcast and sleety day in December. At the time, York's population was fewer than one thousand people, many being in the military. In 1793, Colonel Simcoe, the first Lieutenant-Governor, proclaimed York as capital of the new territory of Upper Canada. De Puisaye perceived its beautiful natural harbour, and the two large wooden defensive blockhouses that dominated its eastern and western ends. The town extended up to the Don River in the east and the large edifice of Fort York had been built right on the waterfront to the west of the town, just opposite the entrance to the bay. From the barques he could view just one church spire near the centre of the town.

De Puisaye and each of his companions were assigned a lot of land along Yonge Street at Windham, about fifteen miles north of the town. Government officials provided them with rustic shelter for the winter and seeds and tools for the spring. They set about felling trees, clearing brush and building log cabins, initially with great enthusiasm, and about twelve cabins were completed. Much of the enthusiasm vanished in the spring when the rains and mud rendered the roads all but impassable. None of the group had had experience with sowing, growing and cultivating foodstuffs and pasture.

Claude visited de Puisaye in his sparsely furnished log cabin in late spring. He saw that de Puisaye lived alone in the cabin with Susanna. "Well, how have you settled?" he asked.

"Very poorly. Everything that can go wrong has gone wrong." De Puisaye spoke curtly, even brusquely. "We are all exhausted from cutting down trees and clearing brush. Wild animals, bears, wolves, deer, broke through the fences we built and ate all the crops we planted. When it rains, Yonge Street becomes a muddy stream where a boat would be of more use than a horse, so we can travel nowhere. The Government is no help, just tells us to work harder and everything will be all right. I have purchased a lot near Niagara and will be moving there shortly." .

Claude frowned and shook his head disapprovingly. "Monsieur le Comte de Puisaye," he stated with gravitas. "You cannot do that. You are the leader of this group. If there are difficulties it is your responsibility to show the way out and put things right, even if it takes time. Moving to Niagara is running away like a coward."

"It's easy for you to talk like that, Ladouceur," de Puisaye replied angrily. "You have a cushy life with food, warmth and clothing provided to you. I have had to fight in the world for everything that I have got. Everyone from kings and governments, to colleagues and so-called friends in the army, to servants and underlings are trying to destroy me. Only dear Susanna here has been faithful to me. Last year we secretly got married." He moved over and gave Susanna a solid hug.

"And you have been so good to me, Sir." Susanna bowed her head obediently in de Puysaye's direction after they had disengaged. "I will do anything for you and follow you anywhere."

"So there you see, Ladouceur. Susanna and I are off to Niagara next week and will make our home and fortune there."

Claude again shook his head sadly, decided he had nothing more to contribute, bid adieu to Susanna and de Puisaye and returned to York on his horse. He did not see de Puisaye again but kept in touch with the rest of the émigré community at Windham for the next few years. It did not prosper. In 1802 during a lull in the war between England and France almost all, including de Puisaye, returned to Europe. Most remained in England and a few returned to France. Only two of the original group, Laurent Quetton St. George and Michel Saigeon, remained in Upper Canada and made a success of their lives as pioneers.

When the émigrés left Upper Canada, Claude returned to Montréal and remained there until 1816, carrying out teaching and pastoral duties as ordered by the Sulpician Superior. He kept in general touch with Laure and Thomas and felt relief that Laure seemed to come to terms with her marriage to Thomas. With pleasure and satisfaction, he watched Claudine growing up into a beautiful young woman with poise, wit and assurance. Only Laure and Claude himself noticed her physical resemblance to Claude. He made a point of seeing her as frequently as he could and developing a fatherly relationship with her. He did not check with Laure whether she ever discussed her paternity, but realised this would be a delicate matter as long as Thomas remained alive.

When peace returned to Europe in 1815, he decided to return to the land of his birth. Claude left Montréal on the first ship bound for England in the spring of 1816. He sadly said farewell to Laure and Claudine stating we would keep in touch with them by letter and perhaps return to Montréal in the future. He spent a few days in London, went on to Dover then crossed the Channel to Calais. From there he took the coach to Arras and immediately walked to the home of Pauline and Charles Cavigneau and rapped loudly at the door.

Chapter Twenty-One

Arras, Summer 1816

Charles Cavigneau's insides felt like the bottom of a birdcage. He had a numbing headache, pains in his chest and stomach, absolutely no energy and a constant sickly feeling without the relief of vomiting. Some days, he would find himself running frequently to the toilet. Other days passed when he would sit for hours and be unable to pass even a pellet. Remembering what he considered Dr Poirier's poor treatment of Demy, he had no trust in the doctor's expertise, so he decided to visit Anton Methot's Apothecary Shop on the rue Wacquez-Glasson not far from the Église St. Jean-Baptiste. Using two walking canes, he wound his way slowly to the shop and told the apothecary his story. On entering he sensed the distinctive, unpleasant chemical smell, and saw the central counter with a beautiful antique balance-scale housed in a wood and glass case resting on the side. Behind the counter were columns of brown shelves and drawers, each with a large clear label indicating its contents. Apothecary Methot himself, dressed in a flowing yellow and brown gown, head covered with a feathered headpiece, stood behind the counter.

"I have just the remedy for you, Charles," Methot replied, with extravagant assurance. "I will give you two prescriptions. The first is this red arsenic powder that I made by boiling arsenic with sulphur and nitrate, evaporating the fluid and we are left with this powerful powder that stimulates the heart and the kidneys."

"Are you sure? The arsenic does not sound right," replied a dubious Charles.

"Absolutely; arsenic in small quantities is a stimulant, not a poison. Look at this letter of appreciation from a customer cured by this concoction. The second prescription is in this bottle and is administered by a Clyster syringe. It contains a mixture of white wine, syrup, whale blubber and egg yolk. The syringe is included in the price. It may be difficult to inject it yourself so ask your wife to help. The mixture will restore mucus to your intestines and aid digestion and bowel action."

"Thank you, Monsieur Methot," replied Charles shaking his head as he envisaged this scene and pondered whether, after all, he should have taken his chances with Dr Poirier. Nonetheless, he paid his bill, took his package and wandered slowly back home. That night he took the foul-tasting arsenic powder but decided to wait until next day before proceeding with the enema. The following morning he inveigled Pauline into administering the Clyster and got himself into position, on elbows and knees with bare bum high in the air. Pauline inserted the nozzle into his anus and just at that moment they heard a loud rapping at the door. "Wait a minute," Pauline called out loudly, while quickly injecting the mixture into Charles' rectum, causing severe discomfort to the defenceless Charles. Their visitor could not have heard her reply because a minute later the rapping was repeated even more forcefully. Eventually she completed the procedure, laid down the syringe and hurried to open the door, leaving Charles groaning helplessly on the bed.

In the entrance she saw a middle-aged but fit-looking man with a clerical collar whom she did not immediately recognise. "Pauline. Claude Ladouceur, back from Canada!" the visitor said.

"You are back and alive!" she exclaimed. "I cannot believe it!"

"I am alive only because I left. I would be under the ground if I'd stayed," he replied. His face appeared thin and weather-beaten and, while still handsome, he looked older than his fifty years.

"Come in and sit down," said Pauline excitedly. "I am just busy with Charles who is not well. Help yourself to coffee in the kitchen. I'll be just five minutes then you can tell us your story."

"I would love that," Ladouceur said, as he went into the kitchen, found the biggin, coffee grounds and kettle, and prepared himself a cup of coffee. Fortunately he was familiar with the drip-brewing technique of the biggin, recently invented with the assistance of the Archbishop of Paris, in which boiling water percolated through a filter, vastly improving the coffee flavour.

Pauline returned to the bedroom to help Charles clean up and dress, which took closer to thirty than five minutes, and the two then joined Claude who recounted the story of his travels since his departure from Arras in 1796. Charles appeared wan and doddery from the after effects of his clyster injection.

"How did you find the Canadians? Do they still speak French?" enquired Pauline.

"They do, and they welcomed me with open arms. They are a God-fearing people. For two years, I taught in the seminary in Montréal where I met some interesting people." Claude paused for a moment as his mind flew back to the joys and sorrows of his relationships with Laure and Claudine. He composed himself and continued, "They then sent me to minister to the faithful in the small town of York on Lake Ontario, and in an area they now call Upper Canada. A group of French-aristocrat refugees led by Joseph-Geneviève, Comte de Puisaye settled nearby around twenty years ago, but they were unable to tolerate the cold and the primitive conditions so most returned to Europe, while I went back to Montréal, although returned at times to York. After the peace of 1815, I came back to France this summer."

"You were fortunate to avoid war and be far from Europe. The War has bled France white. Tens of thousands of men were killed on the battlefield, including young Jean Lupin and Bernard Festigny both of whom lived nearby here in Arras. They disappeared in the wastes of Russia," said Charles, shaking his head and moving restlessly in his chair. His arse remained very sore.

"We had our war too," Ladouceur said, and the couple with him at the table both gave him a look that said, yes, war, always war, wherever you go. "Will you tell us about it?" Charles asked.

The weary priest seemed about to say, 'later', but then decided to tell the story now. "Well, I don't know how much reached here, but perhaps you are aware that the United States, those former English colonials, decided to support France against England. Obviously they had simmered a while, rather like your excellent coffee, Pauline. About four years ago, I would think, yes, four, the Americans, as they now call themselves, came north and invaded Canada, hoping to force it to join them and free them, as they thought, from the English crown. Although a small group of Canadians fought alongside the United States soldiers, the great majority stayed loyal to the English king, would you believe, having no love for the blood-soaked, anti-clerical Bonaparte or his Revolution." Charles nodded his vigorous agreement. Ladouceur took a sip, moistened his lips, and quietly belched in pleasure at the realness of the coffee, then continued.

"The cursed war, as all wars are, touched the hem of my cassock while I was in York, when the Americans plundered and burnt the town, and the British blew up the fort as they evacuated. They led us out and then told us to survive as best we could. I made it by living in the wilderness like a savage. It was not, by any means, pleasant. I ate things I never want to eat again. A few months later a French-Canadian general, de Salaberry, with, let it be said, assistance from les sauvages, the Ir-Oh-Quois, even defeated an American invasion army at a town called Chateauguay and lost but two men. In the end, after a lake of blood had been spilt, we prevailed. Canada will not become an American state, at least not for now." By this time he had emptied his cup. "Pauline, do you have more coffee? It is excellent."

"Yes of course, Claude. I am glad you enjoy it," she replied, refilling his cup.

Charles indicated by waving towards it, that his cup needed filling too, although his mind was already full with his friend's news. "What does that war mean for the French in Canada, Claude?" he asked. "Will they end up calling a cochon a pig?"

Ladouceur smiled at his friend's rather weak humour. "You must remember, Charles, they are no longer French in the sense of belonging to the new France. In a curious way they believe they have maintained the French faith and values of the ancien regime. True, they speak the same language as us, already with an accent, rather like my grandmother's, but they are evolving, becoming a culture unto themselves. Remember, it is over fifty years since they were a French colony."

"And Mother Church?" Pauline asked, appearing at his side with genuine concern in her voice. She had seen enough heresy to last her a lifetime. Claude laid a hand on hers. "I am glad to say the Church has remained powerful in Québec. Yes, the habitants have sworn allegiance to the English king, but their education will continue to be in French in schools run by the Church. And the French legal system prevails, though they are governed by an English administration. How all this will turn out, God only knows." All three crossed themselves.

"It is truly a remarkable journey you have undertaken, Claude," said a visibly impressed Charles. "It must have required courage to live for years in such uncivilised conditions."

Suddenly Charles winced and doubled over with a cramp in his stomach, crossing his arms as if to protect it. Pauline jumped up and put her arm around his shoulder, "What is it Mon Cherie? Can I get you a hot brick from the oven? It will dull the pain."

"Yes please, dear," he groaned, while rubbing his stomach. Pauline kept a brick warm just for emergencies like these. She rushed to the kitchen got the brick, wrapped it in cloth and brought it to Charles who placed it on his stomach, as the cramp gradually subsided. He slowly straightened up, and then, addressing Claude, took up the conversation again on a different topic. "They falsely accused our eldest son, Demy, of theft. For punishment he spent twelve years on the Bagne at Toulon. We thought we would never see him again, but last year he appeared, like you, on our doorstep, more dead than alive. Now, he seems unwilling to accept life in a civilised society, so works for nothing as a mere stable hand on my son-in-law's farm."

Pauline moved closer, tutting. "Charles is giving you the wrong impression," she said, firmly. "They treated Demy like an animal when on the hulk, worse even, surrounded by suffering and death. They snuffed out his spirit. He might have taken his own life without his faith and the blessed help of a fellow-convict, a priest. But while working near the Armory at Toulon, he developed affection for an animal, a horse. I am hoping working with horses he loves will help restore his spirit."

"As you can see, Reverend Father, Pauline has a soft, woman's heart." Charles spoke with thinly disguised disdain in his voice. "Demy is a man, and when a man is hit he gets up, wipes the blood off his body, and gets on with his life. I have no patience with whiners. Look at me. This morning I had a humiliating and painful procedure, a Clyster injection, and now I have severe stomach cramps. Yet here I am, an hour later, up and as strong as an ox." Charles' hands trembled as he made these avowals.

Pauline gritted her teeth and pursed her lips, but remained silent.

"It is a difficult situation for you both," continued Claude. He sympathised with Pauline but remained reluctant to take sides in their conflict. "I understand what Demy has gone through. Under the conditions that exist on the Bagne, I'm sure you're right, that it required courage to survive, and a different type of courage to return to civilization. You are right also, Pauline, that his experience with horses will assist that adjustment. We can only pray that God will restore the fortitude he both needs and desires."

"You're right that he *needs* fortitude, Claude, but I see no indication that he *desires* it," replied Charles, raising his voice, while stressing the two words. His face became flushed and veins stood out visibly in his neck. "He has been sitting around here for six months doing nothing but dwelling on his misfortune. He seems to believe that because he has been mistreated, the world owes him something in return. So he sits on his arse waiting for that payback. Of course he will wait until he dies because no one will come through the door and say, 'Hey, Demy, here is a thousand francs to make up for the bad treatment you had on the Bagne'. Even if that happened he likely would deem it insufficient, so would remain disgruntled."

"You are being very unfair, Charles," Pauline proclaimed shrilly. "I'm surprised you have so little care and understanding for one who is your own flesh and blood. He has been through hell. He has returned, alive. No one returns from hell. You should get down on your knees and thank God for that fact. You've had a sheltered life. I've struggled to raise and care for you and our children. I can imagine you after ten years on the Bagne. You would not survive — you would die or be killed. A man needs two qualities to survive that life, faith and the ability to know when to retreat. You have faith, but you do not know when to retreat!"

"Well, I would rather die than survive and be a burden." Charles spoke stridently, clenching his fists and looking at both his wife and Claude as if to say, 'this is my final word on the topic.' To emphasise the point, and forgetting his maladies in the madness of the moment, he stomped angrily out of the room, and out of the house, banging the doors so loudly that the windows rattled.

Pauline looked at Claude, shook her head helplessly and burst into tears. After some minutes she composed herself and added, "I do not usually argue with Charles. He never admits he is wrong. When it comes to protecting my son, however, I shall fight like a bitch with young puppies. Anyway, I know I am right about Demy. He is not a bad boy. With time I believe he will find his feet again, and I know that Clementine and Marcel will treat him well. It is good he has found a connection with horses. They will lead him back to contentment."

"I hope you are right Pauline," replied Claude sympathetically. "There is some truth to what Charles is saying, however. Despite his difficulties, Demy is not exempt from making a decision. In fact, if you look at it carefully, he has made a decision, albeit a small one, in agreeing to go to Marcel's farm. In my long life as a priest, I have seen many people go through a multitude of troubling times, including poverty, family breakups, illness and death. There is never an easy solution, nor a solution that fits every situation. You have acted wisely in allowing Demy to live on your daughter's farm and work with horses. This is a sign that God is responding to your prayers. It is like a small miracle. It appears to be a natural event but God is using nature to make things happen."

"What about Charles and me?" Pauline whimpered in reply. "We've been married over forty years and have never disagreed as violently as we do now. Our journey's end is now not distant. We cannot spend our remaining time in endless conflict about our son?"

"You said yourself that he never admits he is wrong. Therefore, you will not convince him that you are right, and he is wrong about Demy. It would be best if you say little. Give God time to work his little miracle, and you will find that much will change in your life as well."

Pauline smiled through her tears, shook her head sadly, and then hugged Ladouceur thankfully. "I hope — I think — you are right... "

A loud rap on the front door interrupted her sentence. She opened it and recognised two neighbourhood children who said excitedly, "Madame, Madame, come quickly! Monsieur Cavigneau fell and hurt himself in the street. He cannot get up!"

She followed them quickly and found Charles lying on the cobblestones a short distance from their house, surrounded by a small group of people who were trying to help. She pushed her way through, got down on her knees next to him and found him moaning in pain, sweating profusely and clutching his chest.

"Charles, what happened?" she asked anxiously. "Did you fall? Are you hurt?"

"Pauline, my chest, my chest! I've a crushing pain."

Pauline took a cloth out of her breast pocket and wiped the sweat off his brow and face. She took his hand, held it up to her cheek and said, "Charles, my darling, my dearest, what can I do?"

He gripped her hand tightly and whispered, "I know I'm going. Good bye. I've done my best. Demy, it's a pity... I did my best, goodbye... goodbye... "

"Charlie, my Charlie. Don't go! Don't go!" she cried, shaking his shoulders in a vain attempt to revive him. He did not hear her and these were his last words. He fell back, lost awareness and expired in her arms.

A messenger delivered a letter to Clementine the following day. Brief and to the point, it read:

'Clementine: Your father died suddenly yesterday. As you know he has not been well but the way it happened was a terrible shock for me. The funeral is in two days' time. Could you come?

(Signed) Your Maman.'

Charles' unexpected death evoked a jumble of emotions for Clementine. She knew her father as a good provider with a generous nature but that remained the best she could say of him. She felt overwhelmed by memories of punishment and pain connecting her father with her childhood. As an adolescent, she had rebelled against this austere atmosphere with but partial success. Efforts to deal openly with these matters as a married woman accomplished little.

She approached Marcel for his opinion. "Cherie: do you think I should attend Papa's funeral? Maman wants me to go. Perhaps I should, but have little love for that man despite him being my father. I should feel sorrow and am guilty that I do not."

"I cannot tell you what you should do, Clemmie darling. I never knew him the way you did. I believe he had respect for me as I did for him. He treated women differently from men. He hated what he saw as weakness in people which is why he had so much trouble with Demy. He saw Demy as timid, even cowardly, and perhaps he saw women also in that manner so treated them with disdain, as he treated Demy."

After a brief moment's thought she replied, "I believe you are correct, Marcel, all my life I fought to prove to him that I am forceful and tough, but in the end it accomplished nothing. He had a firm belief that a woman is born weak and can never change and Maman did not help by allowing him to run her life."

"It is strange," Marcel replied thoughtfully. "You had a father for whom you had little love or respect and I have no father yet long to have known and loved him!"

"Yes, that's curious," she agreed. "Our natures seem to tell us that something different will always be better yet often it is worse. We would all be more contented if we accepted our fate without complaint."

"I am not able to do that," he replied quickly. "I shall remain disgruntled until I know the identity of my father so will continue the search though I know not where to begin. I must also add that you have no need to prove your strength to me," Marcel added with a smile. "You have shown it to me repeatedly."

"You are teasing me," she replied with a laugh while at the same time playfully pushing him on the shoulder. "Marcel, you have persuaded me to go to the funeral. It would be weakness to run away. Will you come with me?"

"Yes, of course I will." They arranged for Monique and Alexis to come to the farm and care for the family and livestock. Clementine took Demy aside and told him their father had died. She expected a shocked reaction, perhaps even a terror attack but he merely looked away and said nothing. She perceived his expressionless features and the glazed, faraway look in his eyes.

That afternoon Clementine and Marcel left for Arras to attend Charles' funeral.

Several weeks went by. During the rest of the summer much activity took place on the farm. Demy adjusted quickly to his duties in the stable. He developed a special attachment to a six-year old foal called Maia, but had difficulty with Con Brio, a stallion.

Con Brio was restless and high-spirited, and spent much time in the field pacing up and down the fence line, trying to access the mares, loudly neighing his frustrations. On one occasion he attempted to bite Demy's hand while being brushed. "I think Con Brio would be quieter if he had a home in his meadow," Demy suggested timidly to Marcel one day. "Why don't we build him a stall? We can even place some sawdust on the floor so he can lie down comfortably because he likes rubbing his back on the ground."

"That will not make any difference," replied Marcel authoritatively. "Horses are used to being outdoors on their legs. He is high-spirited by nature but we must do something so we can try building the shelter, as you suggest."

271

So Marcel built a stall for Con Brio in his field. It contained not only a bed of sawdust but a bucket of water and a trough of hay as well. This had a soothing effect and the horse soon stopped pacing the fence line. Marcel complimented Demy on his creative idea.

Demy's night terrors and attacks of agitation became less frequent. One afternoon Marcel and he were in the stable discussing the stallion, when Demy suddenly changed the subject and asked, "Where is your father?"

For a moment Marcel felt nonplussed as he had never before discussed personal matters with Demy. He stammered a reply, "I never had a father... I mean, I had a father ... but never knew him. He disappeared before my birth. I tried to find out about him but no one would tell me. I do not care about it anymore and do not want to know." After a few moments' silence during which he recovered his composure, he added, "Why do you ask?"

"You never talk about your family. I met your oncle Alexis and tante Monique. Clementine told me Alexis is your mother's brother. I asked him to tell me about your father but he said I must ask you." After a moment's silence he added, "My father was hard on me when I was little and I wondered if they were all like that."

"They are not all like that, Demy," Marcel replied firmly. "I know your father treated you roughly as he did your sister, Clementine. It seems he had the idea that the only way to teach children right from wrong is to punish them — that they must be hard and tough like he is himself. I believe you have much anger inside because of this, like a kettle that is boiling but there is no outlet for the steam to escape. You are not the only ones to have a father like that. Although I never met my real father, two men have been like fathers to me: one was a priest called Father St. Amour and the other is my uncle Alexis whom you have met. St. Amour was a wonderful, gentle man whom they executed during the Revolution because he refused to sign the oath of loyalty. I still miss him," he added softly, bowing and shaking his head.

Demy pondered this information for a few moments then said, "It is strange. It seems the way my father treated me helped me endure the Bagne but it has not helped me adjust to life back home."

"You are right, that is curious. It will take time. We all have scars from our childhoods but they are not visible, they are written on our souls. Perhaps our horses will teach you how to deal with people in France, by providing an outlet for the steam of your anger to escape!" Marcel added with a smile.

"I think that may be," Demy replied doubtfully, and Marcel saw a flicker of a smile cross his features. He also noticed his eyes going into repeated spasms as he looked away.

Music remained a key part of Marcel's family's life. Despite his low regard for Father Lepire, he continued his membership of the church choir. He had a mellow but firm baritone voice and sang solo parts when required. Both François and Charlotte joined the youth choir and Charlotte especially showed such musical talent that Marcel purchased a piano. Twice weekly a teacher came from the town to give her a lesson. She made excellent progress and performed on several occasions before a small group of family and friends. Amongst other pieces, she played a Minuet by Mozart and a recently composed Bagatelle called Für Elise by Ludwig van Beethoven, a Viennese composer in the process of becoming famous. Marcel sometimes sang at these private performances and, accompanied by Charlotte, would sing his signature tune, Monsieur de Turenne by Jean-Baptiste Lully.

Clementine and Marcel observed that Demy loved Charlotte's performances. He would sit for hours listening to her practice her scales and pieces, eyes closed and body motionless, seemingly relaxed, as if lost in another world. He even asked to sit in on Charlotte's lessons and although she initially was dubious, even embarrassed, she accepted his presence when she realised that he did not interrupt the process. Marcel did not interfere, knowing instinctively that, as with his work with horses, music would help Demy reconnect with society. Pauline and Charles had told Marcel that Dr Poirier had recommended Water Therapy at Spa as his preferred treatment for Demy's nervous condition. Perhaps the combination of work with horses and enjoying music would prove superior to Water Therapy – and be much less expensive!

Maia's foal was born early in the morning of the first day of 1818. She pushed the foal out while lying down on a bed of straw, then licked and nuzzled her. Marcel and Demy were both present and they watched silently for twenty minutes or more as the newborn foal struggled to stand up and take its first stumbling steps, and then find the teat. Maia licked up the after birth.

"Is it not a wondrous sight, Demy?" Marcel asked rhetorically, as they watched the foal orientate itself to its strange new world.

"Yes," said Demy simply.

"Many years ago I watched a dog give birth to puppies." Marcel gazed at Maia and her foal, not watching Demy. "But that was different. A puppy's eyes are shut and it is a week before they can walk. What makes a mother care for her young? Look at Con Brio. He does not even know that he has sired a foal. He is a father and does not know it. Not only that but we have to protect the foal from the father. He can get aggressive especially when they live in confined spaces like here."

There followed a prolonged silence during which the pair watched the foal learning how to suckle. Demy eventually replied with a simple, "Yes."

Marcel turned and looked at Demy and saw his expressionless face. His head and eyes looked away into the middle-distance, not even watching the foal. He appeared to be gazing through the wall of the stable, his facial spasm repeating itself every few seconds. Marcel wondered to himself if Demy had even heard his musings about animal birth.

Inwardly Demy's thoughts were in turmoil. He heard what Marcel said but could not respond. He thought he might say the wrong thing and that Marcel would laugh or even shout at him again. If that happened he might lash out and punch Marcel. Should he hit him now before that smile turned into a laugh? He clenched his fists, and then unclenched them again. Both the fist-clenching and the facial spasm seemed to ease some tension, so he repeated these gestures involuntarily. A long way off he heard the voice of a loud-mouthed guard shouting at him to get back to work.

"Did you hear him shouting at me?" he asked, his face contorted with anxiety, while pointing in the direction of the fields.

"No I did not," Marcel replied calmly. He watched Demy intently, trying to understand what ailed him. "What did you hear?"

"The guard yelled at me to get back to work but I am working!" he cried out. "He is always yelling at me whatever I do." His face still in spasms, Demy felt himself back at the Bagne, clearing the trees as a forced labourer around the armoury at Toulon. Maia was Bonita, Marcel the guard and the stable his prison.

"Demy. You-are-here-on-my-farm-at-Vimy-in-France," Marcel spoke slowly and deliberately, emphasising each word. He looked in Demy's general direction but deliberately avoided his eyes. He knelt on the floor of the stable and began stroking and petting the foal gently as it nuzzled Maia's udder.

"Help me care for this new baby animal, Demy. It needs affection and stroking."

For a few moments Demy did not respond. He looked from side to side as if seeking a way of escape, fists still clenched and face contorted. Then deep inside his soul something seemed to register. This is a baby horse. Bonita never had a foal. It is cold in the stable; it was not cold on the Bagne. Marcel spoke to him softly and kindly, not loudly and brutally. No one spoke like this on the hulk. He heard only shouts and orders. He knelt down and placed his hand on the foal's rump. He felt it move back and forth as it struggled to grasp and hold the teat. His face opened up, then relaxed as the spasms gradually ebbed. They continued kneeling beside the foal in silence for a few minutes while Demy reoriented himself to his surroundings. The only sounds came from Maia and her foal, the licking and the nuzzling.

"Is that better?" Marcel asked eventually.

"Yes, the foal is small and gentle," Demy replied quietly. "It feels good when I stroke its warm, soft, skin."

"That's right Demy," replied Marcel. "It's good for you and the foal, and we're helping the foal get yoked with her mother." As Demy's agitation subsided they sauntered slowly and silently back to the house.

Dinner that night turned out to be a joyful affair. Louis-Marcel, Jean-Baptiste, François and especially Charlotte were excited by the foal's birth. They had spent the day watching the young animal, desperate to hug and stroke it.

"What shall we call him Papa?" called Louis-Marcel at the top of his voice.

"First it is a girl not a boy. What shall we call her?"

"I want to call her Gigi," said Charlotte loudly.

"No!" countered Louis-Marcel strongly. "That would suit a goat, not a horse, what about Petite because she is so small."

François, always more reserved in his opinions, said, "Let us wait a few days. Once we get to know her we will think of a suitable name. What do you think Maman and Papa, and you Oncle Demy?"

"I cannot think of any name that would suit a baby horse," Demy replied timidly.

"I agree with François," said Clementine. "If we wait a few days the right name will come to us. It is important to get the name right. It will stay with her a lifetime. No one changes their name."

She glanced guiltily at Marcel who flinched, though only Clementine noticed. He felt unsure whether she was serious or just teasing him. Either way he did not like it. So often a serious stab lay hidden in a light-hearted jest. He gave her a severe look that meant "shut up". Marcel then leaned back in his chair, and ponderously took out his box of snuff that he knew lay in the left-sided pocket of his breeches. He had begun using snuff several years previously as a substitute for pipe smoking because the latter caused him to cough. Despite this, he had not been able to give up the pipe completely.

He sprinkled some snuff powder in his right palm, took a pinch between the thumb and index finger of his left hand, applied it to each nostril and inhaled deeply, while the spicy smell wafted through the room. He followed this up with several resounding sneezes. Although the family had watched this portentous ritual many times, they remained quiet, as if they felt profound thinking was taking place which they must not interrupt, exactly the intention that Marcel wished to convey.

"I've given the matter much thought," he intoned eventually. "We will call her Belle Bonita. Belle because she is so beautiful, and Bonita to remember the loyal and sturdy horse that Demy had when he lived away from home."

In response, there were several grunts of approval, and one dissenting groan from Louis-Marcel. Demy said nothing but Marcel noticed he gave a wide smile that Marcel had never seen before. His tics and spasms vanished, he looked at Marcel for a moment, his eyes shining, and nodded as if to say 'merci mon frère; je t'aime'.

Chapter Twenty-Two

Late Autumn 1820

As part of his quest to become Mayor of the Commune of Vimy, Marcel visited Monsieur Jacques Wawrin, Prefect of the region, who made the final decision. Elections for mayor that had been enacted during the Revolution were abandoned during the Napoleonic era. Marcel knew that Raymond Batarse also had an interest in the position. Batarse had lived in Vimy for seven years, had married a former mayor's daughter and built up a successful farm implements business. Marcel believed his own credentials were stronger, however, being a well-known, longstanding resident of Vimy, a respected member of the parish and owner of a reputable horse farm.

He met Wawrin by appointment in Arras, in his office on the south west corner of the first floor of the Hôtel de Ville on La Petite Place. It being market day, the Plaza was as busy and boisterous as a beehive on a spring morning. As he entered Marcel saw the prefect seated in a large chair behind an outsize desk in the centre of the room. After introducing himself, Marcel sat down in an upright chair opposite the prefect and speaking slowly and resolutely, he said, "Monsieur Wawrin, as you know I am here because I'm interested in the position of Mayor of our Commune. I have lived in Vimy my whole life and know all the citizens by their first names, including your good self. I have established a horse farm that, in the opinion of many, is the best in the region. Although I had but a limited education, I am able to read and write and will use the position to represent the interests of the citizens of the Commune, ensure the administration runs smoothly and act for the Government to its local citizens. I know that ensuring security is all-important and will attempt also to improve education for children. I would love to attract a doctor to our community and I believe, indeed I know, I have the organizational ability to accomplish these goals."

"Those are all essential requirements for the position, Monsieur Juin," Wawrin responded approvingly. "I have good reports about the quality of your horses and the cleanliness of your farm, signs of an efficient mind. If you are as adept at the politics of village leadership as you are with the horse, not dissimilar to some men around here, you will be an excellent candidate for the position. As you are aware there are other candidates to be, um, vetted, so we shall make our decision in the next two months and let you know."

After signing a cumbersome official document that Wawrin had prepared for the candidates, Marcel left Wawrin's office and talked to himself about possibly obtaining additional recommendations from influential members of the community, men such as Doctor Cadieux and Father Lepire, but decided this was not necessary and possibly even unfair. He wanted to ensure he won the position in a clean contest.

Meanwhile, even as Marcel commenced his campaign, Raymond Batarse was scheming behind the scenes. The same day he filed his application for mayor, he decided to go and see Madame Eulalie Tricheur, the widow from whom he had bought the farm implements business seven years previously. Madame Tricheur had relocated since then to what outwardly seemed one of the most imposing houses on the Rue Principale in Vimy. It stood two storeys high, and twin white porticos stood like sentinels either side of the front door, with a faux balcony above. The home was equipped with replicas of Louis Quinze furniture and wallpapered throughout with dark floral, vaguely regal designs. Although she had never remarried, Madame had invested the profits of her husband's business wisely, perhaps even a little fraudulently. She enjoyed living comfortably with her two younger children who were yet to marry. Batarse walked to her house and rapped on the door.

"Madame, it is my pleasure to visit you again," Batarse said as he entered, speaking as if syrup was dripping from his tongue. "I love your new home. You clearly have excellent taste when it comes to your home furnishings and décor. I trust you feel as well as you look. You have not aged a day since I first visited you seven years ago!"

Madame Tricheur beamed with pleasure at the compliments.

"Let me waste not a moment more of your time," Batarse continued, "I have come to request your advice and perhaps your assistance. You may know that the Commune of Vimy is seeking a new mayor. I am interested in the position and believe I have all the required qualifications. Marcel Juin is also putting his name forward and I speak to you knowing of your long residence in the community and the esteem in which you are held by the citizens of Vimy. I know Juin's farm is an apparent success, but the few times I have visited him he has been extraordinarily rude and abrupt. Moreover, he employs a crazy relative to care for the horses and pays him nothing. I have heard it said that he is mean and cheap with his other employees. For the good of Vimy it would be totally improper for him, a man of mean spirit, to be mayor. Can you help me make sure he remains, as it were, unseated?

Madame Tricheur thought for a few moments. Her beady eyes shifted from side to side and a faint smile flickered over her features. She then said, "I agree with most of your sentiments about Juin and have heard that he pays little to his farm labourers. I do not like him and do not see him as mayor. I will see what I can do."

Batarse looked firmly into Madame Tricheur's eyes and added in a scornful voice, "I am prepared to do whatever is necessary to ensure Juin does not become mayor. Let me know if you need any, um, financial assistance in your endeavours."

As usual, the mention of money moved the corpulent woman forward in her chair. "I will," she said. "It will not be easy because he is well respected elsewhere in the community. But, I shall give it some thought. Let us see what can be done."

Batarse held in check a smile of triumph. "Thank you, Madame. I value your help, he said, almost kissing her hand but thinking better of it, and with fervent, insincere farewells Raymond Batarse took his departure from Madame Tricheur's home. The moment he walked out of the front door Tricheur's sixteen year old daughter, Rose-Anne, entered the room and said to her mother, "Maman, I listened to that man talking to you. I don't like him. It seems like sugar is coming out of his mouth but underneath the sugar it sounds more like poison. Do not do business with him." Rose-Anne spoke quietly but earnestly.

"What nonsense, child." Eulalie Tricheur replied vehemently. "What do you know about men at your age? Monsieur Batarse bought our business seven years ago. He has developed it successfully and is now the wealthiest man in Vimy. He is dependable and responsible and will make an excellent mayor for our town. I shall do all I can to help him reach that goal." Continuing to mutter angrily, she left the room to avoid any response from her daughter.

A few days after Batarse's visit, Madame Tricheur needed a new closet installed and sent for Alain, the carpenter. After agreeing on the details of the installation she remembered her agreement with Batarse and said, as he closed his account book, "Alain, how well do you know Marcel Juin?"

Alain clenched his fists and replied, "I cannot stand the man. I want nothing to do with him." That was exactly what Madame Tricheur wanted to hear and she told him about the race for mayor between Juin and Batarse. "Do you know anything about Juin that would help Batarse get the job?" she asked.

"Yes, I may indeed know something about him that would be useful," Alain said, fingering a hammer in his belt. "What do you want me to do with it?"

"The decision is being made by the Prefect in Arras. Could you communicate your information to him? I shall give you his whereabouts and let him know of your impending arrival." She took a step closer to the tradesman. "Can you tell me, now, what it is you know?"

Alain's face clouded over, and lines, straight lines, appeared on his brow. "I would rather not tell you what happened between us. It was a long time ago, but I can say he has a shady past and it would disgrace the office if he became mayor of our town."

Madame Tricheur made an unsuccessful attempt to conceal her glee. "And, as I mentioned, would you be willing to share your shaded secret with the Prefect?" she asked, with just a hint of complicity in her voice.

"What is it worth to you, Madame?" Alain sensed that he could even the score with Marcel and also make a good profit. "If I have to travel to Arras, it will cost me at least a day's work. It will be very inconvenient."

"I can offer you one hundred francs."

"I will require five hundred, cash, paid before my departure."

"Five hundred it is then. I will arrange that," Madame Tricheur replied, without hesitation.

Two months later, just a few days before Christmas, the Prefect pinned the following notice on the bulletin board outside the Hôtel de Ville in Vimy:

ANNOUNCEMENT
Monsieur Jacques Wawrin
Prefect of the District of Arras
(Pas de Calais)
Is pleased to announce that

MONSIEUR RAYMOND BATARSE

Has been appointed Mayor of the Commune of Vimy

Signed: Jacques Wawrin,
20th December 1820

Word of the announcement spread quickly in the community. Marcel went to the town hall himself and stared at the notice in shocked disbelief. I spoke to the Prefect myself and had every reason to believe I was the

280

favoured candidate. My credentials were impeccable, a lifelong resident of the community, loyal family and friends, a respected member of the parish, support from Church authorities. How could I be passed over for this position in favour of someone foreign to the community who has refined the art of deception? As far as I know, none in the community who would influence the decision were aware of my illegitimacy. In any case, I have more than compensated with my conventional family and religious life. And with the restoration of the monarchy I thought my reputation as a royalist would be an advantage. How could this fast-talking parvenu who does not even speak proper French, WIN? He slammed his fist into the palm of his hand as he contemplated the implications of this information and then noted ruefully that the announcement had been made, no doubt intentionally, just prior to the Christmas season festivities, making it more difficult to question or contest the decision. Head bowed, he slowly and dejectedly returned home.

Clementine, staring out the window, knew from his face a hundred paces away the outcome of the election. She expressed much sympathy. "Who knows what goes on behind closed doors when these decisions are made?" she said. "Money was involved, I'm sure. Batarse has no scruples about how he uses his cash. You have enough money too but don't like spending it, nor do you know how to use it to your advantage." She had a way of getting quickly and cuttingly to the point.

"I suppose you are right," Marcel said sadly. "But I will admit I wanted that position badly. I could have accomplished so much with it. That limp horse Batarse will likely be there for years, as there is no term limit; clearly, knowing where to place your money counts for far more than trustworthiness and accomplishments."

Just then, a man on horseback appeared at the gate. Marcel and Clementine recognised Raymond Batarse. He alighted, tied up his horse, and approached Marcel with his hand outstretched and a smug smile on his face. "Bonjour Marcel," he said, with a damp and weak handshake. "I am sure you have heard of my appointment as mayor. I know that you too were interested in the position so I came to visit to express my commiserations. In the end, I believe my experience as a senior officer in the army may have swayed the Prefect. Can I count on you for your gracious support in important decisions that have to be made in our community?"

Marcel clenched his fists and with difficulty resisted the temptation to smash Batarse's face. He forced a smile and said, through tightened teeth, "I shall do no such thing. You are on your own, my friend. If there had been a fair process, or an open election, the result would have been different. Justness does not count for much in our community. It is gold that speaks, and to whom you display it. The decision, I know, is final. I shall no longer involve myself in community affairs and will confine my activities and pleasures to family and my horses." Marcel noticed Batarse shaking his head and giving a self-satisfied smile. He grabbed Clementine's arm, turned around without an au revoir, and together they marched indoors. Still smiling, Batarse mounted his horse and cantered off.

Christmas that year was a sombre affair for the family. Clementine invited Monique and Alexis for dinner. In their late-sixties, the senior couple looked their age. Monique, nearly blind, had to be led wherever she went. Alexis, overweight, legs and back crippled with arthritis, needed two canes to get around. A next door neighbour helped them with meal preparation and house cleaning functions.

Clementine and Marcel's four children were lively and now healthy. Louis-Marcel, aged twenty-four, engaged to be married to Marie-Marguerite Lebeau, was outgoing and, like his father, cared for horses. He had become the chief assistant and Marcel's likely successor on the farm. Jean-Baptiste, now twenty, had an erratic tendency in the way he did things and spent much time at the tavern, but he had recently switched liquids and joined a local family business of well-diggers. Marcel expected him to settle down. They were proud of François, aged eighteen, who studied well and showed excellent results. He aspired to attend the seminary in Amiens to become a priest. Charlotte, aged thirteen, had miraculously recovered from her serious illness of five years ago. Clementine still did not know what caused her recovery; whether Dr Cadieux's ministrations, Father Lepire's masses and blessings, or just her youthful strength and resilience. Clementine had a shrewd suspicion that the talisman inside Dr Cadieux's stethoscope was the key therapeutic ingredient. She and Marcel thanked God daily that her health had been restored. She had resumed her musical studies and performed well in both voice and piano.

After dinner Alexis took Marcel aside to a corner of the living room for a tête-à-tête. They sat side-by-side on an arm chair as Alexis was not able to stand. "What happened about the mayoralty race? I felt sure you would be nominated. You had all the qualities."

"I thought so too but apparently the Prefect saw differently," replied Marcel bitterly. "I suspect some unknown source put pressure on him. No one talks so there is no way of knowing. The secrecy makes it harder to bear. After the announcement Batarse came over, gloating. I nearly socked him. I should not say this but he is a mean and malicious man. I fear the direction he will lead this community."

"He came to visit me before the announcement," Alexis said, his hands shaking, "not knowing that I am your uncle. He asked me to sign a letter supporting his nomination. When I refused he offered me a hundred francs to sign."

"What did you do?"

"I signed and pocketed the money," he said with a smile. Marcel's face fell in shocked disbelief, when Alexis added quickly, "No, no, just jesting! I showed him the door, told him to never come back, and said I would tell all my friends not to sign his letter either."

"He is a singular man." Marcel spoke slowly. "He fought in the Imperial army for many years. Otherwise no one knows where he comes from. Don't you find he has the most impenetrable accent? He will not reveal from where he came. Though I dislike the man fervently, I have a strange fellow-feeling with him as we both have dark origins. Few people know about my background and I believe it played no part in the mayoralty decision."

"I agree," Alexis said, shaking and nodding his head sequentially. I never discuss it and no one I know mentions it. Perhaps someone does know and conveyed this information secretly to the Prefect. If so, that could have swayed the decision. We will never know. Talking of knowing, Marcel, what about your children. Do they know you had no father?"

"That is a good question, Alexis." Marcel took a pinch full of snuff – both the action and the drug it contained helped relieve his tension – then continued. "To tell the truth, I have done nothing about informing them. I go through periods when it worries me and others when I put it out of my mind and refuse to consider it. As for the children, they have not yet asked questions so that makes it easier. One day they will realise that their mother had two parents but their father had but one, or at least only one they knew about. I shall have to deal with the matter. I do not wish to do what my mother did to me, and keep silent."

"I have been thinking much about her lately," replied Alexis pensively. "She was a delightful woman, beautiful and generous. Despite being my young sister I loved her like a mother, especially after I lost my mother. It amazed me how she could turn that awful gruel we had to eat into an edible meal! Sometimes I think she must have been raped. It can only be shame from rape that would make a young girl hide what happened."

Marcel was speechless with shock. The idea that he might be the product of a rape had never crossed his mind. He had considered the possibility that his father might have been a philanderer, counting the number of women he seduced just as a soldier would notch up the number of men he killed on the battlefield. But to think he might have been a rapist repulsed him! Unwittingly, Alexis had given him another topic to prey on his mind.

"Would you and the family not have noticed signs of injury if she had been raped? Bruises, bleeding or blemishes?" he asked anxiously, his hands trembling.

"I don't remember any. Besides, she could have hidden it unless severe. Women have means of concealing physical changes in their appearance, though not always successfully. Monique tried to hide the scars of small pox on her face with little success. Do not let this bother you, Marcel. It happened long ago. Those who took part are dead and nothing further can be done."

"You do not understand, Alexis. To know my origins is vital for me. It makes a big difference whether my father was an aggressive rapist who mauled my mother, or whether I was conceived in an act of love, even if illicit. Though I can never know my father I still have emotions about him. I would like these emotions to be pleasant and good rather than bitter and evil."

"You must place that all behind you and get on with the rest of your life, Marcel. It is a pity you did not win the mayoralty race. You would have had something to take your mind off it all."

"Thank you for your advice, Alexis. I plan to focus on the farm and the family and may seek other distractions."

After Alexis' departure Marcel went to the washbasin in the kitchen. Although his hands were clean, he scrubbed them vigorously for a long time using a brush, soap and warm water.

"Papa, a strange thought came to me last night and I would like to speak to you." Louis-Marcel, now twenty-four years old, had approached his father when alone in the small room in the south-east corner of the stables that he called his office. The office had two doors and two windows, one door and window connecting the office to the outside, and the other connecting it to the stable interior. The office furniture was simple but stylish. Pictures of horses hung on three of the walls and on his desk stood the figurine of the horse rearing towards the sky that he had carved when hiding in the cave on the Vimy ridge as a young man of eighteen.

"Sure, Louis-Marcel, you must have been wondering about Belle Bonita and why she has been stumbling, as if she is ill. Perhaps you have a solution to propose?"

"No, Papa," replied Louis-Marcel firmly. "It is not about horses, it is about you." Marcel winced momentarily. He was not accustomed to discussing personal issues with his children.

284

"What is it, Louis-Marcel?" Marcel replied sharply. "I shall answer as best I can."

"We have seen much of Maman's parents, grand-père and grand-mère. We also know Alexis, your uncle. Why have we never met your mother and father? Just as important, why do we know nothing about them? What happened to them?"

Marcel sensed an assertive note to his son's questioning. As he always did when in a quandary, he leaned back in his chair, reached into his pocket, found the snuff box, and for the next few moments took and inhaled it deeply as he pondered how best to respond. Numerous sneezes followed, and that allowed further thought and delayed his reply to Louis-Marcel's questions. The latter, meanwhile, said nothing as he watched his father's every movement.

"It is a good question," he said, finally. "And you have a right to know. My mother's name was Marie-Anne Lachêne and her father, Gabriel was Tante Catherine's brother. Marie-Anne and my father never married. In my seventh year my mother married another man, her cousin called Hubert, also Tante Catherine's son. My mother died one year later in childbirth and the baby also died. I never knew or met my father and to this day I know not who he is. That is my story."

During the extended silence that followed, Louis-Marcel digested this information, and then his face clouded over as he realised its implications. "I am shocked, Papa. So I am the son of a bastard! I wish now that I had not asked!"

"You will learn in life, Louis-Marcel, if you have not already learnt, that wishes are rarely granted in the way you expect, and sometimes, for this reason, it is best not to make wishes. I have dealt with the matter of my mother and father and it is no longer a problem for me. Women and men get together, have babies, then die, but life goes on." Marcel attempted to look calm as he uttered these words.

Again, in silence, Louis-Marcel imbibed his father's story. "Papa, for me it is hard to believe that you did not try to find out more about your father. Did not your mother or Uncle Alexis tell you?"

Marcel shifted uncomfortably in his chair and his eyes were focused into the middle distance behind his son. He then looked down at the table and replied softly, "My mother promised to tell me but died before she did. Alexis knew nothing as did my grand-père Lachêne, whom I asked before he died. My mother was a lovely and loving woman but had a stubborn streak. She died with her secret so we never can know."

Louis-Marcel then ventured, with a gloomy tone to his voice, "I suppose you are right Papa. I now know a little about your mother, and am always glad I met Maman's parents."

Following another lengthy silence Marcel looked his son in the eye and said, "Louis-Marcel, there is one other thing I must tell you. If you seek out your birth information you will discover that the name you have now is not the name you were born with. You were born Louis-Marcel pierre. They gave me the name 'pierre' because of an uncle who died before my birth. After Jean-Baptiste's birth, I changed our family name to Juin because it seemed more fitting. It is necessary for you to know but I ask you not to talk of this to anyone."

Louis-Marcel crossed his brow as if to question his father's need for secrecy. "I do not understand Papa, and I do not understand why you did that."

Marcel repeated firmly, "That is something I would like to keep within these walls. It is no one's business. I am telling you only because it is written down on your birth notice and I would rather you hear from me than find out elsewhere." Marcel did not wish to prolong the ordeal of confiding in his son, so rose from his chair, and with a reassuring pat on the back, hustled him out of the room.

It was a while before Marcel composed himself and left the office to return home.

Chapter Twenty-Three

Vimy, July 1824.

Louis-Marcel had been courting Marie-Marguerite, very properly, for two years. She hailed from Arras, being the youngest daughter of Adam Sonnette, a minor revolutionary in his youth, and his wife Agathe. Adam was distantly related to the Robespierre family and had established a successful business producing equestrian equipment, through which he had encountered Marcel. The two couples met on several occasions to arrange the wedding of their offspring. Details of the dowry were difficult because both families were well-to-do and close with their money. Eventually, the issues were settled with contributions from both sides. The Sonnette family would donate a cedar kist filled with linen, while Marcel and Clementine would host and pay for the wedding.

Eighteen year old Marie-Marguerite was an attractive, demure young woman with long braided dark hair covered by a brown bonnet. As was customary with eligible young middle class women at the time, her family kept her out of the public eye until a suitable marriage partner could be found. She dressed conventionally and felt at her happiest when following the rules. Both she and Louis-Marcel left all wedding details, including selection of partners, to their parents. Marcel and Clementine wanted the wedding to be the event of the year in the region. The invitation list included all notables in the area, including Dr Vincent Cadieux, the mayor of Vimy, Raymond Batarse and his wife, Madame Eulalie Tricheur, Father Claude Ladouceur and many others. Marcel felt relief that Batarse sent his regrets, pleading a prior engagement, but Madame Tricheur accepted the invitation. Well-known in the community as a moneyed widow, Marcel knew nothing about Tricheur's involvement in the selection of the Mayor four years previously. Celebrities from Arras who attended were the mayor, the prefect, Jacques Wawrin, who had selected Raymond Batarse over Marcel in the Vimy mayoralty race, and Dr Jean-Paul Poirier, the noted physician.

With the help of her mother, Marie-Marguerite made the wedding dress. She selected a light beige coloured muslin outfit with a high waistline and widely puffed sleeves. The dress extended below the ankle line so that the lower edge of the back of the dress acted as a small train. The dress had a stellar pattern woven into its fabric. Louis-Marcel wore a drab, dark suit with long pipe-like pants and a wide coat extending to his thighs.

They married on a lovely warm summer's day at a Nuptial Mass celebrated by Father Lepire in the church of St Martin in Vimy. It was a dignified and formal event. Adam Sonnette proudly processed up the aisle to give his daughter away. All heard Louis-Marcel swear his vows but Marie-Marguerite's voice was barely audible. During the service, incense that burned and swung in the thurible wafted through the church, permeating its every corner. At the end, and with the organ as accompaniment, Charlotte sang a beautiful rendition of 'Ave Maria', the music composed by Johan Sebastian Bach. Many in the congregation wept as her pure tones echoed through the church. After the ceremony, the guests walked to Les Érables for the reception, there to be welcomed by the bride and groom and their respective families who all had journeyed from the church in four-wheeled carriages.

Wine flowed freely at the reception and Jean-Baptiste, amongst others, imbibed to excess. With the hubbub of conversation and clatter of dishes, glasses and utensils, everyone spoke loudly to be heard, which in turn raised the noise level in the house even further. In the midst of these festivities Jean-Baptiste stood up and broke into unsolicited and unaccompanied song. Blessed with a strong voice, he rattled the plates, and the din of dialogue in the room rapidly dwindled. His pitch was as shaky as a loose cart wheel, but there was no mistaking the words of the lyric, which he accompanied with strongly suggestive gestures, using his arms and body. With a ruddy face and considerable gusto he sang,

'She then took me down to the cellar
And filled me with Cognac so quick
I'd not been there many moments
When she asked for a look at my whip
She held it and viewed it a moment
Then laid it down with a smile
Young man, by the look and the length of your slash
We could drive the best part of a mile.'

As he completed the verse, some in the company burst out laughing and applauded while others, especially women, appeared shocked and placed their hands over their mouths in horror. For a moment Marcel seemed nonplussed, unsure whether to smile or be angry. He looked over to Clementine to see how she had reacted and saw her shaking her head. So, not quite steady himself on his feet, he crossed over to Jean-Baptiste who was receiving thumps on the back from his male friends, placed his hand on his shoulder and said, quietly but firmly, "Jean Baptiste, now, now, please stop singing. This is our home, not a tavern, and this is a wedding party, not a drinking contest. There are many women and important people present, as well as a couple of priests. Respect them and their sensitivities."

"I don't see why, Papa," Jean Baptiste replied loudly, waving his arms even more. "Look, they seem to be enjoying it."

"It is best you stop," repeated Marcel. Jean-Baptiste was about to ignore his father and start the next verse when he looked over towards Clementine and noticed her scowling and shaking her head at him. He knew better than to cross her.

The whole episode may have blown over and been quickly forgotten except at that point, Demy let out a loud and piercing scream. He had been sitting alone in a corner and had not drunk any alcohol, nor had he socialised. Jean-Baptiste's bawdy song seemed to trigger a deep memory. "The guards are singing and shouting," he yelled, his eyes and face contorted by spasms and tics. "They're coming to get me and kill me. The crowds! The convicts! The guards! The guns! I can hear them shouting and singing. Help me. I'm not going. I am not going!"

Both Clementine and Marcel rushed up to him, while wedding guests nearby moved aside and allowed them space to deal with the commotion. They knelt down beside Demy, each grasping one of his hands while Marcel said earnestly, "Demy, you are at Les Érables, our horse farm in Vimy. This is Louis-Marcel and Marie-Marguerite's wedding. We are helping you. No one will take you away. You are safe with us."

Demy began wailing loudly, tears pouring down his face, and then buried his face in his hands, "I can't take it anymore. I never stole any money. It's too much, too much. I loved André. I loved Richard and they both died. I loved Bonita and she died. I want to go away. I want to die too. There is no one left."

Clementine said resolutely, holding his hand tightly, "Demy, you are my dear brother. We all know you did not steal and sending you to the Bagne was a gross injustice. We love you and care for you."

With his eyes firmly closed and shaking his head Demy wailed loudly, "Nothing gets better. I can do nothing more, except the horses. I love the horses. Only they help me."

"You're quite right, Demy," replied Marcel soothingly. "Our horses are happy when you are with them. I'll be back in just a moment." He rose up from the floor, went to the bathroom, found a packet of Laudanum powder, dissolved it in a glass of water, returned to the living room and offered it to Demy. "Here Demy, have this drink of water. It will help you relax and sleep." Demy drank the potion, sat quietly for a few minutes then fell back into an exhausted sleep. They left him on the couch for the night.

During the whole episode Louis-Marcel and Marie-Marguerite looked on helplessly and silently, while Jean-Baptiste withdrew to his bedroom and fell into a drunken sleep. Meanwhile the wedding guests, bemused by the family fuss, quietly left the house and returned to their homes, with nothing more than a nod, minimal eye contact, and a farewell salute of the hand to Clementine and Marcel. Lepire left quietly, but Madame Tricheur could not resist a parting bolt. On the doorstep, with other departing guests swirling past her like a retreating army, she turned and planted her two large feet, "Monsieur Juin, this wedding would not even respect a low-down tavern in Paris. I can only thank the Lord, once again, that you did not become Mayor of our town. You are a disgrace, and would have brought everlasting shame on us all." She put her nose in the air and sniffed her way out of the front door.

Louis-Marcel and Marie-Marguerite then also quietly took their leave. They said au revoir to their parents and, hand in hand, each carrying an overnight bag, walked to the village tavern, Le Cheval Blanc, where their parents had rented a room for their wedding night. Both were naïve in matters of intimacy. They undressed and bedded in darkness and fumbled and groped in the gloom for hours before Louis-Marcel's arrow finally found its mark. The exercise was exhausting and satisfying for neither, and they fell asleep weary, locked in each other's arms.

Father Ladouceur remained behind after all had gone. Because he lived in Arras, he would not be able to travel home in the dark, and so he accepted Clementine's invitation to remain at Les Érables that night. The three, suddenly realising that the recent events had proved tiring, collapsed into chairs. "Well, we cannot exactly call that a successful wedding party," Marcel said with gentle irony to Clementine and Ladouceur after the final guest had departed. "I so do not like our family business being spread around town like that. And, you know, Madame Tricheur's insulting parting comment makes me wonder if she did not have something to do with me not getting the mayor's job."

"I was thinking the same thing," Clementine said, nodding in agreement. "I have never trusted that Madame. Outwardly she seems so upright, so conventional, but when you scratch the surface she is hollow inside. Her house and furnishings are imitations, not real - cheap and fake." She sighed deeply and then waved a hand as though knocking Madame Tricheur away. A wry smile came on her face. "I suppose the wedding party could have been worse, for example if there had been a fight between Jean-Baptiste and Demy. I am still shocked that Jean-Baptiste would sing that disgusting song at his brother's wedding, but what could have happened to Demy tonight?"

"It is strange, Clemmie," Marcel replied. "It is several years since he has had one of his spells. I thought he had got over them. He mentioned the singing and the crowds. Jean-Baptiste's song must have stirred something in his soul connected to the Hulk."

Ladouceur was anxious to be of counsel. "I'm sure you are correct, Marcel," he said, moving forward in his chair. "Some people who have had shocking events in their past lives, and this one is certainly shocking for Demy, they never adjust. It is a wound that has become inflamed and never heals. There is pus just under the surface, and a little scratch releases it, again. For Demy, Jean-Baptiste's song became the scratch."

"He is not the same Demy I knew when we were young," Clementine said, a well-worn sadness catching in her throat. "Although shy even then, he is much more distant now. He never speaks to me unless I say something first to him, so it's hard to know what he is thinking. He never addresses me by my name, nor smiles, laughs or cries, and until tonight he doesn't even get angry though I'm sure he has much anger inside, as I do." Ladouceur, hearing this, opened his mouth to speak, then closed it and sat back.

"Yes, I've noticed that too," replied Marcel. "Yet he is good with the farm animals, and also about things I ask him to do, as long as I speak quietly and respectfully. I try to be like a caring older brother. I have become fond of him, partly I suppose because I feel deeply sorry for him. I would love to do more to help Demy."

"You are already doing a great deal, Marcel," Ladouceur said. "If you had not been here and allowed him to live on the farm someone, likely his father would have sent him to La Maison de Force at Arras, where they send the lunatics from the region. Believe me, he would not have lasted long there. He may not be happy here on your farm, but there, he'd most likely have died from ill-treatment or perhaps even killed himself." The priest crossed himself.

"At times when I was young I thought I might be heading there myself," Clementine said with a smile. "In a way Marcel saved me from that joyless ending."

Marcel squeezed Clementine's hand. "We've had rough times but also good times that helped us live through the rough ones," he said. "You've helped me too, Clementine. When young I was shy like Demy, though not as bad; with your lively nature you brought me out of myself. I know at times I can be demanding and ungenerous and for that I am sorry."

"We have to make the best of what we've got," Clementine said, squeezing back on his hand. "I hope Demy will be better tomorrow, once he has had a good sleep. I wonder, Claude, if you could talk to Demy in the morning. Perhaps spiritual suggestions will help him. Both Doctors Jean-Paul Poirier from Arras and Vincent Cadieux say to send him to Spa for a water cure but we cannot afford that. In any case I believe what we are doing for Demy here on the farm is more beneficial than a spa."

"Yes, I will do that with pleasure," replied Ladouceur, as he rose and retired to his bedroom for the night. Clementine and Marcel also went to bed and hugged each other with affection before falling into an exhausted, thankfully dreamless, sleep.

The following morning Ladouceur invited Demy to go for a walk with him on the farm and in the nearby woods on Vimy ridge. "Demy," he said as they passed through the gate, "I saw you became very perturbed last night after Jean-Baptiste sang his song at the wedding party. What happened?" Demy did not respond for a few moments, then said, "I do not like noise, and singing or shouting. Everyone seemed to be shouting last night. First it reminded me of the, of my time in Toulon. Then all of a sudden I found myself there again, with guards before me yelling orders at us, striking us, prisoners moaning and groaning in pain. I knew I was not there but felt as if I was. I was so helpless and hopeless on the hulk. Complaining never helped because they would just strike you all the more, harder, so you forced yourself to keep quiet. Here, I can shout and scream, makes me feel good, as if I'm getting revenge on the guards."

"I understand," Ladouceur replied, recalling his own time in Canada under confinement, the everyday cruelty of it. "It is like steam, a head of steam that has to escape from a boiling kettle. Confine the steam to the pot, it will explode. We are going to have to let you scream so the steam can escape. Let you boil over."

"Yes, that is right," said Demy, looking over quickly at the kindly man, then away. "And as time passes, the screams, the rages, the nightmares are less than before. But I still get as angry as ever when people call me 'cross-eyes'. Even if they don't call me that, I know what they are thinking by the way they are looking at me, looking at my eyes. I was born with a curse. If not for my eyes, they would not have blamed me for stealing from Plouffe's shop. I would never have been sent to the Bagne."

"I fear that is true, Demy," Claude said, nodding and crinkling the lower part of his face with sympathy and affection. "There is no justice in this world, only in the next. We have to wait for our next life to even things up, but it is not easy- waiting, hoping. That is why you feel as if you are in this kettle, this trap. Yet I can also see you have come a long way since you first returned from Toulon."

"Father Claude," said Demy, stopping his stride and turning to face Ladouceur, startled by Demy's forthrightness. Never before had Ladouceur heard Demy address someone by their name. "It is eight years since I returned from there. Eight years. I have had a lot of misfortune in my life. And I have had good fortune, perhaps in equal measure. I know that coming to Les Érables has saved me from a terrible fate, like being sent to the asylum in Arras. Clementine, my sister, is good to me and Marcel is like a brother. The horses are my companions. But can I stop blaming fate for all my unhappiness, put it behind me and get pleasure from what is happening to me now? I'm beginning to think I can."

"If you could do that it, oh, it would be a huge step forward," replied Claude punching his right fist into the palm of his left hand. He resisted the urge to place his arm around Demy's shoulder, sensing Demy would misinterpret it as assault. "I know that Clementine and Marcel are so very fond of you and value your work on the farm. It will make them happy to see you happy. It is also something to thank God for."

"I will try," replied Demy, fervour in his voice. They continued the rest of their walk in silence and returned home.

On the other side of the village, a glass of sauternes in her hand, Madame Tricheur told Rose-Anne, her daughter, about the wedding reception chaos and what a triumph the evening had been—for her.

Chapter Twenty-Four

Vimy, June 1826

Marcel's fiftieth birthday came and went with little fanfare, yet he had reason to be pleased with his life and accomplishments. From his beginnings in penury, he had built up a horse farm that was a showpiece for the region. Outside the family circle, with a few exceptions, his wife, four sturdy children and family life were widely admired as ideal. The farm provided a good income but Marcel still kept a close eye on expenses. His early experiences in poverty, and his lack of desire to return there, had made him cautious with his finances. He and Clementine were able to visit Paris periodically for brief vacations, happily leaving care of the farm and horses to Louis-Marcel and Demy. He had come to terms with his defeat in the mayoralty race, even seeing it as opportune, enabling him to devote himself without distraction to farm and family.

The four children were doing well. Louis-Marcel, increasingly, took over direction of the farm. Marcel loved teaching him about horses and Louis-Marcel soaked up horse knowledge like a towel soaked up sweat. Jean-Baptiste worked for a Vimy well-digger, François attended a seminary in Amiens preparing for the priesthood, while Charlotte pursued her career in music. He loved them all and was fiercely proud of their accomplishments.

Marcel was beginning to feel, and show, his age. His brow had become increasingly furrowed, and his beard, though neatly-trimmed, was now almost white, as was the hair on his head, though to a slightly lesser extent than the beard. If he looked carefully in the mirror, he imagined he could still see an occasional auburn hair, a souvenir from his youth. He had developed a visible pot belly. His older friends and relatives had all gone, Catherine, Pauline and Charles many years previously, Alexis and Monique only during the past year. In particular, he had difficulty adjusting to Alexis' death. He had been like a friend and father blended into one. At bleak moments, he rued the fact that he was next in line for the cemetery.

Despite external appearances, Marcel had been getting more disgruntled with Clementine, though he was unsure when or how it began. The home atmosphere felt joyless, with him being irritable and yelling at her, and she back at him, over the most trivial of events. At heart, he knew the problem for him was sexual. Satisfied with neither the frequency nor the intensity of their relationship, he had attempted more than once to discuss the topic with Clementine, but she brushed it off and changed the subject to the children, or what he would like for supper. He knew her also to be loyal and faithful to a fault. Moreover, she had retained her youthful beauty. The fossette in her left cheek, present as a child, had morphed into a long shallow crevice and when she smiled her whole face, and especially her eyes, radiated pleasure.

These mounting frustrations were compounded by the fact that he had never had an intimate relationship with any woman other than Clementine, whereas he knew, or strongly suspected, that she had had at least one relationship prior to their marriage. He secretly even envied her experience in this domain. If he did nothing about the situation, he knew, his disgruntlement could only become stronger. Perhaps going to a prostitute would be the solution, he pondered? There were none in Vimy, at least as far as he knew. Locating one would require going to Arras or Amiens, a return journey of up to a day or more. How would he explain such absences to Clementine? He knew there would be no joy in the exercise, and one could pick up serious diseases in brothels. Worst of all, he would actually have to pay for the privilege of attending. I have no idea how much they charge, but I am sure it is more that I am willing to pay.

He decided the situation could only be remedied by an affair. But who, where and how? What about the fact that it was morally wrong and that he would have to answer for it before God and the confessional, let alone Clementine? He was well aware of the Church's teaching that, even by planning to have an affair he had already sinned in thought, if not yet in deed. His desires overcame the scruples, and he decided that while he would continue to attend mass as usual with the family, he would stop going to the sacraments. He also stopped singing in the choir, claiming, untruthfully, that singing hurt his throat. These changes puzzled Clementine and she asked, while preparing for their evening meal, "Marcel, why have you stopped going to confession and communion? Why have you stopped singing? I have not noticed anything wrong with your throat."

"I am not comfortable with it anymore. I am rethinking my relationship with the Church."

"Why do you not go and talk with Father Lepire?"

"No, I cannot talk with him. He thinks and talks only about himself, he suffers greatly from the sin of self-pride. Give him a mirror and he is happy." He then added, after a pause, "Do not concern yourself with this, Clemmie. I will be all right."

She stopped skinning the rabbit and turned to him, her knife still in her hand. "It does not sound all right to me," she said. "Perhaps you are sick. Go and talk with Dr Cadieux. I insist. Perhaps you are just in need of a tonic?"

"I am well, quite well. I do not need a tonic. Please do not ask me any more questions," Marcel said, in a voice filled with impatience and a few drops of guilt.

A few weeks went by during which Marcel scrutinised and surveyed the women of Vimy. While he did not neglect the farm, he made certain that Louis-Marcel and Demy were there, supervising the animals, giving him time to roam the streets of the town, sometimes on horseback, sometimes on foot.

One morning while walking down the main street he saw in the distance a woman he felt sure was Thérèse. He recalled her as his flame when, more than thirty years previously he had rejected her obvious advances. This event occurred shortly after he had emerged from hiding in a cave for six months to avoid being drafted into the army. Now is the time to rectify my ill-advised snub. He hurried around a back street so that he could encounter her face-to-face, as if by coincidence. When they met there was a look of simultaneous recognition on both sides, and they embraced each other. She certainly looked older and plumper, but her eyes twinkled and her face beamed with a growing succession of smiles at seeing him.

"Thérèse, it is years since I've seen you," Marcel said as he again hugged her fervently. "Where have you been?"

"I got married to Guy Marais who came from Amiens so we lived there. He died six months ago. We had no children because I had woman's troubles." Thérèse shook her head sadly then added, "A woman without a child is only half a woman. I envy those who come with child each time their husbands look at them."

Marcel smiled at her wit, and then thought about the struggles he and Clementine had had to reduce the frequency of their pregnancies. I must be one of those men whose wife comes with child every time I peek at her. He judged it best not to voice these thoughts. "But you look so well," he ventured, eyeing her from top to toe.

"Woman's troubles, you know, don't show on the outside," she replied indulgently, then added, "But they can still cause much inner turmoil. After Guy went, I had no reason to remain in Amiens and anyway don't like big cities, so decided to come back to Vimy where I have family and friends. Guy left me an inheritance so I bought a small house on the other side of town." Thérèse smiled and then lowered her eyes and head coquettishly, "What about you?"

Marcel wondered how much of his life story he should reveal. He decided to be brief and business-like. "I married Clementine thirty years ago. We have four children, three boys and a girl. We lost a three-year-old daughter some years ago to diphtheria. I own a horse farm called Les Érables that has been modestly successful. My eldest son and my wife's brother Demy, who has a nervous problem, help me with the farm work. Otherwise I'm keeping well."

"It seems you've had a cold life. You're not happy with Clementine?"

Marcel felt nonplussed by her perspicacity and pondered before replying. "She is good to me and I care for her and we both love our children. We have our differences but I am not about to leave her." Having no taste for discussing personal matters he did not elaborate.

"Poor Marcel," Thérèse replied sympathetically. "Perhaps it will get better with time. You've been together so long now." After a brief silence she added, "It is strange coming back to Vimy after having been away for so long. Things have changed, yet they have not changed. Trees and buildings look different even though I know they are the same. And of course everyone looks older. I am the only one who has not changed," she added with an ironic smile.

Marcel laughed at her little joke. He thought to himself, I wonder if she would say 'yes.' He looked deep into her eyes, noticed her lower lip quiver slightly with anxiety and comprehension, then said, with trepidation, "Can I come over and visit you one evening?"

"Why, yes, of course," she said, then blushed demurely. "Come tomorrow night. We can have une petite boisson together and talk about old times."

"That will be great, Thérèse." He smiled at her as they bid au revoir.

Marcel spent the rest of the day distracted. Preoccupied by thoughts of Thérèse he went for a walk up Vimy ridge, forgetting that he had made an appointment with Louis-Marcel and Demy. One of the mares had come into heat, and that afternoon Con Brio, the stallion, was scheduled to serve her. When Marcel failed to show up Louis-Marcel and Demy continued with the arrangements alone. Marcel returned from his walk just in time to see Con Brio mounting the mare. He paused and watched from a distance and in admiration, at Con Brio's impressively large penis.

That night at table Marcel said little. As they were washing up in the kitchen after dinner he said casually to Clementine, "Oh, I met an old school friend, Roger Tarbeau in the street today. He moved to Arras but is back in town for a few days. He invited me out to dinner tomorrow evening at the tavern. I shouldn't be back late."

"That's all right dear. I am sure Demy will help with the cooking and cleaning up."

"Yes, it will be nice seeing him again after all these years," he said with as much composure as he could muster.

"Yes, I am sure," she replied gaily.

Marcel heaved a sigh of relief that she had not pursued the questioning. He had a line of responses ready but they were not needed. He went to bed early that night but felt excited and restless and slept fitfully. He dreamt that a parishioner had spotted him entering a brothel in Amiens and had reported this to Clementine who, in revenge, had placed some poison in his coffee. The poison did not kill him, but had permanently paralysed all four limbs, rendering him bedridden for the rest of his life. He woke up in a cold sweat and trembling and could not settle the rest of the night.

Next day he wrestled with his conscience and wondered if he should call off the whole adventure. Eventually he decided he had come this far with his plan and it would be cowardly to back out. He remained unsure how to get to Thérèse's house. If he walked he would arrive back late and exhausted, but walking could be done far more covertly. Riding on horseback would be far quicker but would risk being seen and recognised. Eventually he decided to ride and hoped there would be a secluded area behind her house where he could discreetly leave the horse while inside.

Late in the afternoon he saddled his horse and took a roundabout route to Thérèse's home, so that he approached it from the far side of the town, thinking this would help deceive anyone observing or following him. Near the house, he found a run-in shed provided with water and hay where he tied up the horse. He saw the house was small, even by the standards of Vimy. It contained one bedroom, a tiny kitchen and the living and dining areas were combined into one with a large stone fireplace on the outside wall. Furnishings were sparse but of good quality and the floors well carpeted. He spied a shelf of large books against the living room wall. On closer inspection he saw they included all twenty-eight volumes of Denis Diderot's Encyclopedia. "I didn't know you could read," Marcel said with surprise, flicking his eyes towards the books.

"When I found I could not bear children, I went to school in Amiens and learnt how to read and write," Thérèse replied matter-of-factly. "I love knowing things. These books contain the sum of all human knowledge. It gives me pleasure to read through the topics. I'm a great admirer of Olympe de Gouges, whom they stupidly executed during the Revolution. She argued that women were equal to men in all things and should be given political rights equal to men."

"Mm, I see. I've not heard of Olympe de Gouge," responded an obviously impressed Marcel, nodding his head and crinkling his brow. He removed one of the volumes from the shelf, paged through it slowly and admired the numerous spectacular engravings of anatomical parts, complex engineering structures and many other subject matters. He then embraced Thérèse and she offered him a glass of wine. "I should have done this thirty years ago," he added. "My life has been a chronicle of wasted time and missed opportunities!"

"I cared for you then and I care for you now," Thérèse replied, hugging him firmly. Thérèse was shorter and plumper than Clementine and Marcel noticed the weird experience, for him, of holding a woman with a different physical form from the one to whom he was long-accustomed. "I had a secret admiration for you when we were young," she continued. "I loved your strong features, your long auburn-tinted hair and beard, and quiet nature. I was disappointed when you turned me away."

"We will just have to make up for it now," Marcel said with a smile. "In those days I tried to be good and suppressed my desires. Now that I am older and more devilish I am learning how to express them!"

"I love to feel and hold you, Marcel. Guy was not very affectionate, even before he got sick. My skin has been starved of sensations since he died. I want you to nourish it again!"

Marcel felt his passions rising as he listened to Thérèse's words of ardour and longing. Concerned also as to how long his horse would last without drawing the attention of neighbours to its presence, he gulped down the rest of his wine and said, "Why wait any longer? Come, let us bed!"

By the time he returned home later in the evening, he found Clementine sound asleep and he slipped silently into bed without disturbing her. As he lay in the dark, eyes wide open, brooding about what he had done, he had feelings that mixed intense satisfaction with intense guilt, in approximately equal measures. The satisfaction felt real. Not only had he enjoyed the experience but he had a sense of accomplishment that he had overcome his suppressed desires, knowing the risk being taken. The guilt also felt real. He had broken a strict moral and social code that had become deeply embedded in his heart, infinitely aggravated by the need to deceive Clementine.

As they sipped coffee next morning Clementine asked, "How was the dinner with your friend last night?"

"It went very well. Roger has a textile business and is seeking to expand into the surrounding region," he lied. "I will assist by providing him with contacts. He plans to come to Vimy every week so I shall be meeting with him regularly. It is possible this will develop into a lucrative business for me so it is worth pursuing. He is a quiet man but full of ideas and energy."

Marcel spoke as smoothly and steadily as possible, but felt his armpits and the palms of his hands dampen with sweat, so much so that he thought he would start to smell. He hoped Clementine would not notice, and as soon as possible he went outside in the fresh air to take off his tunic and breathe and relax.

His tryst with Thérèse continued for several weeks. Clementine did not pursue him with questions following his weekly nocturnal absences and he began to believe the arrangement could become a regular part of his life. The hours with Thérèse were satisfying and he wished they could be extended. He also knew that if they were prolonged he risked being found out, and he could not contemplate the effect this would have on Clementine and the family. He suspected she would throw him out, at the very least.

He found leading a double life also personally demanding. He drank more wine, had stomach cramps, ate less and lost weight. He was tense and irritable, and even burst into tears on occasion, for the most trivial of reasons. Clementine noticed and one day said, "Marcel, you are not well, you are not yourself. What is the matter?"

"It is nothing, Thérèse. I am fine."

"My name is Clementine," she replied angrily. "Who is this Thérèse? I have noticed also that these days you make no demands on me in bed. Are you having an affair, Marcel?"

"No, of course not! Where would I find the time, let alone a woman? I have been worried about business arrangements with Roger. It looks like it is not going to be as successful as I thought. I believe he may be going in the wrong direction but I don't know how to break that news to him."

"Why do you not bring him home here to meet me? I am a shrewd judge of men, their needs and their ambitions. I would size him up for you very quickly."

"No, that would not be a good idea," he responded quickly. "He is a busy man and would not have the time. I shall have to deal with it myself." Marcel noticed Clementine looking at him suspiciously. He shifted uncomfortably but said nothing more.

Realising now that, because Clementine's suspicions had been raised, there was a big danger of the affair coming out into the open, he decided to break it up. Next day he rode to Thérèse's house. She came out to greet him as soon as he arrived, full of smiles. Without dismounting he said, "Thérèse, it is all off. I cannot continue living like this. It is hurting Clementine. It is harming me. I am not coming back to visit you."

"I'd be very disappointed Marcel. I love you and you have made me happy. Why do you not leave her and come and live with me?"

"I cannot do that. It is not only my wife, whom I still love, despite our difficulties. I have children who respect me --- at least I think they still do. I have Les Érables that is the envy of the region. I am an esteemed member of the parish — at least I used to be. I care for you also. You too have made me happy, in some respects anyway. I love visiting you and being with you. We have so much to talk about. I would love for us to continue to meet like this but I am not prepared to desert my family and my farm."

Thérèse stared down at the ground for a few moments, and then without looking at Marcel, said, "Do what you have to do. It is your life. I thought you cared about me. Now I realise other things are more important to you." She turned around and strode firmly back into her house without a farewell greeting. Marcel remained motionless for several minutes wondering what to do. Eventually, downcast, he flicked the reins and walked the horse slowly back home.

For the next few weeks Marcel remained at home and tried to regain Clementine's trust. He helped her with household chores and took her out for walks on the forest trails. He resumed their sexual relationship though found it dull and monotonous after the illicit and novel excitement of Thérèse. He attended to farm affairs with Louis-Marcel and Demy and continued grooming the former to take over the farm one day. François was away in Amiens for most of the year and spent little time at home. Charlotte loved her music studies, and she too needed little guidance.

But Marcel had not forgotten Thérèse. Although at the time he last left her house, it had been his firm intention to break off the affair, he began yearning for her again, wondering how he could bring her back into his life. Then, almost as though he had willed it, an opportunity presented itself when Clementine decided she wanted to visit family and friends in Arras for a weekend. Marcel excused himself from the trip on the basis that he had to attend to farm affairs. She had barely left in the carriage when he saddled his horse and rode off to visit Thérèse. They hugged when he arrived.

"You said you were not coming back," Thérèse said with an ironic smile.

"I meant it when I said it. The passage of time excites the dream so I came back," Marcel replied, grinning with excitement and expectation.

"What about your wife, family and farm?" asked Thérèse. She spoke quietly but her sarcasm was unmistakable. "Have they suddenly become unimportant?"

"In spite of them I could not stop thinking about you. My life there seemed incomplete without you." Marcel made a chopping gesture, using the edge of his right hand and hitting the palm of his left hand.

"What would she say if she heard you?"

"She would be disappointed, to say the least." Marcel felt increasing discomfort with the interrogation. "She is already disappointed in me. This would add one hundredfold to the disappointment."

"Listen to me Marcel. We have talked a lot about you and your problem," Thérèse spoke quietly, clenched her fists, and looked directly into Marcel's eyes. "Let's talk a little about me. I am a widow, alone, with few means at my disposal. I am fairly young, not unattractive, am witty and would like a life partner. You are telling me firmly that you will not leave your family but you obviously want to continue our little dalliance, because it suits you, and gives you an outlet for your frustrations. I know you have religious and moral sensitivities, though they are not much in evidence when you are around me. I don't care anything about the morality of what we are doing but if we continue our arrangement, my chances of getting a partner are nil. Moreover, if our arrangement is discovered, who will be blamed? It will be me, totally. You will meekly return to your wife who will forgive you. I, on the other hand, will be vilified by the community for seducing a married man. If it is your intention to stay with your wife, it is my intention to end our affair."

Marcel struggled silently with her strongly-stated position. He felt trapped and did not know how to reply. He opened his mouth as if to say something and closed it again. Thérèse then continued, "Without words, Marcel, you have responded to what I've said. Come to bed with me now this last time. After you leave tonight you are not to return."

Clementine returned late on Sunday to find Marcel lying gloomily on his bed. "What is it my darling? Are you not feeling well again?"

"I'll be all right. I missed you," he lied.

"Poor little sweetie," she said cheerfully. "I am back now ready to care for you and get you strong again. Would you like me to make you one of my hot soup specials?"

"I would like that."

Clementine continued chatting gaily to Marcel while she prepared the soup, bringing him up-to-date on family affairs in Arras. Marcel listened with half an ear, making grunting noises of approval any time a break in the stream of words occurred.

Marcel went to work on the farm next morning and returned home for lunch. As soon as he entered the door he knew a storm was breaking. Clementine stood beside the kitchen table with a broom in one hand, and the other hand on her waist. Her eyes and face were fierce with fury. "I had a visitor this morning," she said, lips tightly pursed and with venom in her voice, "Alain, the carpenter. He informed me that he saw your horse outside

Thérèse Lagrange's house late on Saturday. Do you continue to lie to me that you are not having an affair?"

"I did lie to you. I did have an affair with Thérèse. The affair is now over. I am sorry I hurt you," Marcel replied quietly, looking down on the floor.

"Oh, how can I ever trust you again?" she screamed. "Men hurt me when I was young. I fell in love with you because I thought you were different, but you are the same as the others. You are worse than them because you pretend to build trust and then you destroy what you have built by lies and deception. At least the others never pretended. You despicable dog!"

She rushed at Marcel with the broom and started beating his arms and back. He did not retaliate, but fell down and crouched on the floor with his arms over his head for protection, moaning and crying in pain. Clementine also cried and screamed and continued beating him vigorously, using both arms on the broom for several minutes until she fell exhausted on the floor next to him. Their weeping gradually subsided and Marcel reached over, took her hand in his and through tears said, "Clementine, I know what I did was very wrong. I am sorry. I mean it when I say it is all over. Thérèse only wants me if I leave you and I will not leave you, so it is finished. I have seen her for the last time."

"How can I know that?" Clementine cried through tears. "How can I ever trust you again? You love her but you do not love me. You must go with the woman you love."

"It is not as simple as that. I thought I loved her but it was not true love, only passing passion. Even though I have hurt you badly I love you with a deeper love because it started a long time ago and has endured many tribulations. You are the mother of my children. I love them, you through them and them through you. I want us to stay together."

The pain in Marcel's heart at that moment was greater than the pain in his back from the thrashing. He chose his words carefully now. "I know I betrayed your trust and deserved the pounding," he continued, softly and with feeling. "I know that trust is more than a matter of words and for me to merely promise to make amends is insufficient. It is only time and my actions that will heal the wound. For what it is worth, and I know my promise has little value at present, I am through with the affair and assure you I shall remain faithful to you."

Until that moment Clementine's hand had remained limp in Marcel's. For the first time he felt a faint tightening of her grip. They were still lying on the cold, hard wooden floor and Marcel's arms and back were burning and bleeding from beatings with the broom. A splinter from the wooden floor had pierced the skin on his back, adding to his drastic discomfort. He struggled to stand up and helped Clementine rise. They hugged each other and Clementine then cleaned and dressed Marcel's wounds.

Marcel made his peace with God by going to confession. He dared not go to Father Lepire at the local parish church as he neither liked nor trusted him. So he went to Arras and sought out Father Claude Ladouceur. "How many times did you commit adultery?" asked Ladouceur in the confessional.

"Six times, Mon Père. I also lied and mislead my wife."

"Is it your intention to not sin again?"

"Yes Mon Père. That is my full intention."

"Adultery is a serious sin, not only before God but before your fellow men because it harms others. Your sin is especially serious because of the deception involving your wife. For your penance you are to attend daily mass for nine consecutive days not including Sundays. Every day for one month you are to carry out at least one act of Charity towards your wife. Finally, you are to make a generous donation to the poor house here in Arras." Marcel saw that Ladouceur's voice and hands trembled as he spoke and gave his blessing.

"Thank you for hearing me, Mon Père," replied Marcel, with a feeling that a weight had been lifted from his shoulders.

Ladouceur ended the confession with the injunction he had used many times before, "Now go in Peace and sin no more." He had rarely known it to come true, but in this case he suspected it might. It just might.

Chapter Twenty-Five

Summer 1832

"I am sick, Maman."

Late one afternoon, Jean-Baptiste returned home early from his job as a well-digger. Aged thirty and still unmarried, he lived at home with his parents. Jean-Baptiste enjoyed wine. Every few weeks he would go on an alcoholic binge and for several days would be hung over and inaccessible. He did not, or could not respond to the entreaties of Clementine and Marcel, who ended up putting up with his binges as best they could. After returning home following his most recent drinking bout, Marcel heard Jean-Baptiste mutter, as if to himself, "I'm a failure. Jacqueline rejected me. Maude threw me out. I'm good for nothing." Marcel understood but did not respond. He knew about Jean-Baptiste's disappointments in love. He and Clementine had even tried to arrange a wedding for him but plans foundered when Jean-Baptiste got drunk and threatened the father of the prospective bride.

"You look pale. It must be the drink again," replied Clementine sternly. She then changed her tone to a plea. "Jean-Baptiste, you are harming yourself. If you do not stop it will kill you. Your father and I care about you and hate to see you destroying yourself. Could you not find something else to occupy your time other than the tavern?"

"I have not had wine for a week, Maman," he replied, his face flushed with anger. "It is not booze. I am sick. I have pains all over my body and have no strength in my limbs. I feel cold but my body is hot."

Clementine shook her head sadly as Jean-Baptiste took himself to bed.

Later that evening he started vomiting and developed severe diarrhoea that continued all night, keeping all awake with his painful moans. By morning he felt and looked very ill, with a parched, dry throat and sunken eye sockets. His pale skin had a bluish tinge that gave him a ghost-like appearance. Although very thirsty he would vomit if he drank even a mouthful of water. Marcel sent urgently for Dr Cadieux, Vimy's only medical doctor, who visited that afternoon. By that time Jean-Baptiste was barely conscious. As Cadieux entered the bedroom he sniffed the miasmic odour pervading the air and immediately made his diagnosis.

After completing the examination he took Marcel and Clementine aside and said gravely, "I'm afraid he has cholera-morbus, Marcel. An epidemic of this condition has struck our region, spread from the east. There are many cases and deaths and there will be many more."

"I am shocked Doctor," Marcel replied. "He is but thirty years old and has his whole life before him. Is there nothing we can do?"

"There is no treatment other than replacing the fluid that the patient loses from the intestine. You have to provide him with plenty of water, even if he brings it up. He likely will not survive. Keep the windows in the house open for fresh air and keep everything clean. That will at least prevent others from getting infected."

"I too, am overcome by that news but we'll do as you say, Doctor," added Clementine, shaking her head disbelievingly. "What brings about this awful disease?"

"At present we do not know. Some physicians think it is caused by bad air. I myself believe it is caused by an animalcule so small that it cannot be seen. Look after him as best you can," the doctor added, while replacing his hat, picking up his case of drugs and instruments and making for the door. Jean-Baptiste could not keep down the small amounts of fluid he swallowed and died later that evening. Clementine held his hand and heard him mumble plaintively, to no one in particular, "Bring me a woman. I want to see Jacqueline before I die!" before losing consciousness.

Shortly after the funeral Demy developed the same symptoms. Clementine and Marcel followed the treatment orders recommended by Dr Cadieux for Jean-Baptiste but, as with his case, they had no effect. Demy withstood the effects of the disease with remarkable equanimity. Perhaps helped by his near-death experiences while a prisoner in the Bagne, and knowing he would likely die, he remained calm and in control despite the pain in his belly, the diarrhoea, and the foul effects of the nausea and vomiting, and even apologised to Clementine for causing her so much trouble. "Say farewell to Belle Bonita for me," were the last words he uttered before expiring.

Three funerals were held simultaneously on the day of Demy's death which astonished Father Lepire who normally had but one funeral every three to four weeks. Now there were up to four every day. He, the funeral manager and the gravediggers could not keep up the pace. They were under pressure to bury each victim quickly, on the day of death if possible, because of fear that the corpses could transmit the disease to the living. Panic spread rapidly through the town.

Mayor Raymond Batarse decided to convene a meeting of eminent citizens, the first ever of its kind, to decide how the epidemic should be handled. Lepire, Dr Cadieux, Marcel and Madame Tricheur, amongst others, were invited. He held the meeting in the Deliberation Room of the Mairie, the biggest in the building. A large rectangular table centred the room with thirteen comfortable armchairs ranged around it, five on each of the long sides of the table, two on one short side and but one on the other short side where the mayor himself sat. A gavel rested on the table near his right hand. Large ceramic ash trays were located on the table at every seat and a distinctive hand painted floral design decorated each of them. A clerk who recorded the deliberations of the meeting sat on the mayor's right hand side.

"We have a problem," the mayor intoned pompously, by way of introduction. "There is a deadly disease affecting our community and some people are panicking. I do not wish things to get out of hand. At all costs we do not want it to affect commerce and travel. As mayor I have worked hard and been successful at making Vimy a regional centre of commercial activity. If it becomes known that this town is diseased it could have disastrous effects on trade. We must control all information that is disseminated about this disease."

What nonsense, thought Marcel. Batarse has done nothing for this town. Few people have heard of Vimy and it is no commercial centre. He must be in a panic to call a meeting. He will not listen to a word we say. For the moment he did not air his views. He felt irritated not only by what the mayor said, but by his pretentious manner and yet again by that unidentifiable accent. He knew if he said something in his present frame of mind it would be provocative and profitless.

Dr Cadieux spoke next, in an authoritative tone, while knocking his pipe on the ashtray to empty its ash contents. "The disease we have in our community is called cholera-morbus. There is an epidemic of this condition and we are not the only town affected. Indeed, it may be afflicting the entire country. We shall accomplish nothing by trying to hide the truth. To do so may make things even worse, by not explaining to people what can be done to prevent it. We do not know what causes cholera-morbus. Some authorities believe ..."

"You say you don't know what causes the disease, Doctor," interrupted Father Lepire. "I do know what is causing it! We are a sinful community and God is punishing us. Through this affliction, he is calling us back to His Truth and His Love. I agree with Mayor Batarse. There is no need to make any announcements. What we need is to call the people to prayer and ask forgiveness for their sins. Once this is granted I know the disease will disappear!" Lepire banged his fist on the table for emphasis.

"If you permit, Father Lepire, and for your information I will complete my little speech that you interrupted," replied Cadieux, patiently. The meeting waited while he unhurriedly refilled his pipe with fresh tobacco, and lit it. He then continued, gravely, "Some authorities believe it is caused by bad air circulating in houses. Personally I believe it is caused by a tiny, invisible animalcule. I also believe it can be prevented by having plenty of fresh air, a nourishing diet and drinking clean water. It is up to us to let our citizens know about these recommendations."

"While I respect Father Lepire's opinion, particularly as a member of his congregation," said Marcel quietly though firmly, "I do not believe that prayer alone will be sufficient. There have been many epidemics of plague and other diseases in the past, and prayer alone never caused them to vanish. We have not had to face this condition of cholera-morbus before. Diseases are a branch of medicine, not theology. Dr Cadieux has admitted that medicine does not yet have all the answers, but perhaps he does have some. The measures that he has proposed are simple, easy to propagate and they also make sense. While I am not against prayer, I believe strongly we should do as the doctor recommends. Let us try both, thereby doubling our chances… "

"Dr Cadieux and Monsieur Juin are both talking nonsense," Madame Tricheur interrupted, voicing her strongly held opinions, while slapping her hand on the table. "Medicine obviously knows nothing about this disease. The doctor is just speculating. He is also exaggerating its severity to throw us all in to a panic. No one in my home has taken ill. I agree with Mayor Batarse. We will reduce the so-called panic by not making any announcements about what is happening and what people should do, which will merely instil more fear."

"I thank you gentlemen and ladies for attending this meeting," Batarse voiced from the chair, with the clear intention of terminating the heated discussion, and to reserve any decision or action entirely to himself. "I shall consider your opinions and take action in the next twenty-four hours."

Batarse outwardly gives the appearance of being smart and considerate but he is also foolish, thought Marcel. He will take note of none of our opinions, other than those he wants to hear. He makes decisions based on personal whims and expediency rather than reason, and has the fool's ability to ignore facts. I know this epidemic will end badly.

Two days later the following notice appeared on the board outside the mayor's office.

ANNOUNCEMENT

THERE IS NO BASIS TO THE RUMOUR THAT A DISEASE IS
RAMPANT IN OUR COMMUNITY.
I URGE ALL CITIZENS TO LIVE THEIR LIVES NORMALLY
NO ACTION NEED BE TAKEN

RAYMOND BATARSE
MAYOR OF VIMY

Meanwhile the deaths, funerals and burials continued at an alarming pace. Each street had at least one every day and a miasmic odour pervaded the town, sickening even the healthy. With two deaths already in his home, Marcel followed Dr Cadieux's recommendations to the letter and instructed Louis-Marcel to do the same. Louis-Marcel had married Marie-Marguerite, a young girl from Arras, several years previously, and with Marcel's support, they had bought a house nearby on the outskirts of the town. They had two young children, P'tit Marcel and Caroline, aged four and two respectively.

The morning after the Mayor's announcement had been posted, Louis-Marcel rushed up to Clementine's home. "Maman, come quickly. P'tit Marcel is sick. He is vomiting and his stomach is running. Marie-Marguerite is crying and in panic, fearing he has the cholera-morbus that killed Jean-Baptiste and Demy."

By the time Clementine arrived P'tit Marcel seemed to be delirious. He moaned and cried, recognised no one and his arms and legs were flailing as if trying to keep demons away. Clementine noticed that his tongue was bone-dry, and his skin had the pale-blue hue she had seen on Jean-Baptiste and Demy. She tried to force some water down his throat but he coughed it back. He became limp and died in her arms several minutes later. There had not even been time to call Doctor Cadieux.

Clementine and Marcel felt devastated by the death of their first grandson and Marcel's namesake. At the gravesite, Marie-Marguerite wailed and wept and had to be restrained physically from leaping into the pit as the grave-diggers lowered the small white coffin. Cadieux prescribed a dose of Sydenham's Laudanum for her each night for a week.

Marcel had noticed, from bitter first-hand experience, that cholera-morbus attacked mainly the weak. Jean-Baptiste and Demy both had health problems before being struck by the disease. P'tit Marcel was a child and he knew of several older men and women in the street who had succumbed. He went to Dr Cadieux's office to discuss this idea. He noticed a strange odour in the room, not unpleasant, that seemed to be a mixture of spirits and camphor. A desk occupied the centre, surrounded by three chairs, and near the window stood a high couch covered by a crumpled-up sheet. The wall behind the desk contained a glassed-in wooden closet, from floor to ceiling, and shelves lined with bottles, in various shapes and sizes, filled with potions, herbs and remedies.

"There is something in what you state, Marcel," replied Cadieux after hearing Marcel out. "I have noticed it as well. Those who are very young, old or already ill or feeble appear unable to resist the contagion. It attacks the weak. That is why good food, fresh air, exercise and clean water are so important in prevention. They help build strength. I am shocked by the mayor's announcement. He ignores facts and the announcement can do nothing but harm. It is curious how he calls a meeting to get our opinions and then takes no notice of what we say."

"I have noticed that approach is common amongst politicians. Many advised Napoleon not to invade Russia, and call off the campaign to defeat England, but he ignored this advice and brought disaster on himself and the country."

"People in the town are wiser than the mayor believes," Dr Cadieux added, speaking in low tones, choosing his words carefully. "They know what is happening and are taking their own precautions. I have seen many of them in medical consultation myself and have given the same advice over and over again so the word is getting around. Besides, as I told the mayor, we are not the only place affected. The epidemic is widespread in the country and according to the medical journal I read, many thousands are dying every day. I believe that facing periodic scourges of this nature are the eternal lot of humanity. Almost half the population of Europe died in the plagues of the fourteenth century. What we are experiencing now, so far, is a minor pinprick compared to what our ancestors went through."

"I know little about history," Marcel replied. "Unfortunately, I had little education when young and still do not read easily."

"Here is another thought," Dr Cadieux went on, scarcely seeming to hear what Marcel had said. "In reading history I have noticed that periods of exceptional creativity follow social unrest and agitation. The Golden Ages of Pericles in ancient Greece, and Augustus in Rome, for example, followed intense political turmoil. Similarly the Elizabethan period in England during the sixteenth century that produced Monsieur Guillaume Shakespeare and other great artists. Apropos our present problems, Shakespeare had some words of wisdom, 'When sorrows come, they come not in single spies but in battalions.'

310

"Our own Revolution," Cadieux continued, "despite its excesses, provoked a deluge of creativity, in the arts, in science and in industry not only in France but in Europe as a whole. The steam engine and the railway that have just been invented will transform our society and the world. There is always a positive way of looking at disasters," he added with a smile. "They seem to bring out both the best and the worst in human nature."

Cadieux's ideas fascinated Marcel. Although well-versed in current and recent political events, he had a tenuous knowledge of bygone times. "That is amazing," he replied weakly. "I never knew those things." His mind flew back to his visits with Thérèse, and his admiration for her knowledge and reading of Diderot's Encyclopaedia.

Marcel decided to change the subject to a topic he did know something about. "Because of my daughter Charlotte, I know much about music. As you know she is a musician and a pianist and performs regularly in soirées musicales in private homes in Arras and Amiens. I have a good singing voice and she accompanies me on the piano so we perform together. She has developed a passion for a Viennese composer called Louis van Beethoven. She performs much of his music including some of his sonatas, and even to me it is very beautiful. Apparently this man Beethoven died recently."

"Yes, I heard that," replied Cadieux. "He died of a dreadful disease called dropsy, a painful ending for the poor man. I also read that he was totally deaf. How is it possible for a man to compose music and not hear what he is writing?"

"I cannot understand that either, Doctor," replied Marcel. "Somehow, perhaps, the music must have existed inside his head. Beethoven composed nine symphonies. Two or three years ago Charlotte discovered that all these symphonies were being performed in Paris by the Orchestre de la Societé des concerts du Conservatoire conducted by François-Antoine Haberneck, a famous conductor. She persuaded me last month to accompany her to Paris for a performance of his Ninth Symphony."

"I have to say the music is unforgettable." Marcel gesticulated to emphasise his points. "Charlotte, God bless her soul, burst into rapturous tears when she heard it. It is powerful and nothing like you have ever heard before. Moreover the symphony tells a story, a story about passion, joy and about the universal brotherhood of Man. Politicians who are fighting each other and declaring wars should take note. Beethoven has a message for them all."

Marcel noticed Dr Cadieux's eyes gazing at him intently as he spoke. "I would love to hear it," Cadieux replied. "I know little about music other than folk music and that of the gypsies. I would love to know more. If there is another performance, let me know. I shall accompany you to Paris. To get back to our topic, is there anything more we can do about Batarse and the epidemic?"

"I do not think so," replied Marcel. "Nor can we rely on Lepire with his theological explanation of the epidemic. Over the next few days I shall go around the town and knock on as many doors as I can. I am well known. I shall speak to families individually and pass on your message about how to prevent and treat the disease. If you don't mind, I shall quote you as my authority," he added with a rueful smile.

"I have no objection," replied Dr Cadieux, laughing. "But I am no authority. Medicine still has huge areas of ignorance. With time we will get the answers. While we wait, we have to use our common sense." Cadieux extended his hand, thinking the conversation over, but then noticed that Marcel was about to speak again, although with some reluctance.

"Mm… before I leave, Doctor, I would like to ask your advice about a personal medical matter," he said. "You have likely noticed, without me advising you, that I am losing control of the fingers in both my hands." Marcel showed the doctor his hands. "You notice that the three outer fingers in each hand are curled over like a claw and I am unable to straighten them. As you can see and feel, the palm of the hand is thickened and hard, almost as hard as bone, yet there is no bone there. The fingers are painful, and they greatly interfere with my activities including horse-riding. Can you tell me what is wrong and whether there is any remedy?"

Dr Cadieux examined Marcel's hands and said, "I have seen this condition just once before, in a man your age. He had quite severe arthritis and used a cane, and I thought it might be pressure from the cane on the palm of the hand. That man also drank far too much wine. In his case I inferred that a combination of all of these features — arthritis, cane-use and wine, caused his condition. I can see you do not have arthritis and do not use a cane. Are you a secret drinker?" he asked with a smile.

Marcel smiled in response, "I like my wine but in my opinion I am not a sot. You may talk with Clementine if you wish to confirm this."

"That will not be necessary. I know you well enough. I have not seen or heard colleagues talk about this condition so know little about it. Meanwhile I would suggest you massage the hand and the fingers with oil, and attempt to stretch them to break down the tissues to straighten the fingers. I shall make some enquiries and do some reading and if I hear of anything I shall let you know."

"That is kind of you, doctor. Can I pay for the consultation?"

"That will not be necessary. I have found our conversation illuminating and that will be payment enough. Au revoir, Marcel."

"Au revoir, Monsieur le docteur.

Meanwhile the epidemic continued and more lives were lost. Both the bakery and the butchery closed down when their proprietors died in the epidemic, leaving bread and meat unavailable. Mothers lost daughters, sons lost fathers. Children whose parents had expired appeared at street corners, dressed in rags, begging for food and handouts. They were a pathetic sight to behold. Both Marcel and Doctor Cadieux carried out their low grade publicity campaign about dealing with cholera, informing every citizen they met about the importance of fresh air, hygiene and clean water, while Raymond Batarse sat in his office at the Mairie with a self-satisfied smile, congratulating himself that he had rescued Vimy from ruin.

It took many months, and many deaths, before the epidemic gradually subsided.

Chapter Twenty-Six

Summer 1834

"Marcel, I have some news for you," Dr. Cadieux said. The doctor had turned up on Marcel's doorstep obviously anxious to talk. He had practically run past Marcel and taken a seat near the open window. A blissful summer day, the sun streamed through the window into the living room. Marcel was about to offer him a glass of wine when Cadieux began speaking, his corpulent eyebrows rising up like caterpillars, his voice trembling with fervour. "I have some exciting news for you Marcel," he said, "I attended a medical meeting in Paris this last week and heard a presentation by Baron Guillaume Dupuytren. He is one of the leading surgeons in France. King Louis XVIII granted him a baronetcy many years ago, not that that will hold much water with you." Marcel agreed that it was not an endorsement to which he gave much credence. "Well, be that as it may, the eminent doctor gave a fascinating presentation and in it described a condition of the hand that he treats with surgery and it is exactly the disease that you have! He illustrated many patients in his lecture. The fingers of their hands were curled over in the shape of a claw and the hand is useless, especially for workmen. He treats it by cutting fibres under the skin and this releases tension in the fingers so they can be straightened. The operation is very painful, even with the use of alcohol or opium."

"Interesting," Marcel replied guardedly after some silence, still staring at his hands, as if staring alone might release the tension. "But I am not sure that I want surgery. To be cut. You know I am getting old and have less need of the dexterity of youth. The condition, though bad I'll admit, does not seem to be getting worse. So I've concluded that the devil I know is preferable, and I may as well live the rest of my life with it. But thank you for coming straight to me. Did you learn anything about its cause?"

Cadieux's face could not mask his professional disappointment at his potential patient's reluctance for surgery. "Dr Dupuytren himself thinks it is connected to arthritis. I spoke to one of his assistants who made more sense. He has noticed a number of cases in the same family — a father and son, brothers and sisters. The condition does occur in women, although less frequently than in men. Are there any in your family who have the disease?"

"I have no family," Marcel said, almost wearily. "My mother died in childbirth when I was seven years old. The baby died as well so I have no brothers and sisters. I never knew or met my father. My parents never married."

During a momentary silence the doctor wondered how to respond to this surprising news. "I did not know that and would never have suspected it of you."

"Why not?" Marcel said. "It is not rare for young unmarried girls to become pregnant. As a boy I was teased mercilessly for being a bastard and it toughened me up. But I am still a bastard!" he added, with a half-smile.

Cadieux sought to explain himself. "I am surprised only because you seem so wise and knowledgeable. You have made a success of your life, your farm, family, children and grandchildren. I somehow imagine bastards as being failures in life, from beginning to end."

"It depends on how you define success," Marcel said, raising his hands as if holding the word in front of him. "It is true that I have had success in my horse farm, have a wonderfully faithful and loyal wife and I am very proud of my three children and their accomplishments. I have also failed in some adventures I have undertaken, including several close shaves with death and serious thoughts of suicide when I was eighteen. I am now not far off from death which is the ultimate failure I share with all humanity. I can only hope and pray for success, however you define it, in the hereafter." Dr Cadieux listened to this with his mouth half open, and eyes wide, saying nothing.

Marcel continued his self-reflection, anxious perhaps that if he pass it on one more time, his story might live on in the memory of another. "Here is another detail that will interest you. My name has not always been Juin." Marcel recounted the story of his origins to Cadieux and ended by saying, "to my eternal chagrin my mother died before giving me the identity of my father. She was just a simple country girl, but also quick-witted and had a stubborn nature." Marcel's voice had dropped as he spoke of his mother. Cadieux turned an ear towards him. The sun shone, lighting up the side of his face, as Marcel continued, "As you know, the Revolution introduced a new calendar. I had little sympathy for the Revolution or the calendar and this, combined with hatred of my father for deserting us, and my dubious origins, led me to legally change my name to Juin, the month of my birth in the old calendar." Dr Cadieux continued to say nothing, seeming to imbibe the implications of Marcel's tale. "I do not know why I am telling you all this. Since my uncle Alexis died there is no one other than Clementine who knows my story, and she, bless her generous heart, accepts me as I am, with all the flaws."

"I wish I could help track down your father," Dr Cadieux said eventually. "I would not know where to begin."

"It does not matter anymore. It is so long ago. He must be dead by now. I do not think about it much but talking, as I am now, stimulates the imagination. I shall probably not sleep much tonight. Can I offer you a drink before you go?" Marcel said, and Cadieux realised that his erstwhile patient wanted to be alone with his thoughts.

"Thank you kindly, but no," he said, rising to shake Marcel's hand. "I must leave now as I still have some patients to visit. If you reconsider the repair of your hands, and wish me to research further a possible route for that to happen, please let me know. And my thanks for giving me that somewhat knotted, though fascinating biographical story. I hope one day the truth will unravel for you. I shall make my own way to the gate."

As anticipated, Marcel did not sleep much that night, as silent as fear in the wide wilderness. He churned over the events of his life. I have much to be pleased and proud about. What could I have done differently? He thought to himself. I ridicule people who have done stupid things, but I too have done my share of stupid things; his failure in the mayoralty race, his affair with Thérèse. These actions reminded him of the words of Jesus in the Bible, 'Why do you notice the splinter in your brother's eye but do not perceive the wooden beam in your own eye? How can you say to your brother,' Let me remove that splinter from your eye," when all the time there is a beam in your own? You hypocrite, remove the wooden beam from your eye first, then you will see clearly to remove the splinter from your brother's eye.' Despite these wise words, uttered eighteen hundred years ago, he knew of few people, himself included, who acknowledged and removed beams from their own eyes, but never hesitated to point to splinters in the eyes of others.

Then, as he heard the shrill crescendo song of the nightingale drifting through the open window, he had a memory flash and sat bolt upright in bed. The clawed hand! He was eleven years old, working as a stable boy on the Count's farm. Pierre Tremblais was visiting and came to ask him to care for his horse for the day. Pierre asked him about his age, activities and family. Marcel was not accustomed to anyone speaking to him kindly. Pierre Tremblais had a clawed hand and he seemed so interested in me! Dr Cadieux told him that Dupuytren's disease could occur in members of the same family. "Is it possible that I am his son?" he wondered aloud in the silent bedroom.

"What did you say?" Clementine asked irritably next to him. "Are you talking in your sleep? You must be dreaming. You are disturbing me."

"I am sorry ma Cherie. I have just had a strange idea. I talked loudly without meaning to. I shall sleep now."

Yet he still could not sleep, his head trying to contain his expanding thoughts. He quietly slipped out of bed in order not to disturb Clementine, and went out the front door. It was a warm, windless, night with no moon. The nightingale continued its lovely song in a tree nearby. He sat on the bench he had built when his hands were still supple, and gazed up at the stars. Shining like a brilliant white beacon above him was the planet Jupiter and he recalled the words of Father St.Amour: 'Jupiter is the father of the Roman gods. He symbolises all fathers.' He said out aloud, "As Jupiter is the link between St.Amour and me, now he may also be the link between me and my real father!" He then thought, Pierre! My mother gave me that birth name because of Pierre Tremblais, and pretended it was because of my dead uncle with the name of Pierre. It all fits. It is remarkable!

For an hour he sat, thinking over the implications of these developments and how he should deal with them. Eventually, shivering and heavily fatigued mentally, he returned to bed, cuddled next to Clementine in spoon-like fashion to regain some warmth from her body. She grumbled drowsily, "Why are you so cold? Where have you been?" Once warmed, he fell into a deep and dreamless sleep.

With revelation comes action, but what action? Marcel knew that Count la Fortune, owner of the Chateau, had been executed during the Revolution, the Countess and children had disappeared, and the Chateau had fallen into such a state of disrepair that it had to be dismantled and destroyed. How repugnant were the excesses of the Revolution. He knew also that his mother had worked as a maid for the Countess. It seemed a logical possibility, perhaps even a probability, that she and Pierre had met at the Chateau and had a relationship. But how could he shift through the ruins of that great house and prove what, at present, was only supposition? As far as he knew, the beautiful artifacts, furniture and records had all been destroyed. Somehow, he had to show that Pierre Tremblais visited the Chateau in September 1775, nine months before his birth. Is it possible a Visitor's Book exists and that he signed it at the time of his visit? Even finding this evidence would not prove that Pierre was his father, but it would make this much more likely. He decided to visit the Mairie to see if records had been saved from the Chateau. Early next morning, with Clementine still in the dark as to his sudden change of mood and speed, he told her that he was going to the Mairie to seek musical scores for Charlotte and cantered off to investigate. As he entered the

317

building he met Batarse in the corridor. The man's face, already a muddy puddle, became stirred and his frown threatened to drag the corners of his mouth down to his chin. "I am not accustomed to seeing you at the Mairie, Juin," he said, foregoing any words of welcome. "If you are seeking employment, the Mayor's job is not available." Marcel watched the frown reverse to a sarcastic smile as he spoke. Never trust a man who finds his own venom amusing.

"You may keep your position, Monsieur le Maire," Marcel said, emphasising the words 'le Maire' with a mocking tone. "I have no wish to sit in the seat you have soiled. You have brought discredit to an office that is the most distinguished in the region. Your decisions and acts during our epidemic of cholera-morbus were deplorable. Likely there are dead citizens who voted for you that would be able to vote for you again if you acted more swiftly and with greater concern," he added with dark irony.

"You are talking nonsense, Juin," replied Batarse angrily. "A mayor has to think of bigger issues than the health of citizens. Vimy is an important centre of commerce. We have travellers passing through who spend money and bring wealth. If they hear there is an epidemic disease in town they will take their gold elsewhere."

"Firstly," replied Marcel, disdainfully, "Vimy is not a major centre of commerce in the area, and second, the epidemic became widespread and affected other towns to an equal extent. Travellers with their gold will not avoid this town if the disease is present everywhere. More likely, they will not travel at all."

Marcel noticed Batarse clenching his fists and moving as if about to punch him. He had sized the mayor up physically more than once in the past. Although Batarse appeared slightly taller and heavier than Marcel, he also was slower and less muscular. Marcel judged that if it came to a fist fight, that he was both stronger and fitter and would not likely be at the losing end. Besides, his hands were already fists.

Batarse must have come to a similar conclusion because he relaxed his fists and muttered angrily through clenched teeth, "I will not forget or forgive you this insult, Marcel Juin. You are a contemptible person of no consequence. I shall not miss an occasion to dishonour you in public." He turned his back on Marcel, went in to his office, slamming the door so forcefully that something within fell and shattered, followed by a weak, unimaginative oath. Marcel smiled quietly to himself. The person who loses his temper first also loses the argument.

Then, as the steam of the mayor's choler cleared from the corridor, he remembered the purpose of his visit, to find the Visitor's Book belonging to the pre-Revolutionary Chateau. Turning on his heel Marcel roamed the building until he found a clerk, an old man with a severe hunch, in an office barely wider than his shoulders, writing slowly into a large book. It took Marcel several attempts at explanation to make the man understand his mission, but finally comprehension flooded the old man's face and he rose, there being barely any difference in his standing and seated heights. Walking as slowly as a plough horse, he lead Marcel to a large storage room at the rear of the Mairie filled with old furniture, books and chattels, not only from the Chateau but from many other homes and churches ransacked during and after the Revolution.

"What are you looking for in this mess?" asked the clerk, as he unlocked the door.

"My daughter is a pianist and I am looking for musical scores for her," he lied. "I know the old chateau contained a piano, and the Count's daughters were musicians. It is hard to find scores for Charlotte and they are expensive."

"Go ahead," replied the clerk. "I wish you success. Just let me know what you find and take so I can authorise it legally. You will have to pay of course," he added with a smile. Many in the community knew of Marcel's reluctance to part with his money.

"Yes, of course," said Marcel without hesitation.

Cheap old furniture, cabinets and clutter filled the large storage room, all covered in dust and all in total disorder. The air smelt musty and stale. For the next few days Marcel sorted through the mountains of old books and papers kept in disarray. To his surprise, he did find old musical scores, including two volumes of the piano Sonatas of Mozart that he placed aside to take with him after completing his search.

Amongst other papers he came across a livraison of municipal and mayoralty material. This room must be used to store town records, he thought. As he leafed through the documents he found one file entitled "Raymond Batarse," that contained forms completed when Batarse joined La Grande Armée in 1801. It included personal information required on application. Under the heading "Lieu de Naissance" the response listed "Ville de Québec, Canada" and following the question, "Nom du Père" stood the reply, "Père, Inconnu." Marcel gazed in shock and wonderment at this information, his mouth half open. Just like me, Batarse has an unknown father and is a bastard! And that accent is because he came from Québec. How come I, no one, ever thought of that possibility! He shook his head disbelievingly.

He continued his search. The following day he found what he sought, a beautiful black, leather-bound volume, covered thickly with dust, with its title written in large, gold, calligraphic lettering, Livre d'Or, Chateau de Vimy. With feverish excitement he turned to the entries for September 1775, and there it stood: 'sept septembre, Dix sept cent soixante et quinze: (signé) Pierre Tremblais, Arras' inked in angled and clear, cursive style. A shiver speared his spine as he read those words. Pierre visited the Count's estate on September the seventh, exactly nine months before Marcel's birth. It fitted perfectly! He thought about the brief contact he had had with Pierre in the stables at the Chateau when aged eleven. What a poignant moment! Father and son communicating with each other briefly, the only time they would ever be in close contact on this earth, yet neither aware of their blood relationship!

Then he remembered Uncle Alexis telling him when hiding in the cave that Pierre had been executed in Arras, on the same day as St.Amour. He ground his teeth and clenched his fists in fury at this thought. "The bastards," he said loudly, before realising what he had said. He shook his head and smiled ruefully at the ironies of language. I am calling the revolutionaries 'bastards' insultingly when I myself am one! He needed to watch his use of words more carefully. After wiping the dust carefully off the Visitor's Book he replaced it in the same spot where he had found it, took the Mozart sonatas he had located, reported their discovery to the clerk, paid the required amount and went home.

So, Pierre Tremblais came from Arras, thought Marcel. He placed a personal advertisement in the Arras newspaper, L'Echo du Nord, as follows:

Would any surviving children of Pierre Tremblais,

Executed during the Revolution,

Please contact

Marcel Juin, Les Érables, Vimy.

A week later he received a letter from a woman who introduced herself as Annette Tremblais-Marceau. He went to visit Annette and noted she appeared about the same age as himself, perhaps a year or two younger. A thin, wizened woman, she had white hair and wrinkled features that betrayed a traumatic life. In response to his questions she told Marcel about Tremblais' business success, his fondness for horses, his time as a young man in the French Army in La Nouvelle France, and his awful death on the guillotine.

"I am surprised by your visit, Monsieur Juin," she said. "May I ask why you have an interest in Pierre Tremblais?"

"That is a good question, Madame," he replied adopting a serious tone. "You see, Madame, I was born illegitimate in Vimy sixty years ago. My mother died when I was young without giving me the identity of my father. I have carried out some investigations and have reason to believe that I may be the son of Pierre Tremblais, your father. In other words, I may be your unknown brother!"

Marcel described to Annette his brief meeting with Tremblais as a boy, his observation of Tremblais' hand deformity; that he now had the same condition and that the disease could occur in families. Finally he described his discovery of the Visitor's Book at the Chateau signed by Tremblais exactly nine months before his birth.

"That is a remarkable story," replied Annette after a moment's silence, while she assimilated the implications of what Marcel had told her. "Papa did have the clawed hand. He never complained about it but I am sure it interfered with his activities, especially horse-riding. You will notice that I have the condition as well, although it is quite mild." She showed Marcel her hand deformity and Marcel showed her his. In her case only the little finger of the left hand was involved, curled over so that its tip touched the palm of her hand, whereas the three outer fingers in both of Marcel's hands were affected, curled over and fixed into the palm of his hand.

"Is that not extraordinary," she said with awe in her voice. "I know nothing about the disease and have not enquired because it is not serious enough for me. I considered that I might have got it from Papa but never thought more about it.

"I remember that he used to visit the Chateau to go hunting with Comte la Fortune at Vimy," she continued. "Although Papa was a loving man he and Maman were not happy. She was a vain woman and not affectionate and I would not be surprised if he sometimes strayed when away from her. After Papa's death the Revolutionaries evicted Chantal from our lovely home and she, my brother and I lived in a tiny shack outside Arras. Maman could not cope. She'd had a pampered life with no experience of living hand-to-mouth. Her morale became pitiable. Within months she developed galloping consumption and died soon after.

Now that I look at you closely I can see a physical resemblance. You have the same round face, the same deep set, widely spaced, bulging brown eyes, even the same hook on your nose! Allow me to show you some portraits I have of Papa."

She took Marcel by the arm and drew him to the dining room area. On the walls he saw three large and beautiful portraits in oil colour of a man, one of his head and shoulders, the second on horseback and the third with his wife and two children.

"There you see Pierre Tremblais in his prime. They were painted by Charles Desavary shortly before the Revolution when Papa was about forty-eight years old." Annette said with assurance, while gesturing with her hands.

Marcel gazed at the paintings in wonderment. While scrutinising the head and shoulders painting of Pierre, Marcel thought he was looking at himself, now just a few years older than Pierre when the artwork was created. The widely spaced eyes, the nose and hair colour. Only the mouth was different. He knew that came from his mother. He recognised the horse that Pierre was mounted on as the same one he brought to Vimy on his visit in the summer of 1787.

"It takes my breath away to view these paintings, Madame." He continued to observe the paintings in silence for a few minutes then turned to Annette at last and said, "I have one other question for you, Madame. In what year was our father born?"

"In 1740. He was just fifty-four when executed. Why do you ask?"

"I have a silver medal given me by my mother before she died. She said it would remind me of my father but she told me nothing about him. Now I know he gave it to her because it has the year 1740 inscribed on it so it must be his baptismal medal. I shall show it to you the next time we meet." Marcel felt a chill going through his body when he heard about and saw his physical resemblance to Pierre Tremblais, the final, firm confirmation about the accuracy of his conclusions. As Marcel eagerly continued to probe, Annette provided him with many anecdotes about their father's life. He was pleased to hear that Pierre was, like Marcel himself, both a successful businessman and a talented singer. "He loved singing, especially old army songs," Annette said. "His favourite, his signature tune, was 'Monsieur de Turenne' by Jean-Baptiste Lully." He sang that many times at home when I was young."

"That is extraordinary, Annette! I too sing that song with my daughter Charlotte accompanying me on the piano."

"Marcel, I have something else to show you." Annette moved across the room to her desk, bent over to open the bottom drawer from which she took out a writing pad, already yellowing with age. She gave it to Marcel and said, "We found this amongst our father's papers after his execution. It's the journal he wrote as a young soldier in La Nouvelle France. It will interest you."

Marcel took the proffered journal, opened it and gazed in awe at the writing, the same neat cursive style he'd seen in the Visitor's book at the Mairie. "Can I borrow it, Annette?" he asked. "I shall return it when I next visit."

"Why, yes of course." She smiled with pleasure and continued, "I know you will enjoy reading his own story about his childhood and life in the Army."

At the end of their discussion they gave each other an extended and tearful hug. "It has been remarkable meeting you, Annette," Marcel said as he disengaged, while continuing to hold her hands in his. "For my whole life I have been chagrined, sometimes to the point of raging, because of not know anything about my father. I now feel relief that I know about him. Not only that, but I have also acquired a sister!"

"And I am pleased and excited too, Marcel, not only for you but for me as well," Annette replied. "I married but never had children and my husband died some years ago. Although I sometimes see my brother's children they have their own lives. I am thrilled to have a long lost brother and would like us to meet again."

"And I too," Marcel responded. "I shall be back to visit you"

Marcel left Arras and rode slowly back to Vimy with a profound feeling of solace and satisfaction.

Several cycles of the moon went by. Clementine noticed that Marcel appeared unusually quiet, but not unhappy as he would periodically smile contentedly to himself. "You're acting strangely, Marcel," she said. "Is there something the matter? Are you sick, like Demy?"

"No I am not sick. I have been thinking about my background lately. You know about it. It embarrasses me. I wish I could do something about it."

Clementine noticed he shifted uncomfortably in his chair, avoiding her gaze. "I think you know or you fear something you are not telling me," she said pointedly.

"As always, you are right. You can see right through me. I am not ready to talk about it yet. I will when I am ready."

Clementine shook her head and took Marcel's hands in hers, "I am concerned, Marcel, because I care about you. You are not doing any good by holding it to yourself. It just creates more anxiety."

"Talking about it can also create anxiety and I have not decided yet which way is better, to talk or not to talk. When I decide I shall do what I have to do."

Clementine thought to herself, I know that Marcel has discovered something important. It can only be about his father. It has been on his mind his whole life. I wish he would tell me as I know I can help him. Knowing Marcel as she did, she resigned herself to accepting whatever decision he made. He was as stubborn as some of his horses. If Con Brio did not wish to drink at the trough you could not force him to do so, even though you knew him to be thirsty. Like horse, like master.

In fact Marcel had decided what to do. He would not talk to anyone in the family but he would talk to Dr. Cadieux which he did a few days later. Marcel went to see Cadieux in his office, his last patient of the day.

"What can I do for you, Marcel?" asked the doctor. "As one of my favoured patients I usually visit you at home."

"It is kind of you, Doctor, but today I prefer to come here," Marcel replied. "I have done investigating since we last spoke and have a story to tell. I need someone with good ears. And I don't want snoopers!"

"It is a remarkable tale," the doctor said after hearing Marcel out. "It must be a relief to know now the identity of your father. It must be exciting for your family also."

"You are right, Monsieur le docteur," replied Marcel with a smile. "It is a big relief, not only to have the identity of my father, but to know that I was born through an act of love, not rape. I feared the latter possibility and could not have handled it. Annette told me Tremblais was a loving man and the fact he gave my mother three artefacts in silver that commemorated his baptism proves to me he loved her.

"As for my family I do not wish them to know, at least during my lifetime," Marcel continued after a momentary silence. "It makes me uncomfortable to talk about it with them. A few years ago I told Louis-Marcel about my illegitimacy, and he appeared deeply embarrassed. I cannot go through that again. You may tell them after my death. It will not be long in coming. I have this bad cough and have trouble getting my breath. I smoke more than is healthy, which makes my cough and breathing worse. As you know I also use snuff. I started snuff because I thought it would help me stop smoking but it worked only briefly. I love my pipe," he added ruefully.

"Nonsense, there is nothing wrong with smoking a pipe or taking snuff," Dr Cadieux said authoritatively. "I have smoked for years, ever since dissecting corpses as a medical student studying anatomy. Smoking was the only way we had to disguise the dreadful odour of decomposing bodies. Despite the smoke I am as healthy as a horse!

"I still do not understand why you do not talk to your family," the doctor added, "especially your children. They have a right to know even if you or they are embarrassed."

"I will think about it," he lied. In his mind he knew he could not talk to anyone. He realised the doctor spoke logically yet it surprised him the imperious strength of the desire to tell no one in his family about the discovery. He did not understand it.

As Marcel expected, the condition of his lungs deteriorated over the next few months. His cough became worse, he brought up an increasing amount of

324

phlegm, and he would become short of breath even if he went out on short walks. At home he spoke little but loved listening to stories from others and especially enjoyed hearing Charlotte practising and performing on the piano. She was learning one of the Mozart sonatas from the score he had found in the storage room. He also loved his walks in the open air. The feeling of the wind in his hair and ears, the warmth of the sun on his face and arms, the aromas of the blossoms and pollens, birds singing in the trees, and knowing that he would not be able to experience the outdoors and nature for much longer, gave him much secret satisfaction.

Yet he knew he was not well. He would pick at his food, could consume only broth and no solid food, and lost weight, causing much distress to Clementine, who helplessly watched his condition deteriorate. Marcel could no longer go horse riding, a major sacrifice because horses had been his lifelong passion, and would spend most of the day in a rocking chair outside the front door, puffing away at his pipe or inhaling snuff, in between spasms of coughing and wheezing. The slightest exertion resulted in shortness of breath. During these attacks he struggled to breathe, and became seriously uncomfortable. He made several half-hearted attempts to stop smoking but would quickly resume, either because of some commotion in the household that caused conflict and tension, or because Dr Cadieux would visit and reassure him that smoking had nothing to do with his lung condition.

In September, 1837, Marcel Juin took to his bed knowing that the end could not be far off. It was a tranquil, moonless night. Through the open window he could smell the fresh nocturnal air wafting up from the garden. He listened to the nightingale's beautiful song. With a sense of peace and wonderment he looked up and saw and admired the beauty of Jupiter, shining brilliantly in the still, starlit sky.

EPILOGUE
Clementine

Vimy, November 1837

"It is but a week since Marcel died and I am managing. It is not easy but it is helpful to have the family around. The smells he left behind are especially powerful. Aroma from his clothes and the boxes of snuff and pouches of tobacco make it appear that his spirit is close by. Nights are bad when I am alone in bed and cannot sleep. He seems still to be there even though I know he is not. It is strange — at times I hear him breathing, even coughing, next to me. When alive, I could not sleep because of the noises he made. Now I cannot sleep because of the noises I imagine him making!

"I am not so sure about his holiness. It is true he built up a successful family farm and appeared as a loving husband and father. I cared for him and loved him deeply but I knew him better than anyone. This is not the occasion to make a list of his faults but he certainly had some. For example, I am puzzled by his relations with our mayor, Raymond Batarse. He came close to hating that man, and hatred is not exactly a Christian virtue. I know that Batarse defeated him when he wished to be mayor, and like all politicians, Batarse was two-faced and self-serving. But that does not explain the strength of Marcel's anger and jealousy of him. He could not say a kind word about him.

"Other than to see my children healthy and happy I have no remaining aspirations. I will have time to reflect and pray. I shall prepare my soul for its transition to the next world and rejoin Marcel. After his death, Dr Cadieux visited us and explained all about Marcel's discovery that Pierre Tremblais was his unknown earthly father. This explains his curious behaviour during the last few months of his life. I knew he had a secret and encouraged him to tell me but he refused. It appears he refused to talk to us just as his mother refused to talk with him as a boy. A strange coincidence! We can be thankful that he spoke to Dr Cadieux else we would never have known the truth.

"My life has not been a bed of hay. I had a wounded childhood with few soothers and could easily have ended up on the street or worse. Marcel rescued me or I would have drowned. In a way I rescued him as well. When

326

we met he was tight, solitary and nervous, and I exuberant and reckless. Outwardly we appeared an ill-advised mix, yet we complemented each other in curious ways. A big task in marriage is learning how to love your spouse even though at times you dislike or even hate him or her. I believe we accomplished that. Our marriage was like a horse and rider combination — it is the horse that provides energy and muscle for the pair, which was me. It is the rider that gives direction and provides aims; that was Marcel. Neither can function without the other. A horse without a rider wanders around without aim. A rider without a horse makes little progress in getting to his destination. We had rough times when I ill-treated him or he ill-treated me. Our devotion and dedication carried us through. At the end we were the better because we resolved these differences. Now he is gone and the horse no longer has a rider! Where will it go and who will give it direction? I know I can rely on my own resources as they have served me well in the past. If my faculties fail I can count on my children to give direction and support. I know I can count on Father Ladouceur for spiritual nourishment, and Dr Cadieux for bodily repair. When the time comes for me to meet my Maker, I shall be ready."

Louis-Marcel

November 1837

"The night before his death Papa gave us each a gift and I received the silver chain. That night he also asked us to speak to Dr Cadieux after his death but did not indicate the subject. We assumed it concerned his illness but it turned out that Papa had discovered who his real father was. Personally, I was not, and still am not interested, even though Papa told me last year about his illegitimacy, I have no desire to know any more about that man Pierre Tremblais. I am ashamed about being the child of a bastard and will tell no one about this matter. I will especially say nothing to my children about it even when they come of age. We have had two more children since P'tit Marcel died and will likely have more. I do not wish future generations to know about this brand on our family name!

"I have noticed that my fingers are also beginning to curl over like Papa's. It seems that family tradition is holding true into our generation. It is not yet severe but if it gets bad, I shall have to consider surgery.

"When François and I went to register Papa's death at the Mairie, Batarse acted strangely. At first he smiled and seemed lively, as if pleased that Papa had died. Later, when I gave the required information about his family, and

327

the fact we never knew the name of his father, Batarse trembled and shook like a stipule, so violently he could scarcely write down the words in the record book. He no longer smiled. Dr Cadieux told us that Papa discovered that Batarse, too, was a bastard, born in Canada. Like Papa. To me, the whole story is weird, even bizarre. I do not understand it.

"As to my future, it is simple. I will remain here in Vimy, care for the farm and my family, keep Maman company and care for her as long as she needs me. Papa made a success of Les Érables and I plan to build on his accomplishments."

François

Montréal, summer 1840

"After Papa's death I spoke to Father Claude Ladouceur and told him of my wish to go to Canada. I knew he lived there for the whole of the Bonapartist period. He described remarkable events in Canada including being in the town of York during the War of 1812 when the Americans destroyed the fort and he spent weeks surviving in the wilderness. He confided that during his time in Montréal he fathered a child with a married woman called Laure. At the time it astounded, even shocked me, that a priest could father a child. The child, a girl, was named Claudine and Ladouceur gave me her coordinates. Poor man! He died suddenly shortly after Papa's death. When I arrived in Montréal I immediately went to see Claudine.

"She had become the Mother Superior in a Convent and received me warmly. When a young girl she was raised in the belief that the father of her brothers and sisters was also her own father, Thomas. But when Thomas died – Claudine being then about 18 years old – her mother told her that Ladouceur was her real father. She knew and remembered Ladouceur well because of his visits during her teenage years. Though shocked at first she accepted this because she had loved him. The desire to follow in his footsteps strongly affected her decision to become a nun.

"So far I am free of the Dupuytren's disease that has affected my brother Louis-Marcel. I do not mind if I do get it because it will not change my life.

"On his deathbed Papa gave us each a gift. I received the medal. I looked closely at the medal and saw it had the date 1740 inscribed on it. So it belonged to my grandfather and his parents who struck it to celebrate his birth and baptism! If alive now he would be one hundred years old! It is incredible! Why did Papa not tell us about it himself? All this is wondrously strange. I do not care much about Batarse and his origins but wanted to know more about Pierre Tremblais. Quite suddenly we had a new grandfather. I went to see Papa's half-sister, Annette Tremblais-Marceau and she told me many stories about him, showed me his portraits and gave me his journal to read. I was fascinated to hear tales about my grandparents and would love to have known them and met them. I am proud of my grandmother for caring for and raising a son while being single, despite the turmoil of the times, and proud of my grandfather for the stand he took during the Revolution. In their own ways they both had great courage.

"Three years ago, before I arrived, there was a small revolution here in Canada. With the support of some English-speaking Canadians from Upper Canada the French-speaking community from Québec, now known as Lower Canada, rose up against the English Governor. They called themselves Les Patriotes. The Governor ordered the army to suppress the rebellion, which they did brutally, and many of its leaders were executed. I fear for the survival of the French community here.

"I wish to pursue my ministry in the New World, to the Canadians who speak French, and perhaps even to the native Indians. Canadians are very receptive to visitors from France as they do not get many these days. The Church has made great efforts to bring the Word of God to the native Indians but so far with indifferent results."

Charlotte

Paris, summer 1840

"I love music and am making it my career. Other than teaching or tutoring, it is not easy for a woman to have a profession as a performer of music. Nevertheless I shall try. I have managed to obtain a student position in the Conservatoire de Musique in Paris. I have a great admiration for Adolph-Charles Adam, my teacher, who is a distinguished composer of Ballet music. Like Adam I am devoted to the music of Beethoven and learnt recently that Beethoven had a pupil in Vienna, a French woman called Marie Bigot de Morogues. She returned to Alsace in France, and became famous as a teacher and a pianist. So it is possible for a woman to succeed in music but she has to work hard, even harder than men do to attain success!

I am learning to play a sonata of Beethoven's called the Appassionata. It has intensity and passion, typical of the sort of person that Beethoven himself, was. I hope to perform it in a recital at the Conservatoire next month. Maman will be there with Louis-Marcel and Marie-Marguerite. It will be exciting playing in front of my family! I wish Papa could hear it.

"Before he died Papa gave us each a present to commemorate him and his parents. I received the ring that I treasure and wear on the ring finger of my right hand. Neither Papa nor we can be blamed for an act that took place many years ago between our grandmother and grandfather. Like François, I am thrilled to hear the story about my grandparents and their bravery. Life is difficult now; it must have been dreadful then.

"I do not know if I shall ever marry. In a sense I am married to my music. Not many men would like that. Someday, perhaps one will come along who loves music like I do.

The End